Follow a Star

Christine Stovell

Published 2014 by Choc Lit Limited
Penrose House, Crawley Drive, Camberley, Surrey GU15 2AB, UK
www.choc-lit.com

A CIP catalogue record for this book is available
from the British Library

ISBN 978-1-78189-136-0

Printed and bound by CPI Group (UK) Ltd, Croydon, CR0 4YY

Follow a Star

To my guiding stars, Tom, Jen and Caroline,
with love.

Acknowledgements

My sincere thanks to the following:

Jan and Roger Smith, for their generous hospitality, for updating me on the pleasures and perils of the North Sea, and for the loan of their charts (which are in a safe place!)

Margaret and Richard Masson, for happy memories and dreams shared on *Hephzibah*.

The band, Clocks – Tom, Rich, Ed and John – for the VIP passes.

Gillian, my daughter-in-law, who wanted a different kind of hero.

Jill Shearer, for her unstinting support and for keeping a weather eye on my astrological chart.

The Choc Lit team, my editor and my fellow ChocLiteers.

Sarah and Mandy; writing buddies, cheerleaders and twin pillars of support – thanks for propping me up!

My family and dear friends for bearing with me.

And most of all to Tom, who took me to sea in a little wooden boat and my beloved daughters, Jennifer and Caroline, who joined in the adventure.

None of this would have been possible without you.

Chapter One

May Starling stood outside the deserted railway station on what should have been a pleasant July evening, wondering what had happened to the man who was supposed to be meeting her. There wasn't a car in sight. Certainly no sign of the new silver Jaguar that Cecil Blythe claimed she wouldn't miss. Nor was there, she thought looking round for a crumb of comfort, a cheery line of cabbies jostling for her custom.

There were three texts on her mobile, all from Aiden, which she ignored, and when she tried the number for Cecil Blythe it was unavailable. Perhaps he'd gone straight to the marina and was now so engrossed in his new toy he'd forgotten all about her? May squinted up at the blue and peach summer sky then down at the empty street curving over the crest of a hill. From the brow she'd probably be able to see the sea. If she was really lucky she might even spot a cluster of masts or the gleam of white hulls glowing apricot under the evening sun. Or she could stand there, checking her watch and phone every few minutes, until Cecil Blythe remembered he was supposed to be collecting her.

Hefting her bag over her shoulder, she set off, telling herself some vigorous exercise would settle that fluttering feeling of anxiety batting at her fragile hopes with insistent wings. Her sense of disquiet had grown on the journey. Squeezed on to the cramped train from outer London to the south coast with dozens of office workers at the dog-end of the week, her nerve endings prickled every time a blank stare slid over her, only relaxing when whoever it was turned their attention elsewhere.

But it was ridiculous to imagine that anyone would even notice her, let alone recognise her. They all had their own lives to get on with and weekends to plan. Who'd be looking for her here? Not Aiden, anyway; the great outdoors was the last place he'd expect to find her. So she could loosen up, use the brisk walk to regain her perspective and enjoy her adventure. If Cecil Blythe's new boat had been berthed in one of the marinas closer to the mouth of Portsmouth's historic harbour, she wouldn't even have needed a lift, but Jollimarine, some four miles up one of the sleepier creeks meandering off from the main body of water, was a lot less accessible by land and public transport.

It couldn't be that hard to find, could it? Logically, all she had to do was to follow the road downhill to the sea until she got her bearings. Striking out, though, it seemed to be a very long road. And now that the few houses grouped around the station were behind her and fields widened out either side, it was lonely too. Lonelier than she would have wished …

Careful what you wish for, wasn't that the saying? And oh, how she'd wished for her dream to come true. If only she'd realised that shooting for the moon would send her spinning back down to earth. If only someone had warned her about … May gradually became aware that she wasn't alone any more. So far as an old Land Rover Defender could creep along, this one was. And right beside her. May took a quick sideways glance at a male face turned towards her then stared fixedly ahead.

Ohmigod! A kerb crawler. Here she was out in the middle of bloody nowhere and someone was after her body. He was probably some sex-starved farmer. She'd read about all these lonely men, forced to advertise for 'housekeepers', unable to attract girls from the city to their isolated acres. He shouted something. She caught the word 'darling' and hurried on. He roared ahead, stopped the car and, before she knew it, was blocking her path, six foot plus of lean muscle and broad-shouldered with it. May was not looking forward to running away from someone who looked as if he spent all his time wrestling bullocks to the ground. Especially not one with that hair colour. She whimpered.

'I hope I haven't got this wrong,' he said, running his fingers through the offending mane. 'Are you May Starling?'

Having conjured up an image of someone small and wiry, she was taken aback that her prospective skipper was so much taller, more energetic and, frankly, ginger-looking than she'd expected. Somewhere along the line, she'd also overestimated his age. The man in front of her was in his prime and bristled with vitality, like a Rhodesian Ridgeback eyeing up a rabbit. Slap in the middle of two hundred acres he probably wouldn't look quite so strapping, but most boats would feel pretty confined with him aboard. 'You must be Cecil Blythe,' she said, recovering herself.

'I'm Cecil's nephew,' he said, pulling on the Land Rover's passenger door which opened with ominous groans. 'We need to talk.'

It didn't feel like an invitation so much as an order, and not a particularly friendly one at that. There wasn't another soul in sight, but if she could hoof it back to the station, at least she could always hammer down someone's front door if he made a nuisance of himself. 'I don't think so,' she told him, starting to ease her bag off her shoulders in case she had to make a fast getaway. 'I don't know the first thing about you.'

'Bill. How's that for starters?' he said, looking exasperated. 'Bill Blythe. And you're quite right not to trust me,' he continued. 'We're complete strangers, aren't we? Whereas you've done your homework and you know all about Cecil.'

'Enough,' May nodded, with more conviction than she felt.

'His age?'

'Well, I know he retired early.'

'That's true,' Bill agreed pleasantly. 'Cecil did indeed retire early, when he was fifty-two. Twenty years ago, in fact.'

May tried to sound nonchalant. 'Many people sail at that age. He's obviously fit enough to sail from Portsmouth, round the east coast and up to Little Spitmarsh or he wouldn't be contemplating it. I daresay he's factored sufficient breaks into the equation. At a steady pace it'll take, what, a week at most? So, I'm not especially bothered about your uncle's age; it's a delivery trip not a blind date.'

'I'm afraid Cecil had quite a different impression, especially from the tone of your reply,' he told her, pushing one hand through the untidy red-gold thatch in apparent disbelief. 'The excitement was too much for him.'

'Oh God!' May dropped her bag. 'Is he …?'

'Stable. A suspected heart attack. The hospital's keeping him in while they run more tests, but getting himself in such a state of agitation isn't helping.' He shot her a look of sympathy before his blue gaze clouded over. 'I blame myself really. Cecil's been talking for years about buying this boat if it ever came on the market. I should have known he was serious. He sailed her when he was a young man and I think he thought this was the way to recapture his youth. I didn't realise he'd tracked her down until he showed me that ridiculous ad. Even then I didn't think anyone would be daft enough to reply.'

May chewed her lip. If only she hadn't been in such a

hurry to get away. Maybe she should have calmed down a bit before pressing Send. 'Your uncle's ad wasn't *that* bad,' she said, more to convince herself than the man in front of her. How did it go now? *Sea fever? Skipper, early retired, with comfortable yacht waiting, seeks friendly female fellow-rover. If you must go down to the seas again, let's test the water together!* 'I would have given a wide berth to anyone expecting anything other than the sea to shake his cabin.'

As for being daft? Even though she'd been feeling slightly reckless, she *had* made very sure to avoid the fifty-something millionaire looking for a 'sexy adventuress to spoil in exchange for no-strings fun.' May stared at her bag and examined her conscience. Her e-mail, as far as she could recall, had been a light-hearted attempt to distinguish her reply from all the others. Given how wretched she'd been feeling at the time, she thought it was quite an achievement. For once in her life she had acted entirely on impulse, but unlike other people who managed to get away with it, this had all blown up in her face. Any other woman would probably have found themselves preparing to sip champagne on the sun deck with the Solent's answer to George Clooney.

It was suitable punishment, she supposed, for her uncharacteristically impetuous behaviour that she'd inadvertently responded to the fantasies of a fragile old fraud. If that wasn't bad enough, she had nowhere to stay. Having thoroughly burned her bridges with Aiden, and her parents planning a rave, who on earth could she land on for a week without being discovered?

May pulled herself together. 'I'm terribly sorry about your uncle. It was precisely because his advert made him seem like a man with a sense of fun that made me think he'd appreciate a humorous reply – I had no idea that anyone would get hurt as a consequence.'

'"I must go down to the seas again, to the lonely sea where I can handle myself pretty well on a boat as you'd know if you give me a try."' Bill quoted. 'So far as Cecil was concerned he'd got a fast yacht and a fast woman to match.'

'Oh, come on,' May said, defensively. 'It was supposed to be amusing.'

'Yeah, well don't take up writing poetry for a living, will you, or you'll end up with all kinds of strange followers,' he muttered.

May shot him a look to see if his barb was deliberate, but judging from his expression he was just thoroughly hacked off. And probably worried sick about his uncle too. She picked up her bag and struggled to redeem herself. 'I don't suppose there is anything I can do to help, is there?'

There was a long pause during which May waited for him to tell her that she had done quite enough already.

'The bit in your reply about being able to handle yourself on a boat—'

Put like that, it didn't sound too clever; she really hadn't been thinking very clearly when she'd sent that reply.

'I assume that's a reference to your sailing experience,' Bill said gruffly.

May longed for the ground to swallow her.

'Since this boat means so much to Cecil, I'm going to make sure that it's waiting for him as soon as he's better,' he continued. 'It'll give him an incentive to get well.'

'That's kind of you.' May was relieved Bill sounded so sure of Cecil's recovery. He might even give her a lift back to the station instead of getting her charged with attempted manslaughter.

'No.' He smiled at her as he took her bag and threw it in the Land Rover. 'It's kind of *us*. You signed up for this trip too. Remember?'

Chapter Two

Exactly *what* had Cecil been thinking? Bill saw May Starling's pale lips part in alarm as her bag landed in the back of the beaten-up Defender where it dislodged a coil of salty old rope that let off a soupçon of aroma of dried seaweed. May stood at the side of the road making sad kitten faces at him with innocent honey-brown eyes that didn't fool him in the slightest.

'Your carriage awaits, Madam,' he said, with an exaggerated sweeping gesture, leaning back against the passenger door which squealed in protest. She turned a cool gaze on him, the sad kitten act dropped as she weighed up her options. Not quite the impressionable old man with money to splash around she'd been expecting, he thought, almost laughing at her sheer transparency. Next would come the excuse, the urgent appointment she'd suddenly remember once it dawned on her that her meal ticket had been cancelled. He got ready to retrieve her bag. An extra pair of hands to ensure the safe delivery of Cecil's precious boat would have been useful, but he strongly suspected that it would be no great loss doing without this particular first mate. He got the feeling that May Starling was used to other people running round after her, not used to hard work, in which case the walk back to the station would do her good. What a pity it was downhill.

'Hold on a minute.' She walked round to the back of the car, pulled out her phone, mouthing the registration number as she tapped it in and fired off a text. 'Just so people know where to find me.'

Bill stood back as she swung herself into the passenger

seat, his amazement temporarily forgotten as he registered the denim shorts moulding one peachy posterior and the lightly tanned, shapely legs. He slammed the door with unnecessary force, annoyed with Cecil and irritated with himself for the unwelcome revelation that the dormant goaty gene had apparently just surfaced in him.

'You work around boats, then,' said May, jerking her head at the pile of marine debris behind them on which her bag sat, playing king of the sandcastle.

'Oh this isn't mine,' he shouted above an engine that sounded as if it ran on shrapnel before checking the rear mirror and pulling away. 'I persuaded the guy who runs the yard at Jollimarine to lend it to me. I came down by train yesterday. I didn't fancy leaving my own vehicle at the yard.'

'I thought all these south coast marinas were rather smart. You'd think you'd get good security for the rates they charge so that boat owners don't have to worry about their posh cars while they're away.'

Bill smiled to himself. 'Mine's not very posh,' he said smoothly. 'But I need it for work. It's a white Transit which takes all my tools.'

'Ah,' she said, sinking a little further into her seat.

Well, that had killed the conversation. One minute there you were anticipating a champagne cruise with a silly old fool with more money than sense, the next you found yourself press-ganged into doing nautical service with White Van Man. He almost wanted to apologise for trampling all over her fantasy. A couple of miles along the road and he could feel harsh reality sinking in when, out the corner of his eye, he saw her face turn towards him. He whistled tunelessly to himself as her gaze travelled slowly from the top of his unruly hair that needed a cut, over the thoroughly loved turtle-green hoodie and grubby grey canvas trousers and down to his battered brown work boots.

'You *are* qualified to sail this boat, aren't you?' she said, at last.

'Trust me,' he grinned. Little Spitmarsh didn't have many natural assets, but it did offer plenty of opportunities for messing around in boats. In theory, at least, when he wasn't booked up with work for weeks. There weren't many property developers who could still turn a profit in the straightened economic climate, but Matthew Corrigan, the man he'd been working with for the last two years, had achieved it through sheer hard graft and not being too greedy. An unfair amount of natural charm seemed to work wonders too. Beside him, he could sense May Starling's lingering doubt quivering in the air like a taut string.

'Anyway,' he added nonchalantly, 'you're the one with all the experience, aren't you? So, together, we'll be just fine.'

Her gaze snapped back to the windscreen and she folded her arms and clicked her heels together. Perhaps, like Dorothy, she was wishing herself back home, except those weren't ruby slippers on her feet, but deck shoes. An affectation, he wondered, part of the pretence? Or maybe she really did know something about sailing? The trip would be a lot less stressful for both of them if he didn't have to worry about instructing her. But if not? She was about to find he was going to go right ahead and put her to work anyway.

'So, tell me a bit more about the boat,' she asked, 'you've checked her over, right? Made sure she's seaworthy?'

'Well,' he began, clearing his throat, 'we're nearly there so you'll see for yourself soon enough.' The truth was that the last couple of days had left him wrung out and wondering which way was up. His preparations might not have been as thorough as he'd have liked. All that had persuaded him to leave the old man's hospital bedside was his uncle's anxiety about the boat he had just bought and his concerns for his crewing companion. Cecil's flagging spirits had only lifted when he'd extracted a firm promise from Bill to get the boat to him without any further delay. And although he'd left Cecil resting a little more comfortably, Bill had his own worries, like the sixteenth-century farmhouse he was currently working on. The demanding project had only been saved from slipping behind schedule with help from his mate Matthew, but even knowing he didn't have to cope entirely unassisted hadn't made it any easier to relax.

Three changes on the five-hour train ride to Portsmouth meant he'd done little more than catnap on the journey. The fatigue had really hit him once he'd checked into the nearest hotel, where he'd slept so deeply he'd woken dazed and disoriented. Getting his head round charts and tide tables again had taken some doing. By the time he'd done that, found the boatyard and made a brief inspection of Cecil's Folly, as he nicknamed her, it was mid-afternoon and it suddenly occurred to him that Cecil's crew would be on her way. He'd made a quick call to Matthew's wife, Harry, who ran her own boatyard in Little Spitmarsh, to beg her to persuade the miserable old sod at Jollimarine to lend him the Landie, then dashed up to collect the woman sitting reluctantly beside him.

Bill made a show of concentrating on locating the blind entrance into Jollimarine to ward off any awkward questions and hoped that neither of them was in for any more interesting surprises.

'Right,' he said, pulling up on a stretch of gravel, 'this is the place. Cecil's boat's been moved to a temporary berth on the visitors' pontoon as we're not staying long. Do you want to leave your bag here for a minute whilst we go and find her, then we'll unpack properly later?'

Outside the car, he paused for a moment just to compose himself and enjoy the sight of the evening sunshine gilding the silvery creek in a golden light as the low water lapped the shore. Apart from the distant hum of motorway traffic carried in the light breeze to remind him how busy the south-east was compared with his quiet East Anglian bolthole, it was surprisingly peaceful. May Starling stood silently beside him and he couldn't decide if she too was absorbing the tranquillity of the evening or was simply occupied in her own thoughts. This voyage probably wasn't quite turning out as she'd expected either.

What he did know, though, was that she was standing close enough for him to be acutely aware of the warmth of her body and her delicate, cotton-fresh scent. If he'd needed proof that he was working too many hours round sweaty men on construction sites, this was it. But with Cecil likely to take up what little spare time he had left, May Starling's every move seemed set to remind him that the chances of him resuming anything like a social life were a remote prospect.

'Come on, then,' he said, pushing his hair back off his forehead along with his second thoughts about his crew and indicating that she should go first. He could do this; he was a strong man with self-control, not some freak who got off on sniffing defenceless young women. The denim shorts sashayed in front of him and Bill instantly regretted the gentlemanly conduct that was making him feel decidedly ungentlemanly.

To be fair to her, he thought, concentrating on not losing

his footing on the wooden pontoon jutting out across the water like a miniature pier, she hadn't exactly overplayed her attributes. As far as he could tell, she wore hardly any make-up and her light brown hair was subtly sun-kissed and fell in natural waves to just beneath her shoulders. In her baggy cream cardigan worn over a stripy T-shirt she looked wholesome and ordinary, familiar even; the very essence of the girl-next-door.

'You'd better lead the way now,' she said, standing back.

A variety of boats bobbed on short mooring lines before them, like dogs impatient for a walk straining on their leads, some with elegant pedigrees, others a little less well groomed. The springy boards bounced beneath his tread and all of a sudden he remembered the hotel bedroom he'd woken up in that morning and the king-sized bed he'd stretched out in before resigning himself to the cramped conditions of a small wooden boat. A boat, he noticed, seeing it squatting in its visitors' berth, which now looked even smaller when he thought about the practicalities of sharing with a complete stranger and a female one at that.

'She's a little beauty, isn't she?' he said, with what he hoped was a hearty degree of conviction.

'How quickly do you think we can get to Little Spitmarsh?' she asked, one hand sliding up to her temple. 'Three days? Four?'

Hmm. That rather indicated he hadn't sounded convincing enough. He stole a quick glance at her other hand, the one still folded across her body, and found himself ridiculously satisfied to find it ring-free. Not, of course, that that particular detail was relevant in any way. They were just two sensible adults getting on with the job of delivering Cecil's boat to Little Spitmarsh. How he would deal with Cecil after that was another issue, but it comforted him to think that when he stepped ashore his next task would be a whole lot easier if he didn't have to deal with an irate husband or fiancé waiting on the quay to add to the mess he was already struggling to clear up.

With the boat still resting in the berth at Jollimarine the next morning, May sat up in her sleeping bag – the ones they'd had to rush to buy before the last shops shut once the rudimentary arrangements on the old wooden boat became apparent. Bill had gallantly let her have what was described as a sleeping cabin, but really boiled down to a couple of thin foam mattresses on a V-shaped shelf lining the boat's forepeak. There was no door, but the previous owner had hung a curtain to divide what was essentially an open-plan interior and afford some notional privacy. On the other side of the curtain, Bill, she supposed, was still stretched out on one of the long settee berths.

It was strange that in her not entirely extensive sailing experience – she'd deliberately been a bit vague in her reply about exactly how many sea miles she had under belt – she'd somehow failed to appreciate the true cheek-by-jowl nature of life aboard. Yet, one night of having Bill Blythe just metres away was rather more disturbing than she'd imagined. Especially now, when her bursting bladder was insisting that she did something about emptying it pretty sharpish.

May stole a glance round the curtain. The saloon – the main cabin serving as a multi-purpose living space – was flooded with light but otherwise unoccupied. Despite her first appearances at the end of a tiring and frustrating day, *Lucille*, as the boat was named, was rather lovely. The patina of her teak interior gleamed richly, and a painted white ceiling – deckhead, she corrected herself, remembering the nautical term – created a sense of airiness and space. Sunshine streamed over the gimballed brass oil lamps that swung gently with the boat and scattered the morning light over the terracotta and jade cushions softening the long settee berths. An antique French barometer, mounted on a bulkhead, insisted that the day would be *Beau*.

On the compact stove in the minuscule galley space, a polished kettle was noisily trying hard to come to the boil. The perfect cover, thought May, since the boat loo – heads, she reminded herself – was a tiny enclosed space with cardboard-thin walls, which, to May, felt horribly like peeing in public. Perching carefully, so as to avoid unnecessarily broadcasting what she was doing, she was disconcerted to hear Bill moving about on deck sounding like the giant about to climb down the beanstalk.

Despite a certain amount of tension, she accomplished her mission then had to struggle with the complicated arrangement of pumps and levers which worked the flush. Overhead, the footsteps stopped abruptly, leaving only the sound of a squeaky pump and water gurgling round the bowl. May's red face peered back at her from the small speckled mirror over the doll-sized basin as she tentatively tried the tap, which coughed out icy water. Hearing Bill, doing his Big Foot impression, about to make his way below deck, she hastily dried her hands on her fleecy top since there was no towel on the rail – something else to add to the growing list of provisions required – and prepared with some apprehension to take a fresh look at *Lucille*'s substitute skipper.

Her impressions the previous evening had surely been coloured by a tumult of emotions. Perhaps now that she'd had some rest and could think rationally he wouldn't look quite so tough, rough and red-haired? And he had displayed a touching concern for his uncle, so he was evidently a caring man. She turned to see long legs in dirty-grey workman's trousers coming down the steps of the companionway to an accompaniment of snatches of something that sounded like a Foo Fighters anthem. Great, so she was being cast adrift with someone who fancied himself as a bit of a stadium rocker – boy, it was going to be a long voyage!

But the scowl forming on her face faded as something else began to drift, like her concentration, as she noticed that Bill's long legs were followed by rippling stomach muscles and broad shoulders defined by a clinging dark T-shirt. Toned arms appeared and, ah, as Bill ducked his fiery head under the hatch – that hair. No, definitely not her type.

Chapter Three

'So, you're awake at last,' her crew mate observed, clearly skilled in the art of stating the obvious. 'I even filled up the water tank while you were out for the count and you didn't stir.'

'Good morning to you too,' said May. 'What do you want? Congratulations? For succeeding where every herbal sleeping pill on the market has failed?' She really hadn't expected to drift off so quickly, not with Bill driving them home with his snoring the minute his head touched the pillow, but the gentle rocking of the boat had proved surprisingly soporific. The snoring, too, had settled down into a rumble of contentment which was rather reassuring. Swaddled in her sleeping bag, all cares left behind, she'd felt snug and safe.

'Save the sleeping tablets for when you're back on dry land,' Bill advised, eyeing her keenly. 'I can't have you sleeping like a baby if there's an emergency.'

'I won't let you down,' she insisted, 'so don't fret about me being out for the count when I'm needed. In any case, I understand from friends who know, that babies wake up every two hours screaming to be changed or fed. Sleeping like a baby could be useful if it means waking at regular intervals. At least you know I won't miss my turn to be on watch.'

'Is that a fact?' he nodded, studying her in a way that was starting to make her feel quite self-conscious about her bed-hair and morning breath. 'Well, I'm sure you're quite capable of getting washed and dressed all by yourself, but I can make you a bacon sandwich, if you like. There's a shower block in the boatyard. Just don't take all day about it. I managed to blag the use of the Defender while we provision the boat, so we need to make some serious passage plans. We'll try a shakedown cruise towards the harbour mouth so we can assess the boat and how she handles. Provided there are no major problems, I'd like to get away tomorrow morning. Does that suit you?'

'Fine,' May shrugged. 'The sooner the better.' It dawned on her that Bill was so preoccupied that he wasn't remotely aware of her appearance; she could have been standing there stark naked with her head shaved for all the notice he was taking. He was staring past her now, frowning at a point past her right shoulder through one of the cabin's narrow windows.

'Wind's up,' he grunted.

She toyed with the idea of saying 'Never mind, we're all friends together now,' but managed to restrain herself and went off to dig out her wash bag instead. Bill Blythe was in for a surprise if he thought she was the type to keep him hanging around. Her two tours of the country had, if nothing else, taught her to get ready in double quick time. Not, she decided, tucking a micro towel for speedy hair drying into a cloth bag along with fresh clothes, that she had any intention of reliving those memories. Her glory days were in the past and that suited her just fine. Even if everyone who claimed to want the best for her was applying all sorts of pressure to persuade her to change her mind.

'That's one thing we don't need to buy,' he said, waving a frying pan at her as she waited to get past him and up the narrow companionway stairs. He slid back more lockers to reveal a comprehensive range of kitchen equipment and crockery left behind by *Lucille*'s previous owners and nodded with satisfaction. 'This lot will be fine for a quick rinse over.' He gave her a sharp look. 'Cecil was insistent about reimbursing us for any expenses we incur, but he's not made of money.'

May felt a hot wave of humiliation wash over her, but bit back her retort. Bill was bound to be protective of the ailing uncle who had given him such a fright, so rather than defend her case, she would prove to Bill through her practical approach and hard work that she was more than prepared to put right any wrong she may have unintentionally caused. Since she was standing next to the hanging locker – the storage space for clothes – she opened it to see what was inside and to bury her burning face somewhere cool.

'Empty,' she announced, feeling composed again. 'I wonder where the life jackets and wet weather gear is, then?'

'*Lucille*?' someone shouted outside.

'Oh bugger,' said Bill. 'It's the bloke who's lending me the Defender. I hope he doesn't need it back just yet.'

They went up on deck where a grumpy Scottie dog was standing on the pontoon sniffing *Lucille*'s prow. With the dog was an equally grumpy man. 'Parcel for you,' he said, tossing it to Bill. 'This arrived at the yard a couple of days ago.'

'It's for Cecil,' said Bill, shaking the parcel by his ear and frowning at the stamp. 'I'd better see if it's anything important.'

Not wanting to look as if she was prying, May went below to find something useful to do. There was the sound of ripping paper then Bill's voice, a little strained, as he rejoined her.

'It's for you.'

'Me?' She gazed at the square package with some trepidation. It was small, about the size of a jewellery box, beautifully wrapped and bore a gift label. *For May, welcome aboard. With thanks, Cecil.* Behind her, she could feel Bill bristling with curiosity. Whatever the box contained there was no point in hiding it. The boat was too small for secrets. 'Oh,' she gasped, 'how very sweet of your uncle!'

A little silver starfish pendant dangled on a thread-like chain. When she held it up a pinprick of a diamond right in the centre twinkled and glimmered in a shaft of sunlight, a more evocative and poignant symbol than Cecil Blythe could possibly have known. From falling star to fish out of water in one text. Smiling wistfully, she turned to Bill only to see his mouth set in a grim line. Without knowing exactly how she'd offended him, it was apparent that his mood had taken a turn for the worse because of her.

'What is it?' she asked.

'No wonder there's no life jackets or safety gear,' he said crossly. 'Cecil was too busy trying to make a good impression on you. It must be true that a stupid old fool and his money are soon parted!'

May placed the pendant carefully back in its box. 'I'm genuinely sorry about your uncle, but all I did was volunteer for a delivery trip. This,' she said, offering it back to him, 'wasn't prompted by me, and, of course, I couldn't possibly accept it.'

Bill narrowed his eyes at the woman standing in front of him looking like butter wouldn't melt.

'Why not?' he scoffed. 'Not good enough for you? Were you hoping for something with more bling?'

What was her motive for signing up to go to sea with

an elderly stranger unless it was some sort of financial gain? It wouldn't be the first time a woman had tried to take advantage of Cecil's soft nature. One of his uncle's neighbours, a new divorcee looking for an easy way to make up the shortfall in her income, had made quite a nuisance of herself until Bill warned her off. If May genuinely wanted to feel the sea breeze in her hair, there was more excitement to be had crewing on a racing yacht, more company on a tall ship, and more luxury on just about any other vessel you'd care to pick.

He hated the thought of the gentle, kindly soul to whom he owed so much being taken for a ride. If, on the other hand, Cecil imagined he could boost his morale and regain his youth with an attractive young woman as his shipmate, he really, really hoped his uncle wouldn't die before he could give the daft old so and so the bollocking that was coming. He exhaled slowly.

May had lowered herself onto the nearest settee berth, the unisex fleece she was wearing unzipped just enough to show the swell of her breasts above the camisole top she had on underneath. Feeling his body start to appreciate the view, Bill tore his gaze away, profoundly irritated that he was even capable of such an inappropriate and untimely response to the situation.

'Look, how about I take you back to the station when you've had your shower,' he said, making it clear it was an instruction not an offer.

She went still. 'What?'

It was never going to work, this trip. However disturbing it was to think of Cecil getting swept away by thoughts of a light flirtation with May, it was even worse to discover the same madness now seemed to be afflicting him. He'd always thought of himself as a normal, healthy male with reasonable and balanced desires, but judging by that rather speedy reaction, he was beginning to get ideas, if not into his head then somewhere lower down. So if May, going innocently about her business in baggy pyjama bottoms and an oversize fleece, was bringing out the beast in him, being holed up with her for four, maybe five, nights would make for a long and painful voyage.

'Well,' he said, trying to sound fair, 'it's not as if this is the largest boat in the world.' And if the cabin of a small wooden boat felt this confined tethered to a pontoon where either of them could just walk ashore, how would it feel at sea when there was no escaping the unpredictable combination of weather and waves which could cook up a storm of emotion without warning? 'I ought to be able to manage her single-handed. I mean, it's not what you signed up for, is it?' he blustered, trying to ignore the colour draining from her face and the hurt expression. 'Look at her – she's hardly a luxury yacht.'

'I wasn't expecting luxury,' May replied, dropping her voice. 'I only wanted to get away for a few days.'

'May, this isn't a cruise,' he explained. 'We're not sightseeing or calling in at picturesque little harbours along the way. I simply want to get this boat round to Little Spitmarsh as soon as I can. So get yourself ready and I'll drop you at the station with enough money to cover your fare and any other expenses you've incurred, and on the journey home you can plan a proper holiday.'

No sooner had the word 'holiday' entered his head when the image of a bikini-clad May stretching those golden legs out on a sunlounger insinuated its sensuous way into his thoughts as well. How long now since he'd had anything like some rest and recuperation? Since moving to Little Spitmarsh to be closer to Cecil again, his working days had been long and his evenings short and increasingly spent keeping his uncle company. Even then, he'd been unable to lift the old man's spirits. Nothing Bill could do seemed to stop time weighing heavily or make the nights less fearful.

Worse still, his uncle's general anxiety seemed to be matched by a visible physical decline. Realising that the old man would become even more dependent unless he had something other than morbid thoughts about his failing health to engage him, Bill had been happy to talk about Cecil's boat-buying plans. In theory. What he hadn't appreciated was that the old boy had every intention of putting them into practice. Then look at what had happened.

No wonder his imagination was doing its best to divert him. When his hands began to tingle in anticipation of smoothing warm suntan oil over silky skin, Bill shook his head, came to, and only realised that he must have been standing there glaring at May when he noticed her dismayed expression.

She stood up and picked up her bag. 'Don't worry about the lift,' she told him. 'I'm perfectly capable of making my own way back to the station. Besides, you've made your feelings about me quite clear, so I wouldn't want to have to put you to the inconvenience of sharing a small space with me for a minute longer than necessary. If it makes it easier for you I'll take everything up with me to the shower – and then you won't even have to look at me!'

She drew herself to her full height, which brought her, he guessed, to just under his chin. 'But when you're out in a big sea with the wind tearing at the sails and you find yourself wishing you had someone to help you reef them in, look inside that hot red head of yours and ask yourself what's really bugging you. Me? The person who could have been there to assist you if you'd given me a chance, or'—she nodded towards the jewellery box—'should you be directing that anger somewhere else? I didn't respond to your uncle's ad because I saw a chance to con a vulnerable old man. I needed—' She shook her head. 'Never mind my needs. Maybe you should ask yourself what your uncle needs. Why he's so lonely that he has to buy company for his boat trip and sweeten her with trinkets? Perhaps *you* should be doing more for him?'

Any sympathy he might have had for spoiling her plans evaporated. He opened his mouth to tell her exactly how mistaken she was, but she turned away to the forecabin and quickly swept her wash bag and the few possessions she'd unpacked into her rucksack. Before he could do or say anything, she then pushed past him and climbed the companionway. He felt the boat tilt as she hopped nimbly off the side and couldn't stop himself going over to the window to see if she was really on her way.

A choppy wave, slapping against the bow, almost knocked him off balance as he squinted along the pontoon until May disappeared. Hot red head indeed; after insinuating he had a temper to match his hair colour, she was the one who'd flounced off. Duracell. Copperknob. Animal – his nickname at school, after the drummer in the Muppets. He'd heard them all and none of them bothered him. It certainly didn't matter one jot what May Starling thought of him; she was a complication he could do without.

Though, if he was completely honest, it was going to be a much longer and far more tiring haul getting *Lucille* round by himself than he would have liked. The first few days of adapting to the cycle of being at sea were always challenging; checking the boat's position, keeping her out of danger and on course. There were hazards to face: wind farms, underwater cables, huge cargo ships … even the cabin seemed to have turned a moody face to him as the sun went in, making the dark teak look surly and uninviting.

'You'd better appreciate this, Cecil,' he said out loud. The old rogue had certainly caused him some trouble, Bill thought, shaking his head. Right now, he was undecided about whether to hug him or shout at him first when he next saw him. Except that bawling the old boy out wasn't the way to thank the man who had taken him in after his mother's death and given him security and stability.

Seeing his uncle looking so vulnerable, his skin papery beneath the thin hospital gown, had evoked a small boy's confusion and fear. He'd been unable to save his mother, but clutching Cecil's hand, so frail and arthritic in his, Bill promised to do anything to give the old man a reason to live. Just knowing that the boat was on its way would give him something to look forward to. Pottering about on the backwaters of Little Spitmarsh would perk him up no end.

In his pocket, his phone started to ring. 'Yes,' said Bill. 'Speaking. Cecil Blythe's nephew, that's correct.' Then he sat down and listened intently whilst the woman on the other end of the phone gently explained the situation.

Chapter Four

May had a crick in her neck from fruitlessly trying to dry her hair under the hand drier in the cell-like shower block. It was still damp at the crown, but the long walk back to the station would take care of that and hopefully give her time to think about what she would do when she got there. Remembering there was a hair band in the bottom of her wash bag, May scooped up her thick hair, glad to have something to tame it before it turned into a total frizzball. She stretched the band and it promptly snapped.

She leaned against the washbasin and counted to ten. Dammit! How had she become so inept that even the simplest things were beyond her? The trouble was she'd got too used to people running around fixing her hair and make-up, working their magic to conjure up an illusion of perfection. Wasn't it about time she stood on her own two feet again? She stared at herself, a blurred image in the polished steel. The real May was in there somewhere; all she had to do was find her.

In her pocket, her phone pinged. Another message from Aiden to add to the growing list, but nothing, she noticed, scrolling in vain, from her parents. Perhaps one day they'd surprise her and offer the sort of good, old-fashioned parental guidance she'd really appreciate right now. Yearning for familiarity nevertheless, she tapped the screen. There was no reply at Soul Survivor, the dippy hippie shop her mother ran, and when May tried her parents' home number she got Kurt Cobain who intoned 'Hello' fifteen times before Cathy's bored voice stated, 'Cathy and Rick. Here we are now. Entertain us.' May told them all she was alive and kicking. Unlike Kurt Cobain, she thought, ending the call, who if he'd known that he would feature so heavily on a middle-aged suburban couple's answerphone would probably have shot himself even sooner.

So where did she go from here? It seemed as if she couldn't even run away without ballsing it up. Right now it would be the easiest thing in the world to go back with her tail between her legs, before it was too late, and beg Aiden to make it all better for her.

'May!'

Someone lunged towards her the minute she got outside, but the initial shock lessened at the sight of golden sunshine gleaming on bright red hair.

'Bill!' She scowled. 'I told you, I don't need a lift.'

'No, I know you don't,' he mumbled, scratching his head, 'but the thing is, I need you.'

Huh! So Bill had chickened out of doing the trip by himself after all.

'What use could I possibly be to you? We've already established that my purpose was to sit around looking decorative whilst your uncle did manly stuff steering the boat, only breaking off to lavish expensive gifts on me.' She swung her bag over her shoulder a little too heartily and staggered which ruined her stage exit until she recovered herself and managed to walk.

'Please don't go,' she heard Bill say. Shrugging, she strode away determined, for once in her recent history, to stick to her guns but he caught up with her easily. 'I'm sorry. I was out of order. Please come back.'

'But Bill,' she cooed, 'you're not old enough for me. I'm only interested in sailing with a sugar daddy.' She gave him a sideways glance. Definitely squirming.

'Look, I was wrong to jump to conclusions, but I

was only trying to protect Cecil. I still am – please May, whatever you think of me, I need to get this boat to Little Spitmarsh as soon as possible, and it would be so much easier with your help. My uncle's taken a turn for the worse, and I desperately want him to see this boat before it's too late.'

'Oh god, Bill,' she said, instantly capitulating. 'Why didn't you say? Of course I'll help. It's what I came for, no matter what you think.' Besides, as she later acknowledged to herself bleakly, sitting beside Bill as they set off to buy provisions for the voyage, it wasn't as if she was spoiled for choice of places to go.

In the small outer London borough of Ebbesham, in the bedroom of a thirties semi-detached house whose twin had been disfigured by the addition of a shoe box of an extension obliterating any nod to its Arts and Crafts origins, Cathy Starling reached out and ran her hand over her bedside table until it traced a familiar outline. She placed a cigarette between her lips and stuck her hand out again until her fingers found the lighter. She lit up, drew deeply and reluctantly opened her eyes.

A fleeting moment of wondering if her eldest daughter's sudden urge to run away to sea would bring her to her senses was almost immediately blotted out by an acute sense that it was time to get her own life back on track. Only a glamorous rock chick could get away with proclaiming that fifty was the new thirty. By that reckoning it still meant that in four years' time she would be forty. Whichever way you looked at it, getting old stank. A cylinder of ash dropped on to the crumpled purple bedding. Unconcerned, Cathy flicked it on to the floor then hauled herself into a sitting position. It wasn't that she was losing her figure; there wasn't any extra flesh on her long bones, but something was definitely wrong with her skin. These days it looked as if someone had screwed it up very tightly but hadn't managed to smooth it out again, and when she pinched the top of her thigh it just sat there for a while. Like a favourite pair of knickers washed too many times, all her elastic had gone.

Wedging her cigarette firmly in the corner of her mouth, Cathy picked her old silk kimono out of the discarded clothes beside the bed so she wouldn't offend herself as she passed the mirror. A firm subscriber to the view that eating healthily was what invalids did, Cathy toyed with the idea of having a shot of Southern Comfort for breakfast but rejected it in favour of something hot: black coffee and another cigarette.

Somewhere along the line her supernova had become a black hole, sucking up her youth and the best years of her life. How had the Seventies turned into pushing sixty? Rick hadn't helped either, vetoing her weekend rave because he had to get up early for a roofing job. Of course, if he ditched the sudden interest in cycling and his new carbon fibre bike, he might have a bit more energy. And last night, he'd even been too tired to make love because he'd knackered himself on a pointless twelve-mile ride. Was she really married to a MAMIL, a middle-aged man in Lycra? What next, for fuck's sake? Blinking back tears of self-pity, Cathy ground the end of her cigarette into the dregs of her coffee and left the cup on the side.

If she didn't get her act together she'd become completely invisible. People used to say she looked like a young Cher, after the nose job, of course, and heads would turn when she walked down the street. May didn't realise how lucky she was. Why make a fuss about all the attention in a profession where the average shelf life was very short indeed? Where you could count the number of older women still in the game on one hand. Only someone as young and fresh as May could take her looks for granted, Cathy thought resentfully. Nowadays no one took any notice unless she was wearing a particularly short skirt, and then the odd, battered carload of lads might hoot at her back then retreat with shocked faces, looking as if they'd tried to pick up their own mums, once they'd seen her face.

But if there was no turning back the clock for her, she now stood a fighting chance of rejuvenating the shop. As a teenager she'd been thrilled and inspired by a couple of daring visits to Sex, Malcom McLaren and Vivienne Westwood's punk boutique. Unfortunately safety pins and tartan had gone out of fashion by the time she was in a position to open her own shop, so she'd stocked up on ultra-feminine, floaty fashion and called it Soul Survivor instead. That was fine until people stopped buying floaty dresses, when she'd given up on fashion and resorted to selling scarves, cards, scented candles and a few vaguely mystic, quasi-spiritual bits and bobs full of promises that even she had doubts about. No wonder she was bored. But just when she was staring down the barrel of gun, facing the fact that nothing could save Soul Survivor when customers had the entire internet to choose from, the cards had shuffled in her favour.

Ebbesham borough council, stung by a shopping satisfaction survey describing it as 'just another suburban clone town', was now popping up temporary shops and pumping out free Wi-Fi. Far from being seen as an embarrassing anachronism, Soul Survivor was being heralded as an example of the town's quirkier enterprises. Her overdraft, which had crept up during the lean years, no longer gave her such bad vibes, thanks to a most unexpected guardian angel, a new commercial landlord with a far more laid-back attitude than the previous bloodsucker, who had stepped in at just the right time. The planets were in perfect alignment and this was her chance to shine.

Leaving the house she was nearly flattened by a teenage boy on a skateboard who added insult to injury by calling her a stupid old bag. 'Stupid' she could cope with, 'bag' even, but 'old', no way. 'Death will come!' she shouted after him and was gratified when he was so busy putting his fingers up at her that his concentration lapsed and he nearly castrated himself on a bollard. 'Have a nice day,' she wished, passing him doubled up on the ground. Hers was getting better by the minute.

A workman, lounging in the doorway of Soul Survivor when she arrived five minutes late having stopped to buy tobacco for her roll-ups, also nearly got the sharp end of her tongue.

'Call this customer service,' he jeered. 'I've been waiting here so long I thought I was going to take root.'

She was about to tell him what he could do with himself until, getting close, she saw, even without her glasses, who it was. 'Oh, what do you want?'

'That's a nice thing to say to your old man.' Rick wrapped his hand round her waist and Cathy let him pull her towards him and stopped feeling quite so prickly. He'd worn well, she thought, sliding her hands up his face. Time had filled him out a bit and there was more grey than brown in his wild curls, but the heavy-lashed dark gold eyes still made her weak at the knees.

'Hurry up and open the door, before people stare,' Rick said, pressing his crotch against her.

Picking at the dried mortar on his T-shirt, Cathy pretended to push him away. 'But you're filthy.' She grinned.

'So my missus tells me. My clothes are dirty, but my hands are clean, and you'll do very nicely. Listen, I didn't drop by just to talk. I can pick up the mobile and do that. Now are you going to open the bloody door or am I going back to my roof?'

She loved the way he undressed her, gently peeling off each garment with throaty noises of appreciation as if he saw her with new eyes every time. He pushed her into the changing room and drew the inky blue curtain around him then lifted her on to his thighs, her back against the wall, so they could watch themselves in the mirror. Having admired her slender legs gripping his muscly bum and been reassured that her small breasts were still worthy of their silver nipple ring, Cathy lifted her head, tossed back her long hair and concentrated on more important things.

'Oh God! Oh God! Oh GOD!'

'Oh Christ, my legs!' said Rick. 'That's what you call a knee-trembler.' Ever the gentleman, he reached out for one of the long floaty scarves that people seemed to buy but never wear and slid it between her legs as he eased out. Cathy made a mental note not to put it back on display.

'I thought you were showing off a bit,' she teased, watching him trying to rub some life back into the tops of his legs. 'I've got some juniper oil in the shop somewhere. S'posed to be good for overexertion. Don't go away.' Backing out of the changing room her smile froze when she found that neither of them had remembered to put the 'Closed' sign on the door, and she was being regarded with some confusion by a Miss Marple-alike.

'Are you some sort of protestor?' asked the little old lady, bearing her handbag in case of attack.

'No, absolutely not,' beamed Cathy. 'I'm—'

The little old lady waited.

'I'm—,' Cathy looked down at the ends of the scarf still tucked between her legs. 'I'm Salome in our amateur dramatic production and I was just practising my dance of the seven veils.'

A flash of the old lady's very white teeth signalled her approval. 'And do you sell tickets?'

Cathy's mind went blank. 'What sort of tickets?'

'For the show. It looks like great fun!'

Seeing Rick's rigid feet and bare ankles protruding from the changing cubicle, Cathy rose to the challenge of making them quiver. 'No, unfortunately members of the cast aren't allowed to, but you will be able to buy them from the library in a couple of weeks. Five pounds is the usual price, but it's half that for students and senior citizens. Quite a bargain, wouldn't you agree?' A muffled guffaw from behind the curtain told her she had hit the spot.

'Splendid! Now I'd better not hold you up any longer. Keep up the good work!'

Hastily locking the door before Miss Marple remembered what she'd originally come in for, Cathy surprised a sober-suited businessman who was staring in at the window display. As he shot off looking somewhat pink about the gills she wondered whether, after her impromptu streak, he would be more or less likely to buy the Blue Heaven massage oil he'd been eyeing.

'You might have to practise that dance in front of me later,' Rick grinned, zipping up his jeans.

'Oh yes?' said Cathy, spotting her knickers at last. 'And what do I get on a plate?'

'My balls if I don't get back to work soon.'

'Better get a move on then, I prefer them where they

are.' She straightened up and looked at her husband. 'That was fun, wasn't it? Like the good old days.'

'So I'm past it, am I?' He rolled his eyes. 'Not you as well. I get enough from the blokes on site calling me bleedin' granddad.'

'Oh don't be so daft!' She wrapped her arms round him and buried her face in his neck. The old hurt was still there no matter how careful they were not to prod the scar tissue. 'I do wonder where the years have gone.' She sighed. 'It only seems like yesterday that the girls were babies. Now Stevie's at university, and May ... I hope she comes to her senses and realises just what she stands to lose in this bid for what she calls freedom. Doesn't she realise how many girls must be lining up to take her place?'

Rick held her away slightly. 'Don't be jealous of May. It's about time she got off the treadmill. I hope she's having some fun at last. I won't be sorry to see the back of Mr Bloody Obnoxious either.'

'I know you've never liked him,' sighed Cathy, thinking that no blokes were ever good enough for their daughters so far as dads were concerned. In any case, it was probably better to steer him off the subject of Aiden. 'But her catching a boat makes me feel even more that we've missed ours.'

Picking one of her hairs off his shirt, Rick paused for a moment then turned to her. 'Right, then,' he said. 'This is what we'll do. First of all we'll get shot of this place. That'll free you up. I can get casual work anywhere. We'll put the house on the market and while we're waiting for a buyer we'll go off in the camper van and have a look at places. We could start off in Cornwall and work our way up through Wales and the west of Scotland and we'll keep looking until we find somewhere that feels like home. We could go off to France, if you like, or maybe travel for a while. It's up to you.'

Cathy was feeling a touch of cold about her own feet now. 'But what will we live on?'

Shrugging, Rick headed for the door. 'Something will turn up. Anyway, money doesn't matter. Isn't that what we've always said?'

Blowing a kiss at her through the window, he ran off in the direction of the car park, leaving Cathy staring after him in dismay. After years of casting herself as a free spirit anchored by the ties of domestic duties, the reality of being unleashed to take off in any direction had suddenly lost its appeal. It was all very well pretending money didn't matter until you ran out. Then look at what had happened. Now, when she could almost touch her dream of success, she was suddenly reluctant to give up on the idea of becoming a successful businesswoman with cash to splash. And, she thought, catching sight of her reflection in one of the mirrors, she could get some Botox and fix her frown lines.

At last she collected herself sufficiently to change the sign on the door, then leant against it whilst she surveyed her domain. This was her world, the place that she'd created. How could she give up on it now, when better times were just around the corner? Someone banged violently on the glass panel, almost sending her into orbit. A customer! Right, she'd think about what to say to Rick later, but first she would attend to her business.

'I've been down the library and they've never heard of your production.'

Great, just what she needed, a vengeful Miss Marple.

'You need some publicity, my dear. It'll be a crying shame if no one sees your performance. Now give me some leaflets and I'll make sure they're distributed for you.'

Trust her to get lumbered with a persistent old biddy. What a drag! Once the makeover was complete, Soul Survivor would be so intimidatingly sophisticated and glamorous that no daft old bat or teenage girls hoping to nick nail varnish would dare cross the threshold. Until then, she'd just have to assume her Death Stare to put them off. May really didn't know how cosseted she was! Perhaps a few days in the real world fending for herself would help her appreciate what she was turning her back on. It was also about time she stopped being so inconsiderate and let them know exactly where she was. The sooner the better, for everyone's sake.

Chapter Five

It wasn't until *Lucille* took off backwards, aided by a sudden gust of wind, that May asked herself if she shouldn't have been more thorough about establishing Bill's credentials. Their course seemed to be set in a slow but relentlessly determined arc across what felt like a very narrow stretch of water separating her from other vessels. Looking to Bill to settle her doubts about the advisability of this manoeuvre, she found him tight-lipped but with a wild-eyed expression which was only matched by that on the faces of various yachtsmen popping up on decks as *Lucille* veered towards their expensive gel coats as gracefully and unpredictably as a pig on roller skates.

What a time, thought May, frantically wondering which boat to fend off first, to discover that she was off to sea with a complete nincompoop!

'You're cutting it a bit fine, aren't you?' she suggested.

Gaining momentum, *Lucille* seemed to have set her sights on a close encounter with one particularly beautifully kept model whose skipper was now so near that May could see the tears brimming up in his eyes.

'Get ready to fend us off, just in case,' Bill said, with a studied nonchalance that wasn't very reassuring. Unable to bear it any longer, May lunged over *Lucille*'s stern determined to push them off or be crushed in the process. Bracing herself to take the strain, she waited for her arms to snap like twigs at any moment. She closed her eyes, preferring not to watch a grown man cry, and got ready for the inevitable collision. Just seconds away from unpleasant phone calls to insurance companies, *Lucille*'s engine let out a farty roar whereupon she seemed to remember herself and, quite meekly, allowed Bill to steer her out of trouble.

'There are dinghies with more horsepower than this,' he muttered defensively as they began to snake their way to where the narrow creek joined the wide main channel which led, eventually, to Portsmouth's harbour mouth. 'Not that we were ever really in danger of hitting anything,' he continued, not quite meeting her eyes.

May was too busy weighing up which was most likely to draw them to the attention of the local coastguard as a shipping hazard first: the little wooden boat or her skipper? But once they'd shaken out the sails and cut the engine, taking it in turns to steer with the smooth wooden tiller, she could feel herself relaxing. They spent the rest of the day simply getting to know the boat, tacking backwards and forwards across the lively green waters of the wide channel safely upstream of the busy harbour mouth.

Watching the sails fill and listening to the *shwoosh* of the bow wave caressing the hull, May's worries seemed to slip away in the salty air. To begin with she was simply grateful to have snatched some precious breathing space, somewhere Aiden couldn't mess with her head or make her feel guilty. But soon she was too busy concentrating on finding out what *Lucille* could do and trying to impress Bill that eventually she even stopped wondering what might be waiting for her back on dry land.

Bill, too, looked happier once he was satisfied that their provisions had been securely stowed, the safety equipment was to hand and everything was in order to cast off at first light. 'We'll stop at Eastbourne first. That's nearly sixty nautical miles, which is quite far enough, especially while we're getting attuned to the boat,' he told her when they tied up on a temporary mooring to take a break. Spreading out a nautical map on the chart table, he showed her the route. 'It's another sixty nautical miles from there to Ramsgate, which is the best port from which to cross the Thames Estuary, then we'll head up the East Anglian coast.'

'Okay … and *Lucille* averages what speed?'

'Let's say about four knots.'

Walking pace, thought May.

'So tomorrow we'll have an hour or two of slow progress, but then the tide will take us all the way to Sovereign Harbour in Eastbourne. By my reckoning we'll probably do the whole trip from here to Little Spitmarsh in three passages, possibly four. Is that okay with you?'

Long enough for her to catch her breath, short enough to see there was an end in sight if their tentative truce broke down. She nodded and relaxed while they cast off again and pottered along the peaceful channel in the evening light, looking for a convenient place to tie up for the night.

'This'll suit us,' said Bill, pointing to a string of visitor moorings beneath the silhouette of the battlements of a medieval castle dominating the lonely shore line. 'We're not in anyone's way here and it'll be quiet. What are you like with a boat hook?'

'I've always been good at picking up buoys,' she replied, responding to his better mood but receiving a rather old-fashioned look in return. She grinned back at him before digging out the long hook to catch hold of the float attached to the mooring buoy. After her initial doubts, she was reassured that Bill was a perfectly competent yachtsman who wouldn't lose his head at the first sign of trouble. And if he regarded her simply as an extra pair of hands to bring the boat round, someone who was only there on sufferance, they'd probably rub along fine. No one else knew where she was, or how to find her, which was the most important thing.

If *Lucille* hadn't been as fretful as a hen on the wrong nest, agitated by a choppy current beneath her and a gusty wind above, May might have relaxed. As it was she slept fitfully, afraid of oversleeping, apprehensive about the journey and aware of Bill, on the other side of the curtain in the saloon, moving about in an equally disturbed sleep.

A summer storm of Shakespearean proportions jolted her awake just as her eyelids were getting heavy. She lay stiffly, listening to the roaring wind tearing at the rigging and the sound of water rushing past her just the other side of the hull as it set the wooden boat skittering and leaping about on the mooring buoy. A flare of white lightning lit the cabin as she clambered from her sleeping bag to investigate and found Bill dragging on wet weather gear.

'I'm just checking the mooring,' he told her above a cacophony of thunder and torrential rain beating on the coach roof. 'I'm not planning on going to sea until this lot blows over, but if we're not secured we might end up there anyway.'

Unless they were mown down by one of the much bigger vessels entering or leaving Portsmouth Harbour first, May worried. 'Hang on,' she said, 'I'll come with you.'

Bill looked ready to protest until the boat, having reached the end of its tether, pulled up with a jerk that nearly sent them both flying. 'Make sure you wear a safety harness and clip on to the lifeline, then.' He added, 'We'll make it the rule to wear life jackets and a harness whenever the situation calls for it. And remember, one hand for you and one hand for the boat when you're moving around on deck. I don't want to have to fish you out of the water.'

Dressed to round Cape Horn, they fought their way on deck together and into the full force of the squall. The current, rushing past at a terrifying speed, roared its malevolence and, in the dark, seemed set to sweep away anything in its path. May bent her head and held on for dear life as she followed Bill to the bow of the boat. A rivulet still found its way down her neck and she struggled to breathe as she gulped in the deluge driving against her face. Bill's hood had blown off and his wet hair was plastered to his head as he knelt down to try to adjust the thick ropes which were straining with the tide. May crouched beside him, her numb fingers reluctant to obey as, together, she and Bill slipped and slid on the greasy deck, fighting the current and eventually succeeding in lashing a new line to their mooring.

After their pounding from the elements, it was relief when they finally got back below where the saloon was calm and cosy and the oil lamps created a warm, comforting glow.

'Thank you,' said Bill, hanging their coats up to dry. 'That was so much easier with another pair of hands.'

Droplets slid down the bronze coils of his wet hair, which glistened like seaweed in the lamplight. May was reminded of a merman in a hoodie, but with rather more 'man' than 'mer'. More man, certainly, than anyone thinking she was paired up with some ancient mariner would be happy about. And yet, she was surprised at how quickly she was relaxing with someone she barely knew.

'Look at us.' He grinned, catching her staring. 'We're drenched before we've even gone anywhere. Sure you haven't changed your mind about this voyage?'

'It's all part of the experience, isn't it?' said May, watching as he took a bottle of malt whisky out of a locker.

And it was lots better than the alternative. Aiden wouldn't have been smiling; he'd have been telling her what a state she looked.

'Yep, you can say that all right,' Bill agreed. 'One moment you're peering through drizzle under gloomy grey skies and the next the sun is sparkling on turquoise sea. One day you long for the wind to pick up so you can sail properly and another it's blowing a gale and you wish you'd put another reef in to stop all that sailcloth flapping about wildly.'

May couldn't wait. For all that she was soaked through and shivering with cold, she could feel herself coming alive again at the promise of freedom and what the next few days would offer. Was it wrong, she wondered, to be secretly pleased that worrying news for Bill had stopped him putting her on a train?

'Where did you learn your sailing?' she asked. From what she'd observed it was an expensive hobby; how could a bloke like him afford it?

'Blame Cecil,' he said, finding a couple of glasses. 'When I was little he was always poring over charts showing me where he'd been. The names caught my imagination: The Swinge, Cap de la Hague, the Bay of Biscay. I wanted to see those places too.'

'Not for me, thanks,' said May as he unscrewed the bottle. He paused and raised an eyebrow at her. She'd seen how easily far too many people in her line of work had drunk themselves into oblivion, or succumbed to other temptations, to want to go down the same route. 'I don't drink alcohol,' she explained. 'So you were always close to Cecil?'

'Cecil took me on when I was eleven, after my mum died,' he eyed her over his glass then stood up and lit a match under the kettle. 'Hot chocolate?'

'Sorry, that must have been very tough for you.' She

passed him a mug while he opened one of the sachets of instant drinks they'd bought earlier. 'I'll do it – you don't have to wait on me.'

'Sit down,' he waved her away. 'It wasn't easy, but it was a long time ago.'

It didn't make it any less painful though, she surmised. And now Cecil's life was in danger too. Despite Bill's calm façade, he was probably desperate to get through the coming days without incident.

'It will give your uncle something to hold on for, knowing the boat's on its way,' she said quietly.

'Abdominal aortic aneurysm,' Bill said, shaking his head. 'At least the hospital discovered it in time. It could have ruptured. But that explains why he'd lost so much weight. It was making it difficult for him to eat.'

'So now they have to wait for him to regain his strength before they operate?'

He sat down, as if contemplating his uncle's illness was hard to bear. 'And to decide exactly how to repair the damaged section of the aorta. If he's lucky they'll be able to avoid opening him up and will be able to fix it with keyhole surgery, by threading the graft up through an artery in one of his legs. The advantage, of course, is that he'd recover much quicker. And there are fewer complications.'

He took a deep breath and May was almost moved to reach across the table to give his hand a reassuring squeeze, but the kettle began to whistle and he stood up.

'What about you?' he asked, pouring hot water into the mug. 'Where did you learn to sail?'

May was thankful his back was turned. 'Well, I joined a sailing club at university and took a basic skills course.'

'That's a sensible starting point,' Bill agreed. 'From there, you increase your knowledge with sailing experience.'

Did a couple of outings on other people's motorboats count too? She certainly hoped so.

Bill smiled as he set the hot chocolate down on the small table between them and May smiled back, suddenly noticing that he was really quite good-looking in a red-haired way. If she was half the woman he'd got the impression she was from her response to Cecil's ad, she might have contemplated assuaging all the hurt with a quick fling. Except, she wasn't like that, was she? Besides, he was worrying himself sick about his beloved uncle and her confidence had been so badly dented that she'd run away to sea to lick her wounds. Not exactly a recipe for uninhibited lust.

Warm at last, if not dry, she unfolded herself and stretched. Bill's sandy brows lifted; for some reason she'd really got his attention. Looking down she saw that where her hair had dripped there were two large wet patches which had turned her thin white T-shirt to cling film. 'Oops,' said May, quickly folding her arms. 'One cold front too many, eh?'

Bill was sitting outside the next morning, watching a silver sheet of stratus cloud stretching across the sky, when muffled stirrings from the cabin beneath him told him May was awake and put him on notice to assume his poker face. The sun wasn't up, but looking at May's sheepish expression, when she eventually stuck her head out the hatch, he was sure her crimson face would make a convincing substitute.

'Morning,' he said, congratulating himself for keeping his cool. 'Care for a cooked breakfast?'

As unexpected and delightful as the revelation of her wet T-shirt had been the night before, Bill was determined, as he followed May back down the companionway, that he was going to make damn sure to forget he'd even seen it. It had certainly drawn the previous evening to a rapid conclusion. Taking her mug of hot chocolate with her, May had scampered back to her cabin pretty sharpish, leaving him staring at the space she'd left, nursing his whisky and mentally naming boat parts whilst he waited for his vital signs to get back to normal. First he'd tried telling himself he was sitting on the settee berth looking at the table. The table that could be lowered to convert the settee berth into a *double bed*. No, that didn't help. Floor? Yep, better; the cabin sole. And the space under the cabin sole? Bulge. Flip, no; bilge, *bilge!* Wet locker for willies. Bill shook his head. Wellies. Names of valves to let water in and out? Seacocks. Suddenly even the most innocent places were laden with innuendo.

Bill directed his attention back to making breakfast. Last night, it had taken another hefty dram for his blood to redistribute itself and he certainly wasn't about to risk any sudden movements now. Not when there was hot fat spitting on the two-ring gas burner.

'Sausage?' he asked.

May blinked then nodded.

'Beans? Bacon?'

'Wow! Do you always look after your crew this well?' May asked, scanning the table and searching round for cutlery.

'In a plastic box in that locker,' he said, indicating the direction with a nod of his head. 'It's going to be a long, demanding day, so we need to keep our strength up.'

The gas burners were making it warm in the cabin. May fanned her face and unzipped her fleece just enough to throw his good intentions to the wind. 'How do you like your eggs?' he asked, before he could re-engage his brain.

He was sure he heard her snigger, but she quickly covered it with a cough before replying and setting out knives and forks.

'All right,' he said, when they were sitting down to eat. 'Some dos and don'ts before we set sail.'

'I thought we'd been through all the safety checks and distress calls.' May took a sip of tea.

'This is more about sharing a small space,' he began.

'Size isn't everything, it's what you do with it,' May surveyed him innocently over her mug. 'We're grown-ups, aren't we? Provided we respect each other's need for privacy at crucial moments, we'll be fine. Hey, at least you can pee over the side which is more than I can.' She returned to her breakfast and tucked into a mouthful of sausage.

'You mentioned sleeping tablets,' he said, trying not to let his attention wander. 'As skipper, I need to know if you're on any other medication so I know what to do if anything goes wrong.'

She laid her knife and fork down. 'Thank you for your concern, Bill. But, I'm perfectly sane, if that's what you're asking. I might, when I've had a lot on my mind, occasionally take a short course of herbal sleeping pills just to break the pattern until I'm sleeping normally again, but I understand your concerns and I promise not to use them on this trip. And I didn't reply to your uncle's ad because I was daft, as you put it, but because I needed a complete change of scenery. Nothing wrong in that, I take it?'

Bill shook his head, though he was longing to ask what scenery she was so keen to take a break from.

'The only thing you need to know,' she went on, picking up her cutlery, 'is that I'm perfectly fit and well. Anything else is none of your damn business.' She stabbed a fork into her bacon and he winced.

'May, I wasn't asking for a GP's report,' he tried to reassure her. How to explain without giving away exactly what he was feeling – like telling her that he was a strong man but regular viewings of her wet T-shirt might have him taking bites out of the timber hull? 'Look, all I'm trying to say is that it's easy enough to be pleasant and polite to each other when conditions are calm—'

'—but you want to know if I'm a crazy banana who might turn psycho on you when the going gets tough,' May scoffed. 'Don't worry. You don't need to hide the flares and the harpoon gun.'

Bill held up his hand. 'All I'm saying is that when you're dealing with the unpredictability of the open sea and everything the elements can throw at you, feelings can run very high. We should both be aware of that. It's better to let those emotions out so we can deal with them as they arise rather than keeping them bottled up.'

Her hair had fallen across her face as she concentrated on her breakfast. Since he couldn't read her expression, he hoped this was a sign of assent.

'At the same time,' he began carefully, 'being shaken around in a small boat together can create, erm, an unnatural sense of intimacy. When you're sharing such an intense experience, it inevitably brings you close. But it would be a mistake to compare those heightened emotions for anything that would feel the same on dry land. Not, of course, that you're unattractive – far from it – all I'm saying is that we should be able to share our thoughts without prejudice. What happens on the boat, stays on the boat.' And hopefully that would cover an uncontrollable boner or two as well.

He paused but only heard the sound of May chasing a forkful of baked beans round her plate.

'Excellent,' he rounded off. 'I simply want to get this boat round to Cecil. I don't need any complications and neither, I strongly suspect, do you.'

'No problem,' said May, her flushed face bare of make-up and devoid of guile. 'Is it me or is it roasting in here?' She stood up to throw off her fleece and Bill was relieved to see that she was wearing a thick enveloping T-shirt. And no bra, a deliciously slow-mo suggestion of wobble told him as she sat down again.

'That's better,' she smiled at him. 'So. Got something you need to get off your chest?'

Bill swallowed and desperately tried not to think about what he would like to get off hers. That T-shirt, for a start. He dragged his gaze back to the table more grateful than he had been for anything in his life that it was there. If it started to collapse now there was every chance he could keep it up all by himself. And without using his hands.

Chapter Six

'Clear!' May shouted from the pulpit, the safety rail at the front of the boat, as she let go of the mooring lines and watched the yellow buoy slip away. Bill, at the helm, gave her a thumbs up. She paused for a moment to catch her breath before making her way back to the cockpit. No turning back now; they were stuck with each other for better or worse. At least she didn't have to worry about driving Bill crazy with desire. Not unattractive indeed. Talk about faint praise. He probably, like Aiden, had taken one look at her without her make-up and noticed how piggy her muddy hazel eyes were and that her mouth was too wide. An acquired taste, Aiden had called her once, but not one, Bill had made it crystal clear, that he was willing to try.

A choppy, unsettled tide meant that what should have been a straightforward exercise became a frustrating thrash as they motored slowly towards the narrow mouth of Portsmouth Harbour. 'Wow! Look – HMS *Victory*!' May couldn't help exclaim, catching sight of the tall rigging of the famous old warship beside the historic dockyard. Seven hundred large oak trees, each of them about one hundred years old, were supposed to have gone into its construction. 'And *Warrior* too!' This was where Henry VIII's flagship, *The Mary Rose*, was constructed, the place Admiral Nelson left to command the fleet that won the battle of Trafalgar! Gosh, she really was part of maritime history now.

'Never mind that,' Bill shouted, steering into what felt like a marine rush hour, 'just keep an eye on what everyone else is doing, will you?'

The trouble was that with huge freight ships, passenger

ferries, military vessels and a variety of small crafts all funnelling towards what was beginning to feel like a very small exit, May was running out of eyes.

'Bill!' she shouted, straining to be heard above the commotion as she gesticulated at the ferry bearing down on them.

'I'm trying to get out the way!' Bill roared back. 'Ideally I'd like to get close to the western bank where the current curls back on itself so we're not punching against it.'

'So? Go a bit faster, then.'

'This is as good as it gets,' Bill said, with a quick look over his shoulder. 'It's a sailing boat, remember, not a motorboat. This engine's not built for speed.'

No, it was apparently built to chug along at a rate of acceleration so stately that even little old ladies shopping at nearby Gunwharf Quays could easily outpace it. Now May remembered that the *Mary Rose* had sunk here, almost in this very spot, and that Admiral Nelson was mortally wounded in his fight to confirm his country's naval supremacy and received a hero's funeral for his achievements rather than a hero's welcome. Great! She didn't actually want to be part of maritime history that much. She closed her eyes as the ferry slid past them, its stern wave sending them bucking wildly as *Lucille* crabbed westwards.

In a minute, she told herself, waiting for her head to stop spinning, the motion would get better. It was fear making her feel queasy, wasn't it? Worrying that you were about to be sunk without a trace or that your vessel might take out a smaller craft wasn't good for you. No wonder her legs were shaking and her palms were clammy. But even when they finally made it out of the hectic harbour and into the comparative calm of the Solent, she needed to concentrate. The slim strait, separating the mainland and the Isle of

Wight was, after all, a busy recreational area for water sports in addition to being a major shipping route. It was also, she was beginning to realise as *Lucille* started rolling on a wallowy sea left over from the storm, subject to some complex tides.

May's stomach started rolling along with the boat, and her face, she was sure, reflected the green waves. Bill frowned at her, but it was impossible to say anything to reassure him since she was too afraid to open her mouth. Unzipping her jacket, she took great lungfuls of sea air and tried to let her body go with the flow. It duly did, although not in quite the way she hoped. It was all very humiliating and not, she thought, given Bill's earlier observations about her, exactly guaranteed to send him suddenly crazy with desire.

'Here,' he said, passing her a bottle of mineral water.

Having sluiced out her mouth and wiped her face she felt marginally more human. 'Let me steer for a bit. I'll be all right now.'

'Sure?' He stood beside her, showing her their course and waiting until she was comfortable before sitting down.

'I'm sorry about that,' she mumbled.

'Don't apologise. Lots of sailors are sick before they get their sea legs back. It puts a lot of would-be yachtsmen off for good. You're brave to come back for more.'

May was relieved to use her nausea as an excuse not to respond to that one. Bill probably didn't want to hear that she hadn't really been at sea enough times to find out how prone she was to seasickness.

'You've got guts,' he told her, sounding impressed.

'Yes, mainly over the side decks.'

'May! Don't you know how to take a compliment?'

He was so near the mark that, for a horrible moment, she was afraid she would cry. 'Try a few more,' she said, hoping he would put her watery eyes down to the aftermath of barfing over the side. 'I'll see how I get on.' Risking a quick glance in his direction, May found that for once he was smiling. Simultaneously she noticed the sun had come out; why else would the day seem suddenly brighter?

By mid-afternoon it was so hot that May, sweltering in her jeans, had swapped them for shorts and a sleeveless T-shirt. Hair piled up under a baseball cap, she stood at the helm guiding *Lucille* over the undulating green sea. There wasn't a breath of wind in the sky, just the occasional wispy cloud trailing past the mast. This is what she had come for: to be away from land, to watch the waves turning over like molten glass and not let herself think about …

'Beachy Head,' said Bill, pointing out the chalk headland that was a notorious suicide hotspot just when she was trying to let go of all her negative thoughts. Even on a beautiful, benign day like today, there was a sense of despondency about the place. She'd read somewhere that the top of the cliff was studded with fingernails where suicides changed their minds seconds after jumping. It was an image that was hard to shake off. Shuddering, she looked away to where a recent landfall had created a chalk pier stretching out to sea, but even that felt, to her, as if the cliff had thrown itself at the lighthouse, unable to take any more.

'It crumbles at an average of a metre a year,' said Bill nodding towards the towering headland.

Rather like her with Aiden, thought May.

'The sea attacks from the bottom and ice from the top until the chalk comes away in great chunks. That white face is actually caused by constant erosion.'

Yes, she knew how that felt too.

'But of course it makes the most wonderful reflective surface,' Bill went on. 'Ghostly grey in the moonlight, blood red in the sunset or, like today, brushed with golden light. We're lucky to see it from the sea like this, not many people do.'

Those unhappy times could be sloughed away, May told herself firmly, and with them her previous life. Here, at sea, she could breathe freely.

'… just as not many people know that I quite like talking to myself.'

'Bill! Sorry, I *was* listening.'

'Come on, it's not too far to Sovereign Harbour now,' he said, touching her lightly on the shoulder, bringing her back to the present. 'You've done enough for a while, I'll take over.'

Stretching her stiff back against sun-warmed wood, she sank back gratefully and studied him from beneath her peaked cap. 'Was it difficult for you to drop everything to do this?'

'I cleared my diary when Cecil was taken ill. I'm self-employed so all I'm losing is money.'

May congratulated herself on her supreme lack of tact. An unpalatable thought crossed her mind. 'But what about your wife and six children?'

'My wife divorced me because she didn't like the hours I was putting in setting the business up. We never got round to having children,' he said lightly.

Tipping the peak of her cap a little lower, May closed her eyes, lifted her face up to the sun, giving all the outward signs that she was relaxing so that Bill would let her off the hook and not ask about *her* private life or the sudden interest in his. She had, after all, just been making conversation. What was it to her if Bill was married with ten children or single and fancy-free? Even so.

* * *

Their stay in Sovereign Harbour, if May didn't include the scary lock at the entrance to the marina, passed uneventfully. After fifteen hours at sea both she and Bill had been glad to eat a hasty meal then retire to their respective bunks. Now, after another long day at sea and another night in a harbour, May came to with a start and it took her a few seconds to remember where she was.

The first part of the passage from Eastbourne had passed smoothly enough, but the next twenty miles had felt like an eternity of punching against the tide. Progress had been punishingly slow and the elements unkind with sudden squalls that had them hastily donning wet weather gear. The forecasts had warned of a 'bit of a blow', but an unseasonal gale had arrived from nowhere, along with a couple of tsunami-like waves. May had been relieved when, after negotiating some of the busiest shipping lanes in the world, they managed to slip into Ramsgate just before the wind rose.

From somewhere nearby, a fishing vessel was playing Dutch radio full blast, featuring many hits that really should have been buried in history. With her luck, she was only seconds away from hearing 'Chillin' in the Park', the single that would haunt her for the rest of her days. But for now, she realised, sitting up in her berth, she was free of all those associations. Who, round here, would ever link the woman she was now to the girl she was then? A glance in the mirror showed that, if anything, she had travelled forwards, not backwards, in time. A pillow-crumpled shiny red face framed by wild hair peered back at her. Feeling like her own granny after a bad sunbed treatment, May went up on deck just in time to bump into Bill, who was fresh-faced and sweet smelling from a trip to the showers.

'Feeling better this morning?' he asked perkily. 'You

were a bit subdued last night, but – see? – we made it before the storm. Although how soon we can leave remains to be seen.'

It wasn't fear that had crushed her, not of the elements anyway. What had really made her stomach churn was the menacing tone of Aiden's latest text. They were so hard to ignore once she knew they were there, but so far she'd managed to resist the compulsion to respond.

Conscious of exuding a mephitic cloud that would shame the most unsavoury drunk, May brushed aside Bill's all's-right-with-the-world offer of tea and grabbed her shower bag and change of clothes. Lowering herself on to the pontoon, her suspicion that she couldn't look anything less like a pop princess was confirmed when, even though they had been at sea for goodness knows how long, none of the men working on the fishing boat looked up until she skidded on a bit of fishy debris and narrowly saved herself from a cold plunge.

Looking behind to see if anyone else had noticed, she saw Bill standing with a small band of gale-bound sailors on the pontoon, all hoping, presumably, that their yachts wouldn't disintegrate before their eyes whilst they dodged ten foot walls of spray and tried to rustle up some Dunkirk spirit. Behind them, May suddenly saw, her eyes widening in alarm, several small boats reeling into the harbour to escape the gale were also being forced to take cover from a massive, top-of-the-range luxury yacht named *Valhalla* roaring in and rapidly running out of marina.

On board the smaller yachts, once their owners knew they were out of danger, white faces lit up with ghoulish interest at the prospect of seeing several hundred thousand pounds' worth of yacht smash into unyielding concrete. In contrast to open-mouthed spectators standing idly by, there was great activity on board *Valhalla*. Figures in expensive matching Henri Lloyd wet weather gear jumped about frantically flinging ropes over the side whilst their skipper barked expletives and steered straight at the pontoon.

'Over here!' bellowed Bill.

May froze as he raced to catch a wildly thrown line then braced himself to take the impact of the still speeding yacht. 'Let go!' she screamed. If he didn't drop the line now he would either be dragged between the yacht and the pontoon like a human fender or lose his fingers trying to hold the rope. 'Please, Bill! Don't be a hero!'

Jerked out of their inertia by her cries, some of the men standing round sprang forward to help. There was a heart-stopping moment when their efforts seemed set to fail, but with the very tip of its nose about to be kissed by concrete, they managed to drag the line round a mooring cleat and *Valhalla* shuddered to a halt.

The exhausted men sank to the ground and May made a beeline for Bill. 'You idiot!' she told him, taking his hands and turning them over to examine large weals across his palms. 'Fancy putting yourself at risk like that for morons with more money than sense. They probably won't even thank you for it!'

'On the contrary, darling,' came a breathy voice from behind her. 'The skipper is very grateful to you for saving his new toy. And if the skipper is happy, *I'm* happy.'

They looked up to find one of the expensively liveried crew next to them. Bill seemed about to brush aside any thanks until the bright red storm hood was drawn back to release a curtain of glossy mahogany-brown hair which made May even more self-conscious about her own unkempt locks. Wide blue eyes under sweeping lashes gave the other woman an air of innocence which was somewhat at odds with the predatory curve of her lips. She was also surprisingly strong as she elbowed May out the way. Evidently she had decided that Bill was weak with shock and needed reviving, since she proceeded with some very thorough mouth to mouth. Ooh! Bill would hate being shown up like that!

'Thank you,' she purred, releasing him at last.

'The pleasure,' said Bill, grinning from ear to ear, 'was all mine.'

'Paige!' someone roared from the deck high above them. 'What the fuck do you think you're doing!'

Glaring down at them, the skipper was not a pretty sight. With his grisly skull-like face topped with spiky yellow hair he had the look of a man who owns one nightclub too many.

'Don't talk to me like that, Thunder!' Paige returned shrilly. 'Can't you see this poor man has been injured!'

'What's that, babe?'

'Deaf as a post,' she told May, shaking her head.

'INJURED!' she bellowed. 'Looks positively ACTIONABLE to me!'

'Nothing we can't sort out over a few stiff ones I hope? Get him over here now.'

The skipper's neck retracted into the black offshore jacket that marked him out from his crew. He reminded May of a sporty tortoise. Did they head off to warmer places for the winter, she wondered, or did Paige paint his name on his back, pack him in straw and leave him in a box at the back of the garage? But, wait a minute, May screwed up her eyes to get a better look at the man on deck. Her heart sank as she realised she hadn't misheard: the woman standing next to them really had called him Thunder. It was definitely time to make herself scarce.

Chapter Seven

Bill couldn't help grinning at May's frosty expression. 'Forget about it,' he told the woman pouting her luscious lips at him. 'I was happy to help.'

'Let me, at least, put something on those hands for you,' his Florence Nightingale purred, with a look that suggested she might like to put something in them too.

'I'll go off for my shower, then, shall I?' May huffed.

Bill turned an interested gaze on her. Surely her cute little nose hadn't been put out of joint because the lovely Paige was flirting with him?

'But darling,' he protested – and immediately got her full attention – 'you know how prone I am to fainting when I feel pain. You'd better come with me.' He hooked hold of her arm before she could escape and leaned forward to hiss in her ear, 'Come on, it'll be fun. I want to see what you get for your money inside a yacht like this. It's an Oyster and they don't come cheap!'

Despite the earliness of the hour, the skipper was initially too busy pouring himself a drink to take much notice. Bill took no offence as it gave him plenty of opportunity to gawp at all the American oak joinery and blond faux suede upholstery lining the saloon. Besides, he had some sympathy for the skipper; he'd need a drink too if he'd narrowly avoided writing off such a valuable yacht.

Cecil would love hearing the story later. He only wished his uncle could have been there to see it too as it would certainly have perked the old boy up. Though not, he thought, feeling his eyebrows raise, quite as much as the sight of Paige casually discarding her wet weather gear to reveal a tiny pair of white shorts and a hot pink polo shirt, which was at least a size too small and was unbuttoned to show a lot of tanned cleavage as she leaned over him with a first aid kit.

Taking no notice whatsoever of this fleshfest was a young man with his head obstinately stuck in a car magazine.

'Thunder's son, Blaise,' Paige explained, following his puzzled glance. 'Bit of a petrolhead. Adores anything with wheels.'

'Pity I don't like you, then,' snarled Blaise, sotto voce so that his father couldn't hear. 'You're always taking Dad for a ride.'

Reminding them of why they were assembled, the luxury yacht rocked with the impact of the next gust outside.

'Blast!' complained Thunder as most of his drink landed in his lap.

'Yes, sweetie,' said Paige, dabbing at his crotch whilst Blaise pulled a look of disgust. 'But it should blow through soon. Let me get you another one. Anyone else?'

Coming to at last, Thunder straightened up and suddenly noticed May who was poised for flight at the other end of the settee. 'Sorry to cause you so much trouble, babe.' He smiled, which made him look slightly more human than reptile. 'I hope we haven't held you up. When are you and your bloke hoping to get away?'

May, who was still clutching her shower bag, gave him the ghost of a smile in return. 'I don't think any of us are going anywhere just yet. And he's not my bloke.'

'I see,' he nodded.

They fell silent. May's gaze roamed over the spacious saloon flooded with light from twinkling ceiling lights and generous windows. It lingered on the sensuous curve of the wood, the pale blue silk cushions adorning the deep seating areas, the pop-up plasma screen TV and entertainment centre. And while May studied the boat, its skipper was studying May.

Bill wasn't sure he liked the way this encounter appeared to be going. Maybe his initial instincts about May were sound? Perhaps such a conspicuous display of wealth suggested a better alternative to a further voyage on *Lucille*? But then May didn't look anything like Paige; her hair was naturally tousled in that sexy messed-up-in-bed way, her face was endearingly pink from the sun, not the colour of fake bake and, he couldn't help but notice, as she went back to dressing his hands, the perfect bowl-shaped pertness of Paige's breasts rather suggested that her assets weren't all thanks to Nature's bounty. May's charms were all her own; she wasn't Thunder's type, surely?

He narrowed his eyes as Thunder opened his mouth and turned back to May.

'You don't half look familiar, babe,' he said, searching May's face. 'I swear we've met before.'

'Right that's it,' Bill said, leaping up. 'We need to see how *Lucille*'s doing.'

Waving away Paige, who now that she had got hold of him seemed reluctant to discharge her patient, Bill clung on to May and pointed her in the direction of the companionway.

'Talk about the cruise from Hell!' groaned May when they were safely out of earshot.

Unwinding the bandages that made him feel like an extra from *The Mummy*, Bill paused to throw her an amused look. 'Comfortable surroundings and a sugar daddy to pay the bills ... sure you wouldn't like to swap boats?'

'If that's supposed to be a joke, it's not remotely funny,' May said hotly. 'I've told you before, I needed a break, I was in a hurry to get away and I certainly didn't mean to raise poor old Cecil's blood pressure so desperately.'

He was about to come back at her with a withering retort when he noticed her eyes were brimming with tears. Flip! This wasn't turning out as he'd intended, it was just that seeing the hideous Thunder come on to her like that with all that guff about being sure they'd met before had made him feel ... he struggled for the right word ... protective of her.

'May?'

She fanned her face with her hand and shook her head. 'I'm going for my shower, then I'll see if I can find the laundrette. I might as well get on with something useful if we're here for a day or two.'

'Good idea,' he nodded, thankful for the reprieve. 'Is there anything I can do?'

'Yes,' she said, so vehemently he took a step back, 'you can cut me some slack.'

The constant frapping and jangling of rigging lines against the metal masts of stranded yachts knelled an end to their passage plans; even in Ramsgate's all-weather harbour, little *Lucille* still bounced around like an egg in a cauldron of boiling water. May concentrated on channelling her energy into getting everything shipshape so they'd be ready to set off as soon as conditions were even halfway tolerable. Keeping herself out of trouble by dealing with the pile of washing was easier than defending herself against Bill's grubby accusation, since she had no wish to explain what lay behind Thunder's sudden sense of déjà vu. The only dirty linen she had any intention of making public was the load going into the coin-op machine in front of her now.

She shook her head. However brave she tried to be,

thinking about Aiden was still like probing a fresh wound; every time she poked around to see how the new tissue was coming along she made herself bleed again. The washing was beginning to blur and not just because it was spinning. Rather than shed more tears for Aiden, May decided that once she'd bundled the washing into a drier, she'd set off for a spot of retail therapy.

What she found was that like so many tired seaside places, shunned in favour of more exotic destinations, the town reflected years of steady decline. It wasn't shopping temples that were keeping the pubs and restaurants open, but towering turbines, the development of offshore wind farms and the construction work that came with them which were creating regeneration. An ill or good wind, depending on your point of view. Perhaps it was passing a shop selling the same sort of new-agey knick-knacks her mother stocked that had set-up some psychic connection, but, whatever it was, it was both a comfort and a surprise to May when her phone rang and she saw it was her mother calling.

Most of the time Cathy pretended to be far more laid-back than she really was. Although, the fact she'd screeched, 'For fuck's sake May, have you thought about the risks?' at a level only dogs could hear when May had told her about her sailing trip showed she was still capable of being shocked, even if it hadn't been quite the reaction May had hoped for. Not only that, Cathy had been topless sunbathing at the time and had tugged on her tie-dye top so furiously she'd nearly yanked her silver nipple ring from its mooring.

Listening to her now, she could imagine Cathy in Soul Survivor with the blue door open and cannabis-scented joss sticks, at least she hoped it was joss sticks, streaming into the warm air. She'd be sitting by herself at the counter wearing a pair of cheap reading glasses which always slipped down her nose. A gossip magazine – left, she always said, by a schoolgirl customer – would be spread in front of her and, as she bent her head, a fine white seam along the parting of her ferociously dyed jet hair would show.

'I'm fine, Mum,' she assured her, picturing her face, always gentler in repose, assuming its harder, angular proportions as she rattled off another question.

'No, we won't go anywhere until it's safe. Then it should be one passage, a long one admittedly, to Little Spitmarsh. When? Depends how quickly the storm blows over. Another couple of days, I reckon. Yep. Love you, Mum. Mum?'

No answer. Cathy had gone, but it made May smile just to know her mum had been thinking of her. She was surprised that her mother had sounded so delighted when she'd picked up, as if she was genuinely missing her and sorry she wouldn't be home soon. It was unusual for someone who'd never shown signs of Empty Nest Syndrome to sound even faintly clingy. Yet beneath the aggressively black hair and smoky eye make-up was an insecure woman who had struggled to find her own niche in the world.

For all Cathy's feigned indifference, she loved her daughters, but because of her own upbringing found it hard to express her feelings. Rick, of course, she adored. May always had the feeling that if something ever happened to her dad, her mum would find it difficult to carry on without him. Considering the pair of them had been in their mid teens when they'd met, she sometimes wondered how they'd managed to stick together. For all the lean times when money had been scarce and with faults on both sides, somehow their relationship worked. How had May managed to make such a mess of her own love life?

Consoling herself with a double scoop of Italian ice cream and a totally superfluous chocolate flake, May parked herself on a bench overlooking the harbour to juggle with the problem of trying to soak up as much sun as she could whilst making her ice cream last as long as possible. Even then, the gusty wind imprisoning them in the harbour was against her, snatching strands of her hair and whipping them across her mouth. As she did her best to fight it and see off the threat from a couple of interested gulls wheeling above her head watching her with beady eyes, she barely registered the footsteps coming towards her until it was too late.

'I've been looking for you, babe,' said Thunder, sliding on to the bench next to her. 'Paige wanted to get her nails done, so I took a stroll into town with her and saw you go by.'

May braced herself for what she knew was coming, but at least Bill wasn't around to witness Thunder's epiphany.

'It was doing my head in wondering where I knew you from,' he said, searching her face, 'and all of sudden, it came to me! Of course, you look different without the stage gear and the fancy lighting – but, it is you, isn't it? You're Ch—'

'Ah, May. This is where you've been hiding, is it?' said Bill, towering over them and making her jump. He pulled something out of his pocket and dangled it under her nose. 'By the way, you left these behind.'

May could have kicked him. Of all the pairs of knickers spinning round in the drier he'd ignored her industrial-strength comfy old faithfuls and picked out one of the few pairs that didn't give you a visible panty line because there was no panty to see and which she only wore when all else failed.

Bill raised his eyebrows as she snatched back her knickers and glared at him.

'Easy, man,' said Thunder, hastily withdrawing. 'The little lady and I were just having a chat. I didn't realise you two were an item.'

'We're not!' May insisted. What the hell did Bill think he was doing? However timely his intervention, she was blowed if she was going to let Bill Blythe play Big Brother with her life.

'We may not be an item, May,' Bill ground out, his eyes glinting. 'But we do have some unfinished business.'

Growing paler by the minute, Thunder turned to May. 'Now look. If you two have got stuff to sort out I'll leave you to it.'

'What the hell has it got to do with you anyway?' she exploded as Thunder beat an unflatteringly swift retreat. 'Who do you think you are, sneaking up on me like that!'

'Whoa! Steady on now. In twelve hours' time,' Bill said, pointing at his watch, 'we can get on our way again. The wind's dropped sufficiently, but there's still a heavy swell out there and we'll need our wits about us.'

'Are you trying to tell me I'm incompetent?' May snorted.

'Let's just say your mind's not on the job,' Bill said pleasantly. 'Well not the job of preparing to go sea, anyway. It was your choice to do the laundry, so I thought I could rely on you to complete the task. If you can't even get through a pile of washing without getting distracted, how do I know you'll concentrate when we're sailing?'

'Shape up or ship out? Is that what you're saying? Fine.

That suits me just fine. I'll just collect my belongings and then you can find someone else to deliver your bloody boat.'

'Not my bloody boat,' Bill shouted after her as she marched off in the direction of the harbour. 'Cecil's. And she's no good to him if we lose her at sea.'

Keep walking, May told herself; it's not your problem, he's Bill's uncle, nothing to do with you. Except for the fact it was her who'd replied to his e-mail, built his hopes up and agreed to deliver his boat … She stopped and waited for Bill to catch up.

Bill rewarded her with a grateful smile. 'Look, I'm sorry if I came on too strong, but I've just spoken to the hospital …'

He broke off and swallowed hard. May couldn't help but touch his arm seeing how he was struggling to contain his emotions.

'What's happened?' she asked gently.

'Oh, hopefully nothing too bad,' he said, 'but Cecil's developed a chest infection which is giving slight cause for concern. They can't operate on him until he recovers.'

'Then we must make sure we get away as soon as we can. I don't mind if it's a bit lumpy out there,' she assured him, 'so let's make sure everything's ready so we can cast off at first light.'

'Thanks,' he said, surprising her by taking one of her hands in his, 'and I'm sorry if I spoilt your fun just now, but I think you'll thank me for it in due course.'

'Let's just drop the subject, shall we?' she said shakily. Coming so close to being unmasked by Thunder was unnerving; if he shared his discovery with the world, she'd be hunted down for sure. The sooner they got away, the better, and it would certainly make the rest of the voyage easier if she could maintain the status quo with Bill until they went their separate ways. Better a row about the washing than the battle she had yet to face about her washed-up career. 'I don't know about you, but I'm not in the mood for cooking. Let's find somewhere to eat this evening. And just to show that there are no hard feelings, you can pay.'

'What?'

She gave him a watery smile. 'It's the least you can do, but don't worry, I'm not expecting dinner at the Ritz. If I was any good as a gold-digger, Bill, I wouldn't be standing here with you. A curry will do fine.'

Chapter Eight

In Soul Survivor, Cathy was more relieved than she would admit that her eldest daughter was safe, well and happy. At least she could forget her immediate worries about May pitching about in a little boat somewhere at sea with a complete stranger. May had always been the reliable one in the family, her feet firmly on the ground even when her career was at its height. When she'd taken off like that, Cathy had to admit, it felt like a slap in the face to everyone who'd supported her through some early setbacks. She made another phone call to share the good news then sat back and relaxed. Now she could press on with her plans for the shop's most successful incarnation ever.

With perfect timing, the interior designer she'd called in to give her some initial thoughts and a quote for the rest of the work arrived just as she'd finished her calls. Vintage with edge, she already decided, hoping he would help her realise her vision. None of that pastel cupcake crap. She was impatient to see what he'd come up with.

'Think *Marine* – à la Edgar Degas – with the understated hues of pearl and dove,' he was urging while she frowned at a colour chart with what seemed to be fifty shades of battleship grey.

Cathy tried screwing up her eyes, wondering if it was Toby's training which helped him see the aesthetic qualities in such a depressing palette. She might have gained a little financial wriggle room, but refitting the shop was stretching the budget, so she had to be confident she was investing for success. Staring at these all day was liable to make her feel as if she'd been incarcerated in the asylum wing of a cold war prison. Rick would go bonkers too, if he knew what she was doing. As disloyal as she felt not asking him and his mates to do the shop, she knew it would always be the last job on his list. And once he was presented with a fait accompli, surely he wouldn't be anything other than impressed?

An unexpected lump came into her throat at the thought of achieving something to make her family proud. What if 'mum's old shop' became achingly cool? She could imagine the press coverage, her and her daughters, reporters asking if they were sisters. Everyone would sit up and take notice of her yet. Feeling cheered up at the thought, she silently intoned her favourite Buddhist chant and visualised her plans coming together.

'An eye-catching display at the front of the store is essential,' Toby was saying.

Really? And she was paying an extortionate hourly rate to be told the bleeding obvious?

'And you'll need to position the counter to steer customers in an anti-clockwise direction.'

'Some kind of ley line thing?' she wondered and saw his eyebrows shoot up.

'It encourages them to spend more,' he explained, looking piqued when her mobile phone interrupted them.

'Soul Survivor,' she said in her shop voice, 'how may I help you?'

'Eh?' said her husband. 'Don't tell me you've actually got a customer?'

'May I call you back, Richard?'

Toby looked at her approvingly, eager for her complete attention and at that rate she'd ensure he'd got it. 'I'm going to show you a statement wallpaper you'll adore,' he confided in a loud whisper, tapping on the top of one his mood boards.

'Cath?' Rick persisted. 'Stop messing about, will you?'

'I haven't got time to chat,' she hissed.

'For fuck's sake, Cath, I don't want a bleedin' chat – I'm in A & E and I thought you just might like to know!'

'Jesus, Rick!'

Toby's eyebrows rose above the mood board he was clutching to his chest.

'What's happened? Are you all right?'

'Yeah, of course I'm all right; fit as butcher's dog, me. I thought I'd just go for a ride in an ambulance for a laugh!' Rick moaned with heavy sarcasm. 'Listen, I'm fine, but I had a bit of brush with that chalet bungalow I've been working on. I came off the roof, see?'

Toby was not best pleased to be informed, when Cathy ended the call, that she needed time to study his mood boards in different lights, but eventually let her persuade him to return later in the week. Rushing him out of the shop, she dashed round to the service entrance at the back of the shop where there was just room for her to park her Mini and fought her way into the gridlock of cars in the one-way system.

It was only when she was at the traffic lights in the town centre that she began to feel annoyed and wondered if she'd really needed to put everything on hold. It wasn't the first time, by any means, that Rick had come a cropper. Most of the time it was his own fault for taking a stupid short cut, and he was still capable of using a phone, so he was conscious at least. Except, he wasn't getting any younger; at pushing sixty he was too old to be rolling around on the ground, especially when he'd skied off the top of a house first.

Work was patchy enough these days. When her husband quoted for a job, some clients didn't recognise the experience and maturity that came with age. She drummed her fingers on the steering wheel, took a deep breath and turned Primal Scream up loud. The poor old sod was probably more shaken than stirred. Most likely she'd find him sitting there forlornly hoping for some pretty young nurse to dress his wounds. Hah! He'd be lucky.

Cathy swore under her breath at the hospital car park rates that amounted to plain extortion. The longer they kept hanging around, the more money you had to part with – which was especially galling when you didn't want to be there in the first place. Barging through the automatic doors of A & E and seeing no sign of her husband amongst the bruised, bleeding and bandaged masses, she marched up to reception.

'Oh, you'll probably find him waiting for an X-ray.' The young male receptionist, looking to Cathy suspiciously like a schoolboy, smiled sympathetically. 'Go through the double doors there and follow the signs.'

Cathy nodded her thanks. She'd begin by giving Rick a piece of her mind for wasting her time and then she'd make up for it by being nice to him.

'By the way, he's in a wheelchair,' the receptionist added. 'It's just precautionary, so don't be alarmed. Your daughter's with him though, so at least he doesn't have to wait for a porter.'

Cathy frowned as she pushed through the doors and prowled the corridors. Definitely not May. Stevie, then? But Stevie wouldn't have got there from her uni in Brighton already, surely? Cathy shrugged, it had to be Stevie. Maybe she'd been up visiting her mate in Dorking? Cathy could see the lines of chairs that marked out the waiting area and searched the backs of heads for her younger daughter's straight black hair. May, with her light brown waves, took after her dad, and there he was. Beside him, holding his hand and looking into his eyes with deep concern, was not Stevie but an attractive young woman Cathy had never met before.

'Rick!' she snarled, marching over.

'Oh, hello love,' he said, looking a bit flushed. 'I'm sorry to be a nuisance, thanks for coming up.'

'Here, do sit down,' said the attractive young woman, patting Rick's hand and standing up.

'I'm not a geriatric,' Cathy snapped, glaring at her.

'This is Miss Edwards, my client,' Rick said wearily.

'Call me Bekah,' said the young woman, returning Cathy's gaze with a bit of a smirk.

Cathy narrowed her eyes back, noting every detail from the lustrous blonde locks, through the deceptively innocent jersey top in a witty Boden-print clinging to lovely young breasts and long slim legs in lemon skinny jeans.

'I expect you'd like to go now,' said Cathy.

'Oh, I'm not in a hurry,' the woman smiled sweetly, 'but now that you've arrived at last, I don't suppose Rick needs both of us to be here.'

'Yeah, well thanks for looking after me,' Rick said, fishing in his pocket and pulling a note out of his wallet. 'Please take this and get yourself a cab home.'

'Let me know how it goes, will you?' she said, brushing the money aside. 'You've frightened me enough today. I don't want to lie awake tonight, tossing and turning and thinking of all the dreadful things that might have happened to you.'

To Cathy's fury, the other woman leaned over and kissed her husband firmly, enveloping him in a cloud of scented blonde hair so Cathy couldn't see exactly where the kiss had landed. With a little wave and a coquettish smile over her shoulder, she headed off, leaving every man in the waiting room craning his neck to watch her neat bottom in the tight lemon jeans bobbing off along the corridor.

'Well?' Cathy said, feeling more and more like a bitter lemon.

'Oh, don't give me all that again,' Rick moaned. 'We're old enough to be her mum and dad. You should be grateful to her for coming in the ambulance with me. At least she was concerned about me, which is more than you seem to be.'

'I didn't know what to expect. I was worried, that's all,' she said, fumbling to balance her oversized bag. 'What's wrong, then?'

Rick sighed. 'They want to take a look at this ankle and make sure I haven't busted my head. Load of fuss about nothing. I landed in a clump of pampas grass which took most of the fall.'

Cathy stiffened. 'Pampas grass? Isn't that what people plant as a code sign to show they're swingers?'

Rick snorted. 'You think I'd swap you for Bekah Edwards? Do me a favour! I couldn't keep up with that one. She's what you call high-maintenance. You want to see some of the ideas she's got for that place – smart lighting, climate control, fancy wet room, recycled glass tiles. She should have just pulled the lot down and started again.' He shook his head, and Cathy, feeling a twinge of guilt, began to hope his head wasn't busted instead of longing to bust it herself.

'Besides,' he said with a grin, 'if I was going to trade you in, I'd swap you for something decent. A crate of Scotch or a new racing bike, maybe.'

'Hmn, well you won't be going out on the bike with a broken ankle. And the Scotch won't help your head either.'

Rick reached across to squeeze her hand and as he did so knocked her open bag, and the colour chart with Toby's business card stapled to it floated to the floor in front of them.

'Remember what that lovely nurse told you,' she reminded him when they were back home, hoping to distract him from any awkward conversation. 'Rest, ice, compress, elevate. At least it's only a badly sprained ankle. A couple of days and you'll be back to normal – provided you don't do anything silly.'

At this rate, she wouldn't need any ice; the atmosphere was chilly enough.

'Cathy, why didn't you tell me about doing up the shop? No more secrets, we agreed,' he said, wincing as he lowered himself on to a chair across the kitchen table from her. 'Then you had the flaming nerve to storm into the hospital looking at me as if I'm the one doing something suspicious.'

So that's why he was sulking. 'I only wanted to prove that I could do something for myself,' she said, blowing out an exasperated breath. She decided that attack was better than defence. 'Besides, if I left it to you it'll never get done, will it? I mean, look at the state of the house,' she snorted, waving her hands at the dated kitchen units, the half-tiled walls, a wire hanging out above the cooker where a new hood was supposed to be. 'Nothing's finished!'

'And why do you think that is?' he said, banging his mug down. 'It's because when I come home, having worked my bollocks off, I'm too flipping tired to start here.'

'Not too tired to go out on that stupid bike, though,' Cathy couldn't resist adding. 'Don't you think I've got enough worries with you flinging yourself off roofs without worrying about you getting hit by a bus as well?'

'Well at least if I get knocked off the bike, you can console yourself with the insurance money. That ought to pay for a new kitchen *and* the shop refit.'

Cathy flinched. None of it mattered without Rick; he was the reason she was doing whatever she could to keep them afloat. He gave her a sad smile. 'What's got into you? The state of this place has never bothered you before. We always said it wasn't about appearances. It was what we did together that mattered.'

'It is,' she insisted, comforted. 'I'm sorry, Rick. Everyone else in this family gets a fuss made of them – you with your grateful customers, Stevie with her mates, May, well, we all know about May – and no one notices what I do. I just wanted you to be proud of what I've done.'

'Yeah, but where's all the dosh coming from, babe? Please don't tell me you borrowed any money.'

A wash of betraying colour flooded her face as Rick looked up suspiciously.

'Relax, Rick, will you? I've paid a small deposit and negotiated a temporary rent reduction.'

'What? From that little shit! I wouldn't trust him as far as I could throw him.'

'Don't be like that.' Cathy sighed. Aiden stepping in at just the right time when the shop premises had unexpectedly come for sale had proved a sore point for Rick and festered like a wound ever since. Personally, she thought he ought to be grateful, otherwise she would have had to cut her losses and walk away from Soul Survivor. The previous landlord, who'd found herself overstretched during the recession, had been getting a little too greedy. 'That's just your pride talking. He's only trying to help us out. I mean, what else is he going to do with the money? It's not as if he's short of a bob or two. Don't worry, it's all under control.'

After what she'd done today she was certain of it. One phone call, that's all, just to keep everyone in the loop. What harm could a phone call do?

Chapter Nine

Tired of lying in her bunk, May pulled on her fleece, crept past Bill, and went up on deck. Huge clouds still scudded across the dark sky and the telltale ribbons tied to the shrouds showed that the wind direction had budged in her favour. Running with the tide, it would probably take one final push to reach Little Spitmarsh. And at least they were getting away from Thunder, and anyone else who might recognise her. Bill didn't need to know who she was or why she'd run away – although his suspicions about her being a gold-digger were irritating as well as hurtful, especially when she was more of a Sugababe than a sugar baby, but why risk making a simple trip complicated?

In her mind, she scrolled back to the day she'd finally decided that enough was enough. It was at the sound rehearsals for the opening day of the inaugural Ferrington Farm Festival on the South Downs, only the month before, when she'd finally been pushed too far. A hot June day when the air was sticky and claustrophobic. Already nervous, because she'd never felt comfortable on stage, she'd been unwise enough to read some of the press reports in the build-up and see the derisive comments about how ill-matched she was to the other acts. 'Like the comedy invitee on Strictly Come Dancing,' one of them read, 'but at least you'll know when to time the queue for the portaloos.'

When Aiden's text had come through, she'd pounced to open it. She'd figured he must have read the adverse press too, so had sent her a loving message to make her feel special. What she saw instead tore her apart, her self-esteem so destroyed that not only had she been unable to perform but barely able to leave the house for the next month. After four long weeks of mental torture and recriminations, she'd finally seized her chance to escape.

'You can't sleep either, then?' said Bill, from the companionway. He took the stairs and sat down next to her in the cockpit. He was still warm from his sleeping bag and seemed such a reassuring presence that for two pins May, who was feeling haunted by ghosts of the past, would have huddled into him for a hug.

'I expect it's that I'm afraid of oversleeping,' she admitted, not trusting herself to meet his gaze in case she gave anything away. 'We don't want to miss the tide, do we?'

'No,' he agreed in a quiet voice. 'We don't.'

Maybe he'd been right to warn her about the emotional dangers of close-quartered living, because being around him had given her a sense of what life could be like if she hadn't got herself in such a mess. Bill, earning a living with his hands, doing the decent thing for his elderly uncle, made her wish she could cast off, sail away for good and start again. Leaning towards the comfort of his body heat despite herself, May's attention was drawn to a narrow window on the boat across the pontoon where something she couldn't quite identify appeared to be waving at her. What was especially intriguing was that although every vessel on the water was gently rocking from side to side, this was a definite up and down movement and quite a fast one at that. Even knowing that it was terribly bad manners to stare into someone else's yacht didn't stop May standing up to get a better look at what was happening on board *Valhalla*.

After puzzling at the sight for a minute, May felt herself go bright red as she realised that she was looking at Paige's unleashed breasts. If Paige had any qualms about bedding Thunder, she was doing an excellent job of disguising her reluctance. Oh, well, it took all sorts. Maybe she really did fancy him? Omigod! May gasped as, instead of seeing Thunder's wizened head rearing up from below, it was Blaise revelling in Paige's embonpoint.

'I don't think Thunder need have any fears about Paige mothering Blaise,' she said weakly. 'Smothering him possibly.'

'Yes,' agreed Bill, who didn't sound as if he was entirely concentrating on what she was saying. Moving away she was nearly knocked sideways by a sudden gust of wind and only prompt action by Bill stopped her falling over the guardrails. Some men would have been so engrossed in the revelations on the boat opposite that she could have toppled unnoticed over the side, and it wasn't a good night for a swim. It was an endearing thought.

He was wearing his shabby green hoodie and had a not quite fresh smell that was much closer to the just-showered end of the spectrum than the rank-as-a-polecat end and which she found surprisingly attractive.

'May, about earlier, I'm sorry. I was suspicious of you to start with – I had to be, for Cecil's sake. And I definitely wasn't comparing you to Paige; you're funny and sweet and ...' his voice dropped as he mumbled self-consciously, '... naturally sexy.'

Aha! That was it. Watching Paige's antics had obviously made Bill a little hot under the collar. Which was unlucky for him as she wasn't about to play that game. Was *this* what he meant when he likened life aboard a small boat as being an emotional pressure cooker? Boy, was she about to put him in his place!

'And hurting all over by the looks of you,' he continued,

giving her a brotherly pat on the back. 'It's none of my business to know what you're running away from, but I want you to know, May, that you're safe with me.'

Safe again, May told herself, taking a quick glance over her shoulder into the soft nacreous morning light which transformed the harbour into a shimmering, ethereal city on a rolling, quicksilver sea. Both it, and the crew of *Valhalla*, were disappearing into the distance, much to her relief. Although, while she could be certain of avoiding unwelcome revelations out at sea, there were other dangers ahead – sandbanks, sudden pockets of poor visibility and the busy construction traffic to-ing and fro-ing from the massive offshore wind farm – however, Bill assured her there was no chance of them being chopped up by a rotating turbine.

Scanning the horizon with the icy breeze lifting his copper curls, Bill wouldn't have looked out of place in an outdoor clothing catalogue. Even his expression was suitably enigmatic. A black body warmer over his hoodie and dark twill trousers was his only nod to the glacier-fresh morning whilst May shivered in a jacket and fleece and the kind of woolly hat she would have curled her lip up at anywhere else but here.

Catching herself wishing she had something more becoming to wear, May realised she was in danger of falling into her old habit of trying too hard to please. Aiden liked her to dress according to his tastes, but that didn't mean she needed to solicit Bill's approval for everything she wore too. Whether Bill liked her or not was of little consequence; once *Lucille* had been delivered the chances of bumping into him again were only slightly higher than winning the lottery two weeks in a row.

May remembered to check the compass bearings, before she steered them back to where they'd come from. The break in the weather, which had given the opportunity to move on, also meant the wind had turned fickle, forcing them to rely on the very sluggish engine. Slogging out towards the North Sea keeping a sharp lookout all the time for shallows in one direction and freight ships in another was quite a test of endurance. Over the centuries countless boats and ships had been lost there and, after rough weather, old wrecks had sometimes surfaced, bleak reminders of lost lives, only to disappear when the sands shifted again and swallowed them up. Well, May decided, she wasn't an old wreck yet and she had no intention of letting herself be swallowed up either, so the only option was to hold her new course and see what lay ahead.

'Ready about,' she shouted to Bill, watching him uncleat the sheet to the mainsail as the wind picked up at last. May hoped she sounded less nervous than she felt. Steering the boat up through the wind was potentially hazardous and she was particularly mindful of reading somewhere that most accidents at sea were caused by a wildly swinging boom, the heavy wooden spar at the foot of the mainsail holding it in place.

'And, lee ho!' May ducked as the boom swung over her head and prayed that Bill had also taken avoiding action. She'd much prefer it if he wasn't knocked unconscious or, worse still, flung over the side. Bill probably would too, she thought, throwing a quick glance at where he was supposed to be and finding, to her relief, that he was still on board. Proving there was nothing like a well-executed manoeuvre to forge a sense of teamwork and togetherness, just as there was nothing like a bad one to set sparks and mutual recriminations flying, they beamed at each other like proud parents as *Lucille* responded beautifully to the change of tack.

'Well done,' Bill murmured. 'How are you feeling?'

'Oh, fine,' May responded heartily.

Bill considered her for a while. 'You know, before my ex-wife left she told me she'd got so used to eating alone, sleeping alone and finding things to do on her own at weekends that she didn't need to come second to the business any more. She said she had all the tools to build her own life and that's what she intended to do. It was over. No discussion. No turning back. Finished.'

His bleak expression made May wince.

'While I'd been working all hours trying to secure our future she'd decided she could do without me. I couldn't believe that she was gone; every time the phone rang I thought it would be her asking to come back. When it finally sank in that she meant it, I was so hurt and so angry that I took it out on every woman who crossed my path. I thought that I could use them the way I'd been used. Any more close encounters and I'd have been invited to join the crew of the *Enterprise*.'

May had a look to see if he was boasting. He wasn't.

'Anyway, when I finally stopped punishing totally innocent people I realised that it wasn't entirely my ex-wife's fault either. The fact was that I'd put the business first because it *was* more important to me than being with her. Somewhere along the way I just assumed that her priorities were the same as mine. Looking back, I never even stopped to ask her what she wanted and she didn't tell me until it was too late.'

Too late! The lovers' death knell. It brought a terrible lump to her throat just to think about it. 'Oh God, Bill,' she croaked. 'That's so sad. You must miss her so much.'

Bill looked staggered. 'My marriage broke up because neither of us cared two hoots about the other. We could have spent the rest of our lives being totally indifferent to each other if Suze hadn't found the guts to walk out the door and give us both the chance of a fresh start.'

Now *she* felt used. 'So if everything's so wonderful why the hell are you dumping all this on me?'

'May! What do you think I'm trying to tell you?' He dragged a hand through his ruffled hair. 'Look May, it's not difficult to guess that you're running away from something; you wouldn't have signed up for this trip if you hadn't been in a hurry to get away from something or someone. But whatever it is that's troubling you you'll probably find it'll work out for the best anyway.'

Fighting to control her trembling voice, May turned to him. 'Bill,' she mumbled.

He looked up at her, the harsh lines of his face softened with compassion, watching her with eyes that inkily reflected an ominous sky.

'Yes, May?'

Suddenly all the blood seemed to rush back to her head at once. 'What the FUCK has it got to do with you?'

Giving way to a lava flow of hot angry tears May was forced to abandon the helm whilst Bill quickly hove to. Apart from the occasional tear which had, very rarely, trickled through her guard, she hadn't really cried for months and now that the floodgates were open she couldn't stop. Lost in her own misery May hardly noticed what was going on around her, but gradually became aware of the solid, safe, comforting warmth of another body against hers and strong arms holding her tight.

Squinting up, May had a watery vision of a broad chest and a firm, masculine chin. Bill! Bill's arms were holding her close to him. Bill was pulling off her ridiculous hat and sliding his hands through her hair. Bill's lips were bent to her ear, telling her softly that everything was all right. Bill's voice which seemed to have developed a throaty break and, like the tender caress of his fingers on her cheek, was making her forget all kinds of essentials, like how to breathe.

If she held herself very still maybe he would forget she was there and she could remain pressed against him, suffused in the scent of warm male body, feeling the rise and fall of the wall of his chest beneath her fingers. Certainly Bill seemed in no hurry to let her go. In fact one hand was clasping her closely to him whilst the other moved over her back in a slow, sensual caress that stopped her tears and sent shivers down her body. Any more of this and she would start to think he was quite enjoying holding her.

'May?'

Lifting her head warily, in case she woke up, her heart skipped madly as she met his gaze. Hardly daring to move, she told herself that any minute now he would release her, but hoped against hope that he wouldn't. Her hand shot up before she could stop it and the next thing she knew she was trailing her fingertips over his face, the harsh lines of his cheekbones, his warm mouth.

'Oh, May!'

Wow! She didn't know she had a pulse *there*, but now all kinds of strange places seemed to be throbbing. His fingers pushed her hair back from her face and she couldn't believe that his touch, as he stroked the soft skin behind her ear, could give so much pleasure. His mouth caressed her skin, her eyelids fluttered and the small sound that could either have been denial or pleasure turned into a banshee wail of alarm as she noticed the huge hull of a bulk carrier filling the horizon as it bored down on them.

'Shit!' Seizing the helm, Bill moved fast. 'Life jackets, quickly!' he ordered May as he coaxed *Lucille* into going about. 'And the grab bag too.'

Her body moved but her brain stalled. The grab bag? The grab bag was there for emergencies. Packing a grab bag was one thing; water, chocolate, flares and space blanket etc. Yes, packing it was fine; quite fun really to throw in the Mars Bars never dreaming for one moment that she might actually end up bobbing around in the sea trying to eat one. A glimpse over the side at the sinister green water swirling around them made it even harder for her to fasten her life jacket. She really, really did not want to end up down there.

Several thousand tons of grey metal moved steadily towards them, determinedly pushing the waves aside. In comparison *Lucille* was beginning to feel about as robust as a snail in a bus lane. Some very unwelcome pictures of shattered boats and limbs flooded her imagination. So much for the Mars Bars; knowing her luck she'd probably break both arms on the way down and not be able to unwrap one anyway.

'Is it going to hit us?' she asked, hoping that Bill would laugh and tell her not to be such a silly girl; couldn't she see it was *miles* away? But Bill remained silent, keeping his eye on the huge great monster slicing almost malevolently through the water towards them.

'Is it—'

'I heard you,' Bill snapped tersely. 'Just get ready.'

Ready for what? Ready to fall cleanly over the side only to be shredded by the prop shaft of the container vessel?

Ready to be horribly mangled, caught between steel and wood like a clove of garlic on a chopping board? Ready to drift for days in her life jacket and finally be washed up on some distant shore where they'd shake their heads and say 'Poor girl, if only she'd been able to get at her Mars Bar.' How could she get ready to die when she hadn't had sex for weeks? She was practically a virgin again. She hadn't even had time to be kissed by Bill!

'Bill! Kiss me, Bill!'

He shot her a look of sheer exasperation. 'May, this is no time to do your Nelson impression. If you think I'm letting go of anything until this thing's gone past you've got to be joking.'

'You did say "gone past", didn't you?'

Bill grinned. 'Just look, will you? But make sure you're braced until we're clear of the wash.'

Sure enough the massive stern was gliding slowly by, close enough to make out a few tiny faces aboard, but far enough away for *Lucille* to be out of danger. Only when it finally dwindled to bath tub size in the distance did May's nerves feel convinced. Sinking back into the cockpit she thanked her lucky stars, and anyone else who might have an interest, for her deliverance. She could breathe! Flex her toes and fingers! Feel the sun on her face! Hear Bill saying—

'What?'

'I said, about that kiss ...'

Chapter Ten

If only May knew what it had cost him to say that, Bill thought, as his initial relief gave way to guilt and shame as they kept the boat steady so they could take a break.

'What do you mean it's not going to happen?' she said, in a squeal of indignation that was almost ultrasonic.

Bill spread his hands. 'I'm sorry, May. I just think it's for the best.'

'But you *liked* it! If that ship hadn't come along ...'

He had liked it. That was the trouble. All those deliciously soft curves moulding against him were almost a temptation too far. 'And that's another thing,' he told her, struggling to regain control of himself. 'We could very easily have been killed if you hadn't looked up in time. I'm afraid the high sea is no place for high jinks.'

'Huh! Tell that to the Marines!' May's amber eyes sent gold daggers at him.

'Don't sulk, May,' he pleaded. 'It doesn't suit you.'

'And *I* don't suit *you*,' she harrumphed, folding her arms. 'Well, honestly – I always thought that the expression about a ship coming in meant that something nice was about to happen.'

'Not when it's coming into your side, it isn't,' he said, hoping to sound quite stern.

Whatever she was about to say to him was hijacked by the hiccup of laughter, she was trying to pass off as a cough.

'It really isn't a laughing matter.' *She* might be able to see the humour in a near-death experience, but *his* emotions were in tatters. He was the skipper, for crying out loud; it was his responsibility to look after *Lucille* and all who sailed in her. A moment of utter madness on his part had almost cost him Cecil's boat – and May's life.

'I can't believe you turned me down even though we were staring death in the teeth!' she moaned. 'I bet you would have kissed me if we'd been floundering around in the wreckage of *Lucille* together. You would have been so pleased to find me, you wouldn't have wasted time shaking my hand, saying, "there you are." Unless, of course, I'd fallen on to the propeller in which case it would have been, "there you are, and there you are and over there."'

Bill shook his head. Shock. That, of course, was the nub of the problem; the only reason May had ended up in his arms in the first place was because she was desperate for comfort and he was the only other living being in sight. Why else would she have turned to him? As for kissing her? 'It's my job to get you safely to landfall, not to snog you – quite literally – to within an inch of both our lives.'

'What a way to go, though,' May said, not quite meeting his eyes as if she was already having second thoughts about throwing herself at him. Back on dry land, he figured he'd be the kind of guy she'd pass in the street without seeing. Especially if he was mixing concrete or bricklaying. So even if the sight of her breasts rising and falling as her breath steadied was utterly spellbinding, it would be better for both of them if he concentrated on the rise and fall of the waves instead.

As he took another glance at her, May's shoulders started to shake until she could hold it no longer when what started off as a fit of giggles turned, as he would have predicted, into another outbreak of sobbing.

'Poor little duck,' he said, trying to sound brotherly, and using his hands to adjust a sail rather than pulling her into his arms.

'God!' She sniffed. 'No wonder you want to avoid

kissing me if you see me as a short, dumpy little thing waddling around splashing water everywhere. I'm sorry about the tears. I expect it's just an overreaction.' She sighed, shielding her face with her hand as she peeked up at him. 'Either that or I'm going quackers.'

'Oh no, nothing as bad as that.' He smiled at her. 'You're just a bit overwrought at the moment.'

'No shit, Sherlock.' May dropped her hand and glared at him. 'There was I thinking it might be connected with the fact that my whole life just flashed before me.'

'Oh come on,' he said, hoping to jolly her along, 'we missed it by miles.'

She frowned. 'Why do men always say that?'

Bill tweaked the helm. 'Definitely overwrought,' he said smugly.

'On the contrary,' May began, with a withering look. But whatever she was about to deliver died on her lips as she held his gaze. She started slightly, as if something had surprised her. Her lips opened and her pupils widened into black velvet on gold silk.

'Does this mean you've changed your mind about that kiss?' she whispered.

'May, I'm not going to kiss you,' he insisted quietly.

'Spoilsport!' she murmured. 'Why not?'

Bill sighed. 'Because it wouldn't be good for you. And it probably wouldn't be good for me either.'

Bill was right, of course. Their narrow escape had been a sharp reminder about safety at sea and with *Lucille* facing the challenge of her longest, loneliest passage, it was essential to stay focused on what was going on around them. As wave after lumpy wave rocked the little boat as it battled strong currents around the first headland, May's head was already aching and her stomach was tight with nausea and apprehension.

From being impatient to get to sea, she now dreaded the prospect of being out of sight of land. Even the hustle and bustle of the busy shipping traffic and dodging seafarers going about their business, delivering cargo and passengers in and out of ports, seemed preferable now to the desolate expanse of the cold North Sea which lay ahead with its ghostly forts and shifting sands.

At least she still had Bill. Or, more accurately, hadn't had Bill. No wonder she could feel his appalled gaze sliding over her every so often. Probably checking that she was keeping her distance and not about to make another exhibition of herself by jumping all over him. How right he'd been right to warn her about the intensity of small-space living. Clearly that explained her sudden attraction to him.

May scrutinised him as carefully as steering would allow. Great lungfuls of sea air and adrenaline from their near miss must have affected her circulation and pumped her blood straight to her erogenous zones. Good job she wasn't one of those monkeys with the red bottoms or she might still have some trouble sitting down. Imagine, if Bill hadn't put up some resistance, she might have thrown him to the deck and impaled herself on him. What a rude thought! What was it about steering that seemed to set her subconscious running wild and free? Was it the somewhat meditative nature of watching the bow of the boat nose through mile upon mile of undulating waves which allowed her imagination to conjure up such lurid imagery?

Surely it couldn't be anything to do with Bill? She stole another look at the unruly red hair ruffling in the breeze while he went innocently about the boat's business and tried to dismiss the thought. Perhaps all that sea air would have made any man seem attractive. Yet she'd never felt that way about Aiden. Possibly, she had to admit, because she was always a bit too anxious about pleasing him. Especially in bed, where she always felt her lack of experience let her down. Now, when she'd suddenly seen the attraction of no-holds-barred, swing-from-the-grab-rails sex, Bill wouldn't play – which was right and proper and better for both of them, she told herself quickly. Fancying Bill was a complete aberration; that rough and ready red-haired look couldn't have been more of a contrast to Aiden who was so good-looking she always felt quite plain in comparison.

Looking back, her relationship with Aiden was so one-sided it was little wonder she felt so insecure and inhibited. Other women sensed it too, forever elbowing her out of the way after a gig to get closer to him. And who could blame them? He really was jaw-droppingly handsome, so it was hardly surprising she'd been unable to keep him.

'Why the long face?' Bill said, catching her off guard.

One, two, three. Damn, she could feel her nose going red. If only she could cry prettily, like Demi Moore in *Ghost*, all sparkly eyed and dewy. Even worse was the fact the more she tried to stop the more she ran with snot and slobber. Bill, to his great credit, was not repulsed, but calmly found her a handkerchief then fixed the helm and backed the sails to slow the boat's progress. Once it was almost at a standstill, he sat her down and went off to put the kettle on, returning a bit later with a mug of tea and a chocolate biscuit. She couldn't remember Aiden ever bringing her a cup of tea.

'There's sugar in it too,' he said, to explain the plastic spoon. 'So give it a stir and drink it, it'll do you good.'

Nor was Aiden ever that thoughtful.

'Now, what's all this about?' said Bill.

Or so concerned about her feelings. May inhaled slowly.

Spilling the story of her love life – ha! – on the ocean waves with no other vessel in sight and only the hiss of the breaking bow wave and the high-pitched mewing of passing seagulls to break the silence was more therapeutic than she could ever have believed. She had friends who spent good money paying people to listen to them. She should at least offer to buy Bill a Chinese takeaway when they struck land for all the money he'd saved her in counselling fees. Not only was he thoughtful and solicitous, he was such a good listener that he'd barely opened his mouth, except to prompt her here and there or to take a sip of his own tea.

Actually, May thought, feeling the first prickles of unease, it was about time Bill *did* say something. Having just disgorged the last two years of her life to him she expected him to make *some* comment. Okay, she'd omitted to tell him the bit most people were interested in, but still. Perhaps he hadn't heard her after all? Maybe all that time he'd been mentally counting the nautical miles waiting for her to shut up? Maybe he was even asleep? May checked to see if his eyelids were open. He was staring into his empty cup with such a look of distaste that May had a quick look to see if one of them hadn't washed up properly and he'd found something unpleasant lurking at the bottom.

When he eventually met her gaze May was shocked by how angry he looked. The controlled, silent fury was more intense than any outward expression would have been, and for a terrible moment May was afraid that he was angry with her.

'I know it's naïve but at first, I felt it was romantic, having someone there to take care of me,' she said, trying to excuse herself.

'That's not taking care,' Bill growled, 'that's taking control.'

'He'd promised to be there for me. And I was flattered that he was so interested in me he wanted to accompany me on even the most mundane trips. He told me that nothing was more important than being with me. He wanted to know who my friends were, what they did, he asked about my social networks ...' She shook her head. 'I was secretly delighted at how jealous he was when an ex-boyfriend, a teenage romance, purely innocent, flirted with me online. I had to sever contact with him which I felt uneasy about, but it seemed a small sacrifice to keep Aiden happy.'

She shrugged, ashamed of how meekly she'd gone along with his demands.

Bill's face was like thunder, but then he seemed to pull himself together. He reached out and briefly touched her face in a gesture of compassion.

'I don't understand why it took you so long to break away,' he said gently.

May smiled regretfully. 'I asked myself the same question so many times. I guess I just couldn't bear the thought of him being on his own.'

Bill's hand came down on the coaming so hard that even a seagull, deciding whether or not to land on the rear safety rail, squawked and jumped. 'May! You don't owe him a damn thing.'

She took the plastic spoon out of her mug and started fiddling with it. Bill was wrong about that, but she'd gone on about herself for quite long enough now.

'It's the way I left,' she admitted. 'I shouldn't have done it like that, it was cowardly. But I was afraid that if I didn't just pack up, he'd find a way to make me stay. I should have phoned him to warn him that I moved out or at least got someone to make sure he was all right. I mean, I know he's alive and kicking, but he has very few real friends.'

'Oh you *do* surprise me,' Bill said with surprising force. He leant forward. 'May, do you mind if I ask you something?'

'Ask away,' she replied, shrugging nervously.

'Are you quite sure that you're completely over him?'

'Quite.' The plastic spoon she'd been holding snapped in half, making her jump. They both looked at the two pieces and Bill gave a funny little smile.

'Well,' he said sadly. 'Maybe you need more time to think about that one.'

In Ebbesham Cathy Starling was up early since Rick, against the doctor's better judgement, had left the house before seven to go to work. Since she was awake, she'd use the opportunity to gather her thoughts before meeting Toby at the shop. May was supposed to be in Little Spitmarsh very shortly. Should she ring to prepare her for what might be coming, Cathy wondered, or should she let events take their course? On balance, Cathy was in favour of the second option. May might not be best pleased if she knew, although in time, she'd hopefully appreciate that Cathy's intervention was for her own good.

Staring at one of Toby's mood boards, Cathy tried to ignore the pricking of her conscience and stifle the tendrils of guilt wrapping themselves round her heart. During their last phone conversation, it hadn't escaped her notice that her daughter sounded lighter and freer than she had in months. Until then, Cathy had been convinced she was having a breakdown, but now she wondered if all May had really needed was a break. Whatever the case, May couldn't afford to drift for much longer; someone had to take charge.

Jazz was the new black, according to Toby who banished

her Music for Meditation from the shop. Cathy, beginning to question her actions, tried it now, turning up the volume to let Miles Davis fill the air while she waited to feel calmer. Then her phone started ringing.

'Toby? I was just thinking about you, listen – can you hear that?'

But instead of getting warm approval, she heard a nervous cough. 'I'm sure there's a perfectly simple explanation, but I thought I'd tell you in case there's a problem.'

'Sorry, Toby – I'm not with you.'

She heard him clear his throat.

'No, I know you're not. That's why I'm ringing. I'm outside Soul Survivor. I got here a bit early as the traffic was lighter than I expected. The thing is, there were men working on the place when I arrived.'

Ricky! What had he done now?

'Locksmiths, I think. And there's a notice in the window announcing the shop's closed due to unforeseen circumstances.'

By the end of the day, Cathy's disbelief had given way to numb acceptance. She fingered the solicitors' letter that had arrived by recorded delivery and sent her into an impotent rage, knowing that no matter how many times she read it the same message would jump out at her. Aiden had hung her out to dry.

She'd spent hours ringing round trying to come up with ready cash, anything to save her skin. 'Yes,' she got tired of saying, 'the business *was* struggling, but what small business didn't struggle?' But unless Aiden had a change of heart, everything she'd worked so hard for was over. And by the time she'd told Rick what she'd done that might not be the only thing.

The sun was hot on the back of the house so she moved round and sat in the open patio doors that led off the living-cum-dining room and lit a last cigarette as her dreams went up in smoke. Where the walls met the door frame, a wavy seam of lilac paint which a couple of hastily slapped-on coats of more recent jade emulsion hadn't quite covered reminded her of the excitement of buying their first family home. It had, of course, required complete modernisation which was how they'd been able to afford it, but there was a garden for the girls to play in and more space than they knew what to do with after their tiny flat.

'We'll just paint over this Anaglypta for now and lose the beige. I'll strip it all off later,' Rick had promised. 'What colour do you fancy?'

So they'd made the room their own with lilac paint, but somehow they'd never got round to stripping off the old paper, nor so many of the fiddly little jobs that were easy to postpone. Cathy turned away and stared at the overgrown apple tree which had also promised far more than it delivered. Sharp, mottled fruit which fell in a rotten mulch before you could blink. A thumping bass from the house backing on to their garden told her that school was over for the day. The little girls next-door-but-one were pounding their trampoline and shrieking with laughter and the inane banter of a banal early evening game show warbling through the walls from her neighbour's TV coalesced in an unholy suburban cacophony that dropped abruptly from her conscious hearing as a key turned in the front door.

'Cath? What are you doing home? Don't you feel well?'

Rick touched a hand to her shoulder and crouched down beside her.

Chapter Eleven

How had everything unravelled like this? Cathy shook her head and choked back the tears. She'd never been the kind of woman who used crying as a weapon so there was no point in making herself feel even worse by trying it now. All she could do was explain why she'd acted as she had.

'Aiden came round to the shop as soon as he realised May had packed a bag,' she began. 'When she told us she needed to get away from everything, I didn't realise that included him as well. He was beside himself, Rick. I mean, imagine how he must have felt walking in after a business trip to find she'd left without telling him. It was like when …' She stopped and pulled herself together. 'I've got to say I felt a bit sorry for him.'

She glanced towards him, knowing that he wouldn't have a shred of sympathy for the younger man. Why would he when he didn't know how it felt to be isolated, to have to pick your way barefoot over the broken glass of your love life? What else could she have done in the circumstances, with Aiden standing there choking back tears, other than help?

'He was really concerned,' she continued, desperate to make him understand how it felt to be caught between a rock and hard place, 'not for himself, although I could see how hurt he was, but for May. He said he was doing his best to guard her interests but that any goodwill towards her would quickly evaporate unless he could speak to her and agree a way forward.'

'What's he been doing for the last four weeks, then?' Rick asked. 'It's been a month since May backed out of doing the gig at the festival. Didn't he tell us he was taking care of everything? Weren't we supposed to leave it all to him?'

'We've got to be a bit careful, Rick. He pointed out that, in theory, she'd breached her contract, that she was liable to pay him a percentage of her future earnings. Think of what that will mean.'

'For her? Or for you?' Rick asked bitterly.

Cathy clamped her hands between her thighs before she was tempted to reach out to him for comfort she didn't deserve.

'Us, don't you mean,' she replied, since it was partly his fault that it had even dawned on her that it was necessary to safeguard her own future. 'I didn't notice you protesting when she stepped in to pay the mortgage when we couldn't. Listen, he told me May's career was finished unless the matter was resolved. And, he seemed genuinely concerned for all of us.'

He raised an eyebrow. 'Yeah? So what gave you that impression?'

'Well, you remember how apprehensive May was about her appearance at the new festival? Aiden stopped by Soul Survivor in April and admitted that the pressure was getting to both of them. He thought it would widen her potential fan base if she could reach out to an indie audience, but May wasn't having it. She started seeing problems that weren't there, like imagining he was running around with other women and generally doubting his advice.'

Rick shook his head.

Cathy pressed on. 'Because May wasn't listening to him, he asked me to have a word with her, just to encourage her along a bit.'

'Hold on, Cath, he always told us to keep out of May's

business. Always said he was the expert. So where's this going?'

'He said at the time that he couldn't help noticing that the shop needed a bit of work. He knew it was hard with you having to compete for jobs with younger blokes, so he offered a temporary holiday with the rent whilst I sorted myself and improved the shop to help us get back on our feet.'

'How much do you owe him?' Rick asked quietly.

Cathy took a deep breath. 'When he came in this week, he reminded me that I was in debt to him to the tune of three month's rent. He told me it wasn't a problem because of us being May's parents. He even acknowledged that although he hadn't always seen eye to eye with us, he realised that May needed us as much as him.'

'One big happy family, eh?' Rick scoffed.

Now she had to admit how very stupid she'd been.

'He promised me everything would change if she gave him another chance. And even though he'd lost a lot of money because of May's stage fright, he said he was cool about the rent in the short term, provided the misunderstandings and problems didn't drag on. He had an awful lot on his plate, Rick, and May *had* left him to pick up all the pieces. I thought it was only fair when I heard from her to let him know where she was and that she was all right.'

'You did what?' Rick's face was white.

'Yeah. I thought I was helping, but he's thrown it all back in my face. I didn't check the ins and outs of the new tenancy agreement as thoroughly as I should have when I took it over either. I assumed it would carry on as before – only with less hassle.'

She held up her hand. 'I know, I know it was crazy of me

to trust him. So, it turns out there was a forfeiture clause in the lease and because there's no residential accommodation to complicate the issue he's within his rights to change the locks, kick me out and take back what's his.'

'So that's it – it's all gone, has it?'

Cathy appealed to Rick's back as he began pacing the room. 'You know how determined he is, Rick. I was only trying to do the right thing.'

'And look how he's repaid you! Concerned about all of us, my arse! If he was that bloody concerned why would he pull the plug on the shop as soon as you told him where May was?'

She folded herself back into the sofa, not quite understanding how easily she'd allowed herself be taken in. 'Nothing you can say, Rick, can make me feel worse than I do already. He seemed so plausible. Remember what a gentleman he was when we first met him? I used to think it was so romantic, the way he swept her off her feet with surprise weekends away,' she said, thinking aloud.

'No you didn't,' Rick said, spinning round and surveying her with disgust. 'You were jealous. You couldn't stand the fact that May was getting all the attention instead of you. No wonder Stevie saw the writing on the wall and got out before you could cut her down to size too. When did you become so resentful of your own daughters?'

'Oh, don't give me that, Rick.' She got to her feet to face him. 'You know exactly what knocked me for six. I wouldn't even have thought of trying to build a little nest egg of my own before then. I'm not getting any younger and … after you did the dirty on me, I just thought …'

'So this is all my fault, is it?' he snorted. 'One mistake in forty years and I have to pay for it for the rest of my life. For crying out loud, Cath – it's ancient history, must be at least two years now. How many times do we have to go through this? I thought I'd lost it – and yes, I was a stupid old git. Typical midlife crisis. Yep, I'm guilty, hands up. I was flattered because some bird was interested in me, I played away from home and then I realised just how much I had to lose.'

Everything had gone wrong during that lean spell when Rick was out of work. Autumn rolled into a cold winter and the prospect of a miserable Christmas. Looking back, she hadn't helped her husband, going on, as she had, about how they were going to pay the bills. No wonder he'd lost heart and turned to the first person to see him as a man, not a failure. Ironically, the affair had started just when she was breathing a sigh of relief because he'd got some painting and decorating work as a stop gap, until she realised that her husband was doing a little overtime in another woman's bedroom.

'What? When you came home and found all your clothes cut in half and thrown on the drive, you mean.'

His eyebrows lifted. 'Yeah you did do that, didn't you?'

'Someone had to teach you a lesson,' she dropped her gaze to her wedding ring and twisted it round her finger. 'You screwed around, but I'm the one who's screwed everything up.'

Drained, she lowered herself back to the sofa and rubbed her tired eyes. 'I should have trusted you a bit more and Aiden a lot less, but he's always been so charming and protective of May.'

'Too protective,' Rick said, moodily. 'I felt as if I needed an appointment to see my own daughter.'

'Well, she needed some protection, especially last summer when that hit was everywhere and everyone was trying to get a piece of her,' she pointed out. 'I was pleased then that he seemed so keen to guard her privacy. Thinking about it now, Aiden's always been in the driving seat, but until today, I thought he was taking care of her career.'

Silence … except for the muffled news theme from the living room next door. Rick stared out into the garden and then turned to face her. She shivered and finally expressed her growing doubt. 'Rick, you do think May will be all right, don't you?'

Nearly there. As the sinking sun burnished the purple clouds with copper, Bill scanned the horizon for a first glimpse of the fairway buoy marking the entrance to the Little Spitmarsh backwaters. All being well, he'd find both his uncle and his business in reasonable shape and could start getting back to normal. So why didn't he feel happier about the prospect?

Stupid question. Especially when the answer was sitting right beside him, rebounding wildly after the split with her boyfriend. Some men might have taken advantage of her vulnerability, but he wasn't like that. It was hard enough anyway imagining that back on dry land she was certain to laugh and put her sudden attraction to a ginger builder down to the bracing effects of sea air, but he didn't want to torment himself by thinking about the kinds of regrets she might have had, if he hadn't exercised a hefty measure of self-control. The last thing he wanted was for her to look back and cringe every time she thought about him. As for him, he'd always be wondering what might have been.

'I've got a visual on the channel buoy, now,' he said, not exactly ecstatic about it. 'There's plenty of water either side of it for this boat, but we'll still keep it to the port side to be sure. When we're on top of it, we'll turn in and start pottering slowly up to Watling's Boatyard where we'll tie up. There should be enough light for us to see where we're going.'

'Great,' she said, her voice tired and flat after what had been a very long day.

'Great,' Bill agreed, wishing it was.

'It's gone really well, hasn't it?' May said, offering him the ghost of a smile. 'All things considered. Well, most of the time ...'

Her honeyed gaze met his and a knot tightened in his stomach. Hell, of course he was going to miss her; he'd learned so much about her. Like the little puffing baby-breath snores that signalled that she'd drifted off at night. How, sleep-befuddled in the mornings, she'd pad speechless into the cabin until he'd pushed a mug of tea in front of her. He'd miss the sight of those cotton pyjama bottoms that looked so innocent until she bent over to find the milk in the cold store, when the soft fabric stretched and moulded across a bottom so perfectly and deliciously curved, just looking at it made him want to bark like a baboon.

Bill clenched the tiller harder. It was more than just that nature had made such a wonderful job of her; he liked her, damn it, and would miss her company. She was funny, self-deprecating and hadn't baulked once that she hadn't exactly found herself on a luxury liner. Heck, how could he have written her off as some kind of gold-digger? He could read her well enough to be able to tell that she wasn't the type of woman who craved a celebrity lifestyle. No one like that would have been as happy as May, in her casual clothes, sailing the boat in all weathers, her face bare of make-up and hair tied back any old how. She was just an ordinary, undemanding girl. Given what a tough time she'd had emotionally, he was the one who owed her, for enduring some basic conditions and hard work to deliver the boat. She deserved better.

'The whole of this North Sea coast is subject to longshore drift,' he explained, seeing that they were nearly at the channel buoy. 'The sea tears at the land and produces these magnificent shingle spits. This one's huge and distinguished by its cone shape. That's the entrance that winds down to Little Spitmarsh.'

May gave a desultory glance in the general direction of the land whilst fumbling in her jacket pocket before producing a tissue and blowing her nose hard. He hoped she wasn't thinking about that clown of an ex-boyfriend. Bill had a sudden brainwave. Perhaps he could take her for a meal at Samphire, his mate Matthew's restaurant. That would be a great way to thank her. And take her mind off her ex. No one visiting Little Spitmarsh for the first time ever expected to find such a remarkable place in such a sleepy seaside town. The cuisine was outstanding too, thanks to Jimi, Matthew's original and accomplished chef. May couldn't fail to be impressed.

But, wait a minute, Bill shook his head. Thanking May was fine, but impressing her? That was a non-starter. Even if she'd been in the slightest bit interested in him this was not great timing for either of them. He had plenty to worry about with Cecil and all the work that was bound to be piling up. And May deserved someone who would take good care of her. Why risk creating an even bigger mess?

His stomach leaden with disappointment, Bill adjusted the tiller and began to nudge the boat towards its new home. 'What you find,' he started to explain, 'is that this shingle bank produces a back eddy. The longshore drift flips backwards here so you get this huge body of circling water swirling around like water down a plug hole.'

'If you say so,' said May, flatly.

'But don't worry,' he assured her, trying to lighten his own mood as much as hers, 'we're perfectly safe, it's hardly a whirlpool! Before you know it we'll be packing the boat up and getting back to real life.'

She'd gone very quiet, but since the wind was right on *Lucille*'s nose, creating a heavy, uncomfortable motion as the force of the tide gushing out of the channel pushed against the little boat, she might have been concentrating on not being seasick.

'All right?' he asked.

'Not really,' she replied, lifting her eyes to his. 'I'm not sure I'm looking forward to real life.'

The smile that she gave him was so brave and heartbreaking that Bill forgot his good intentions and decided he would ask if she'd like to have dinner with him before they went their separate ways. He took a deep breath, dimly aware of wings somewhere above his head, flapping against the wind, and May's eyes widening with alarm. Then something smacked him on the back of the head and his world turned upside down.

Chapter Twelve

May crouched over Bill in his berth, drawn by the faint groan as he came to.

'What happened?' he grunted.

'Have you really forgotten?' she asked, feeling horribly concerned. This was her fault – they should have called for medical assistance the previous evening, but Bill had been so insistent that he hadn't been knocked out that she'd taken his word for it. Besides, she needed him to shout instructions while they limped into a small inlet where they were able to pick up an isolated mooring.

'May, I work on building sites – I know the difference between a bang on the head and serious concussion,' he'd assured her. 'And since I've been too busy to get it cut, my hair's thick enough to cushion the blow.'

Nevertheless, once she'd made sure he wasn't going to bleed to death either and watched him down a stiff Scotch for the pain, she carried her sleeping bag into the main cabin, taking the berth opposite so she could check his breathing throughout the night and make sure that he hadn't died on her. She stroked his forehead now, as Bill grunted into wakefulness, checking that it wasn't clammy or feverish.

'Bill,' she said gently, afraid that if she wasn't vigilant he might still slip into a coma, 'do you know who I am?'

His eyes flew open and she stared into their black depths, checking each pupil in turn to make sure they were evenly matched. What if there was bleeding inside his skull? He could be dying of cerebral compression right now and it would be all her fault. Come to think of it, his face *was* looking slightly flushed, but how was his pulse? May felt for his wrist, but her attempts to take a reading were somewhat hindered by the throbbing of the blood in her own body. Ah, there it was, but was it full and bounding? How could she tell? And his breathing? She turned the side of her head to his face. Wasn't that slightly heavy too?

'Bill,' she said urgently. 'Tell me who I am.'

His eyes fluttered and he gave a faint moan.

'*Bill!*' she clasped his face between her hands, willing him to give her a sign that he was in there somewhere.

'You,' he said, frightening the life out of her as he suddenly reared up beside her. 'You're the woman who was so nearly the death of me.'

'Me?' May said, recoiling. 'You're the one who told me at the start of the voyage how important it was to always watch for what the boom was doing!'

Nevertheless, he was still looking worryingly uncomfortable. Perhaps he'd sat up too quickly?

'Are you all right, Bill? Shall I make you a cup of tea?'

He winced and leaned forward. May patted him tentatively on his shoulder but couldn't help notice that the area that seemed to be giving him most discomfort seemed to be in his lap region.

'Water would be fine, May, if you don't mind,' he ground out at last. 'I'll be on deck – I think I could do with some fresh air.'

Even though she turned away to give him some privacy as he unzipped his sleeping bag and climbed out, she decided it would be prudent to see if being upright aggravated his pain. He grabbed his trousers and as he shot past, it was evident that Bill's boxers were bulging with an erection that could take someone's eye out. She flopped back against the bulkhead feeling a bit pink and giggly. Blimey, Bill had a second career waiting as an underwear model with a kecks department like that! Trying to think serious thoughts and compose herself while she poured them both a glass of water, May was just about ready to face Bill when he called out to her.

'Come and look at this and tell me what you think!'

May, silently shaking with laughter, bit her lip, and had to steady the glasses for a moment before she spilled water everywhere. She took a deep breath.

'There you go,' she smiled, handing him a glass. Even though he was fully dressed again and all, presumably, was safely gathered in, May couldn't quite dismiss the fleeting image of those hard thighs and black figure-hugging trunks. His hand brushed hers as he took the drink and set a few nerve receptors tingling. When he tipped his head back and the strong muscles of his throat worked as he drained his glass, May was convinced she felt the ground move under her and wondered if she'd missed a bang on her own head somewhere along the line.

She was about to sit down, when he took her arm and pointed over the side at the receding tide. 'We're just about to take the ground again, see?'

Well, at least the bumping about was nothing to do with her but down to *Lucille*, settling down on the bilge plates beneath her hull that kept her steady on dry land.

'That means we're not going anywhere until the water comes back again,' said Bill, 'I'm afraid we're stuck.'

In the confusion of their arrival, May had barely registered where they were, but now, as the sun broke through on what promised at last to be a perfect summer day, she began to absorb the beauty of their surroundings. Selfishly, she couldn't help think that there were worse places to run aground.

Lucille sat in a little creek off the main channel which snaked through a labyrinth of tributaries and islands separated by reedy tufted mud banks which made up the backwaters. With the tide so low, it seemed that on the seaward side the sand stretched away for hundreds of acres. On the landward side, the mudflats gave way to saltmarsh, rough shrubby pasture then the good land above the high tide. Silvery palisades of wooden stakes, remnants of man's efforts to manipulate the sea, protruded from undulating swirls of silty sand stretched up to an endless sky, and right beside them, as the waters receded, the sea birds were eyeing up their favourite spots on a vast rippling sand bank glistening in the sun.

It looked blissful to her, an escape from whatever was waiting for her when she went home, but to Bill, with so much on his mind, it must feel like a prison. She turned back to him regretfully. 'I'm so sorry. If I'd managed to warn you about that swinging boom sooner, you could have been on your way to see your uncle by now.'

She sank down on one of the cockpit lockers, reluctant to believe that her voyage was really at end. 'I suppose I could make a start on tidying up and packing things away,' she offered.

Bill swung round to throw her a look of sheer disbelief. 'Here we are marooned next to a perfect beach on an island that only appears once a tide. It would be criminal to waste such a beautiful day. Come on, we're going ashore.'

Little more than a mile or so from the creek, in a Victorian villa transformed by its keen new owners into a smart boutique B&B, Fiona Goodwin gazed across at Little Spitmarsh's seafront and remembered that she really ought to smile before answering the phone. It was supposed to show in your voice, wasn't it? And heaven knows she was in need of something to give her a lift. Surely it wasn't natural to be permanently exhausted? Was it her age?

Maybe this summer, when Paul turned thirty, he'd feel in need of a holiday too? Her own thirtieth birthday seemed a dim and distant memory these days. Was it really six years ago? The same evening she'd met Paul who was out on a stag do? Maybe she wouldn't have been quite so chuffed with herself for pulling a toy boy for her birthday had she known that he'd end up encouraging her to plough what savings she had into buying the albatross now hanging round her neck.

Listening to her caller, though, Fiona soon found that her smile came quite naturally. Since he'd phoned to make his booking *after* the early morning ordeal of serving breakfast, she didn't even have to rush him and could listen to that beautiful, seductive voice at her leisure.

'Thank you, Mrs Goodwin, you've been so helpful …'

Fiona found herself holding her breath, whilst her unknown guest considered his words.

'… so understanding.'

'My pleasure,' she exhaled, closing her eyes. 'I'm glad I could help and I look forward to meeting you very soon, then.'

In the three years since Fiona and her husband, Paul, had opened Walton House, Little Spitmarsh had seen its financial tide beginning to turn thanks to the opening of Samphire, an upmarket restaurant which was still managing to attract foodies willing to make the long pilgrimage to the bleak east coast. The restaurant had been the brainchild of property developer Matthew Corrigan, who'd certainly shaken the place up when he'd come to town, but he must have got more than he'd bargained for when his path had crossed, quite literally it turned out, with feisty boatyard owner Harry Watling, who was fiercely protective of the business her father had started. Fiona liked Harry, but she wasn't a woman Fiona would ever care to rub up the wrong way, tiny as she was.

Nevertheless Matthew and Harry made a dynamic team. The restaurant and an annual film festival had almost reinvigorated parts of the once seedy town to the point of gentrification, encouraging a smattering of galleries, cool vintage shops and a few of the hardier pilgrims to snap up some of the most attractive old buildings along the seafront as second homes. Twirling a strand of long dark hair round her finger, Fiona tried to guess which of the new category of visitor the man at the other end of the phone would turn out to be. Foodie, film buff or Up-from-Londoner?

He laughed gently. 'Well, I sincerely hope I don't disappoint you,' he murmured in that gorgeous accent that hinted at emerald fields shimmering under the kiss of soft Kerry rain.

'Oh, Mr Cavanagh, you couldn't possibly disappoint me,' she said, looking round to make sure Paul wasn't within earshot. 'All our guests are assured of the warmest of welcomes.' The most fun she was likely to have in a long time was anticipating the arrival of the mysterious Mr Cavanagh this evening. That and a weekly trip to the cash and carry over at Great Spitmarsh. Away from the seafront, their own so-called high street remained snaggle-toothed with vacant units and a depressing number of house clearance shops crammed with the yellowing and dusty possessions of the dear departed, only added to the sense of ghosts lingering in the shadows of any economic recovery.

All the same, she thought, half listening for an echo of

his ripple of amusement even after he'd ended the call, she would feel a bit miffed with her imagination if the reality of the man she'd conjured up turned out to be a disappointment. Mr Cavanagh, she thought, absent-mindedly stroking the phone, sounded romantic too. Lucky the woman, whoever she was, who was about to be surprised with such a thoughtful and caring gesture.

'It was another nappy,' said Paul smugly, leaning over the reception desk making her jump. 'In Trafalgar,' he added, lifting an ominously bulging bin bag. 'Though it got me wondering if we should have named the rooms after battles rather than shipping areas since I thought the blockage was about to defeat me.'

Trafalgar, Lundy, Fastnet, Rockall, Cromarty. Names for the guest rooms to evoke the ritual and the reassurance of the shipping forecast. Respite for the weary. Beacons in the dark. A talisman she'd swum to herself many times when the night ahead seemed too long. Names to hang themes on when they were bringing Walton House back to life. Pale washes of sea green, muted tartans, crisp white sheets, sleek, restful bathrooms and translucent cubes of Hebridean seaweed soap. Everything set for her guests to soil, steal and abuse in return.

'Why do they do it?' Resentment surged through her. 'They wouldn't flush a disposable nappy down the lavatory at home – why do they do it here? They seemed such a nice couple too.' She stabbed at the keyboard, pulling up a screen. 'I'm minded to send them an e-mail and tell them they left something behind. Their manners for a start.'

'Don't, Fee,' he said, reaching over to lay his hand on hers. 'Give them a break,' he said gently. 'It was their first time away with a new baby. You could see they were finding it a shock to the system.'

And no wonder. Where friends had suddenly heard their body clocks ticking, Fiona had heard nothing. When they presented their new babies for her delight, nothing within her had stirred except relief that the responsibility of looking after such a small and helpless person wasn't hers. And when they regaled her with tales of pre-eclampsia, emergency Caesareans, tears and stitches she felt plain horror. Why would any woman willingly subject herself to such a terrifying ordeal?

Fiona silently ground her teeth at Paul's pet name for her when there was so little room left for endearments in the drudgery of her everyday life. 'It would have been a shock to our system too, if you hadn't been able to fix it,' she complained. Paul's hand, she noticed, was still damp. She only hoped it was clean.

'They weren't thinking straight. One of them probably threw it down the loo instead of in the bin, in their rush to vacate the room. I bet they'd be horrified if they knew what they'd done. Don't do anything that would embarrass them too much to make a repeat booking.'

She folded her arms and tried to ignore Paul's beseeching look. He tried a winning smile, which only made her crosser. Did he have to be so bloody cheerful about everything? The trouble with Paul was that he loved his job, loved every single aspect of it. If ever there was an ideal match for the perfect host, it was Paul: loves getting up at stupid o'clock to prepare meals – check; is tolerant and patient at all times with everyone he meets – check; enjoys routine maintenance and downright menial chores – check; has superheroic energy levels and relishes long hours – another check. Nothing about owning and running Walton House ever got him down. With his long legs, spindly frame and ceaseless desire to please, he was like a lanky, overgrown dog bounding around with endless enthusiasm and a constantly wagging tail.

Thinking about the wagging tail would normally have made her giggle, except that their love life had become a bit of joke lately too. It was all very well for Paul, who was something of an early riser and seemed to think it was perfectly fine for him to rush through his idea of a wake-up call. Fiona, however, sometimes felt like one half of an Olympic team constantly striving for a record-breaking time for two people to climax and get showered and dressed before preparing breakfast.

When was the last time they'd shared an evening bath? Sat in scented water, sipping wine by candlelight and swapping sexy stories? Shared a massage and a cuddle and soft, sweet, tender love-making? And the fault was as much hers as Paul's. The truth was that given the choice of sleep or sex, she would have opted for an extra hour of shut-eye every time. At least the morning quickies kept them in touch; left to her, they might not have a sex life at all.

Three years of running Walton House had taken its toll. She longed for a lie-in, for someone to bring *her* tea in bed, to run *her* a long, luxurious bath and supply her with warm, fluffy towels which *she* could then drop on the floor for someone else to launder. Ahead of her was an infinity of running round after everyone else, unnoticed, invisible and taken totally for granted. When had she last mattered to anyone? Someone who wanted her for herself?

Her thoughts drifted towards some unidentifiable, shadowy, mysterious stranger whispering in her ear. Someone who sounded very much like the mysterious Mr Cavanagh.

'Fee?'

She gave a guilty start. 'Oh all right, I'll let them off –

but the next couple who try to flush a nappy down our loo will be for it.'

'That's my girl!' His big, happy grin reappeared, and he leaned in for a kiss. 'Hey, Fee?' he whispered. 'Maybe we should have a baby?'

'And maybe you might like that nappy in your face?'

He walked away laughing to himself, clearly enjoying his little joke. At least, she hoped it was a joke.

Chapter Thirteen

Lifting her face to the sun, May thought how lovely it was to feel golden sand beneath her bare feet and some real warmth on her body again. It had been a bit of a disappointment to discover that sailing was rarely about lolling around on deck whilst the boat made stately progress in light air and benign sunshine. She seemed to have spent a disproportionate amount of time zipped up in her fleece, with her eyes watering as *Lucille* thrashed into a headwind.

Since they'd brought the makings of a picnic lunch with them, there was nothing to do but relax. Leaving Bill, who'd cracked open a tin of beer and was stretched out on the sand reading a political thriller, she went off to paddle and splash in the crystal clear water lapping at the shore. Every so often unwelcome thoughts about what she was going to do next bubbled up like threatening puffs of grey cloud. Much as she tried to bat away one particularly niggling idea, eventually she had to admit that part of her wasn't looking forward to saying goodbye to Bill. For her to imagine there was anything more to their time together than a joint enterprise successfully accomplished would be madness, yet she would always look back on this interlude in her life and remember Bill fondly. And, she thought with a giggle, remembering his sudden haste to rush up for cold air earlier that morning, be slightly envious of the woman who got the pleasure of discovering just how well built a builder Bill was.

Gathering up a handful of white shells scattered like a broken necklace across the sand to take back with her as a souvenir, she returned to where Bill was lying, next to the cool bag, and popped open a can of Coke.

'Oops,' she said, as he started and sat up. 'I didn't realise you were asleep.'

He'd changed into shorts too, topped by a black T-shirt, so May had another chance to study his bare, muscular legs, which she was surprised to see weren't half as pasty as she might have supposed given his colouring.

'I used to burn,' he laughed, seeing the direction of her gaze, 'but as I've got older, I seem to be able to take it more.'

As if to prove it, he sat up and pulled off his T-shirt. May blinked as she registered the palest caramel tan, a dusting of gold hair across an amazingly well-constructed chest and, oh, 'Bill! That bruise!'

He shrugged at the violent purple contusion that wrapped itself round one of his ribs. 'I thought I'd hit one of the lockers as I fell, but there was so much going on last night, there was no time to take a better look.'

'Yikes, Bill. Are you sure you haven't cracked a rib? Let me have a look.'

Worried that he'd hadn't been asleep but hovering in and out of consciousness while she'd been frolicking in the sea, she edged closer and gently placed her fingers on his smooth skin. Probing the area round the bruise, she made a tentative check for any obvious damage.

'Is that sore?' she asked, hearing a muffled gasp.

'No,' he grunted, only convincing her more that he was hiding a serious injury. May fanned her hands across the lines of his ribs and felt him exhale in a shuddering breath he was obviously doing his best to steady. Poor Bill, he was being very brave. Working smoothly and rhythmically from his back to his chest, she continued to map the firm lines of his body trying to locate the exact trouble spots.

Bill let out a groan. She searched his face expecting to find him wincing with pain, then looked straight into his eyes. Eyes that reflected the summer blue of the sky above them with pupils that bloomed under her gaze into pools of indigo. May, suddenly feeling light-headed, swallowed hard. She tried to concentrate, but found her gaze dropping to his lips. Hmm, yes, he was breathing. That was a good sign even if her own breath was becoming a bit ragged.

If she was being honest, she had to admit that from the word go she'd noticed that Bill had a very kissable mouth, with lips that promised all sorts of pleasure. May went still, afraid of breaking the spell. Suddenly all she wanted was to satisfy her burning curiosity about how Bill's mouth would feel against hers. She raised a tentative hand and stroked the lines of his face, running her fingers across the chiselled cheekbones, the straight nose and a jaw that was excitingly rough with gold bristles. And then she ran her fingertip very lightly to trace the outline of his lips, before bending her head and giving her mouth permission to follow her fingers.

Ooh, that felt good! Now she didn't have to wonder any more, May decided, stopping before Bill turned sensible on her. Oh dear, he was certainly looking very serious, she noted, squinting at him. She hoped he wasn't about to give her another lecture about the dangers of living in an emotional pressure cooker. And then he gave a sort of strangled growl and his mouth came firmly down on hers. *Dear lord*, she wondered, feeling dizzy as she closed her eyes and wrapped her arms around him, had she *ever* been kissed before? He smelled heavenly; like warm sunshine on a salty breeze. And he felt divine; heady and exciting. The promise of his hot, hard body pressed against hers suggested all sorts of exciting pleasures as she prepared herself to be utterly transported.

'Damn it, May,' he ground out, breaking away. 'I shouldn't be doing this.'

'Why not?' she panted, wondering why the heck he'd applied the brakes.

He thumped the sand, exasperation blazing in his eyes.

'Because this is not real. I warned you about what could happen when two people are thrown together in an entirely unnatural situation. You're not yourself, May, and I'd be taking advantage of you.'

She knelt up beside him, placing her hands on his shoulders, determined to damp down this particular objection once and for all. 'It feels real to me Bill, and natural,' she insisted softly. 'No one's taking advantage of anyone. Don't we both want this?'

Bill groaned and with a sudden urgency pulled her to him. Reaching up behind her back, he unhooked her bra before sliding each strap over her arms and whipping it away in one swift movement. Gosh, he must have been a demon bra-remover in his teens, May observed, letting him lean her back against the soft sand. She arched up to him as his warm hand slid under her vest to cup her breast and his mouth moved against hers in a slow tantalising kiss that went on and on and—

'Oh, God, Bill – don't stop now!' she begged, as he broke away again.

'May,' he said, breathing heavily as he struggled to speak, 'I've only just begun.'

Then, in a movement that took her by surprise, he lifted her effortlessly into his arms – thus proving, thought May, that there was nothing wrong with his ribs – and carried her towards the boat.

But just a few paces along, he pulled up again. Now what? May, who had been swooning into his arms like a

Victorian heroine silently praying that he would still have some strength left once he'd lugged her halfway across a beach, opened her eyes.

'I can't have been thinking straight,' said Bill, gently setting her down.

Damn it! How unfair of him to discover he was suffering from delayed concussion, not now, not when she was completely losing her mind.

'Are you any good at swimming?' he asked.

May turned to follow the direction of his gaze ... blue sky, white foam-tipped waves shimmering in the sunshine. And, in front of them, *Lucille* – bobbing gently up and down on a rapidly incoming tide. Great, she thought, grinding her teeth, not only had she missed the opportunity of riding aboard Bill's love boat, but unless they were quick about it, *Lucille* would be out of reach too.

Bill pulled up the anchor with a heart that was sinking, but just about intact. Had he and May got any further, he was pretty sure it would have been lost. They'd got back to the boat before it was too late, but Bill was certain he was still in deep water. Wasn't that why he'd warned May at the start of the voyage about the dangers of getting too involved – to protect himself?

But, oh, she was so beautiful and almost impossible to resist; the satisfying weight of her full breasts in his hands, the delicious, accommodating curves of her stomach and a plump little bottom that was as firm and inviting as a freshly plucked nectarine. And when she'd reached up, laced her arms around his neck and smiled at him, her trusting eyes dark with need, he'd never wanted a woman more in his life.

If only he hadn't miscalculated the state of the tide,

things might have been very different. Bill stared up at the water rushing towards the hull and wished that time and tide *would* wait for him. As it was, he couldn't help but be afraid that whatever had flared up between them had run its course. He hadn't felt emotionally so far at sea ever, not even in the early days of his marriage, but what did he really know about the woman standing beside him?

'It's probably for the best,' he tried telling her. 'You might feel differently when we're off the boat.'

May pressed her lips against his throat. 'What? I might realise you're a red-haired builder, you mean?' her breasts jiggled as she laughed at her own joke. She didn't really know much about him at all.

'And I know how much you care about your uncle, to put everything on hold for him.'

All that he knew about her was that she had a barely-mended heart and was possibly – probably – on the rebound. 'And I know you ran away to sea,' he said gently, 'but what I don't know is where you'll go next.' Seeing that she was struggling to reply, he dropped a last kiss on her head and moved forwards to trim the mainsail. Whatever the answer was, he was about to find out.

Some harmless fantasising about her mysterious guest had certainly helped Fiona deal with the hurried preparations for his arrival that evening. Standing in Cromarty, her best room, she looked across with satisfaction at the sunshine turning the green waves from olive to apple, lifting the mood of the sombre North Sea. The pristine room looked especially inviting in the afternoon light flooding through the sash windows, reminding her of how much she'd enjoyed discovering her previously untapped creative side as she brought the old building back to life.

She'd chosen a wash of sage green for the walls, in this room, picking out the cornicing of the high ceilings and the stripped floorboards in a subtle off-white. In the early days she'd fancied herself a style guru of boutique B&Bs and anticipated a deluge of compliments from her grateful guests about her good taste and comfortable beds. But with barely more than ten per cent of their guests staying more than two nights, very few of them bothered to say anything at all about their surroundings, leaving her with the nauseating reality of soiled sheets and towels and a major clean up every day. To think, she'd given up a stressful but prestigious job in local government just to double her working hours mucking out after other people. When would she and Paul enjoy the so-called quality time they'd hoped to find?

Being confronted with the evidence of strangers having sex under her roof was one of the aspects of running a bed and breakfast that still turned her stomach. She eyed the bed with its crisp bedding possessively, wondering what fate had in store for it next. Mr Cavanagh, of the lovely voice, sounded like a man who liked lots of wild sex, and since he had gone to some lengths to time his booking to be sure of surprising his girlfriend, it seemed he was certain of getting it. It would be just her luck for them to be noisy and messy and for him to shed body hair like a gorilla with alopecia. She stood in the doorway, taking one last sweep of her beautiful room in its immaculate glory before sighing and closing the door.

'Home alone,' said Paul, rising from the lovely old Windsor chair at one end of the landing, where he'd clearly been lurking. He moved towards her, his blue eyes dark with intent, and his mouth, which always reminded Fiona of a child's drawing of a smile, came down on hers before she had time to speak. Frantically trying to banish all thoughts of other people's couplings, Fiona struggled to get up to speed.

Predictably unpredictable, a little voice was telling her, since it was only that morning that she'd stopped him rushing out of bed just long enough to tell him how nice it would be if they didn't always make love at the same time and the same record-breaking pace. Reaching up, he slid the band out of her hair and let it tumble round her shoulders. 'Fancy catching up?' he murmured. He looked so shy, for all the talk, that her heart just melted. There was still something of the innocent little boy about her husband that made her feel protective towards him. How could she hurt him by telling him she wasn't really in the mood? Heck, he deserved a treat.

'Give me a minute, then come and get me.' She smiled and raced up the stairs to their private suite on the third floor, giggling to herself as Paul started counting out loud. In the bedroom, she rapidly shed clothes and rummaged through her underwear draw. The first pair her fingers alighted on, big pants from her period week collection, made her pause for a moment. No, not suitable at all, she laughed to herself, dismissing the thought and slipping into black lace and a pair of holdup stockings just as Paul thundered through the door.

'Wow! Look at you! You look fantastic!' he said, beaming. 'Amazing boobs,' he added, cupping one appreciatively. 'I swear they've grown!'

'You're in too much of a hurry to notice, usually,' she scolded playfully.

'I'm going to make up for it now, I promise.' He grinned and was as good as his word.

At the end of what was a very satisfying romp, Fiona

reminded herself of her good fortune. She'd thought it such a romantic place to live when she and Paul converted the former servants' quarters at the top of Walton House into a suite for their private accommodation. Even though the apartment was smaller than their previous flat, it was fine for a couple but completely unsuitable for a family; she shuddered recalling Paul's jokey suggestion.

The further you climbed up the house, the more spectacular the views. She felt secure tucked under the eaves, listening to the wind blowing straight off the sea at the front of the house. Even from the kitchenette at the rear she could look down on a jumble of rooftops towards the light glinting off the creek in the distance and calculate how quickly they could buy a small boat so they could enjoy the freedom of getting away from the pressure of running the B&B without being too far from home. Sometimes she had to remind herself that while other couples talked about it, they had done it; they were living the dream. One day, she thought, sighing as the bell in reception sounded, they might even get the time to enjoy it.

Fortunately she was almost dressed, unlike Paul, who was still stretched out in bed looking very pleased with himself. 'Stay there, I'll go,' she said, her heart swelled with love and affection. She blew him a kiss and tugged her chocolate jersey shirt over her coral pencil skirt as she went downstairs. He was a lovely man even if he did need to be reminded every so often not to spread himself too thin. He was fun to be around and they made a good team, all they needed was a little more time on their own.

Feeling reckless, for once, and uncaring about her tousled hair, flushed cheeks and the fact that she was probably reeking of sex, she sauntered into reception and stopped dead. The man sprawled in one of the leather bucket chairs, his hands cupping the ends of the arm rests and his legs aggressively spread, regarded her with insolent dark eyes and a wicked smile.

'Mrs Goodwin, I presume,' he purred. 'What a pleasure to meet you. I have a booking, the name's Cavanagh.'

Instead of reacting, Fiona just stood there, feeling herself quiver as his gaze travelled over every inch of her body from her dishevelled dark hair to the tips of her gold ballet flats. She almost gave him a twirl, except there was something so sensual and intimate about his inspection, she was a bit afraid of what she might be prepared to do next.

'I'm pleased to meet you,' she stammered, finding her voice. 'I'm sorry, I didn't think you'd be here until later.'

'Clearly,' he said, with a dry amused note in his voice that told her he knew exactly what she'd been doing. And then he stood up and Fiona struggled to hide her surprise. Who would have guessed he was such a pocket rocket? Judging from his voice, she'd conjured up an image of someone dark and handsome, which was certainly true, but she'd been way off in her estimation that he'd also be tall. Well, that had certainly shattered her illusion ... which was probably a good thing. For a moment there, Mr Cavanagh had gone straight to her head.

Chapter Fourteen

May understood that it was probably a good idea for Bill to concentrate on steering the boat, especially if they were to avoid running aground for a second time, but given the intimacy they'd shared, it would have been nice of him to show a bit more interest in what she was going to do next. Or, more to the point, what they were going to do next.

On another day, she would have been charmed by the meandering course through Campion's Creek, past shrubby islands tufted with waves of seablite, purslane and studs of sea lavender. But today all she noticed were the palisades and tidal gates, an overgrown tributary leading to an ancient wharf, timbers cracked and patinated with age. All the traces of past efforts to control the dynamic, shape-shifting landscape only served to make her more aware of her own inability to fight a rising tide of emotions.

'From an age when East Anglian grain and hay for horses were sent by sea to London … and sewage was sent up in return,' Bill observed, following her gaze.

May pulled a face; perhaps she'd been guilty of dumping on Bill? Perhaps she'd frightened him off? The trouble was she didn't know herself whether to be glad or sorry that having to wade out to the boat had poured cold water on their moment of passion. Now they were running out of time.

Willow withies marking the shallows gave way to port and starboard buoys and then to a string of yachts jostling on deep water moorings as the tide rushed them to their voyage's end. The watercourse eventually looped towards a neat spoon-shaped basin where, on one side, a starkly modern restaurant rose above them as they slid past. Huge floor to ceiling glass windows glowing orange in the early evening sunlight and a long expanse of dove-grey decking dotted with seating areas, must have afforded diners both inside and outside with an unrivalled view of the secret waters. Nestled into the opposite curve lay a collection of black-stained weather boarded buildings. Between them, hugging an undulating wooden pontoon, a chattering of colourful boats – some of them classics, some complete misfits – shuffled and swayed on their mooring lines.

'*Lucille*'s found her natural home,' May observed as they slipped through the tidal gate. A happy ending for one of them, at least.

'There's a much bigger marina up at Great Spitmarsh,' said Bill, nodding, 'where they pack all the plastic boats and the motor monstrosities in nice and tight to stop them cluttering up the river and places like this. This is the definitely the best place for *Lucille*.'

May moved forwards to look out for a berth and wait for Bill's instructions.

'May?' he said urgently.

Something in the tone of his voice made her turn to him expectantly, but whatever he was about to say was interrupted by a cry from the shore.

'Bill! Over here, mate!'

A vision in how to do well-worn Levi's, accompanied by one of the oddest-looking little mongrels she'd ever seen, was waving at them and pointing to an empty berth. In ordinary circumstances, May would have been pleased to draw ever closer to such a fine-looking man, but, filled with a terrible sense of time running out, she wished that *Lucille* handled a bit more like a car, so they could take off for another quick spin. Who would have believed at the start of the voyage that she'd dismiss the bloke on the shore for another few minutes with Bill?

'What?' she begged. 'What did you want to tell me?'

He looked at her then back at the shore. 'Just take the line and go forward, will you,' he said, turning his attention back to the boat. 'Matthew there will catch it and tie us up.'

May shot him a look over her shoulder but, failing to catch his eye, went to kneel at the front of the bow. Looking at the guy waiting was making her nervous. She hoped she wasn't about to spoil those achingly good looks by chucking a rope in his pretty face. It didn't help that his scrappy little dog was adding to the confusion by dancing backwards and forwards alternately growling and yapping its head off as *Lucille* wallowed closer. Fortunately the guy on the shore seemed to have a spare hand and managed to catch the line as well as grab the dog just when it was on the point of barking itself off the wobbly pontoon.

'Well done,' the man murmured as May let go of the breath she'd been holding and looked at him properly. Hooded, hazel eyes, sleepy and sexy, returned her gaze and May, who'd been about to jump ashore, almost lost her footing. A dimple in his right cheek twinkled as he smiled and offered her his hand, but suddenly Bill was there too, solid and reassuring, and it was him she turned to. Having successfully secured the boat without loss of looks, limb or dog, and the introductions having been made, May stood back whilst the two men talked, wondering when to pack up and go back to ... who knew what might be waiting for her?

'So, Matthew, how come you're on boatyard duty?' Bill said, running a hand through his too-long hair.

'Just holding the fort for Harry – my wife,' he explained

with a grin that flashed that very cute dimple. Harry? What kind of name was that? May wondered. And what kind of wife?

'She's all right, is she?' Bill frowned.

'Yes, she's fine.' Matthew's smile faded momentarily. 'Good days and bad days, still.' He turned to May apologetically and added, 'Just after Christmas we lost someone who was very dear to us, the old boy who used be Harry's right-hand man here. He was like a second father to her. We've got an apprentice with us at the moment, a young lad who's doing a boatbuilding course. He's great but it's not quite the same ... For a start, he can tie proper knots. At least I can walk round the yard without being decked by a load of timber! Although it's taken some of the danger and excitement out of it too. Mind you, Captain Flint, here, keeps me on my toes, don't you, Flinty?'

Cocking his ear at the sound of his name, the dog rolled over for a tummy tickle, making May feel quite envious as the delicious Matthew bent over to oblige. Just then a pale blue Volvo estate of a vintage that made every other vehicle around them look brand spanking new lumbered into the yard. Matthew straightened up and turned towards it with an eagerness that suggested he was ready for a tummy tickle too. 'Here's Harry now,' he said, his face lighting up. 'She needed to pop over to the marina at Great Spitmarsh, so she took our trainee with her to take a look at the competition.'

A mixed race boy in his late teens got out first, then the driver, who at first sight didn't look much older. A slight woman in a short dungaree dress and vintage blouse with a suitably nautical print, bare brown legs and baseball boots, her short dark hair curling round her face, she waved then reached into the back seat and lifted a squirming toddler on to her hip.

'And here's my pride and joy,' grinned Matthew as the young toddler let out a series of frustrated squeals and started kicking her legs, desperate to get at the dog who was leaping around at Harry's feet.

'May, meet my wife Harry. This is Tyler, our valuable assistant. And this bundle of trouble,' he said to the little girl who was stretching out her arms to him, 'is Georgia.'

Harry smiled a greeting as she handed the wriggly toddler over to her daddy. Wow! Was this slim, pixie-faced young mum really the woman who ran the boatyard? The same woman who'd talked old misery guts at Jollimarine into lending Bill his Landie. May was impressed; evidently there was a lot of punch in the other woman's small frame.

She wasn't what you would call a conventional beauty with her tomboyish looks and wide mouth, May decided rapidly, but her grey eyes were gorgeous and Matthew was beaming at her as if she was the best thing he'd ever seen, so she was doing something right. Looking at their little group, May felt quite wistful for the things she hadn't got, like an adoring husband and a chubby, adorable baby. It made thinking about what she was going to do next even harder.

'How did you get on, love?' asked Matthew.

'Well, it was bit more lively than usual, wasn't it, Tyler?' said the petite Harry stretching up to kiss her husband. 'Normally nothing ever moves in that marina, so it's a bit like waking the dead when something happens! Ancient skippers rise from their cabins, looking as if they've just heard the Trumpet of Doom.'

'Or the air turning blue.' The boy grinned. 'There was a right scene on this enormous luxury yacht that's staying up there.'

'Got in last night,' Harry interjected, 'making the

acquaintance of a couple of beefy-faced trawler men as it did so, when it nearly took the side of their boat off.'

May and Bill frowned at each other; was it a coincidence? Surely there couldn't be that many top of the range yachts in this part of the world?

'Anyway, this grisly old geezer appears on deck and starts chucking women's clothes over the side, but before he can throw the Louis Vuitton holdall into the water, this woman who looks like some kind of model tries to wrestle it back. She starts yelling at him to calm down and that they can sort it out when a young guy joins in and the old boy starts shouting at him "and you can piss off, an' all!"'

'What made it even more entertaining,' Harry chipped in, 'was that it was that old rocker guy, Thunder Harwich, you know, the one who did the comeback show at the Palace on the Pier?'

'You can't knock Thunder Harwich,' Matthew said, grinning. 'The first album I ever bought was one of his. I've even got the special edition LP!'

'Not that that had anything to do with the bosomy woman in a black leather cat suit on the front with a zip you could undo,' Harry observed. 'I'm sure you were only interested in the music.'

Bill opened his mouth to speak but Harry, to May's deep gratitude, pushed forwards to take a closer look at *Lucille*. 'So *this* is what all the fuss was about?' She laughed. 'Well, she's got a lot of charm. I reckon she'll do nicely here, although there's been a pickup in interest in these vintage wooden boats recently. Plastic boats may be easier, but some people are beginning to realise that it's worth putting in a bit of tender loving care for something a bit different. I've had a couple of calls this week from potential buyers asking if anything new's coming on the market. One was a bit of a nuisance actually, behaving as if I could produce boats that weren't there; I had to tell him the only new boat I was expecting definitely wasn't for sale! Your uncle will be over the moon when he sees her. What's the latest on him?'

'Holding his own. The hospital promised to let me know if there was any change.'

Georgia, in Matthew's arms, began to grizzle.

'All right,' said Harry, taking her back, 'we know you're hungry. Come on then, let's get you fed and ready for bed. Tyler, can you put those new sails away for me? And, May, I'll catch up with you tomorrow.'

'And speaking of food,' said Matthew, 'if the pair of you want to eat over at Samphire tonight, I'll see that there's a table. Don't worry about the tab, either. It's on the house.'

'That's very generous of you, Matt ...' Bill began, his eyes raking May's face.

'The offer's there, you don't have to take it up tonight.' Matthew shrugged, looking from one to the other. 'You can sleep on it,' he added thoughtfully.

Grinning, he ran, chased by his dog, to catch up with his wife, and then they were alone again.

When she dared look up, she saw Bill watching her, a frown creasing his brow.

'This is where life's supposed to return to normal,' he said softly. 'But I'm beginning to wonder if I know what normal is anymore.'

'Maybe we should ease ourselves in slowly,' said May, keeping her voice light. 'Perhaps we should spend another night on the boat?'

Around them the yard fell silent, except for the caress of waves breaking against the boats, then Bill bridged the gap between them and wrapped her in his arms. Sighing contentedly, May closed her eyes and snuggled in to him, felt the beat of his heart as he crushed her against his chest, heard …

'Bill? Is that your phone?'

The next morning, Fiona was better prepared for the power of her guest's mesmerising good looks. 'Good day to you, Mr Cavanagh,' she said, with hearty cheer. 'Did you sleep well?'

'I did indeed, Mrs Goodwin. I was exceptionally comfortable in your bed.' He winked, throwing her off guard again. 'And yes, I think it's going to be a grand day.'

Boy, could he turn it on! It was a long time since anyone had made her go that weak at the knees just looking at her. And he really was a handsome devil, no less delicious in the morning light than the previous afternoon; dark curls laced with a distinguished touch of grey at the temples, straight black brows and sensual dark eyes, white, even teeth and a heavy silver hoop in his left ear that gave a roguish edge to his tailored black jacket and crisp white shirt. Cocky with it too, swaggering around Walton House as if he could buy them out with his small change – oh, please, wouldn't that be a lifesaver? – and the car and luggage to suggest there was real money backing up the expensive façade.

Paul, seeing her turn a bit flushed and flustered when their latest guest took his seat for breakfast, was rather less impressed. 'Typical short man syndrome,' he observed, glaring at him through the glass in the kitchen door. 'He's got to chuck his weight around because he's so close to the ground.'

'Yes but anyone under six foot looks short to you,' she'd pointed out, secretly delighted that he was a bit cross, 'and I think a lot of women would say this was one instance when size doesn't matter.'

Just before she'd swept out to take their guest's order, Paul noticed one of her shirt buttons was undone. Having newly discovered her breasts, he didn't seem too keen for someone else to appreciate them, especially one whose height afforded him such a grandstand view. Much as she felt like teasing him by suggesting that their guest could probably blast off her buttons with the force of his smile, she decided it was probably best not to antagonise her husband, who was after all, the person doing the cooking and therefore the one in charge of whatever ended up on Mr Cavanagh's plate. Standing there in front of her handsome guest, however, it did seem as though her bra was tighter at the mere sight of him as if her breasts were about to unleash themselves of their own free will.

Actually, when he sat there like that, decorating one of her dining tables so beautifully, you couldn't tell that Mr Cavanagh was vertically challenged at all. Small but perfectly formed, she decided. And probably a very hard dog to keep on the porch, she was willing to bet, unsure whether to feel envious of or sorry for the girlfriend he was expecting.

'So may I order some breakfast?' he asked, that mellifluous brogue snapping her out of her trance. Fiona felt the blush spreading over her face and picked at an imaginary bit of fluff on her skirt to hide her embarrassment.

'Yes, of course. Sorry, I was …' She gave an apologetic shake of her head, but she could see from the gleam in his eye that he was well used to the effect he had on women. Looking round to see who else was waiting, she caught sight of Paul glaring at her from the door to the kitchen and couldn't resist a bit of sport at his expense.

'Now, what can I get you?' she said, leaning forwards

seductively. There was a pause, whilst Mr Cavanagh held her in his dark gaze and considered the matter with a slow smile. *Phwoar!* He certainly knew how to make a girl's legs shake, didn't he? Not that Paul really needed to worry, she decided, as she took the order back to the kitchen. Oh, their guest was gorgeous to look at and very well mannered, but there was something about him she didn't quite trust. Still feeling quite light-headed, she was trying to decide what it was about him that didn't quite add up as she walked into the kitchen where the heat hit her like a blast furnace.

'About time,' said her husband from a very long way off. 'I thought I was going to have to drag you off him. Any closer and you'd have been sitting in his lap!'

Paul's features were blurred as he turned towards her, adding to her sense of confusion. And just as the room started to spin and her legs buckled under her, Paul raced forwards and caught her just in time.

Chapter Fifteen

Reaching the concrete sea defences that guarded the lane down to Watling's, Bill slowed the van to a crawl and turned off the Foo Fighters. It had been a long worrying night at the hospital, but Cecil had surprised them all. His temperature was back to normal for the first time in days and the chest infection, which had come so close to overwhelming the old man, had suddenly responded to antibiotics.

'We thought we were losing him,' one of the nurses told him afterwards, 'and then you arrived and it was as if he made up his mind to carry on. I think you saved him.'

Choking back his own grief, Bill had sat there holding his uncle's hand and telling him all about the boat. And when he'd finished talking about *Lucille* and there was still no response, he told Cecil all about the wonderful girl he'd met, even though he was certain the old man couldn't hear him. Then, just as the dark night gave way to the pale light of dawn, and he had drifted into a half waking, half sleeping dream, he felt his hand being squeezed and looked up to find Cecil's blue eyes twinkling at him above his oxygen mask.

The old man was struggling to tell him something, so Bill got up and gently lifted the mask from his face.

'Now, young Bill, I hope you've taken good care of that boat of mine, because I'll be checking on her in a few days when I get out of here.'

In the light of his remarkable recovery, the hospital was hopeful that Cecil was fit once more for surgery. But Cecil had one last request to make before Bill went home to snatch a couple of hours' sleep.

'That crew I hired to bring the boat round. May someone. I'd like to meet her to thank her. Will you sort that out for me?'

No problem, thought Bill, grinning to himself as he surveyed the boatyard in front of him. It was going to be a memorable day; he could feel it in the air. Seabird-song danced on the warm wind blowing through the open windows, the indignation of bickering oystercatchers squabbling along the shore, gull ululations spinning in an azure sky and the plaintive piping of a lone curlew. Ahead of him the fresh morning sunshine bathed the boatyard in lemon light and the cluster of small boats herded in their berths jangled and frapped, straining to be set free as they caught the stirrings of the tide. On board one of them was May, waiting for his return.

Glancing towards the neat weatherboard buildings standing black, solid and timeless on one side of the yard, a glitter of sea-green glass revealed that one of the buildings was not as industrial as first glance would suggest. Harry had, as a very young woman fighting hard to keep the boatyard business started by her father, converted one of the boatsheds into living accommodation. Being Harry, she'd carried out most of the work herself, not least because George, her old assistant, was probably more of a hindrance than a help. It was also typical of Harry to stick at a task however daunting, so the boatshed, with its lofty proportions and amazing views, was now an enviable home.

And across the creek was Samphire, its great glass façade elegantly reflecting the natural beauty of its setting. Funny to think that this was the same place that had caused so much controversy in Little Spitmarsh. Some people, like the guys who ran the florist business in town, spotted a business opportunity whilst others, Harry most of all, resisted anything that would threaten the unique character of the sleepy resort. Did anyone seeing Harry and Matthew so at loggerheads then think they would wind up together?

Bill smiled to himself; much as he admired Harry, he wasn't sure *he* would have been brave enough to take her on! For a tiny woman she could certainly throw her weight around, although she had mellowed somewhat since becoming a mother and she was tigerish in her defence of Matthew when she thought he was taking on too much work. Strange what love could do ... Never had he imagined when he'd picked up the woman he'd supposed was a gold-digger at the start of his voyage that he would end up falling in love with her.

The van stopped abruptly as Bill stalled the engine. Wait a minute – fall in love? What was the matter with him? Had he forgotten his own warning about false intimacy, the heightening of emotions that pitting your wits against the elements could bring? Just because his loins ached at the thought of her, or that his lips longed to rain kisses on every part of her, or because the warm feminine smell of her would haunt him for as long as he lived, didn't mean he was in love with her. The only way to trust his feelings, he decided, starting the engine, was by testing them on dry land where he had an invalid uncle to nurse, and a build that needed serious attention before the client threw him off the site. And what chance was there for any relationship that started with so many competing demands? But what was the alternative?

It was only a short roll downhill into the boatyard, but it was enough time for him to work out that it was too soon to give up. Leaping out of the van, he strode purposefully towards *Lucille*, only to find Harry, hands on hips, scowling at a spot further along the creek.

'Everything okay?'

'You tell me.' Harry looked up at him with troubled grey eyes. 'I think your first mate just found herself a new skipper.'

May tensed as her lover and mentor, the man she'd once thought was so perfect, Aiden Cavanagh, reached towards her. 'Why did you think I'd simply let you go like that? Hmm?' he said, twisting her hair back from her face so that she was unable to hide behind it. 'You must have known I'd come looking for you.'

At first, she couldn't believe her luck when charismatic Aiden Cavanagh told her he could take her places. He had, too: dinner at The Ivy, tickets at the best gigs in town, a fairy-tale five-star trip to Paris. Anxious about her talent and ability, she felt as if she'd been sprinkled with stardust when he promised to take her all the way to the top.

Knowing that it would be crazy to complicate a professional relationship with personal feelings, she'd hidden her attraction to him by feigning indifference. But Aiden, with his bedroom eyes and low, lilting voice had worn her down. With hindsight, she realised that holding out on him had made her irresistible. It was typical of the man to want what he hadn't got. All his success hadn't been achieved without a very great deal of determination behind the relaxed façade. Once she'd lived for his praise; now she was wary and afraid of enraging him.

In this secluded coil of the creek, they were quite out of sight of anyone watching from the boatyard, but she still found herself crouching lower in the long grass in case Bill came looking for her. Worrying about the possible consequences for both of them if he was to find her now, she was very conscious of the thudding of her heart. She was anxious too about her dry throat which was bound to make her voice breathy just when she needed to demonstrate that she was relaxed and in control.

If only she'd checked before automatically answering her phone. The first person she'd thought of was Bill, calling her with news from the hospital. But Aiden? Her initial instinct was to wonder if she could cast off in *Lucille* and hide in the backwaters until she'd taken in the fact that he was there, just a mile or two away from her. She dismissed the idea because it would have been unfair to Bill to add a missing boat to his worries. Besides, it was only postponing the inevitable. She wasn't surprised that Aiden had tracked her down, only that he managed to find her so quickly.

'Listen, I understand that you're embarrassed because a lot of people think you've let them down, but you can't just run away from everything, because the word will get out that you're flaky too. If you'd left it to me, we could have limited the damage, but you're going to have to pull out all the stops if you want to save your reputation. You really should have trusted me, May. Am I so much of a monster that you couldn't even face me?'

May closed her eyes, trying to harden her heart against the soft Irish lilt that was trying to carve its way back in.

'Am I, May?' he insisted in a low voice. 'A monster? With no feelings? Is that why you thought it was fine to pack your bags when I was away on business? Did you think, somehow, that I wouldn't notice you had left? Or perhaps you thought I wouldn't care?'

She gave herself time to answer, keeping her face turned away from him, determined not to be won over, and focusing instead on the soothing rhythm of rippling glassy-green wavelets, their foamy crests being held up by the breeze. If she looked at him, saw the mischief and menace in his dark eyes, or the amusement playing across his handsome face, she'd be lost. He could dissect her at a stroke; chief tormentor in one breath, tearfully, tenderly apologetic the next.

Every time she'd tried to end their relationship, he promised not to hurt her again, promised to change, simultaneously implying she was the one at fault. Sometimes, like after her failed gig, she even blamed herself for making him angry. No wonder it had taken her so long to leave. When he reached across and tried stroking her hair again, she shrugged him off and edged away as far as she dared.

Sighing, he lay back on the grass considering his next move before rolling on his side. She could sense him studying her. 'I'd forgotten how beautiful you are,' he said wistfully.

'Oh, you forget every time you go away!' she said, unable to stop herself boiling over. 'Every time some star-struck girl thinks you can give her a leg-up with her career. Or a leg-over.'

Oh, the irony of it! Once upon time, she'd been one of them.

He laughed softly and moved closer to her. Ran his fingers down her spine. 'Ah. So this is what all the fuss is about. You wanted to teach me a lesson.'

He pulled himself up and leaned in to touch his hand to her chin, but she pushed him away.

'May, please,' he coaxed, catching hold of her fingers before she could stop him. 'Okay, I admit that I haven't been a saint, but there's nothing like coming home to find that the woman you love has packed her bags and left to make you take a long, hard look at yourself. We can sort this out, can't we?'

Her head swam as he traced a circle in her palm and a great surge of remembered desire rose through her at his nearness. The heat of his taut body, the familiar sandalwood and spice scent of his aftershave. She recalled how beautiful he'd seemed to her at the height of her infatuation, his dark hair against white sheets, his dark eyes flashing as he whispered a new trick to her, how willing she'd been to do anything to please him. Even now, she was ashamed to discover, he could still evoke a treacherous need within her.

'I've a king-sized bed waiting back at my hotel, so just stop this nonsense and come back with me, will you?' he murmured against her throat, fuelling her arousal.

Don't do this, she warned herself, lifting her head anyway and giving herself away with a sharp intake of breath as he nuzzled against her. How could she help it when he was the one who'd trained her? The man knew where to touch her, how to make her respond.

'There's a fine big bath there too,' he added, as the heat spread through her. 'If you don't mind me saying, you look as if you could do with it.'

May stiffened, suddenly conscious that she'd let herself go faster than you could say man – or in her case, woman – overboard. Along with her designer dresses, her high heels and highlights, she'd ditched everything that gave a girl bounce and shine in the right places. What about her hands? She looked as if she hadn't had a manicure in weeks. Aiden liked her to look understatedly sexy and well groomed and, even though he had a weakness for red, she doubted whether he would be impressed by her torn cuticles and chapped fingers. Only a week ago she would have felt ashamed of the way she must look to him, apologetic even. But something had changed and now she astounded herself.

'No,' she was staggered to hear herself say. 'It's over.'

Aiden gave a short laugh of disbelief as if, without warning, she'd turned round and slapped him.

'Just listen to yourself, will you?' he mocked, shaking his head as if he couldn't comprehend what he'd heard. 'What's happened to my sweet girl? When did you learn to answer back?' He fell silent, watching her with a feline intensity that made her afraid of what was coming. Somehow she managed to stay calm and not rush into a garbled reply.

He sighed, apparently exasperated and threw up his hands in a gesture of defeat. 'All right. All right, if you want a confession, I'll give you a confession. I work all the hours the good Lord sends and when I stop all I want to do is sleep. Sleep. With you in my arms. I'm only human, May. Sometimes the loneliness got too much to bear and, yes, I strayed. But if I ever had another woman, it was you I missed, you I wanted.'

He took her by the shoulders and held her gaze. 'I promise you,' he said, his voice dropping almost to a whisper, 'not one of those other women meant a thing to me. Not one. Say you believe me, will you, May?'

Still the same Aiden; a look of sorrow in his dark eyes and his mouth lifting with a contrite, wicked smile as he waited for her to acquiesce.

A solemn and dutiful child, May had learned to take her place as the quiet one in the family whilst her parents, Cathy and Rick, and her little sister, Stevie, made exhibitions of themselves at every opportunity. Under Aiden's intense gaze, she had blossomed. He'd made her feel wanted and important for the first time in her life. He'd made her throw away all the outfits he said were boring and unflattering and insisted on buying her clothes to reflect the woman he said she was. He'd changed the way she wore her hair and make-up, told her she was sexy, encouraged her to lose her inhibitions. And whenever Cathy or Rick made a nuisance of themselves, pestering her and turning up unannounced, he'd tell them where to get off.

'May?' he said with a hint of impatience, leaning forwards and cupping her face in his hands.

'No, Aiden. Not this time. You mean it now, but it won't last. I won't let you do that to me again.'

He squeezed her face a little tighter, until the pressure became uncomfortable, but she returned his gaze, unblinking until he groaned and leaned his forehead heavily against hers. 'You need me, May. You owe me, remember? You can't just walk away from me.'

Taking a deep breath, May shook herself free. It really was a very quiet spot and now she longed for someone to pass by. She glanced over her shoulder, to the path they had followed to see if anyone was in sight.

Aiden saw her looking and gave a short laugh. 'So you *do* think I'm a monster,' he said in disbelief. He got to his feet and stood over her, his expression unreadable against the sun. 'I'm not the bad guy here, May. It's everyone else. You're confused, that's all. I would never harm you. I want to look after you.'

'I can look after myself,' she said, getting up to face him, which, she realised with a faint shock, was easy to do after spending time with Bill who was so much taller than him.

'We'll see, shall we? For a start, it'll be interesting to see how you'll get by when word gets out that you've unlawfully ended your contract. It may have slipped your mind, perhaps, that assuming you do work again I still have a stake in your future earnings.'

He gave her a sweet smile and pulled her towards him. 'Come on now, May,' he said, stroking her hair, 'you've got yourself in quite a state, haven't you? Now, listen, I'm a reasonable man, I'm not about to force you to do anything you don't want to. I'm happy for you to take a couple of weeks off and get yourself sorted out.'

He released her and fished in the pocket of his black jacket to pull out a card, which he held out to her. 'This is where I'm staying, Walton House. I'll give you two days to come to your senses, then I recommend you come and find me.'

May folded her arms to make it plain she wasn't going to give into his bullying. Aiden tapped the card against his lips and seemingly remembered something. 'It's your poor mother I feel sorry for. She's got herself into all sorts of trouble worrying about you. Shame, isn't it? '

She laughed in disbelief. 'Nice try, Aiden, but believe me, my mother can take care of herself.'

'You think I'm joking? Why don't you call her and find out? Oh, she's in a mess all right, but nothing we can't sort out as soon as you come home. Just don't leave it too long.' He caught hold of her waistband and shoved his hand and the card down the front of her jeans. 'And, May?'

She braced herself for the cutting comment.

'I understand that you ran away to sea to crew on some feeble old man's boat. Is that so?'

'It's really nothing to do with you,' she managed to say.

'Oh, but I think it is,' he said, walking away. 'Imagine how unhappy I'd be if I find out you've been economical with the truth.'

As soon as she was sure she was alone again May flopped down in the grass and stared at the clear blue sky whilst her breath steadied and her soaring heart rate slowed. Aiden had just proved he could find her again whenever he liked, but next time she'd be ready for him. The sun was hot on her face so she rolled over to let it warm her back, glancing at her watch as she did so. High noon, and she hadn't backed down. She rested her chin on her folded arms, proud of her small victory.

Could do with a bath! Hah! A couple of days of topping and tailing at sea where there was no shower hadn't bothered Bill. Cutting loose from Aiden, even for such a short period, had given her enough distance to see his coercive and threatening behaviour for what it was. Severing their professional relationship, with its contractual ties, was another problem altogether. As for the stuff about her mum, well, she thought, reaching for her phone, she could dismiss that nonsense right now.

Chapter Sixteen

Cathy rubbed her throbbing temples while she waited for her daughter to fill the silence. 'Oh come on, May,' she said at last when no reply was forthcoming. 'Let's just see how it goes for now. What else is Aiden going to do with the shop? He's not making any money with it all the time it's sitting there doing nothing. Once he cools down and realises his attempt to cause mischief has backfired, I can probably work something out with him. Perhaps he'll be more amenable to the idea of me repaying the debt at a slower rate?'

May's snort of disbelief was quite audible even through a bad mobile signal. 'You can't negotiate with him because it's not about money, it's about control – you know that! I've dared to show that I'm strong enough to stand up to him, but he's not some playground bully. He'll bide his time and think of another way to try to make me do what he wants. When he does, I want to be ready for him – so, no cutting deals behind my back, please.'

Cathy fumbled for a roll-up, lit it and inhaled deeply. 'May? Are you sure you're not getting the professional and the personal muddled up? You might not want to live with the guy any more, but it's his determination and backing that made you so successful—'

'Oh, and there was I thinking it was my talent!' May sounded very annoyed.

Cathy breathed twin plumes of smoke out through her nostrils and shook her head. This was coming out wrong. 'What I meant was that if you do any more damage to your career, you might regret it later.'

'And you'd know all about that, wouldn't you?' May said in a sarcastic voice that sounded very unlike the sweet, obedient daughter she was used to. 'Being as you've made such a success of running a shop!'

'Some of us,' Cath said, smarting, 'haven't had golden opportunities falling in our lap. *You* haven't had to worry about cash flow problems and juggling suppliers, or wonder which utility bill is most urgent. You haven't had to worry about anything practical. You've had Aiden taking care of all that for you. What little I had, I worked my butt off to get – and now it's all gone! So take a good hard look at what you stand to lose before you walk away. It's all right for you to look down your nose at how I chose to earn my living, but when the money stops coming in, you might have to be grateful for what you can get.'

'This is not,' she heard her daughter say slowly, 'about my career. It's about my welfare, Mum. I thought you'd understand. But fine, if the shop's that important to you, you'd better hope that Aiden's the reasonable guy you seem to think he is.'

The call ended and Cathy took a deep drag of her cigarette. So May had finally learned to stand up for herself. That was good, wasn't it?

May curled up on her side, hoping there was no one else to fight as she was rapidly running out of steam. Her guard went up again, though, as the peaceful burble of wading birds trilling to each other as they scoured the shoreline was broken by a human intervention. The footsteps coming towards her were too light to be Aiden or Bill. She peered through the long grass apprehensively as her bravery suddenly deserted her.

'I had a hunch you might be here.'

Sheepishly, May sat up to face Harry Watling, hands on her hips, regarding her inquisitively.

'This is where I always come when I need time out,' Harry said, tugging at the knees of her baggy dungarees as she sat down beside her.

'It must be tough juggling the business with having a baby,' May observed, as if they were simply making idle conversation instead of watching each other for signs of trouble.

'Sometimes,' Harry agreed, stretching toned, tanned arms out in front of her. 'Although Matthew's brilliant. He's looking after Georgia now ... but that's not why I'm here.'

'Bill,' May said miserably, sweeping her hair back from her face. 'He must be wondering what the heck is going on.'

'He's not the only one,' Harry agreed. 'Your friend wasn't looking very happy either when he roared away in his black Mercedes, disturbing the peace.'

May didn't like the tartness in Harry's voice one bit. 'I don't really see what it's got to do with you,' she said, getting into the hang of defending herself. 'And I don't suppose you'd understand if I tried to explain.'

'I don't *have* to understand,' Harry said, visibly seething. 'What about Bill? Don't you think you owe *him* an explanation? He's beside himself trying to be in three places at once and he doesn't need to be worrying about you. You should have seen him when he arrived back at the yard after a long stint up at the hospital. It was obvious to anyone who cared to look that all that was keeping him going was the thought of seeing you. Only you'd made off with your friend by then and I wasn't about to let him chase after you. He hung around not knowing when and if you were going to return, worrying about work, worrying about his uncle until I told him to go off and do what he had to do. I said I'd tell him when there was news, but it might be better coming from you, don't you think?'

May stiffened. 'Bill and I, we're not— That is, I only delivered the boat with him.'

'Oh really,' Harry said, giving her a withering look. 'Judging by the body language going on between the pair of you last night and the heat coming off the boat, I'd say there was a bit more to it than that.'

They stared at each other, equally cross. Harry Watling could think what she liked, May decided, determined not to give her the satisfaction of a reply when it was none of her bloody business.

Harry leaned forward. 'If Bill was the fuck you'd prefer to forget, you'd better tell him soon and get back to your boyfriend before he gets involved too. So if you've reached dry land and you've discovered you've made a complete tit of yourself, it's kinder for you to tell Bill now. He's got far too much on his mind to waste his emotions on someone who's only been stringing him along.'

'You've got it all wrong,' May said fiercely, stung because she knew Bill wasn't going to like what she'd have to tell him. 'Nothing happened, certainly not what you're thinking, but the last thing I want is to cause Bill extra worry. Getting building work in the current climate must be difficult enough without him being thrown off a site because he's not safe to be there. With all the additional costs he must be incurring caring for his uncle, I know he can't afford to be unemployed.'

Harry was giving her a sideways look. 'May, just what is it you think Bill does?'

She shrugged. 'I don't know what line he's in exactly, but I know he's some kind of builder.'

For the first time since joining her, Harry laughed. 'Don't let that happy-go-lucky exterior fool you. Bill's the renaissance man of restoration buildings! He's a trained architect, part-time lecturer at Great Spitmarsh College and heads up a very successful business which specialises in the conservation and restoration of listed properties. He runs a team of twelve tradesmen who mainly cover the stuff like electrics, plumbing, carpentry, plastering, et cetera, but Bill's very hands on and loves to get involved. He enjoys the practical experience of working on sites, so he just can't keep away from them. No, May, he isn't "just" a builder.'

May blew out softly and leaned back to adjust her impression of Bill in the light of this new information when Harry broke into her thoughts.

'But he's not the only one who hasn't been exactly forthcoming. There's more to you than you've told Bill, isn't there?' she added quietly.

May looked up warily.

'Men!' Harry said with a short laugh. 'They only see what's right under their noses at times. Matthew didn't recognise you either. But that's why that bloke was keen to find you, wasn't it? That's why he asked me earlier if *Lucille* was new to the pool. I recognise his voice now; he's phoned the office a couple of times trying to find out which boats were about. I knew he wasn't a pukka buyer. I thought he might be a competitor sniffing around to see if it was worth buying me out – but he wasn't looking for a boat, was he? He was looking for you. Is he someone in the business, or is it something more personal?'

May groaned. 'It's such a mess! I just wanted everything to stop, for everyone to leave me alone so I could think.'

'Running away from your problems is a race you'll never win. That's what my old assistant, George, would have said,' Harry insisted. 'And my dad used to tell me if you're in a corner, you come out fighting.'

'I'm *trying* to fight my corner!' May replied. It was all very well for the woman whose life looked so rosy and uncomplicated to tell her what to do – Harry had no idea of the battles she was facing. 'But I can't just come out waving my fists. I need a plan of action and a place to stay where I won't be disturbed. What hope is there of me finding that?'

Harry snorted. 'Even Little Spitmarsh is heaving with summer visitors. It used to be a sleepy old-fashioned seaside town too run down for anyone to bother with. When my husband bought the old Spitmarsh Yacht Club and decided to turn it into an upmarket restaurant, things started to change. Sometimes I don't recognise the place myself: arty-farty types visiting the galleries and film festival, food writers reporting on the restaurant. We even have yummy mummies now!'

'You looked quite a yummy mummy yourself when I met you yesterday,' May pointed out. Harry's husband certainly looked as if he thought she was good enough to eat.

'Though not in my grubby work dungarees today, eh?' Harry laughed, her face softening. 'To be honest, I never thought I'd be any kind of mummy, but a lot of things have changed since Matthew came along.'

May thought how lovely it would be to have someone solid to support you; a partnership of loving equals. Then Harry spoke again. 'Tell you what, though, if you're serious about needing some real time out, I might be able to help. Come with me.'

Bill was doing his best to keep his temper and not bombard May with questions. Of course he didn't have any claim on her, or any right to demand to know just exactly what she was playing at. But a week was a long time on a small boat, especially a small boat whose safe delivery offered hope to a very sick man.

Alone with May in the cockpit, he discovered that his doubts about her eligibility as crew were unfounded as she happily followed his instructions, holding *Lucille* on course through all sea conditions whilst he tweaked the sails. The hours spent in companionable silence just listening to the creaking of the mast and the boom, the wind whistling through the shrouds and waves rushing past the hull had been an important time. A respite from his worries and a sense that he could just relax and trust in their excellent teamwork to bring the boat to Little Spitmarsh. Everything he'd wished for in other words. So why had everything changed so abruptly as soon as they returned to dry land?

He was convinced they had the beginnings of a lasting relationship. Had he really misread the signs so badly? Did he mean nothing to her? He glanced across to May in the passenger seat beside him staring silently out the window. The late-afternoon sun cast her in gold light, and she sat there as still as a statue. He hadn't actually expected her to agree to Cecil's request to visit, so fair play to her for giving up her evening to go with him. But what *had* caused his stomach to sink with disappointment was how easily she'd slipped away from him and back to her old life.

Given how quickly her ex had arrived on the scene, he couldn't help wonder if she'd been in touch with him all along. He had his suspicions too about whether it really was over between them as May had insisted. As for all the heat and passion on the boat? Hadn't he been the one to suggest what happened on there, stayed there? If she'd simply been testing her feelings, he guessed she was feeling pretty embarrassed about that now. Well, he still had his pride. If she wasn't going to talk about it, neither was he.

'I can see why there's no coast road to Great Spitmarsh,' she said at last. 'It's just creeks and marshland from here. No wonder Little Spitmarsh is so cut off. Do you miss living so far away from civilisation?'

Bill felt his chest tighten, irritated to be addressed like a country bumpkin. 'People have time for each other here away from the hustle and bustle of big towns,' he said mildly. 'It's not a wealthy part of the world, but I have a roof over my head and enough money to get by. What's uncivilised about that?'

'It's beautiful,' she said, her face flushed. 'But some people might find it too quiet.'

'Not me.' Bill said firmly. 'I've lived in the south. I went there to—' he nearly said 'train' but what was the point in complicating matters. May thought he was a simple builder so he'd leave it at that. '—to find work,' he resumed. 'Later, thanks to Matthew, local opportunities picked up and after my divorce there was nothing to keep me in the south so I came back here.'

'To where you grew up?'

Bill frowned at her interest. Why bother asking questions when they were going their separate ways? 'When Mum died,' he found himself telling her, 'Cecil took early retirement here from the Foreign Office. He bought a small antique shop in Little Spitmarsh – more of a hobby for him, though what he'll do with it now remains to be seen – and I went to live with him.' Bill refrained from mentioning that Cecil had also paid for his education, sending him to the public school where he'd played rugby and met Matthew Corrigan, who was a few years above him.

'And now you're taking care of him,' May said quietly.

Yes, it was his turn to look after Cecil, and he was glad to do it, to repay the old man for giving him a home. But suddenly he wasn't so sure it was much of a kindness to introduce May to him. Making small talk with a stranger, especially one he'd never see again, seemed unnecessarily stressful for a man who was so ill. The sign for Great Spitmarsh General Hospital was looming in front of them, but there was still time to talk May out of her visit. After driving round several times Bill finally spotted a car pulling out of a space and was able to park. 'Are you sure you want to do this? I can always make an excuse for you.'

'No, you don't need to do that,' May said, meeting his gaze properly for the first time. 'If it's going to help your uncle then of course I want to see him.'

Bill nodded and reminded himself that Cecil had especially requested this visit. Anything that helped lift the old man's spirits was good. He just wished he could say the same about his own prospects. He took a deep breath and braced himself to ask another favour.

'Would you mind?' he said, offering her the box containing the little silver starfish pendant his uncle had sent her.

'Ooh, you've got a bloody nerve,' she tutted, thankfully not looking too annoyed. 'Just remember I'm doing this to help Cecil. Here, give me a hand with it.'

She turned her back to him and lifted her heavy hair, and Bill had to fight every fibre in his being not to rain kisses on the soft, adorable nape of her neck. His fingers were clumsy as he fumbled with the clasp, but at last it was done.

'Don't worry,' she told him. 'I'll give it straight back to you afterwards. You can always call hospital security if you're worried about me making off with it.'

'I asked for that, I guess.' Great job, Bill. 'May, I—'

'Joke,' she said, touching his arm lightly. 'I think the way you look after your uncle is lovely. Cecil's lucky to have you.'

And May could have him too, any time she liked, he thought. If she'd only give him the chance.

Chapter Seventeen

Cecil was at the far end of a four-bed bay where all the patients were elderly men and, at first sight, looked similarly insubstantial and silver-haired. If the window suddenly opened, Bill thought, it was hard not to imagine them being blown away like seed heads on the breeze. May was lifting their spirits, judging by the bright eyes following her as she passed by looking fresh and wholesome in skinny jeans and a white lace cardigan over a denim-blue vest top.

His uncle, who had been dozing, looked startled to find May beside his bed. With her hair freshly washed and falling in soft, fluffy waves around her shoulders, he must have been worried an angel had come for him. This evening, Bill noticed, she'd even applied a slick of lip gloss and mascara, though there were dark shadows under her tawny eyes.

'My dear girl – at last,' Cecil said, brightening up when they were introduced. 'Well, this is a pleasure.'

Bill raised the end of the bed so his uncle could sit up. He was happy to see a little more colour in Cecil's face and a spark of liveliness in his faded blue eyes. His uncle had been a sprinter in his youth and, until his sudden illness, deported his rangy frame with a square-shouldered strength and grace suggestive of a much younger man. It was hard to see him so helpless.

'I hope you didn't take offence at my little gift,' Cecil told May. 'It was a small gesture to thank you for making it possible for my dream to come true. I'm afraid one becomes so reliant on other people as one gets older and everyone leads such busy lives, that sometimes one has to rely on the kindness of strangers. And I knew you would be a kind person with a sense of humour from your response to my silly little advertisement. Dear me, some of the other replies made me blush. Some of them seemed to have a very strange idea of what was involved. I was so looking forward to our little trip, but alas it was not to be.'

'They'll get you better in no time,' May assured him. 'Then you'll enjoy the boat even more. She's lovely – and so is this, thank you.' She held up the pendant which twinkled in the light.

'It's only a little thing,' Cecil smiled, 'but I'm pleased you like it. It seemed so appropriate.'

Bill leaned forwards with his iPad. 'I've taken some photos of the boat. She looks settled in her new home, doesn't she?' he said, wondering if Cecil really would regain enough strength to sail her.

Cecil ran his fingers over the screen and immediately started asking lots of questions about the boat, making it clear that he was in no doubt about his prospects. So far as he was concerned he was planning to take the boat out at the earliest opportunity.

'Her weather helm's heavy,' Bill warned him. 'You might want to wait for some light winds so you don't overdo it.'

Cecil brushed this aside as if Bill was still the little boy in his care, rather than acknowledge their changed roles. 'You coped with her, did you, May?' he said, with the obvious implication that if a mere woman could do it, so could he. Bill shook his head. Fond as he was of Cecil, he remained totally unreconstructed.

'I had a wonderful time on her.' May smiled. 'It was an experience I'll never forget.'

'Good, good. I'm looking forward to having a go myself. First I have to get out of this wretched place,' Cecil's voice trailed off and he sunk back against the pillows. Bill could see him struggling to keep his eyes open.

'They'll kick you out when you're well, don't worry.' Bill smiled, smoothing the floppy silver hair back from his uncle's forehead. 'I think you've had enough for one day, we've tired you out.'

'A little,' Cecil admitted, 'but in a good way. We'll talk some more next time, eh, May?'

'Definitely,' she said, with an assurance that made Bill a bit cross.

Cecil's eyelids fluttered again, but as Bill bent to kiss him, Cecil caught hold of his hand. 'We've both found the right girl now. I'll see to *Lucille* and you make sure you take care of May. Don't let her go, will you, Bill?'

Too late, thought Bill.

'Don't worry about anything,' May said, patting Cecil's arm. 'Just rest and get better. I'll see you again soon.'

Back in the van, Bill finally flipped. 'What the *hell* do you think you're playing at, May?' I know the old boy's not exactly compos mentis, but he hasn't lost all his bloody marbles. It's one thing mucking me about, I'm big and ugly enough to take it, but don't think you can string Cecil along too. Can you imagine how disappointed he's going to be when he finds out you've only told him that to keep him happy? It might amuse you, for some perverse reason, to make commitments you've no intention of keeping, but what about the rest of us who have to pick up the pieces when you bugger off again? It's plain cruelty.'

She turned a white face to him. 'Why do you always think the worst of me, Bill? I don't make promises I can't keep. Of course I'll carry on visiting your uncle. Unless of course, you're giving me specific instructions not to see him.'

Bill gave a short laugh. 'I'm just being practical. How are you going to be able to visit Cecil when you disappear back to wherever you came from?'

'I'm not about to disappear,' she protested.

'Oh really?' he said, clutching the steering wheel tightly. 'Your so-called ex has arranged a nice little romantic holiday up here for you, has he? I mean, this may be the arse-end of the world, but even Little Spitmarsh has seen something of revival in boutique hotels. We're practically Kensington-on-Sea now. And how will'—he could barely spit the word out—'*Aiden* feel about you trotting out to visit Cecil? Perhaps you thought you'd bring him along too?'

'Bill!' she yelled at him. 'I'm staying here alone. Harry's caravan was available, so I've taken that for six weeks.'

'Harry doesn't have a caravan – not one that she lets out, anyway,' he snapped. 'Well, technically, she's got one, but she's never got as far as advertising it. It hasn't been used since she had it renovated, and no one's stayed there since—'

'Bill!' May folded her arms. 'She offered the place to me herself. I do know what I'm talking about!'

'She did?'

May glared at him.

Bill fell silent as he let the clutch out and set off on the return journey to Little Spitmarsh. The caravan sat on the fringes of the boatyard. For many years it had been home to Harry's beloved old assistant, George, who had stoutly refused all offers to upgrade his accommodation. In the weeks after his death, the place had almost become a shrine to his memory, especially for Harry, who had struggled to come to terms with her grief.

Matthew had been frantic with worry about his wife

and confided that he thought it was only having Georgia that had made her get up in the mornings. When Harry surprised them, one week in late spring, by clearing the caravan and sprucing up the interior, everyone took it as a sign of her recovery, but no one seriously expected anyone to stay there again.

Now this? Bill dared to smile to himself. No way would Harry allow May anywhere near the place that was almost sacrosanct to her if Harry didn't trust her. And for the entire summer holiday, too. Whatever was going on between May and her ex, she wasn't about to disappear from his life – or what passed for a life, given how busy he was – completely. The winding road which cut its way through the flat, watery landscape leading them back to Little Spitmarsh narrowed ahead of them. Bill pulled closer to the side of the road to let an oncoming car pass. 'You must have a very understanding boss,' he ventured, thinking of the number of clients who were anxious for him to get back to them.

'Yes, me,' she said wryly. 'I'm self-employed.'

'That's handy, then.' Somehow they hadn't got round to the subject on *Lucille*. Either because they'd been too busy or too exhausted. It just proved how little he really knew about her. They had reached Sea Lane and Bill drove into the boatyard. He started to think about suggesting something more pleasant they could do together, like that meal at Samphire, where they could talk in peace. At worst, maybe they could come out of the whole experience as friends? And what a thoroughly depressing thought that was.

But before he could ask, May spoke. 'I meant what I said about being happy to visit Cecil. I can always keep him company while you're at work. It's simple enough for me to catch the bus.'

He managed a weak laugh. 'Why would you want to do that? We'll go together, of course. You don't need to lumber yourself with my uncle.'

He watched her gaze drop to her hands folded in her lap. 'Bill,' she began at last, 'you were right about emotions being heightened on the boat. I was running away from real life when we set sail together, but even then, as it turned out, I didn't manage to run far enough because the person I've been too weak to face is myself. Thanks to Harry, I've got some breathing space and a chance to clear my head. I can't keep making mistakes. I have to be able to live with myself. Everything's happened between us so quickly, that I don't know if I can trust what I'm feeling or not.'

'Then, let's give it a try.' Bill was desperate.

She looked up and gave him a rueful smile. 'Whatever I do next, it's got to be right for me or it's not fair on you. Otherwise, there's a danger we'll just plough on and end up hurting each other. Let's just slow it down, give each other some space and see where we land. And hey, whatever happens, we'll always have those memories of *Lucille*.'

She jumped down and took the path beside the waterfront leading to the far reaches of the boatyard, her bouncy hair shining in the evening light. *Don't let it be over,* he silently begged, waiting for her to turn and smile over her shoulder at him. *Give me a sign.* But he watched until she was out of sight and she never looked back.

May was getting used to the caravan and was beginning to feel relaxed in her new surroundings. After a rare night of uninterrupted sleep, she was just coming to when she was jolted by a heavy thud on the thin roof, swiftly followed by another. Aiden? Had he discovered her hiding place? Two days, he'd said, but was he about to bully her into early submission? Listening intently while her sleepy brain scrambled for a plan, her fear turned to relief as the thudding became a scampering then a loud squawk as war broke out between two seagulls.

'Running away from your troubles is a race you'll never win.' That's what Harry had told her. May sat up in the narrow bed with its cheerful bedspread of knitted coloured squares and looked around. She liked how the space had been sympathetically refurbished without losing its unique character. There was a neat galley kitchen with painted pale green units running along one length, at one end a compact seating area, again kitted out in cool, sea greens, with stunning unbroken views across the creek and, at the other, a minuscule bathroom.

What she liked best, though, was the atmosphere; a strange sense of serenity and sanctuary that made her feel as if the previous inhabitant had handed it on with love. May guessed that some people might have been spooked by that feeling and the secluded location, but it made her feel stronger. She felt safe in this small caravan, isolated as it was. Instead of sitting there waiting for Aiden to make his next move, could she take Harry's father's advice and come out fighting?

Rather than waste any more time worrying about what she couldn't change, May decided it wouldn't hurt to put herself first for a day. Although her break was only a temporary reprieve, every hour away from the pressures of her previous life would give her time to regain sufficient mental strength to face the future. Answerable to no one for the first time in far too long, she relished the thought of some time to herself to wander and explore. Later, if she felt like it, she *would* ring Bill, just to see how his uncle was faring – that was a perfectly reasonable thing to do, wasn't it?

Right now, she had practical matters to attend to. Like silencing her groaning stomach and doing some shopping. The contents of her rucksack had been enough to see her through a week or so but needed supplementing for a longer stay. She'd look out for a new notebook too, just in case she was tempted to start writing again.

Little Spitmarsh, she was quickly realising, was a town of two halves. Towards the seafront, developers had restored many of the lovely Victorian villas, a cluster of cutesy shops selling vintage tat or cupcakes and a smattering of galleries created an illusion of prosperity in the most picturesque part of the town, but the tide of gentrification spluttered to a halt further along the high street, leaving a depressing wasteland of charity shops, the remnants of national retail chains and empty spaces.

Ignoring the rather chichi cafés in the old town, May chose the Paradise Café, with its amazing views across the muddy North Sea. In Cornwall it would probably have been swallowed up by a TV Chef's empire, but here, thankfully, its refurbishment was comfortably low key with stripped floorboards, shabby-chic sofas arranged in pairs and free Wi-Fi. Whoever owned the Paradise Café seemed to be of the opinion that heavy-handed interior design was an unnecessary distraction from the hearty food on offer and the superb views. It was an approach May rather applauded.

Fully equipped with a chunky bacon sandwich and a large cappuccino, she had just settled herself into a sofa with stunning sea views and was looking forward to enjoying the peace and quiet when the doors flew open and what felt like a small army of mummies and babies marched noisily in. May looked at the vacant sofa opposite protectively, wondering what would be regarded as reasonable defence of her territory, when a tall, attractive woman with dark hair approached her.

'Is this seat taken?' the woman asked.

She was several years older than May, she guessed, with a warm, intelligent face. She wore the off-duty clothes of an office worker. A look the older women's magazines called 'weekend casuals'. May made sure that coffee was all that the woman was carrying and wasn't about to spring a noisy baby on her. 'Be my guest,' May said with a smile.

'It's not that I don't like children,' the other woman said, leaning forwards conspiratorially, 'but this is my treat to myself. It's one of the few chances I have to enjoy a quiet coffee and a good read, and it helps keep me sane. My husband and I own a B&B, you see. We wanted to work for ourselves, but it's like being on stage twenty-four hours a day giving a command performance, if that makes sense. Sometimes I need time out.'

The woman took an e-reader out of her bag and made herself comfortable while May watched the mesmeric pattern of the waves and let her mind wander as she ate her sandwich. The peace of their cosy nook lasted all of five minutes.

'I'll grab us a seat!' one of the mummy army yelled, knocking the back of May's new companion's seat causing her coffee to slop into the saucer, as the neighbouring pair of sofas was rearranged to make way for all the buggies.

'Oh my god,' the woman opposite May moaned. 'It's like being parachuted into a postnatal class. I must have read the same passage three times now.'

With the noise levels increasing, May glanced over the woman's shoulder hoping to shame the interlopers into better manners only to be greeted by a nipple blaring at her from across the table whilst one of the babies, who'd got himself into a real temper and was now looking red as well as snotty, calmed down sufficiently to recognise a silencer when he saw it. As the roars of rage turned into slurping and sighing, May hoped that would be the end of it.

'He's a little piglet, isn't he?' Mummy One observed affectionately, looking down at him.

'Oh, tell me!' Mummy Two said with a sigh. 'He doesn't know when to stop! He will keep going until he's absolutely stuffed and then, whoosh, it all comes back again, right across the room sometimes!'

Lovely, thought May, wishing she'd chosen one of the chichi cafés after all.

'It's that first feed in the morning,' laughed Mummy Three, beside her. 'You know, when your breasts are so full, you just think "give me a baby to feed, any baby!"'

'Oh yes!' Mummy Two agreed. 'That's when you feel like a human fountain. Milk spurting in all directions! I managed to squirt Ben *and* the baby in the eye yesterday morning.'

In the ensuing hilarity, the woman opposite May lifted her coffee out of range and took a wary sip, as if trying not to imagine any strange taste to it. 'Too much information,' she mouthed at May, who nodded in agreement. They pulled faces at each other and giggled, determined to enjoy their expensive cappuccinos despite everyone else's best efforts to spoil it. Lifting her cup, May returned her gaze to the sea and blocked everything out except for Thelonious Monk's jazz piano drifting from the speakers. She was about to take a sip when she was hit by a sulphurous wave of full nappy, like rotten eggs scrambled in the Devil's kitchen, and almost gagged.

The dark-haired woman opposite turned a pale green. Dropping her cup, and shoving her e-reader into her handbag, she stood up and nearly tripped over a buggy laden with shopping bags, which tipped over backwards, crashing into the next table and sending a tray of cups and saucers flying. In a chorus of cries and tutting as she staggered for the door, Mummy One's voice was shrill above the noise. 'Well thank goodness Alfie wasn't still sitting in it! Some people are so rude!'

Noticing the woman had left her scarf behind, May decided she too had had enough and hurried outside to find her. Luckily she hadn't gone very far, but was outside on a decked area, leaning on a rail overlooking the sea and taking great gulps of air.

'Are you okay?' May asked, noting the woman was still very pale and clammy.

'That eggy poo nappy nearly pushed me over the edge,' the woman moaned softly. 'I've a nasty feeling that one's going to remain in my nasal memory for far too long. What with that and the wash of mother and baby body fluids flowing far too freely, it was all a bit much for my personal comfort zone. Urgh! Why are babies supposed to be adorable? Sorry, no offence if you've got a family.'

'Not yet,' May said with a laugh, 'but I would like children one day.' A sudden image of having cherubic ginger babies with Bill popped uninvited into her head. She quickly dismissed it and handed the woman her scarf.

'Thank you. If you could chose to have children delivered when they've reached a sensible age, I might be tempted. Otherwise, I can't think of anything less welcome right now. I'm Fiona, by the way, Fiona Goodwin.'

'May Starling.'

Fiona gave her a puzzled look. 'I'm sure we'd have met before if you were local, and yet I can't shake off the feeling I know you from somewhere. It might help my concentration if I could only shake off the smell of that nappy. On the bright side, it just goes to show that I'm not completely inured to human nature from running the B&B. Some things can still take me by surprise!' She cast a quick look at her watch and sighed. 'And on the subject of the B&B, I'd better get back. My husband will be sending out the search parties if I'm not home soon. Can I give you a lift somewhere?'

'Thank you, but I'm trying to find my way round the town as I'm staying here for a few weeks.'

'Oh, whereabouts?'

It couldn't possibly do any harm to tell her, could it? May decided. 'Watling's Boatyard – do you know it?'

'Know it?' Fiona laughed. 'Everyone here knows Harry and Matthew. My goodness, if anyone's been changed by motherhood it's Harry! When Paul and I first moved here, I used to feel quite intimidated by Harry.'

'You and me both!' May said with feeling. 'But you run a business too, I thought Harry would respect you for that.'

'Ah, but it's just a job for me, whereas it's personal for Harry. Her father established the boatyard, that's why she kept her own name when she married, to keep his memory alive.'

May Blythe, May tried it out. 'I don't know,' she said, wistfully. 'There's still something romantic about showing the world you're a couple.'

'I think so too,' Fiona agreed. 'Of course Harry wasn't married to Matthew back then and Little Spitmarsh had been completely divided by his plans to drag the place into the twenty-first century.

'Paul and I decided to support the cause most likely to keep our business afloat – one which Harry had fiercely resisted. And although most people with an economic stake

166

in the town welcomed anything that would see the tide of prosperity turn in its favour, not everyone agreed. Someone even tried to burn Matthew's restaurant down.'

Great, thought May. Just what she needed to hear when she was already anxious about her personal security.

'Our Harry's a far more approachable lady these days, since Georgia came along. Oh, heck – if you're staying with her you must be a close friend of hers.' Fiona clapped her hands over her mouth and May laughed.

'No, it's all right. Harry's dropped a few barriers, but I think it'll be a while before we're besties. I'm renting the caravan.'

'Really?' Fiona looked puzzled. 'Oh, well, if you get fed up with that and feel the need to use more civilised facilities, pop in any time. In fact, pop by soon. It would be great to have a girlfriend to talk to. As much as I admire Harry, she's not really up for girlie gossip over coffee and cakes.' She pulled a card out from her pocket and offered it to May. 'This is us. Walton House.'

Chapter Eighteen

'Was it very bad?' Paul asked Fiona on her return, rushing to help her with the shopping.

'Oh you know,' she said bravely, with a small martyred smile. If they weren't always so busy, she could admit that she'd bunked off without feeling so guilty. As much as she wanted to tell her husband about the woman she'd met in the Paradise Café and the invasion of the yummy mummies, she couldn't because she felt bad about leaving him to do all the work. She'd felt an immediate connection with May Starling, as if she'd known her from way back when, so it was rather disappointing that May seemed peculiarly vague about calling in.

There was too much to do to feel let down for long, though, so she scooped up an armful of towels from the laundry and rushed upstairs with them. Unsure whether or not Mr Cavanagh was in his room, she listened outside Cromarty and was embarrassed when he suddenly opened the door, to be caught still standing there, with her ear practically pressed against the wood. His knowing dark eyes and worldly wise expression gave her the feeling that he could tell just by looking at her what she liked best in bed. She caught his eye and gave him a bashful smile.

'Sorry, I only wanted to bring you these. Just let me know when it's convenient to do your room.'

Aiden Cavanagh gave her a long considered look, and although she was becoming increasingly uncomfortable, she would not give him the satisfaction of being the first to break eye contact.

'Oh, Mrs Goodwin, I'm disappointed. I thought for a

moment you were going to offer to scrub my back,' he said softly, with a half-smile that suggested all sorts of wickedness.

'We do like to offer our guests a high level of personal attention, but that might be taking it a step too far,' she joked, trying to relieve the palpable tension.

He laughed and moved closer. Leaning one arm out against the wall and effectively blocking her path, he regarded her with impish, twinkling eyes. 'Are you sure about that now?' he said softly, making her blush. Ooh, that lovely Irish lilt transfixed her every time, she thought, feeling butterfly wings of desire fluttering in her tummy. He must know what he was doing. She eyed him to see if he was laughing at her, but his gaze was serious as it dropped to her lips.

'I tell you what you can do for me ...'

'Y-yes?' she managed to stammer.

'Just make sure no one's missed any messages for me, will you? If anyone tries to phone me via the hotel or arrives in reception for me, I want to know immediately. Is that clear?'

'As crystal,' she said, feeling utterly humiliated.

'Hadn't you better run along, Mrs Goodwin,' he murmured, since she was still standing there gawping at him, 'before you get yourself into trouble. I mean, what would your husband think if he knew you were hanging around outside my door like this? You should be a bit careful of your reputation, you know.'

Fiona scurried away, her face flaming. Jeez, the man was a menace, she thought, knowing that she'd come very close to making a fool of herself. Thinking about it, wasn't his girlfriend supposed to have arrived by now? Perhaps she'd taken a wrong turning and ended up at the boatyard instead? If she had any common sense, she'd find herself a little boat and set off into the sunset. That would take the wind out of Mr Cavanagh's puffed-up sails.

She flew up to her own room to add the contents of her own laundry basket to the next pile to go in the wash. It was only as she weeded out an assortment of underwear to be washed separately that it crossed her mind that she hadn't worn her period knickers for a while. Occasionally she ran two packs of pills together and missed a break; that might explain it. But what was long overdue was a holiday, a far more likely reason why she'd been feeling so run-down. If it hadn't been for the recent exposure to messy babies she wouldn't even be thinking about the possibility of being pregnant. Brushing the thought away, she rushed back downstairs to put the next load of washing on, then remembered she'd left a bulk pack of loo rolls in reception. Going to retrieve them, she was surprised to see someone standing at the desk. Where was Paul? she wondered. Did she have to do everything? The flash of irritation disappeared as quickly as it had flared up when she realised it was her new friend.

'May,' she said with pleasure. 'How nice! If you give me two seconds I'll fetch us both some coffee and we can enjoy them in rather more fragrant surroundings than earlier. Unless, you've come to take me up on my offer to use the facilities …'

'Thank you,' said the other woman nervously. 'But actually, I've come to see one of your guests. I think he might be expecting me. His name is Aiden Cavanagh.'

Bill hadn't expected to feel May's absence so keenly. He'd hoped that by burying himself in his work, he'd be too busy to miss her and too exhausted when he went home.

It hurt that she didn't feel the same way. If only she'd give him another chance, he wouldn't rush her, he'd try to win her round slowly. He wasn't perfect, but he had to be better than that ex of hers. And sometimes, he thought, standing back to take a critical look at the red brickwork gable of the restored farmhouse, it was possible to love imperfections.

He crossed the flattened rough grass to get a better look at the roof. If you cared enough, you could find beauty in the least promising material. Imagine how the character of the building would have suffered if they hadn't been able to salvage those beautiful old handmade red clay tiles, each one unique and with a different story to tell about its maker.

His first glimpse of the project hadn't been promising either; the farmhouse had been subject to some very clumsy repairs and ugly extensions over the years. Matthew had objected too. 'It's got so many grade listings, we won't even be able to blow the dust away without getting written permission!' he'd grumbled. 'And it's supposed to be haunted.'

That was all right with Bill, who didn't believe in ghosts, although he'd discovered a spirit or two when he got home after May had walked away, the ones that filled your glass and emptied your mind. A passing cloud casting him in shadow, darkened his thoughts. So now it was back to business as usual.

He let himself in to attend to a few snags and carry out a final inspection. Standing in what would have been the all-purpose living room of the original fourteenth-century building, he cocked his head to one side. In the vacuum of silence after all the traffic noise, something creaked above his head. Bill shoved aside the feeling that the hairs

171

on his neck were standing on end. There was certainly evidence of something weird going on, but it was all in his head because he hadn't been thinking straight since he'd met May. The dead didn't scare him, but the living ... the living could really hurt. Just the upstairs timbers, he reckoned, stretching themselves stiffly in the sun. It was too easy to assign some supernatural presence to these old buildings which had an atmosphere all of their own, unlike the soulless clusters of modern homes and spanking new estates.

Once some of the building's worst features, like the ghastly reproduction Tudor window – probably added by some well-meaning Victorian – had been carefully removed, the bones of original structure revealed it could still be lovely, for all the neglect. With sensitive handling and painstaking rebuilding using traditional materials the house was not only breathing but living again.

Only the attics to inspect, accessed by a narrow flight of stairs behind an original blackened door. Noticing for the first time that something was scratched into the wood, he crouched down to take a closer look. Running his fingers across the graffiti, he felt a sense of connection with the hand that had scored those words so many centuries before. 'Remember Me?' some tortured soul had pleaded. Another frustrated, heartbroken sod, he guessed, feeling their pain.

Straightening up, he was conscious of his spine tingling and an almost overwhelming urge to look over his shoulder to make absolutely certain he didn't have company. Sheesh, if he let himself get this spooked out simply because he was alone in an empty property, he'd have to look for a different job, and he was getting a bit long in the tooth for that. There were ghosts about all right, but not here in this rather charming old house. He'd always be haunted by May, but he didn't need an exorcist to tell him she was presently beyond the realm of his everyday life.

Asking for space was like asking to be friends, wasn't it? But if that's what she wanted, he had to accept that his May, the May he'd grown so fond of on the boat, was lost to him.

'I win again,' said Aiden, his dark eyes darting to her in triumph as the fruit machine lit up and started pumping coins into the tray. Not this time, thought May, who felt she'd already outmanoeuvred him twice; once by picking a time to call on him while he was still considering his next move, and then by rejecting his overtures to persuade her up to his room. She was grateful to Fiona Goodwin for her help with that, since the other woman seemed to sense May's unease and hovered in the reception area checking the computer screen – to Aiden's obvious irritation.

Little Spitmarsh pleasure pier – which, she noticed in passing, had a flourishing bill of old rockers still doing the rounds as well as the ubiquitous tribute band – was busy with sightseers, so it seemed a safe enough place to walk with him, but she still had to be wary. Aiden fed more coins into the machine, happy to make May wait until he was ready. She glanced towards the amusement hall's square doorway leading out to the boardwalk which framed the seascape and provided a nearby exit.

'I didn't come here to play games,' she said, 'so you're about to lose the chance for a grown-up discussion before I seek legal advice if that's all you want to do.'

Aiden, in black, looked at ease against the frenetic backdrop of jangling slot machines and flashy fairground rides. With his sloe-eyed insolence and lean, snake-hipped body, he could almost have been one of the boys weaving between the dodgems promising danger and cheap thrills to the prettiest girls. A twitch of his lips as he cocked his head to look at her showed his interest had been piqued; a stray cat coolly assessing a timid pet.

Scooping up his winnings, he followed her outside. May kept walking, inhaling salt air and the cloying sweetness of hot, sugary doughnuts. Along the rails, fishermen were casting their lines for bass and sole. May had no intention of allowing herself to be reeled in, but that didn't mean it was going to be easy to resist Aiden. The sea breeze was chilly towards the end of the pier, so few summer visitors in their light clothes were inclined to linger. May let them pass, waiting until she and Aiden were alone before speaking.

'We can't go on like this,' she said, turning to him at last. 'I'll always be grateful to you for the good times, but surely you can see we've reached rock bottom both personally and professionally. Let's do something about it now before we hurt each other even more.'

Aiden spun round to face her, backing her towards the rails as he moved closer and spread his legs either side of hers.

'I know,' she said taking a deep breath, 'that I'm not what you want me to be at home or at work—'

He made a dismissive sound. 'Do you now?'

'But there have been faults on both sides, I think you'll agree,' she hurried on. 'Maybe we would have been better off not getting involved, but we did. It's too late to change the past, but for the sake of what we had, let's sort this out between ourselves.'

She waited to let the idea take root. If she was being honest with herself, she couldn't regret the early days of their relationship. Aiden would always be a bittersweet love, but her biggest mistake was not falling for him in the first place, but being stupid enough to believe she could change him.

'Here's the thing,' he said, dropping his voice as if he was talking to himself. 'If I let you go just like that, my lawyers might be inclined to remind me of the heavy investment I made in your career ...'

'And mine might argue that you're sitting on a wealth of unreleased material,' she countered. 'Going through the courts would be a waste of money for both of us. Unless you're determined to destroy everything we ever had.'

He made a restless gesture and stepped away from her. May began to feel optimistic. 'Besides,' she added, 'I'm willing to guess that taking into consideration your behaviour and the detrimental effect on my health, most courts would rule that if anyone had breached the contract it was you.'

Aiden's eyes narrowed. 'So this isn't about our professional relationship, it's revenge. Are you're threatening me?'

May bit her lip and struggled for a quick response. 'Aiden, it's over! I can't work with you and I don't want to live with you. I know you've been seeing someone else, so why try to hang on to me as well? Just let me go.'

'You're imagining things.' He caught hold of her shoulders, forcing her to meet his gaze.

'No.' She stood her ground. 'Don't waste your breath. It's not fair to me and it's not fair to Molly.'

May reached for her phone and showed him the text that had arrived just hours before her big moment at the Ferrington Farm Festival, sent possibly in error, but probably as one of his nastier ploys to keep her on her toes, and not to Molly, his most recent signing, but to May. Written in highly explicit language making it absolutely clear about the intimate nature of the relationship, it was the straw that had finally broken her back. She'd gone to the loo, vomited copiously and walked out.

Aiden shifted from one foot to another as if pacing a cage too small for him. 'All right,' he admitted, 'I *have* been seeing her, just to help her along at the start of her career, that's all. You're blowing it out of proportion, May. She doesn't mean anything to me, not like you. Give me a chance to sort it out and I'll prove it to you.'

'I don't want proof,' May insisted. 'I want out. And remember this is nothing to do with my family, so stop using them to get to me.'

'Aah! You got the sob story, did you?' He came over and stood beside her, and leaned back against the rails. 'It's easy to fix, May. The sooner you're back in my bed, the sooner your mother gets her shop back.'

'Your bed,' May said firmly, 'is too crowded for me. Whatever Mum owes you, I'll repay it.'

She started to walk away, but Aiden called after her, 'Oh you will, angel. What's yours is mine – you still belong to me, remember? And the sooner you come home, the sooner you can clear the debts.'

May kept walking, keenly aware of his eyes on her back. She was certain he wouldn't do anything as obvious as following her back to the boatyard, but nevertheless, she felt shaky and needed the reassurance of a familiar voice as she wound through the streets of Little Spitmarsh. *Bill*, a mischievous thought whispered, before May silenced it. How unfair would it be of her to run to Bill, a decent, kind man, when she was so defiled and weighed down by the weight of her personal baggage?

She took a deep breath of the fresh salty air and refocused. On notice boards, layers of old flyers gave a snapshot of a town trying hard to adapt to a revival of staycationers as cash-strapped families looked for alternatives to the Canaries: carnival days and bingo, mingled with art exhibitions and a film festival. It was anyone's guess, she supposed, whether or not these attractions would be sufficient to hold their interest when – and if – better times came.

A few hardy families had already set up windbreaks on the beach determined to make the most of every minute of their holiday. May felt that by standing up to Aiden, she too had drawn a line in the sand. Maybe this marked the start of better times for her? Feeling that she deserved a small reward, she snaffled a few bargains in Little Spitmarsh's retail outlet shop on the seedier side of town. She then decided to splurge on some fat, deep pink peonies from Black Orchid, a very upmarket florists she passed on the way back to the boatyard, where she was served by two men with shiny new wedding rings.

'Mind Kirstie,' one said, as she almost tripped over a dog basket on her way out. 'She's not very happy. She and Phil have had a tiff, and he's gone off for a sulk.'

'Oh, there,' said May, bending down to pat the matronly Jack Russell but thinking better off it when Kirstie bared her teeth at her in return for her troubles. With her tissue-wrapped flowers in one hand, a carrier bag in the other and a handbag over her shoulder, she needed all her limbs to make it back to the boatyard.

Tyler, Harry's apprentice, beaming down at her from a ladder up the side of a boat, greeted her on her return and offered to help carry her shopping back to the caravan. 'Be right with you,' he said, before she could stop him, smiling and complimenting her on her hair as he took her carrier bags.

May smiled back at him. As she came up the high

street, she'd mistaken the sign above the hairdressers as Chimps, until a second look showed her it was actually Crimps – which to her mind was a terrible name for such a modern salon. Nevertheless the temptation to give in to some unashamed pampering was too strong to resist. Intending to pop in just to see how busy they were, she was somewhat apprehensive when the voluptuous manager with her plunging neckline and vertiginous heels directed her to a wash basin. She'd been pleasantly surprised by the result, even though almost anything would have been good after a week of boat hair and coping without any styling tools. Certainly, she'd had to cough up much more in the past at far trendier salons and been left wondering exactly where her money had gone.

'Not your usual style, though, is it?' Tyler added, stopping her in her tracks. 'S'alright,' he went on, without breaking a step. 'I won't say anything. Everyone deserves some space, you more than most. I mean, man, anxiety attacks – that must be crippling in your line of work.'

At the caravan, May reached awkwardly for her bag, wondering if he was expecting a tip. He spotted what she was doing and shook his head. 'You're among friends here. People who will look out for you. Just take the time you need and get better.'

Chapter Nineteen

Restored to his calm, rational self, Bill completed his inspection of the farmhouse without further visitation and walked back into the bright sunlight, pleased that his team had got the balance about right. Sometimes a restored building could end up as pastiche, a smoothed-out featureless copy of its former self. Or conserved to the point of becoming a museum piece; authentic but quite out of odds with modern life. The farmhouse before him was going to make a lovely home for some fortunate family. All the conveniences of modern living, like under floor heating, comfortable bathrooms and a solid wood kitchen whilst retaining enough of its original quirks and curved walls for its personality to shine through. If only he could apply the same skills to people. Was it possible or even sensible to wish he could break through the barrier of May's newly erected façade and catch another glimpse of the funny, endearing May who'd sailed with him on *Lucille*?

Relieved that after all the stress and heartache this project at least had been completed to his satisfaction, he was about to turn the key in the oak front door when a car horn tooted and a battered bottle-green Volvo – the disgraceful old wreck that Matthew still insisted on running – rolled into the drive. Even Harry had caught the vintage Volvo bug, but at least hers was in better condition. The door opened and Matthew's annoying dog shot out and cocked his leg up the new lime plaster on the front elevation.

'Oi, Flinty!' Matthew groaned. 'Sorry about that, Bill, mate!'

Bill shook his head. He was getting fed up of people pissing down his back and telling him it was raining. He was convinced that May hadn't come entirely clean about her ex and disappointed, after all the intimacy they had shared, that she couldn't even confide in him as a friend.

Matthew slapped him on the shoulder, bringing him back to the present with a jolt. 'You've done a great job, mate'

'What can I do for you, Matt?' said Bill, who knew that Matthew's charm assault usually meant work. 'What've you got in store for me now?'

Matthew grinned at him. 'A beautiful old chapel. Built eighteen thirties. Thought it would make a couple of luxury apartments, you know. A mouth-watering combination of sacred and divine.'

'Okay,' Bill said and nodded. 'Where is it? And how soon do you want me to take a look? I'll be free this coming weekend, but next week I'll have my hands full looking after Cecil.'

'Flinty! Will you come here now?' Matthew clicked his fingers in vain at his boisterous mongrel, who was off on a wild scent chase. 'Sorry, Bill. How *is* Cecil? You were up at the hospital this morning, weren't you?'

'Yes, I wanted to be there when the consultant spoke to him about which option to choose for his operation. There are two; both carry risks, but Cecil's desperate to get out on that boat so he's keen for them to take the endovascular surgery route where they go in through an artery in the leg and repair the aorta that way. It's a safer procedure in the first instance ...'

'But?' asked Matthew.

Bill pulled a face. 'The disadvantages are that the graft sometimes splits and there's a higher risk of infection. Just under half the patients who choose that option require further surgery.'

'And Cecil's prepared to take that chance?'

'Yes,' Bill agreed. 'He's keen to get on with his own life, as he puts it, as soon as possible.'

Matthew whistled at his dog who pretended he hadn't heard. 'So what's the problem?'

Bill shrugged. 'I'm worried that the main reason he's doing this is to make my life easier. Not his. Traditional surgery – cutting him open – means he'll have to stay with me until he's fit and well and he's afraid he'll be a burden.'

Matthew leaned back against the car and folded his arms. 'What would you want for yourself, if you were in his shoes?'

'I'd want to be up and running as soon as possible,' Bill replied, but he was a lot younger and fitter than Cecil.

'Well there you are,' Matthew observed, keeping one eye on his dog who was skittering towards them. 'Give the old boy the respect he deserves. Don't treat him like a baby, let him make his own decision. When do they want to do it?'

Bill watched Captain Flint make an abrupt detour round the back of the Volvo. 'On Friday morning, three days' time. They'll do it under an epidural apparently, so the staff can talk to him during the procedure, then he'll spend the next day in the high dependency unit while they monitor him for infection and if all goes well he'll be out on Monday.'

'Just in time for the Little Spitmarsh Regatta the following weekend,' Matthew told him, grabbing hold of Captain Flint as he came up beside him. 'You've got to be there. Fun and games for all the family at Watling's.'

Bill frowned. 'That doesn't sound like something Harry would come up with!'

Matthew laughed, showing off the dimple in his cheek. 'No, you're right, mate. But love is a many-splendored thing and I persuaded her that both our businesses – the boatyard and the restaurant – could do with a boost from all those lovely tourists with time and money on their hands.'

'You're incorrigible,' Bill said as he shook his head.

'No, I'm Corrigan, Matthew Corrigan, remember?' He opened the car door and Captain Flint scampered in. 'That's settled then. Tell your uncle he can take the boat out for a bit of punt, then you can come over to the restaurant in the evening. We're holding a bit of a do to raise money for the local hospice. Jimi's got the most fantastic taster menu lined up – The Regatta Platter. Genius. Oh, and make sure you bring May.'

'I can ask her, I suppose,' Bill said, not convinced she'd accept.

Matthew's eyebrows rose. 'Bill, mate, you give up too easily, that's your trouble. If I can get round someone as prickly as Harry used to be, a sweet girl like May ought to be no trouble!'

Another manic morning rolled around. The trouble was it wasn't only manic Monday but Tuesday and Wednesday too, thought Fiona, surveying the breakfast room with despair. And she was still feeling grotty from whatever was affecting her. Dizzy spells, queasiness, it had to be a bug, she told herself hastily. She couldn't possibly be pregnant. It was enough to make her feel sick just thinking about the possibility. In the office days she would have taken sick leave and stayed in bed. All she needed was a chance to rest and for her body to heal. Instead of being grateful for the business, she wished her guests would all go away.

Mr Cavanagh had been in a black mood since returning – alone, she was pleased to see – from yesterday's mysterious date with May Starling and had snapped at her when she'd accidentally spilled some coffee on the table cloth. Anyone would think he was the one who had to get the stain out, not her.

'Can I get you anything else?' she asked coldly when he grabbed her by the arm and pulled her back.

'My bill,' he replied, letting his arm drop. 'As soon as you like. I've some unexpected business to attend to and I don't want to sit around this dead-and-alive hole all day.'

Fiona hoped for May's sake the unexpected business didn't involve her. She seemed far too nice a person to be associated with such an odious little man. Her latest crop of staycationers were doing her head in too. One glimpse of a property price tag that equated to the cost of the second car in SW18 and they were already mentally eyeing up whole rows of houses and shouting, 'Buy!' These days, there was apparently no better way to demonstrate your green credentials and your abstinence from air miles than by reclaiming and renovating a dear little cottage and filling it with terribly clever junk-shop finds. She looked up to find Paul beside her. He caught hold of her arm and steered her to one side.

'Come on, Fee, at least try to smile, you'll scare away the guests,' he said, only half joking. '"If Momma ain't happy, ain't nobody happy", remember? Look, I can manage here now, if you wouldn't mind seeing to reception. There's a visitor wanting to book in. Lundy's still free although I think we've got a possible taker for Fastnet.'

Fiona headed for reception hoping to find a lovely, quiet, single customer with no family in tow, but her hopes were dashed at the sight of an old and far too familiar face.

'Hello, baby!' said Thunder Harwich, leaning in for a kiss. 'Remember me!'

How could she forget the ancient rock singer who'd stayed with them for the duration of his come-back performance at the Palace on the Pier last summer? Little Spitmarsh's unlovely slab of a theatre was gradually attracting a better quality of acts, but Thunder Harwich, referred to sotto voce between themselves as Mr Undercarriage, wasn't one of them.

'The trouble with Matthew,' said Harry over at the boatyard the same day, wielding a power washer hose like a gunslinger as she sized up a grimy boat bottom, 'is that he can twist me round his little finger. How I let him talk me into holding a regatta here, I don't know. The Spitmarsh Yacht Club used to run an event at the marina, but a lot of them have gone over to caravans now so it's died a death. Along with several of them. There's lot of extra work involved just tidying up the boatyard, so I hope it's worth it.'

From the little she knew of Harry Watling, May didn't think she was the type to let herself be twisted round anyone's finger, not even when the finger belonged to her good-looking husband, and especially not where her precious boatyard was concerned. Having been on the receiving end of Harry's displeasure, May was simply relieved that the other woman was more accepting of her and seemed to be enjoying some female company for a change.

'But the boatyard looks great,' she said, meaning it. 'I love the black-stained weatherboard of the buildings and it couldn't be a lovelier setting. It wouldn't look like a working yard, would it, if it wasn't a little ramshackle in places.'

'It breaks my heart to see some of these old boats never being put to sea. This lovely old girl made by David Hillyard, for example,' said, Harry, looking up sadly at *Maid of Mersea*, 'or this pretty little Stella,' she said, waving the hose at *Evening Star*. 'It's so sad to see them propped up out the water, but all the time no one's buying them and the owners can afford to pay us to store them, what else can I do? If they were mine, I'd drop the price and let someone else get some pleasure from them.'

May couldn't think of anything positive to add. Whilst everyone loved a bit of shabby chic, to her untrained eye both of these boats looked like expensive projects. Why would anyone go to the bother when they could buy a plastic trailer sailing boat and get out on the water at an instant's notice?

'Poor old Cinderella,' Harry sighed, reaching up and patting *Maid of Mersea*'s hull fondly. 'No one's going to take you to the ball, but I can at least make sure you have a clean bottom for the public.'

May guessed that having the public in for a regatta would be challenging for Harry, who, she noticed, kept a close eye on the business and an even closer one on any strangers who turned up at Watling's. But this time, perhaps because they were shouting to be heard above the electric motor as Harry wielded the powerful jet, neither of them heard the man approaching them until it was too late.

Harry turned off the washer while a familiar figure, who must have been sweltering in his black leather trousers and Guns N' Roses T-shirt, stood there grinning at them. 'Well, well, if it isn't—'

'May Starling's my given name. May will do.'

Thunder Harwich nodded and stuck out his hand. May sighed and offered hers and was surprised to find his grip was firm and reassuring. 'So this is where you've been hiding, is it?' he said, looking round with interest.

'And if you know what's good for you, you'll keep that information to yourself,' Harry said fiercely, drawing herself up to her full height somewhere at his chest level and brandishing her power hose menacingly.

'It's cool,' Thunder laughed, holding up his hands in a gesture of surrender. 'I don't blame anyone for wanting to drop out for some peace. In fact it's what I'm planning to do myself. Do either of you lovely ladies know where I can find this bloke Harry Watling?'

'I'm Harry,' Harry said, narrowing her eyes. 'And this is my boatyard.'

Thunder nodded. 'Respect.'

'How can I help you?'

'I'm looking for a boat.'

Harry shook her head. 'Sorry, but we don't have anything in the kind of bracket you'd be looking in. You're selling that monster *Valhalla* up at Great Spitmarsh marina, aren't you?'

'Guilty as charged. But this is more like it; this is what I'm searching for,' said Thunder, shading his eyes against the glare as he surveyed the sunlit creek. 'I didn't know places like this existed anymore. I thought they were all great big car parks crammed full of plastic boats.'

'They do,' Harry acknowledged. 'But you can't keep anything the size of *Valhalla* here – it would take up most of the yacht basin – assuming you could even get it through the channels and even then it would need to be a very high tide.'

Thunder snorted. 'Bloody *Valhalla*. Someone saw me coming when they sold her to me. Saw some egotistical old has-been with more money than sense, looking for a symbol of what a big dick he's got – excuse me, ladies. If anyone's a dick it's me, for falling for it. Nope, the sooner *Valhalla* goes the better. I'm going back to the simple life – a little boat in a place like this would suit me fine.'

From her pocket, Harry's mobile started to ring. 'You can have a wander round, by all means,' she told Thunder as she took it out to answer it. 'The "for sale" boats are clearly marked, but you won't find anything very grand here.'

'It's not exactly a rock star playground,' May pointed out, wandering along the lines of boats with him to give Harry some privacy. 'The facilities are pretty basic.'

He laughed. 'Listen, May, I know about basics. I grew up on the coast not far from here, on an estate in a town that once topped Britain's most deprived table.'

Ah, May thought to herself. That would explain why Thunder's faux transatlantic accent sometimes slipped. He probably saved it for his stage persona.

'That's why I was determined to make a success of myself,' he was saying. 'When I found I had a voice, I knew I could leave the lot behind – even my name – Maurice Cledwyn didn't really fit with my stage image,' he grinned. 'I've got enough royalties rolling in to keep me in clover for the rest of my days, and even after three divorces I've still got a mansion in the Surrey countryside with five bathrooms I never even use. You can only sit on one bog at a time after all. And it won't buy me friendship, or health ... or any more years. What's important to me now is making time to do it properly, to slow down and live life instead of watching it go by.'

'Some might say you'd had plenty of experience,' May couldn't help pointing out. Maurice Cledwyn, eh? No wonder he'd ditched that name. She found herself warming to his self-deprecating manner.

'In a life that was hermetically sealed,' he insisted, rolling his eyes. 'From arena to arena, by tour bus and hotel room, when every place merges into one and you'll do anything to stop the boredom. No wonder it's enough to drive you crazy.' He raised a quizzical eyebrow at her. 'You don't look crazy to me. What happened?'

No, she wasn't crazy, but that was the story that had gone out in the press. Panic attack, stage fright. 'I was never happy being the centre of attention, so it's true that I always got worked up before an appearance,' she admitted. 'I didn't like what I was – the image they created for me. I always felt as if I was wearing another woman's clothes. It wasn't the right place for me to reach a new audience either, not when everyone else was a "serious indie artist",' she said, making a little quote sign with her fingers. 'I would have been laughed off stage had I gone on, so I decided to take matters into my own hands. I did the unthinkable, walked away and hitched a lift back to the station.'

Thunder sucked his breath through his teeth. She could guess what he was thinking – highly unprofessional, career suicide. But the real reason had been more personal and she wasn't going to share that with him. 'As for that song!' she continued. 'It was a joke. Pink Lix Records, who signed me, put out two singles from what was supposed to be my first album and they did nothing. Zilch. No interest at all. So I got given a list of hits and told to write one just like it – "not these touchy-feely girlie songs no one wants to buy," they said.'

Or rather, Aiden had instructed.

'And that was the result – the blandest tune with the cheesiest lyrics I could imagine.'

'And the rest was history,' said Thunder. 'You know every time I saw the video for your single, I always wondered if there was more to you than the public image they created for you.'

'Behind the perfect pout and pink painted smile,' said May, finding she was able to laugh. 'Don't even get me started on the subject of creative control. Imagine if someone had tried to kit Radiohead or Muse out like One Direction?'

'So what happened to the album?' Thunder said, leaning forwards.

'Technically acceptable, but not enough radio hits, apparently. Pink Lix didn't like the feedback from the experimental material we tried on tour. They want me to re-record the tracks until they're satisfied they've got chart potential.'

'So they've extended the option period and got you over a barrel,' Thunder said with a sneer.

'What else can I do? I can't see any escape from my contract,' May felt helpless again. She could run, but for all her talk yesterday, she was horribly afraid Aiden only had to tug the leash to bring her back to heel.

'They don't own you, girl,' Thunder said hotly. 'I'd get someone to take another look at that contract, if I was you. In fact, get it sent to me and I'll get my brief to look at it.'

'I'm not sure it'll do any good, although that's kind of you. I was very naïve when I signed it.' And infatuated. At the time, she'd bowed to Aiden's judgement. He was the person who'd made her career, the one whose record company she was signed to. The puppeteer pulling her strings.

Thunder's face grew grim. 'Got any more of that commercially unacceptable material hanging around?'

'Commercially unacceptable is what I do,' May sighed. 'I certainly wasn't going to let them have any more of my songs whilst they were still trying to recut and butcher the eight tracks I'd given them.'

'I'd like to take a look at what you've got,' Thunder said, surprising her. 'You might not be able to use it, but maybe I can.'

'I really don't think it would—'

'What?' Thunder interrupted softly, 'be suitable for an over-the-hill rocker like me?'

May bowed her head, ashamed that she was guilty of the same sin of judging Thunder by how he'd been packaged and sold.

'It would be my privilege.' She smiled.

'Excellent. Listen, I'm staying at this boutique B&B place, got the card here somewhere,' he said, patting his trouser pockets. 'Why don't you drop by tomorrow and show me what you've got. It's called … where the hell's the bloody card?'

'It's all right,' said May. 'I think I know it – Walton House?' At least she wouldn't run into Aiden. That much was abundantly clear from his latest text. And it would be nice to see Fiona Goodwin again.

'That's the place!' Thunder leaned forward and gave her a fatherly kiss on one cheek. Over his shoulder, she could see Bill, coming towards them frowning. Bloody typical. He was bound to get a rush of blood to his red head thinking she'd arranged a secret assignation with Thunder whilst they were holed up in Ramsgate harbour.

Chapter Twenty

May waited for Bill to open his mouth but before he could say anything, Matthew, pushing Georgia in her buggy and chased by his dog, was approaching from the other direction, a big grin over his face.

'Thunder Harwich!' he exclaimed, looking star-struck. 'I don't believe it! I was a massive fan of yours – I've got all your albums!'

'Worse luck,' Harry said under her breath as she came over to join them. 'Meet one of your biggest fans, my husband, Matthew.'

'Wow! I can't believe I'm talking to the man who sang "Six Nights with Lucifer's Bride"!' Matthew beamed. 'Heck, man, when I was thirteen, I wanted to be you!'

'Yes, well, I'll bet you're glad you didn't turn out like me looking at me now, eh?' Thunder said drily.

Bill looked totally perplexed whilst Harry and May shook their heads at each other. Matthew suddenly went a bit sheepish – probably realised what he'd just admitted to, thought May, until he opened his mouth again.

'You probably get sick of fans and their requests, but if I go back to the house and dig out the *Lucifer's Bride* album, would you sign the cover for me?'

'There's no rush, son,' said Thunder. 'I want to speak to your good lady about buying a boat here.'

'Right, then,' said Matthew, looking down at the buggy. Harry was about to take over when Georgia stuck her arms out to Thunder, clearly hoping to be picked up. 'At least I haven't lost me touch with the birds,' he said, looking at Harry who nodded before lifting Georgia into his arms.

'Aren't you a cutie, just like my granddaughter? Now, be a good girl for me, because I want to talk to your mum about a boat.'

'I'll put you on a waiting list, shall I?' said Harry, folding her arms again.

'Well, that depends,' Thunder began, slightly distracted by Georgia who was babbling at him and trying to grab hold of the diamond cross hanging off one of his earlobes. 'This is the one I like the look of, right here.'

He looked up at *Maid of Mersea* and Harry, much to May's amusement, stepped protectively in front of the wooden props surrounding the forlorn boat.

'All right, you've had your fun. Why are you really here?'

'Straight up, darling, I want to buy a boat!' Thunder said, visibly wilting in the force of Harry's hard stare. 'And this one here's got great character; looks a bit lived in, like me.'

'True,' Harry agreed, softening a little, 'but you do realise you can't just put her back in the water and expect to sail away in her.'

Thunder winced as Georgia successfully caught his earring then gently unwrapped her fingers. 'I'm not planning on sailing off anywhere. I've had enough of big boats, big seas, and mutinous crews. I've come back to the area where I grew up to do a bit of pottering round the backwaters in a little boat that I can manage by myself. And if what you're saying is that the boat needs a bit of tender loving care, well, I've got plenty of time to give it to her.'

'You wouldn't need to do it all by yourself,' Harry said, beadily. 'We offer the full range of services at Watling's to help you get her seaworthy again at a very competitive rate.'

'I'm glad to hear you singing from my kind of song sheet,' Thunder agreed with a big smile despite the very angry-looking left earlobe he was sporting thanks to Georgia's attention.

'Well, well, well, Cinders,' said Harry, looking up at the old boat. 'Looks as if you're going to the ball after all. Do you want to take a closer look?'

'Do I?' Thunder smiled.

'Over to Auntie May, then,' said Harry, removing a surprised Georgia from Thunder and passing her to an even more startled May.

May, who couldn't remember the last time she'd held such a small human being in her arms, couldn't help pressing her cheek against Georgia's head, unable to resist her fluffy baby curls. Would she ever be in a position to think about having children of her own? she wondered wistfully. She caught Bill watching her and felt unexpectedly shy.

'I can't offer to take you to a ball, I'm afraid, only somewhere rather more mundane,' he said as Thunder went off to help Harry put a ladder up the side of the boat. 'I want to ask a favour. Cecil's having his op on Friday and it would really give him a boost to see you before the procedure. I wondered if you'd consider coming up to the hospital with me tomorrow evening to wish him luck. And to thank you for your time, maybe I can repay you by cooking a meal. That is if you're not busy ...' He looked up at Thunder at the top of the ladder who, restricted by his leather trousers, was having a spot of bother lifting his leg over *Maid of Mersea's* guard rails.

'I thought we'd been through all this in Ramsgate,' May complained, rolling her eyes. 'And it cost you a curry.'

'I didn't realise he was famous then!' Bill protested.

'What? So you're accusing me of being some kind of

groupie now, are you?' she couldn't help teasing. She took a deep breath. 'Bill, you asked me who I worked for but not what I did, remember. I suppose I'd call myself a writer.'

'Really?' Bill sounded impressed. 'What do you write?'

'Songs,' she said, after a slight pause.

'Without a musical instrument? How do you do that? You didn't bring anything with you, did you? Not that I saw, anyway ...'

'Well spotted,' she said, and laughed. 'I wish I did have my guitar with me now. I miss not having it. But I can still write. You can sing, can't you Bill? Don't deny it because I've heard you singing "Learn to Fly" enough times!'

He looked embarrassed, as well he might, she thought, given the number of times he'd let rip at the helm when he thought she was fully occupied doing something else.

'There you go, then,' she smiled. 'If you can sing "Do-Re-Mi" you can write a song entirely in your head without a musical instrument. No wonder everyone thinks they can do it!'

'But you must be very talented to make a living at it,' Bill enthused.

May laughed at that. 'When everyone's downloading music for free? At, say one penny per download, that doesn't go very far if there are three songwriters.'

Bill pulled a sympathetic face. 'But you get by?'

'There's more money if the artist is still selling in a physical format, like CDs. And if you get on an advert – but that's what everyone's trying to do.'

'You're young, though,' Bill said. 'I don't want to crush your dreams, but there's plenty of time for you to get your big break. And when you do, I'll be able to tell everyone that the person who wrote it was once sick over the side of my boat.'

'Cecil might dispute ownership with you,' May reminded him. 'I'll mention it when we visit him.'

'And I'll have to cook for you now,' Bill said firmly. 'I don't want to see a struggling artist starve.'

'I'd like that,' she said happily.

'Just one thing?'

'Hmm?'

Bill ran his hand through his thatch of red hair in a gesture that May recognised from the boat, as one he used when he was in a hole and unsure of how to proceed. She felt her heart swell with ... with ... affection, yes affection. That was it.

'About Thunder ... since you're a songwriter and he's a singer, you ought to talk to him about your career. He might know someone who'd be useful to you.'

Oh, he was a sweetie. May was half tempted to tell him about her so-called career, but the sight of Matthew hurrying back with what looked like a considerable collection of vinyl albums under one arm was a reminder of how even the most straightforward and sensible folk could get a little bit star-struck when you least expected it. Just for now, she wanted to enjoy being plain May Starling, accepted for who she was, not what she was. And, yes, she had to admit, she wanted a quiet life and the chance to get back on good terms with Bill, who'd been understandably frosty with her.

'Bill,' she said, shutting him up. 'I appreciate the career advice, but can we just forget about Thunder? You're the one I want to see, especially when you've offered to cook.'

'Really?' Bill beamed at her and May felt her stomach flip and told herself that it was just Georgia, digging her little heels in as she tried to escape.

*   *   *

In Walton House, the next morning, casting her eye over the bookings, Fiona ran her hands over her stomach enjoying the silence as she swung gently to and fro in the turquoise swivel chair behind the curved reception desk. She could see they were in for a quiet couple of days. The two women in Fastnet, apparently besotted with Little Spitmarsh's blend of old-fashioned kiss-me-quick appeal and new café culture, were no trouble at all and took themselves out for most of the day. The three vacant rooms left Fiona feeling torn; it made for a much lighter round of cleaning, but it wasn't brilliant for the bank balance, especially given how much it had cost them to convert the old house in the first place.

Of course, there was Thunder Harwich, who'd turned out to be a bit of star. When he'd booked Lundy for the entire coming month, she prepared herself for some inappropriate touching and lots of tedious boasting about his glory days, but he appeared to be a reformed character. Even his singing, sounding out above the shower as she passed his room, had mellowed since his last visit with far less of the roaring like an injured lion. Never a fan of commercial music, unlike Paul who loved bubble-gum pop, Fiona liked simple acoustic guitar-based music so some of Thunder's more soulful, melodic tunes – even through a couple of doors – nearly brought a tear to her eye … unless of course, that was from something else bothering her. She really ought to find the right moment to talk to Paul when they weren't both exhausted, but hadn't anticipated just how well he and Thunder would hit it off this time.

A smudged shape beyond the greens and blues of the stained-glass panels of the original Victorian front door showed that someone was about to come in.

'May!' she said perking up before it occurred to her that

the younger woman might not welcome her news. 'I'm so sorry, but Mr Cavanagh left yesterday.'

'Believe me, I wouldn't be here otherwise,' May said vehemently. 'I've come to see another of your guests. It seems everyone who is anyone stays at Walton House!'

'It's mainly us or a pub called The Admiral, and I wouldn't even wish The Admiral on—'

'Aiden Cavanagh?' May suggested, her voice tart. 'You warmed to him too, huh?'

'Well …' Fiona struggled to find something diplomatic to say.

'We're not a couple,' May said, apparently reading her mind. 'But just for the record, there's definitely no romantic link between me and the man I've come to see today.' Leaning closer, she added, 'Especially not when he rocks a pair of leather trousers more like Bertie Bassett than Jon Bon Jovi.'

'Mr Harwich?'

They exchanged amused glances. 'That's right,' May nodded. 'I think I'll need a recovery coffee with you after, if you're free when I've finished my meeting.'

'I'll be there,' Fiona said, pleased. 'And in the meantime, I might get five minutes with my own husband. He and Mr Harwich have got quite a bromance going on. They're in the lounge, come through.'

Paul, hunched over a table, was studying an iPad, and Thunder's arm was slung over his shoulder while he also stared at the screen.

'See what I mean about property prices? I've got to get myself back to this part of the world,' Thunder was saying. 'I mean, I've got a bloody lovely house in Surrey – modern Tudor with an indoor swimming pool, state of the art kitchen and a marble hall. But I'm hardly ever there. It's a waste, isn't it?

'What's really getting to me is that I feel bad about my sister. She lives with me, you see, looks after the place for me and she hates it. Hates not seeing anyone, misses the sea and loathes rattling about an empty house all on her own. She really could do with some company so I've got to do us both a favour, put the house on the market and get back to my roots.'

'Hello,' said Fiona. Thunder, she already knew, was a bit hard of hearing, but what was absorbing Paul's attention?

'May, my darling, you made it!' Thunder said, getting to his feet. 'Excellent!'

'Well, I'll get some coffee, shall I?' Fiona offered. At that moment Paul's eyes met hers and instinctively she knew he was hiding something. What on earth was making him so shifty? But then he looked at May and his eyebrows shot up.

'I know you!' he said excitedly. 'You're—'

'Shush,' Thunder interrupted. 'Not right now she isn't, are you, May?'

Chapter Twenty-One

'I shall be very relieved to escape from here,' Cecil said with a sigh.

With a smell of slightly over-cooked dinner and a hint of bed-pan hanging thickly in the hot air, Bill couldn't blame him. 'Not long now, and you'll be a free man,' Bill reassured him and glanced across at May. His uncle had been a bit tetchy when Bill had nipped over to see him at lunchtime, but had recovered himself at the sight of May when they walked into the ward together.

'It's very good of you to give up your time to console a tedious old man when you could be doing something exciting,' Cecil told her with a wan smile.

'Don't be silly,' said May, leaning closer to be heard above the neighbouring patient's TV. Sitting across the bed from him, she clasped Cecil's hand and smiled. 'I wanted to wish you all the best for tomorrow anyway. I'll come up in the morning, if you'd like someone to keep you company before they operate.'

His proud uncle looked a bit tearful, Bill was moved to see, and when he tried to speak again his voice was thin and husky. He cleared his throat and started again. 'Naturally, from the minute one is labelled "nil-by-mouth", the stronger one's desire grows for a cup of tea,' he said, looking with longing as hot drinks were offered to others. 'No, there's no need for you to trouble yourself, my dear. In fact, I don't want to see either of you before the procedure. It may be superstitious of me, but I feel it would be unlucky.'

'Rubbish,' Bill interjected, 'nothing's going to happen. You'll be out the other side before you know it.'

'But which other side?' he pondered. 'So long as it's the angels on the ward and not at the Pearly Gates waiting to greet me, I'll be happy. I refuse to miss the chance to sail my boat now, not when I can almost touch her. Bill, dear boy, we both know there is a risk, however small, so I didn't bring you up here to say goodbye. However, it would very much give me something to look forward to if I knew I was going to see you again when it's all over. Would it be very selfish of me to ask you both to look in on me afterwards?'

Once they had left the hot, claustrophobic ward behind them, Bill had to make sure May didn't feel trapped by Cecil's request. In the car park a single blackbird was singing a fluting melodic song. May tilted her head on one side as she listened for a moment before replying. 'It's the least I can do, Bill, after what your uncle's done for me. If it wasn't for his ad, I wouldn't have …'

What? He needed to know. Wouldn't have realised how much she missed her ex? Unfinished business, May had said. What did that mean? And speaking of unfinished business, as a professional he never walked off a job, no matter how tough it got, and it wasn't exactly helping him to sleep at night thinking about how close he'd come to making love to May.

'I wouldn't have known what a good cook you are.' She reached out and patted his hand. Bill would much rather she found some more interesting parts of him to pat, but he was doing his best to respect her feelings and not rush her into a relationship. 'Sure you're all right about this? I don't mind if you'd prefer to have an early night.'

An early night was exactly what he felt like, but not one that would give him much sleep. 'It'll be good to have company,' he said lightly.

'What's on the menu tonight?'

A couple of rude retorts sprang to mind, but Bill ignored them. With Cecil about to go under the knife, so to speak, it was hardly the right night for romance.

'Wait and see,' he said with a smile, opening the van door for her. 'And don't get grumpy, I know what you're like when you're waiting to be fed.'

'Hey!' she protested. 'Once! Once in a whole week, I might have got a bit snappy when I was particularly peckish.'

Bill walked round to the driver's side and slid in next to her. It was going to be fine, he could do this. After all, he'd managed to keep his hands off her most of the time they were at sea.

In Bill's van they fell into a comfortable silence. May liked that. Silence with Aiden was weighted with portent, the eerie stillness whilst he considered the next move in his cat and mouse mind games. With Bill, she could relax and let her train of ideas take off in any direction without fear of him breaking in, demanding to know what she was thinking. Yet, for all Bill's protests that he was fine about Cecil's operation, his tired eyes betrayed the strain of recent days. He was also doing his utmost to stop yawning, and May started to feel guilty at jumping so quickly at his offer to cook for her. She'd seized it as a chance to recapture some of the easy companionship they'd shared on *Lucille*. If she and Bill could be friends, perhaps it would stop her waking in the middle of the night from hot dreams about what might have been if the tide hadn't turned against them.

Before she could suggest that it wasn't too late to postpone their meal to another evening, she realised that they had left the road. They were following a track which eventually led to an isolated low-slung building in a gently undulating landscape with fields behind and views across the marshes where a rising mist dissolved distant shapes to purple shadows.

'It was almost derelict when I found it,' Bill said. 'Just one of those abandoned farm buildings nobody quite knows what to do with.'

'You live here?' said May. Knapped flint faced the gable end wall of a pretty brick cottage with a roof that sloped steeply down to a small sunroom with French doors leading out to the garden.

'No,' said Bill, 'I only brought you here to impress you. I've got a flashy four-bed place on a brand new housing estate, with a gym in the garage and plenty of room on the drive for my van. Is that what you were expecting from a builder?'

May felt herself blush. At their first meeting she had been guilty of stereotyping him, and it had suited her not to probe too deeply on their delivery trip in case she was forced to say more about herself than she wanted. 'Harry quickly put me right about what you really did,' she admitted. 'Although, I would probably have expected you to live in something more modern, which is daft, given that you conserve old buildings.'

'I didn't even know if I'd get permission to turn it into a residential dwelling. All I knew was that it had a lot of charm and the location was unique, so I took a chance and bought it. Fortunately, my gamble paid off. The planning authorities approved of my proposals and I was even able to add the single storey extension which accommodates my study. Of course, I didn't know then that I might end up housing an elderly relative ... I'm not sure how Cecil will cope here if the worst happens. I've told him I'm bringing him back here for a few days to recuperate, but I guess his long-term future depends on how tomorrow goes.'

Despite her intentions to look but not touch, May reached across and squeezed his hand. Her conscience was telling her that now would be a good time to tell Bill that it would be a better idea if he took her back to the boatyard and caught up with his sleep, but she sensed he needed to take his mind off his worries about the operation. 'The worst is not going to happen,' she said instead. 'Cecil's far too determined to take *Lucille* on the water for that.'

'Thank you,' he said, his expression hard to read in the evening shadows. 'Well, are you coming in?'

A pair of part-glazed hardwood doors in the gable end led straight in to a kitchen-dining room, where something in the duck-egg-blue Rayburn was filling the air with a mouth-watering aroma. Pitted and worn red brick pamment flooring and the exposed beams added to the room's considerable charm and painted a wonderfully inviting picture.

'Wow! You did all this?'

'Mostly. I'd occasionally enlist one of the blokes when they had some down time.' He took a bottle of sparkling water from the fridge and poured them each a glass. 'You don't drink and I'm driving, so we'll have to toast Cecil's health with this instead. Come through.'

There was an opening to the sitting room where a wood-burning stove sat on a raised stone plinth in a large open fireplace and a quirky wooden staircase led up to the first floor. A high white-painted vaulted ceiling reflected what was left of the evening light, flooding the room with deep gold and warming the exposed brick and flint walls of the original building which could otherwise have looked bare.

'Gosh, Bill, this is lovely,' she said with a sigh, looking

round at deep, mismatched sofas and some wonderful dark oak glazed bookcases. Having grown up in a house where skirting boards hung off the walls, the kitchen was only half modernised and the new pipework had never quite got boxed-in or painted, she imagined that anyone in the building trade was like her dad; always too busy or too tired to finish the work in his own home.

'What were you expecting? Some towering monument to my ego?' he shook his head. 'I'm afraid I've been too well trained by Cecil not to waste money. All those hours I spent looking round junk shops and car boot sales for antiques mean that hunting for bargains is well and truly in my genes.'

She was very touched to see that he'd even gone to the trouble of setting a small circular table for supper in the garden room. Her mum was someone who ate to live rather than lived to eat, and Aiden enjoyed the frisson and extraneous pressures created by eating out, especially when he had anything of an audience.

'Have a seat,' he said, pointing to one of the wicker chairs before opening the French doors to the garden just enough to let in some mild air which was sweet with the scent of honeysuckle. May watched as he walked round lighting candles, absent-mindedly noting that he still hadn't had time for that haircut. Tonight it looked more gold than red and as he bent forwards, it flopped over his eyes. He shoved it back off his face and the candlelight picked up the sprinkling of gold stubble and the deeper copper of his sideburns. May badly wanted to run her hands across his face and stroke his rough jaw, but instead she made herself take a sip of water and think about poor Cecil lying in hospital.

'What's happening about Cecil's antique shop?'

'Something else on the to-do list,' Bill said, straightening up, but not before May had got a very fine view of low-slung jeans skimming over his lean hips and firm backside. 'It's always been more of an interest for him than a serious source of income. He roped in the friend of a friend to look after the place on a temporary basis, but I guess it all depends on how strong he feels after the op as to whether or not he decides it's worth keeping.'

He reached across to top up her glass and May found herself breathing in the familiar Bill smell of him as she stared at the base of his throat above the navy shirt.

'Sit tight,' he said with a grin. 'I'll bring you some food.'

May made herself sit tight, especially as the bolt of rampant lust that shot through her made her worry about what would happen if she moved.

As it happened, Bill's wonderful Thai curry and fragrant rice did a terrific job of persuading May's body that there were other appetites worth satisfying besides the need to have hot sex with him quite urgently. The conversation was relaxed too, as they both forgot the demands from other people that came with being back on dry land. There was more room to move in Bill's conservatory than in *Lucille's* cabin, but the sense of both being inside and outside recalled the intimacy they had shared during the voyage.

'So, how are you doing now? Feeling any more rested?'

'Oh, was that a bat, I saw?' said May.

'Probably,' said Bill. 'They often flit round the garden at night. But don't change the subject. How's the broken heart doing?'

May put her fork down. 'It wasn't about my heart, Bill. I hadn't been in love with Aiden for a very long time, I know that now, but he knew how to get inside my head. Not any more though. It's over and it feels good to be back in control of me!'

She couldn't stop herself breaking into a smile, knowing it was true. Bill watched her for a while then smiled back. Lovely, pillar-of-strength Bill. With that wonderful, kissable mouth, she thought, dropping her gaze to it and shivering at what he might do with it.

'You're cold,' he said. 'Let's move back into the sitting room.'

Yes, let's, thought May. The sitting room with its deep, comfortable sofas with plenty of room for two people to get cosy.

'Make yourself at home. I'll bring you some coffee.'

Reminding herself that Bill was tired and needed a rest, May resolved to put aside her wayward thoughts, drink her coffee like a good girl and ask him to take her back to the caravan. Meanwhile, she familiarised herself with the room, scanning Bill's books and belongings whilst he moved about in the kitchen whistling another Foo Fighters number, 'Next Year', she thought, picking out notes that were vaguely in the right order.

'And the song-writing?' he called, making May sit up.

'Oh, well, I've had a couple of rough ideas,' she said as he placed cups on the table in front of her.

'Good, because I thought this might make it easier, whatever you said about being able to write songs in your head.' He disappeared behind her briefly and returned carrying an acoustic guitar. 'It was my dad's. I think he thought I might learn to play it one day, but it's wasted on me. If you can get some use out of it, please do.'

'Oh, Bill.' She shook her head helplessly. 'I can't take this. Not if it belonged to your father, it's too much.'

'He's not dead,' he said, grinning. 'He just happens to live on the other side of the world.'

'Oh.' May frowned. 'But I thought with Cecil bringing you up ...'

Bill sat down on the sofa beside her. 'Dad met an Australian nurse when Mum was dying. The poor guy got pilloried, but Mum had been very ill for a long time and, let's face it, you can't choose who you fall in love with.'

Very true, thought May, nodding. 'But how awful for you to be rejected,' she said, patting his hand and feeling desperately sorry for the small boy that he was.

Bill shook his head. 'It wasn't like that either. Makayla was homesick and Dad, who's an engineer, could see the chance of a fresh start, but I dug my heels in and refused to go, so Cecil offered me a home. It was supposed to be a temporary solution, but as time went on, I felt settled and Dad had started a new family with Makayla, and it became permanent. We never fell out, and I visit every couple of years, I just felt happier here. So, are you going to play that guitar or just look at it?'

He was watching so eagerly that May didn't like to disappoint him. Having dithered about staring at it for a little while, she finally took action. It felt good, she had to admit, to hold an instrument again, and it was a well-made guitar: mahogany with a rosewood fingerboard and a spruce top wood which had mellowed with age, turning its colour from the yellow of clotted cream to a glowing amber. She strummed it experimentally then tweaked the machine heads until it was tuned and felt it come to life with a rewarding sweetness of tone as she played it in.

'Blimey,' said Bill, jolting her out of her reverie. 'You're good at that. Maybe you've got a new career ahead of you!'

'Ooh, I don't think so,' she said, carefully laying the guitar down.

'No, really,' Bill said reaching out to place his hand on her shoulder. 'Start believing in yourself. Don't let that lousy ex of yours keep you in a box. You're a lovely person,

May. You're talented, you're kind – you've got so much to offer.'

May shook her head, helplessly. Bill was being kind too. It was very sweet of him to want to bolster her confidence. He probably wouldn't be half so sympathetic if he knew she'd got herself in a mess of her own making.

'Don't let one man destroy your self-esteem,' he was saying. 'May?' He shook her shoulder gently.

She looked up and met his reassuring smile.

'It's going to be all right.'

May studied his face and hoped he was right. But then she had a feeling Bill could make a lot of things better. There was a long pause as they stared into each other's eyes and then she felt herself moving towards him, just as he leaned forwards to pull her into his arms. Melting in to his kiss reminded her of everything she'd missed about him. That mouth of his was already doing her a power of good, she registered vaguely as the urgent drumbeat of her heart sent let's-get-ready-to-rumble hormones racing round her body. She moaned as his lips broke away from hers, exhaling raggedly as they moved slowly and thoroughly down her throat. Arching towards him, she shuddered as his fingers slowly unbuttoned her blouse, pushed back her flimsy lace bra and exposed her erect nipples.

She had just enough presence of mind left to tug at the buttons of his shirt, shoving it aside, desperate to feel strong muscles and warm skin against hers. Bill groaned and mumbled something as she reached for the belt of his jeans. May kissed him hungrily whilst they began to tear urgently at each other's clothes, then groaned when Bill bent his head to take a breast in his mouth. Oh, lordy, at this rate she was going to come before they'd even finished undressing. Bill was amazing! He could even talk with his mouth full! Eh? Bill froze and at the same time she realised a voice was speaking on his answerphone.

'Bill?' Cecil was saying plaintively. 'Are you there? Sorry to be a nuisance, dear boy, but I've got myself a bit worked up about tomorrow and wondered if we could chat for a little while.'

Chapter Twenty-Two

After an anxious wait the next morning, the consultant popped into the relatives' room to report back to Bill and May about the operation and to tell them that Cecil was well enough for visitors. May went with Bill to the High Dependency Unit but stayed only long enough for Cecil to register that she was there and to say hello, then she squeezed Bill's hand and told him she would wait outside. Even though they'd both protested and urged her to stay, she felt they ought to have some private time together. Cecil looked tired after his ordeal, but the early indicators were that the procedure to repair his damaged aorta had gone very well.

Mindful that the outcome was not so rosy for other patients in the ward, May stifled her smile until she was outside where she was strongly tempted to skip down the corridor. Cecil's phone call, just when she and Bill had been getting on so beautifully the previous evening, might have dampened down the flames of desire that moment, but it hadn't extinguished them. Every time Bill looked at her, her stomach turned over and her knees felt weak. In a way it was exciting, having to wait because Cecil would be convalescing at Bill's house for the next week. It wasn't a question of whether they would make love, but when. In the meantime, May thought, feeling lovely and warm inside, there was a lot to be said for rediscovering the joys of a steamy petting session – and having fun for the first time in far too long.

Her contented sigh was interrupted by a flickering screen above a patient's bed clearly visible through the glass of the neighbouring ward. How anyone got any rest with a constant stream of nonsense from six different televisions it was hard to imagine. What rubbish was on now, anyway? May peered in and gulped. *Aiden!* Or rather, she thought, narrowing her eyes – Molly! Molly Gordon, celebrating her new number one single, with Aiden at her side. Big pink hair, teeny pink playsuit, lovely legs that went on forever and although May couldn't hear what her successor was saying as she began to speak, she scoffed to herself knowing there would be no trace of the mockney accent Molly affected for her singing in contrast to her normally patrician tones. Molly's daddy was someone influential in the Cabinet, which was nice for Aiden. A lot more useful than a roofer and an unemployed shopkeeper as potential in-laws, she guessed, feeling a little bit guilty about her mum.

And although the cameras were pointing at Molly, she was acutely aware of Aiden's presence; the force of that mesmeric dark gaze was so direct that she couldn't be sure she wasn't being watched even when he was safely tucked away on a television screen.

His hair looked nice, though a bit shorter than usual, twinkly smile firmly in place. And his arm possessively clamped round Molly's waist. So much for all those claims about Molly being nothing to him and missing her. The 'glued at the hips body language' clearly showed he'd got over her very quickly. And got on top of someone else, she thought, indignant as her rival turned to him and looked down on him with an adoring smile.

'Yeah, and you're still a short-arse!' she couldn't help muttering.

'Didn't your mother ever tell you not to talk to strange televisions?'

'Bill! Don't sneak up on me like that!' she said, jumping.

Bill smiled and caught hold of her hand. 'Fancy grabbing some lunch? We could have a picnic down by Campion's Creek.'

'It's a perfect day for it, but what about Cecil?'

'Fast asleep, but doing well. It looks as if the procedure's been a great success, but the next few days will be crucial.' Bill frowned and stroked her cheek. 'May, I've got to look at a job later this afternoon; a chapel conversion Matthew's got me involved with. It'll keep me busy over the weekend too. And then with Cecil ...'

'Shush ... what's the hurry?' May stretched up and silenced him with a kiss.

Behind him she could see Aiden staring out of the television watching her with a half-smile and felt ... she tested her heart ... nothing.

The sun was high in the sky, and the silence of the peaceful spot he and May had chosen for an impromptu picnic lunch at Campion's Creek was broken only by the shrill shriek of seabirds. At least it wasn't the shrill shriek of Harry Watling stumbling across them, Bill chuckled to himself. He raised his head with great reluctance from May's mouth, which he'd been enjoying getting to know, and stared into her beguiling gold-brown eyes.

Sunshine warmed his aching back, easing the tension he'd been carrying worrying about Cecil, and May warmed his aching front. Contented and relaxed, he didn't want to move and he didn't want May to move, he simply wanted to lie there, drinking her in, counting the sprinkling of freckles that were appearing like gold dust brushed across the bridge of her nose and her pink cheeks. Except if he was staring at her, it was hard to kiss her, and she was such a sexy and responsive kisser. And also, if they were stuck like this forever, how would he ease the painful hard-on bulging in his work trousers? Flip, it was like being a teenager again, all the pent-up frustration.

'Go!' she smiled, pushing him away. 'You've got work to do.'

'I can think of far more exciting things to do,' he murmured.

May wriggled and giggled beneath him. 'Perhaps we could sneak off to *Lucille* ...'

'I think the fear of Harry Watling knocking on the coach roof or peering down the companionway to investigate a strange outbreak of rocking on one of the boats in her care might cramp my style a bit.'

'Ditto, the caravan.' May sighed. 'Harry does the rounds regularly to make sure I'm not wrecking the place.'

'Well, it did belong to someone very special to Harry, so you're honoured,' Bill told her, his erection wilting at the thought of George. And however tempting the idea was to give in and satisfy the desperate urge to make love to May as soon as possible, he was reluctant to rush the moment.

''T ain't right, 't ain't proper,' George would have said. And he would have been right. He didn't just want to fall into bed with May; he wanted to linger, to take his time getting to know every inch of her, from her golden-brown head to her plump little bottom, down to her cute pink toes and then do it all over again. In short, he couldn't get enough of her.

'And talking of people who are special,' she said, running her fingers over his lips and making him catch his breath. 'Is there anything I can do to help you prepare for Monday?'

Yes, of course, she meant Cecil. He rolled off and helped May to sit up beside him. 'Obviously he'll be in the High Dependency Unit for the rest of the day and maybe tomorrow, so they can monitor him for any signs of infection. The plan is to take him back to the ward for Sunday. Then he'll be X-rayed to ensure the stent's in place with a view to discharging him after the weekend. I've made up the single bed in my study and the district nurses will call in to take over the care of his dressings. By the end of the week he should be fit to go back home.'

'Don't rush him,' May said, holding his hand.

'I don't want to rush you, either,' he said, brushing a strand of windswept hair out of her eyes.

'You're not,' she told him firmly. 'But I am going to rush you back to work before you start losing clients.'

'Yeah? Well you won't write a hit single sitting around on your backside all day either,' he said, standing up and pulling her to her feet. 'Get on with it, so I can boast that you got to number one in the charts with a little help from my dad's old guitar!' He glanced down and thought he'd caught a frown crossing her face, but it was quickly replaced by a smile. And why not? Wouldn't it be great for May, who at times seemed to have so little self-confidence, if she could write the kind of catchy hit song no one could stop singing?

Now, perhaps, after another day of Paul following Thunder around like a star-struck puppy, Fiona finally had her husband to herself. Even so, she lingered in the bathroom, painstakingly wiping off her make-up, brushing her hair and rehearsing her lines. By the time she got into bed Paul was fast asleep, which she took as a sign that her news could wait for another day. In any case, saying the words out loud would only make them true and she wasn't sure if she was ready for the truth yet.

As soon as her head touched the pillow she was wide awake wondering how she could have been so negligent about her own health. So much for her assumption that a couple of pills missed here and there or taken at the wrong time didn't matter. Two positive pregnancy tests proved how wrong she could be. What a mess!

She glared at her husband's sleeping form. It was all right for Paul, business as usual for him. He'd be up and about before dawn, giving the best of himself to strangers, treating the most obnoxious guests as if they were his best friends. Meanwhile she'd be the one looking forward to stretch marks, varicose veins, coping unaided and years of clearing up after yet another person.

This was all Paul's fault, she decided, conveniently forgetting that they'd bought Walton House together and with high expectations of their new life by the sea. If she hadn't been so starry-eyed about him, she would have foreseen she was signing up for a life of drudgery. And if she wasn't so flipping tired all the time, she would have been a bit more diligent about taking her pill. Silent tears of self-pity streamed down her face.

Was this a sign of her hormones creating havoc? For crying out loud, this was one of the reasons she'd dreaded ever having a baby, wasn't it? Because she'd lose an emotional layer of skin, that she would weep at the news and move fearfully through a world where bombs killed innocent children, paedophiles lurked like crocodiles in the sludgy waters of the internet and young women were shot in the head for trying to get an education? What would she be like by the time she finally had the baby? A complete basket case!

'Paul,' she whispered, unable to bear it any longer. He rolled over and pulled her closer, hugging her into his chest.

She lay there, listening to the soft thudding of his heart and ran her hand over his ribs. Not an ounce of spare flesh on him, she thought enviously. Whatever Paul ate, he still had a distance runner's build, but then if anyone cared to count the number of miles they covered in the average week at Walton House, it probably added up to several marathons. She, however, was about to turn into a whale pup.

'Fee?' he asked sleepily before she could say anything.

'Hmm?'

'Do you love me?'

'Hey, of course I do,' she smiled, knowing it was true.

'No matter what?'

She slipped her hand inside the band of his shorts and moved down to cup his sleepy willy.

'I might get the hump if you're about to tell me you've been shagging one of the guests and you're running off together.'

'No,' he said, sounding sad. 'Nothing like that.'

'Then what?' She wobbled his willy, which ignored her.

'Nothing,' he said, yawning. 'Nothing at all. So long as you love me and the two of us are together that's all that matters.'

Rolling her away from him and on to her side, he spooned against her, holding her tightly. Very soon his breathing told her he was sound asleep. Better by light, Fiona told herself. Why tell him something that would mean neither of them would get any rest afterwards. It could wait. Everything would seem better in the morning.

Chapter Twenty-Three

The weathermen had promised the hottest weekend of the year for the Little Spitmarsh Regatta. In the natural harbour next to Watling's, many boat owners were about, eager to put the last touches to their vessels before the Sail In of visiting yachtsmen – 'a handful of boats if we're lucky,' Harry had commented pessimistically – began later in the day, marking the official start of the weekend's festivities. There was a gentle bustle of activity with flags being hoisted and varnish being polished. A warm breeze sent silver ripples shivering across the surface of the water, setting the boats twittering on their moorings. May couldn't think of many prettier locations.

Aboard *Lucille*, May was supposed to be dressing the pretty boat with decorative flags in preparation for Cecil's imminent arrival, but was slightly distracted by the sight of Harry's hottie of a hubby, Matthew, looking pretty decorative himself in his Jack Sparrow costume with a loose white shirt split halfway down his chest showing off an impressive set of pecs. To May's shame, he caught her gawping and winked, making her blush bright red, but at least – thank the Lord – Harry was too preoccupied to have noticed.

'You're lucky I had spare flags in the store,' Harry was grumbling. 'There's etiquette for this sort of thing, you know.'

'What's wrong with the vintage bunting I bought in town?' May said, thinking that the triangles of green and red gingham perked up with some pretty floral fabric went beautifully with *Lucille*'s pale green deck paint.

'It's not a question of stringing up anything that takes

your fancy,' Harry said through gritted teeth. 'Otherwise you might be hoisting a rude or offensive message.'

'What? With old curtain fabric?' May was puzzled.

'Well, I find that floral fabric quite offensive for a start,' Harry told her, grinning at last. 'You're supposed to use The International Code of Signal Flags like these. There's a very carefully composed sequence you're meant to follow, and you should start at the bow to the stern via the masthead. You don't want to fly a message telling Cecil to bog off, do you? Not when he's seeing the boat for the first time!'

May looked at the other boats being dressed to welcome in the visiting vessels. Everyone else's approach looked far more haphazard. 'I don't care what the others are doing,' Harry growled, catching her rolling her eyes. 'We're going to get this right for Bill and his uncle. Especially since you've made such a good job of cleaning her up, don't spoil the ship for a ha'porth of tar.'

Preening a little at Harry's praise – which, she was learning, was hard won – she hoped that Bill and Cecil would be equally impressed. It had been a demanding week for Bill, getting Cecil back on his feet as well as managing his restoration projects. She and Bill had managed a few chaste trysts, which had been rather lovely, but May had been busy too.

Thunder had been as good as his word and consulted his solicitors, sparing her from racking up additional costs in legal fees, so she'd braced herself and started to take the necessary steps towards extricating herself from Aiden's contractual hold on her. Where she had once felt powerless against him, here, away from the pressures of her previous life, she could see him for the bully he was.

Her trips to Walton House had meant she'd got to know Fiona Goodwin better too – though it was a shame that their meeting at the Paradise Café had scarred Fiona so badly it had put her off drinking coffee for good. Everyone she'd met in Little Spitmarsh had made her feel welcome. As the ties to her past loosened, she was suddenly able to leap the obstacles in the path of her creativity as new songs and lines of lyrics kept coming towards her. Bill, she admitted, might have had something to do with it too. She wanted to do justice to his dad's guitar, after all. And since Bill was occupied with Cecil, she'd taken it on herself to get up early to wash the topsides of the boat down and polish her brightwork.

'I couldn't have made a better job of it myself,' Harry added, straightening up and looking round approvingly at the varnished wood gleaming in the sun.

'Matthew! Get some life jackets on those kids,' she bellowed, spotting her husband, who was now surrounded by a gaggle of small children all set to go on a treasure hunt. Matthew grinned and waved a large toy cutlass at them. At least, May hoped it was a toy. Once the children, with some help from their fussy parents, had donned their life jackets, Matthew inspired his merry crew with a rousing talk and dubbed them all on each shoulder, making them swear a blood-thirsty oath of allegiance and threatening to feed them to the sharks at the first hint of mutiny. The cutlass alone was enough to worry May. It was a wonder one or two of the more wriggly children hadn't been beheaded.

'Avast behind!' Matthew roared, making them all giggle and stick their bottoms out, then they set off, with Georgia shrieking like a banshee to be let out of the buggy, Captain Flint yapping wildly and a trail of self-conscious parents bringing up the rear.

'I'm beginning to wonder if I ought to have dug out a couple of adult life jackets too,' Harry said thoughtfully.

'Seeing that one of the dads nearly lost his footing. Although, I know what the problem is …'

May followed the line of her gaze to where a handful of houseboats were moored just beyond Harry's land. 'That's Lola Moult visiting her parents, Carmen and Roy, on *Bella Vista*,' she said, nodding towards a curvaceous dark-haired young woman looking sleek in black jeans and black shirt standing on deck. 'He's not the first man to lose control of his senses at the sight of her. She might have the figure of a prowhead, but she's also blessed with an acute business brain and far too much ambition to let herself get tied down by an early marriage.'

'Darling, what a brilliant idea for a holiday home!' an excited woman squealed loudly. 'A houseboat! Imagine waking up with the waves lapping at the bedroom window. Not just living by the sea but living on it! Perhaps we should try an offer?'

'Isn't she looking pretty?' said Bill as Cecil stopped beside one of the black wooden tubs spilling over with orange nasturtiums Harry had planted up round the boatyard. He eyed his uncle surreptitiously, gauging his fitness. Two weeks was about what the hospital reckoned Cecil would need to make a full recovery. Spooked out by his reading of the possible post-surgery complications, Bill had insisted that Cecil convalesce with him for a full week, even though the district nurse had quietly assured him that his uncle was well enough to return to his own home after a couple of days. He silently ticked off the milestones as they reached them, but still worried about the synthetic graft migrating, or its fabric tearing, or the risk that it would form a dam that would pool and clot his uncle's blood or cause him to have a stroke.

Even though the rational side of his brain accepted that keeping a constant eye on Cecil wouldn't save him from the inevitable one day, Bill was still anxious about this first proper excursion and what the emotion and excitement of the day would do. Cecil, however, had been so determined to be well enough to start sailing again wild horses wouldn't drag him away now. But, Bill wondered nervously, had he pulled up to soak up the view or to catch his breath?

'Are we talking about *Lucille* or your young lady?' Cecil chuckled, patting Bill's hand. 'Both of them are looking very lovely to me, but I have to admit to being particularly delighted to see *Lucille* after all this time. Just look at her elegant lines! I was most envious of the chap who owned her back then. She always turned heads whenever we visited a new harbour. He offered to sell her to me when he packed in sailing and if I hadn't been posted abroad, I would have snapped her up and never have let her go. There's a lesson for you, Bill. It's all very well for your head to give you cool, sensible advice, but you'll never be content unless your heart's in it too.'

Bill looked at May, waving from *Lucille*'s cockpit, her light brown hair lifting as it was caught by a refreshing gust of wind tugging at the signal flags. Her lines were looking pretty good too, in her blue stripy T-shirt and denim shorts. And *Lucille* was looking splendid, thanks to her hard work. He was enormously touched and grateful, and he could think of nothing that would make him happier than he was at this moment … except having her naked in his bed.

Now that Cecil was desperate to regain his independence, it looked as if he and May could have some uninterrupted time together at last when they weren't wrestling with a truculent weather helm, the vagaries of the tide, an overloaded work schedule or a possessive ex-boyfriend.

The kind of thoughts he was having owed little to his head or his heart, but an entirely different part of his anatomy. But as for holding on to her? He'd only known her for a couple of weeks and there was so much more to discover; it was a little soon, wasn't it, to be rushing out buying engagement rings?

Any niggling worries about his uncle's health seemed to be groundless. Cecil was forging ahead, confidently striding out after his confinement and looking very dapper in his Breton red cotton sailcloth trousers and a new checked shirt. He was still an upright, handsome man who moved easily and seemed to have shed a few years along with some extra pounds. A few of the grannies, lining up for tea at one of the refreshment stalls set up around the yacht basin, seemed to think so too. Bill scooped up the cool bag and hurried after his uncle before May decided he was a bit of silver fox after all.

'I should be piping you aboard, shouldn't I?' May laughed, taking Cecil's hand as he climbed nimbly over the pulpit.

She was certainly looking piping hot, thought Bill, curling his arm round her waist and kissing her, and he was touched to see her wearing the little silver starfish pendant. Cecil, very misty eyed, pulled out a very clean white handkerchief and pretended to blow his nose. Moving slowly, he went off to explore the boat, tenderly renewing his acquaintance with the vessel he'd sailed on so many years ago before returning to sit in the sunny cockpit next to May.

'I can't thank you both enough, for everything you've done.'

Bill watched May returning Cecil's smile. Cecil was right to advise him to not to let go of May, who could brighten anyone's day just by sitting there. He thought about the luxury of a long, leisurely evening together, about undressing her slowly ... and, he swallowed hard and steadied his thoughts ... about just how nice it would be to wake up in the morning to see May's head resting on the pillow next to his. With the rest of the summer to get to know her properly, his sensible head ought to approve too.

'The thanks aren't necessary, Cecil,' he said, unwrapping the champagne glasses he'd packed so carefully. 'Just try not to frighten me like that for a good long while, will you?'

If anything he ought to be thanking Cecil. If he hadn't been ill, Bill might never have met May. Although he could have done without the subsequent drama. It was a great relief that Cecil seemed to be over his health crisis and was back to his usual self. He glanced across at him fondly. The old boy certainly deserved to enjoy the future having paid dearly for his dreams of regaining his lost youth.

'May?' he began, removing the gold foil from the *Veuve Clicquot*.

'Just a sip,' she said, smiling. 'Just this once.'

He unwound the wire, lifted off the cage and eased off the cork, letting it fly in the big blue sky and into the creek.

'To *Lucille* and all who sail in her!'

The chinking of glasses was accompanied by cheers from the other boats and ashore as a cluster of small boats appeared in the channel beyond Samphire, led by a Cornish Crabber with beautiful tan sails.

'I can't wait to be out on the water,' Cecil observed wistfully.

'Tomorrow,' Bill told him, 'in the regatta. Until then you'll have to be patient.'

He caught May's eye and grinned back at her. All three of them were learning how to be patient.

*　*　*

Having waited for so long, Fiona didn't know whether or not to be grateful that her guests had gone out, giving her a chance to have a private conversation with Paul at long last. She knelt over a flowerbed doing some much needed weeding while she practised what to say to him. Being pregnant was already changing her. The heightened emotions were probably to be expected, but she was also horribly aware of anything that might threaten the baby, as if she was being subtly manipulated from within. Her initial resentment of her condition was giving way to an unexpected and growing desire to protect her unborn child. Previously innocent foods like soft cheeses, mayonnaise and shellfish now seemed laden with murderous intent. Even a harmless lettuce leaf might have been crapped on by a cat and infect them both with toxoplasmosis if someone hadn't bothered to wash it properly.

She froze and stared in horror at her gardening gloves, but before she could work herself up about anything she might have accidentally brushed across her mouth, a shadow fell across the flowerbed. Looking up, she found Paul standing over her.

'Come on, Fee. Come and sit down,' he said, crouching down beside her and stroking her back. 'I've made some tea.' Then, as if reading her mind as she started running her mental check list of everything she couldn't or shouldn't drink, he added, 'Peppermint for you. I noticed you've started drinking it. Is that all right?'

He straightened up and offered her his hand to help her up. She already felt like Granny Grumps; how would she feel when she was seven months pregnant, she wondered miserably, and what would Paul think of her then? But sitting down on one of the garden chairs on the terrace, she let her gaze rest on the pots full of geraniums, their colours so bright in the sunshine, and tried to feel optimistic. Paul had obviously made a special effort, setting out her favourite bone china cups, given to her by her grandmother, with their oriental themed design of peacocks and peonies. He'd even put a few ginger biscuits on a plate, which he solemnly offered to her.

'Did you want to go to the boatyard?' said Paul, sitting down next to her.

'What? And bump into most of our guests?' she said, smiling. 'No, I'm happy here. Unless you want to. I think Thunder said he was going to have a look round to check on his latest investment.'

'Investment?' Paul said warily.

Fiona swatted away a bug as it flew towards her hair. 'He's buying a boat off Harry Watling. Some old wreck she's persuaded him is a bit of a bargain. I expect she's convinced him to pay for the privilege of her doing it up for him too.'

'I don't blame her. In the current climate everyone's doing whatever's necessary to stay afloat. She's very good at her job, though. I'm sure that no matter what condition it's in now, Thunder's boat will look smashing by the time she's finished with it. But not as grand as the yacht he's been used to – I wonder what he's bought?'

'I thought you'd know all about it, seeing as you two have always got your heads together lately. It's enough to make a girl feel jealous,' she teased, squeezing his hand.

She heard him take a deep breath. 'Fee, there's something we need to talk about. Something serious.'

Oh my god! He was dying! She'd been so wrapped up in herself she hadn't noticed something going wrong right in front of her eyes. That's why he was always so thin no matter how much he ate. Her poor baby was going to be fatherless!

'Paul.' She clutched his hand. 'I'm sure it's not as serious as you think. There have been huge strides in treatment and all kinds of medical innovations. I'm sure we can find a doctor who can do something.'

'Fee, I'm not ill. Although you're probably going to think I'm raving mad. I know that Walton House realised our dream of living by the sea, but Thunder Harwich is very keen to buy it for his sister. She's lonely where they live now and has always fancied running a B&B. He's made me an offer, a very generous one, said it's worth it to him for the time he's saving not having to look around. The thing is, Fee, I've indicated we'll probably accept it.'

'You've what? You've made us homeless! Are you crazy?' No wonder he'd gone to such lengths to soften her up. 'And just what are we going to live on? Thin air?'

'Hush,' he said. 'Just listen for a moment. We knew it would be hard work running a B&B, but I don't think either of us reckoned on how time-consuming it would be. The more I watch you endlessly chasing around and clearing up after other people the more convinced I am that we've made a mistake taking this place on.'

For a moment, she forgot about the baby and dared to start hoping that this unknown sister would love Walton House as much as Thunder seemed to think. 'But this was your dream? Won't you be sad to give it up? You hated working in an office.'

'It was never my dream to unblock the toilets after other people.' He shuddered. 'I hated someone else telling me what to do, which is why I don't intend to return to an office,' he insisted. 'I thought Walton House would give us some free time, but now I'm answerable to other people twenty-four seven instead of from nine to five. I've tried to stay upbeat about it for your sake and I've kept smiling to keep the punters happy, but really all I want is to spend more time with you. I've been contacting agencies for some freelance consultancy work, and although nothing's firmed up yet, I think we can afford to take a chance.'

She nibbled on a ginger biscuit, while she thought of the freedom and all the possibilities now open to them, completely forgetting that some bug might have sneaked through her waterproof gardening glove on to her bare, unwashed hand.

'You know what it's like. There's always one guest or another demanding attention.' Paul sighed. 'Thunder's offer felt like a godsend. I'm certain we'll never get a better one. I know I've sprung this on you, but I thought this would be great opportunity for us to take off and have some fun before we settled down again and start a family.'

Fiona was brought back to harsh reality by a biscuit crumb sticking in her throat. 'Oh Paul,' she choked out at last. 'It's too late – I'm pregnant. It's as much a shock to me as it is to you. But it's happened and now we've got to deal with it. This poor baby wasn't planned, but I don't want it to feel unwelcome. What kind of start in life is that?'

He didn't answer and when she dared look, she realised he was struggling with his own emotions. He gulped and pulled her towards him, clasping her face and raining clumsy kisses on her hair. 'Oh Fee, I've been so worried about you. Especially given how pale and exhausted you've been lately.'

'Paul,' she said, feeling strangely hesitant. 'What are we going to do?'

He leaned back and closed his eyes, and reached for her hand. 'One thing at a time. Right now, the guests are out and we've got the house to ourselves. Let's go to bed.'

Fiona thought about it. It might not solve the big problems but it was a good place to start.

Chapter Twenty-Four

Later, as the sun began to sink on a day of simple pleasures, May sat alone on *Lucille*'s coach roof feeling the warmth of the wood beneath her bottom and the cool evening air ruffling her hair. Cecil had sensibly decided to have an early night, having been on his feet all afternoon watching the procession of classic boats which had arrived from all over the East Anglia coast from Woodbridge and Walberswick to Wells. One by one, they'd trickled along the creek. The Cornish Crabber was followed by a spruced up Dallimore sloop, then a perky little Folkboat with a dark blue hull until fifteen boats, in total, were crammed in around the basin. With everyone relieved to be safely tied up, the party atmosphere was building.

This was how it felt to be happy, she realised, catching sight of Bill making his way through the people gathering for the evening celebrations. That hair marked him out, copper gold in the light, a contrast to the grey of his T-shirt and dark low-slung jeans. He still hadn't found time to get it cut and with its strong wave, it was flicking up at the back now, like Robert Redford playing the Sundance Kid in that old film. Only proper ginger, of course, not namby-pamby strawberry blond, she sniggered to herself. Somebody stopped him, another man about Bill's age, and introduced him to the woman with him. Bill smiled and shook hands, but his impatient glance towards the boat demonstrated his eagerness to get back to her.

May drew up her bare legs and rested her chin on her knees, trying to rationalise the pitter-patter of her heart as Bill came closer. She wanted to believe that everything was going to work out, that Aiden would throw up his hands and tell her she was free to go, and then she'd walk away from her old life without regret. Use the money she had to bury herself up here for good, until the world forgot who she was. Maybe she could wipe the slate clean and start again with someone straightforward, easy-going and as unlike Aiden as it was possible to imagine. A breath of cold wind sent shivers down her back and she pulled the thick, cream cardigan around her shoulders. Someone, she thought, who didn't know about her past and was happy to be with her even when as his seasick shipmate? She hoped so, because the alternative of repeating the same old mistakes didn't bear thinking about.

'Is Cecil all right?' she asked as Bill stood on the pontoon in front of the boat, facing her.

'He's fine. He just wants to make sure he's fit to race tomorrow, although looking at the forecast, I'm not sure there's going to be any wind. It'll be more of a float than a race. Come on,' he said, holding out his hands to help her over the pulpit at the nose of the boat. 'There's a fish and chip van on its way – and it's not just any old fish and chip van. It's been laid on by Matthew's restaurant over there. His chef is superb and I can tell you we need to beat the rush before all those hungry visiting sailors smell the salt and vinegar.'

Even so, a queue had already formed by the time they reached the vintage van with its curved lines and blue and white stripes. A lot of people, it seemed to May, either worked for Bill or he had worked for them and were keen to catch up with his news. Some of his students from Great Spitmarsh College were there; the girls smiled under their lashes at him and the boys showed off, and inevitably everyone's gazes had slid to her and questioning eyebrows were raised.

'Swab my deck, if it isn't Bill and his wench!' Matthew, who was helping to serve and still in pirate mode, roared at them. May very much hoped he wasn't going to make any cracks about catching her eyeing him for hidden treasure earlier in the day. Touch Matthew's loot and she'd certainly feel Harry's boot, she decided.

'Dig out your doubloons for a good cause,' he went on. 'The food's courtesy of Samphire this weekend, but we want to raise as much money as we can for local charities.'

Bill handed over a crisp note and ushered May away, 'Before he comes up with any more pirate phrases,' he explained as Matthew warmed to his theme.

Back on *Lucille* they sat in the cockpit and unwrapped greaseproof parcels of thick wodges of homemade ciabatta filled with spicy fried pollock which were served with a dinky bucket of chips with aïoli. It was the perfect end to the day so why, she noticed, catching him watching her as she licked her fingers, did Bill look as if he was brewing up to say something?

'What's the matter, then?' she asked, nudging him.

'This tasting dinner and entertainments night Matthew's put together at Samphire tomorrow night,' he said at last. 'I wondered if you'd like to go with me.'

'I'd be a bit disappointed if you hadn't asked,' she grumbled, 'but what about Cecil?'

'Why?' laughed Bill, 'is it a condition now that we have to go out as a threesome or has he already invited you?'

'Silly. It'll be a long day for him if he's still serious about entering the boat race in the afternoon. I just thought that if you needed me to stay behind and look after him while you help Harry and Matthew, I'd volunteer.'

'Cecil,' he said, watching her closely, 'has decided he'd be more comfortable back in his own bungalow tomorrow.

I'm going over with him in the morning to check the place over and settle him in.'

'Oh?' she injected a note of disapproval into her voice. 'You'll miss the fun run in the morning. Matthew won't be happy.'

'Matthew can take a running jump,' Bill said softly. 'I might need to save my strength.'

'And why's that?' she said, looking into his dark eyes. He reached a finger inside the neck of her cream cardigan and traced a circle on her shoulder.

'If you don't think I'm being too pushy, I hoped that since we've finally got some time to ourselves, that you might like to come home with me afterwards.'

That was one of the aspects of his character she found so endearing, that he was so considerate about her feelings. Nevertheless she couldn't resist teasing him.

'Oh Bill,' she sighed. 'I wouldn't want to put you to any trouble. The last thing you need is another visitor. Not when you've got the house to yourself at last.' And then she spoiled it by bursting out laughing.

Bill growled and pulled her to him. Then there was a loud bang above their heads and May broke away to the sound of more fireworks exploding, sending stars and little glittering fishes of lights twisting and spiralling in the night sky.

'Blimey, Bill.' She giggled. 'That was clever. If that's what you can do with your clothes on, what will you do when we're home alone?'

The next morning, as the first event of a packed regatta programme drew to a close, Georgia, in Matthew's arms, started kicking off again as she spotted her mum near the end of the 5k Fun Run. Coming in to loud cheers, Harry finished with a very zippy time of just over twenty-six minutes.

'I don't know what you're all so surprised at,' she grumbled. 'I run round the boatyard every day. Besides,' she added softly to May, 'I wasn't going to let another mum beat me in front of Georgia.'

Matthew, behind Harry's back, rolled his eyes. No one, it seemed, was going to get the better of Harry, not even in a light-hearted contest.

Harry had vetoed demands for a crab race on the grounds of cruelty to crustaceans, so there was plenty of time to watch the prizes being awarded and for crews to prepare for Little Spitmarsh's very own round the island race.

'Back to something like normal at last,' Cecil announced, looking proudly over his shoulder at his silver Jaguar gleaming in the car park. 'It's not that I'm ungrateful for everything everyone's done for me, but it's a damn bore relying on other people. You'll be relieved to get your home back to yourself too, I daresay, Bill.'

'Don't overdo things, that's all,' Bill said, helping Cecil aboard. 'Remember what they say about making progress slowly or you'll be back to square one.'

May took Bill's hand as she dropped into the cockpit beside him. His grip was firm and always so reassuring, like his manner when he addressed his uncle. Instinctively, she knew that if Cecil needed him this evening, Bill would postpone their plans to be with him. He was a man who took care of others and she liked him all the more for his unselfish nature. It didn't stop her hoping, though, that Cecil wouldn't need them, or from quietly simmering in anticipation of the night ahead. And when Bill looked at her so tenderly and intensely, May could tell that he was having similar thoughts. For the rest of the afternoon she'd have to try to avoid catching his eye as she needed both her wits and her sea legs to be in full working order, especially when Bill's hot looks were affecting both.

She hadn't forgotten what a big day it was for Cecil. He'd once participated in the Little Spitmarsh Regatta's much larger namesake, the Round the Island sailing race that took place annually in the Solent. Now, he was busy talking tactics with Bill. Whilst they wouldn't be racing against high-tech multihulls and the course took them round Little Tern Island, not the Isle of Wight, no one listening to them would guess that today's event, comprised mainly of weekend sailors in ancient wooden boats, wasn't just as serious.

'That lot look as if they need resuscitating, not motivating,' said Cecil, looking askance at the elderly crew on *Rose of Grimsby*, a North Sea 24 next to them. But his smug expression was masked by one of fury when, in the melee at the starting line, the same crew almost tricked them into sailing off before the starting gun, therefore nearly earning instant disqualification.

'Wiley buggers,' Cecil muttered. 'We'll have to watch them.'

Once through the tidal gate, nerves were tested as the flotilla of little ships squeezed into the same stretch of deep water, all of them trying to avoid the shallows either side of the narrow channel.

'Damn fool,' said Cecil happily as the skipper of *Winkle* steered on to a sandbank, his race over. May, who had been enjoying the sight of the colourful boats cutting through the fretwork of marshes and mudflats, prayed they wouldn't suffer the same fate. Surely this was her and Bill's night? If they ran aground at this state of the tide, they could look forwards to cocoa with Cecil rather than getting cosy at Bill's.

From Campion's Creek the channel split in two, leading to the sea in one direction and to Peregrine Water, a large lagoon easily navigable by all the boats. Simple, May decided, relaxing until the breeze on the big stretch of open water caught the sails and almost swept them into the Folkboat just ahead.

The sea was flecked with the hues of bobbing hulls as the yachts cut through the waters, taking advantage of every breath of wind as they fought for the fastest route round the small island. In the carnage, the Cornish Crabber came perilously close to scraping *Lucille* and Bill had to make Cecil sit down for a while for the sake of everyone's blood pressure. And then, just as they had almost rounded Little Tern Island, the wind died just as suddenly as it had blown up. The sails drooped, the rudder lost power and for a moment it looked as if the current would take them straight on to the narrow shingle shore.

'Shall I start the engine?' May said, recoiling as both Cecil and Bill bellowed, 'No!' at her. Another competitor did, though, so that was another boat out the race.

Afraid of being keelhauled for mutiny, May retreated below to put the kettle on. When she returned with mugs of tea, *Lucille* was pointing back towards the main channel but still drifting. The tea was received with barely a grunt, so she went back down below again and found fruit cake to go with the tea, by which time the boat was drifting very gently downstream towards Watling's along with a sedate procession of so-called racing yachts.

May settled herself against the coamings surrounding the cockpit which made a good back rest and enjoyed the warm sunshine and the sight of the grassy banks passing slowly beside them. Cecil and Bill were still willing the wind to pick up, but the only motion was with the tide, so it was hardly surprising when small clouds of smoke started to rise above the creek as one by one the other crews reached for the engines and chugged back towards Watling's.

'What do you think, Skipper?' Bill said, checking his watch. 'Reckon we'll make it back before we run out of water over the tidal gate?'

'I'm jolly well going to give it a try,' Cecil said, casting a steely eye at the competition. 'Even if we're not going to win.'

Far from looking tired, an afternoon outside had put some colour back in his cheeks, and he was full of plans for solo sailing and exploring the backwaters as soon as possible. Listening to him, May felt a tinge of sadness that the time had almost come to hand the boat back to him, although she hoped there would be more opportunities to sail again on *Lucille*. In the meantime, she could look back on her memories and forwards to the evening with Bill.

'Look out,' Bill warned as the two remaining boats ahead of them collided in a scrape of paintwork as they both made for the centre of the main channel in the approach to Watling's.

As one yacht struggled to get back on course, having been nudged into the shallows, *Lucille*'s sails suddenly picked up in a freak gust of breeze, giving Cecil the chance to nip past her, although it was too late to catch up with the lead yacht which had the clear advantage.

'Second!' said May, turning to Bill and Cecil as the boat made a spritely finish. 'That's wonderful!'

Cecil pulled a wry face. 'You obviously don't know what Queen Victoria was told after the America's Cup, do you?'

May shook her head.

'"Your Majesty, there is no second."' Bill laughed, giving his uncle a consolatory pat on the back.

Shrugging, because she couldn't understand what there was to be disappointed about when they'd all enjoyed such a pleasant sail, May looked at Bill in anticipation of the night ahead. It was a shame that Cecil hadn't won a prize, but hers was yet to come. Then they became aware of the committee boat making an announcement over the loudhailer.

'*Rose of Grimsby* – you're disqualified for fouling *Hazy Daze*. *Lucille* is therefore declared the winner of this year's Little Spitmarsh Regatta!'

May saw Bill turn to his uncle anxiously, and although she too was worried about what the sudden excitement might do to him, a tiny part of her couldn't help but observe that it would be just her luck for Cecil to need another night recuperating at Bill's. Cecil, however, was punching the air, waving to the cheering crowds and was all set to let off a flare gun, until Bill stopped him in time. The photographers on the bank, disappointed not to get some atmospheric red smoke for the benefit of their pictures, looked around for something to point their cameras at, and, before she could do anything about it, Bill wrapped her in his arms and gave her a very long and very triumphant kiss.

Cathy felt positively triumphant now that she and Rick were on their way to Little Spitmarsh. The camper van sitting on their drive had always served as a symbol of how wild and free they still were beneath the wrinkles and mortgage, even though the furthest they'd been in months was a trip to Bognor. But now it provided a means for her to demonstrate that she could be a responsible parent too. The impasse with May had gone on too long and she was determined to do something about it.

She dug in her bag for her tobacco tin and then,

sighing, her reading glasses so she could see what she was doing. It was a bit of a miracle that she and Rick had got through another rough patch that would have seen many other couples dividing up their LP collection. They had talked, shouted, cried – though only because she'd been overwhelmed when Rick presented her with the couple of hundred quid he'd made selling his bike on the hurry to help her raise some ready cash – and then they'd made up.

So far Aiden had ignored every appeal she'd made to him; Soul Survivor remained locked, barred and dead to her. She wished she could assume that meant he'd lost interest in May too. With his latest signing, Molly Gordon, popping up and popping out everywhere, it seemed likely. But then again, this was Aiden, what else might he be capable of? What were the chances now of May resuming her career without his professional support? Well, they'd find out soon enough. Since May was determined to hunker down in Little Spitmarsh, Cathy had decided her best course of action was for her and Rick to go to her and help pick up the pieces.

All the same, with a long drive ahead she decided that the single carriage road in the heart of the Surrey countryside would be a good place to roll a spliff so she'd be nice and mellow in the event of any uncomfortable conversations arising. Getting old was no sodding fun, she decided; the bloody reading glasses were a dead giveaway that you were past it, for a start. Concentrating on trying not to spill everything as they ricocheted off a pothole, she was carefully laying out a tobacco paper when she heard a muffled roar beside her.

'Don't you ever fucking grow up, Cath?' Rick bellowed, fumbling with the panel beside him. 'For crying out bloody loud!'

In the next instant, he'd grabbed everything off her lap and sent it sailing out the window. There was a metallic clatter as it landed in the road.

'My glasses case was with that lot,' she said resentfully.

'Too fucking bad. If you think I'm turning round you've got to be joking.'

She folded her arms. Some dog walker was going to get lucky tonight when he picked up her tin. At the speed they were going, if she was really minded, she could probably open the door, jump out, run back and catch up with Rick again before he'd crawled round the next bend. She'd forgotten quite how sluggish the old VeeDub was and that it was a complete pig to start; perhaps her memory was letting her down too?

Every time they slowed down, she found herself listening as the engine coughed and threatened to stall. When they rounded a bend, she was deafened by a combination of the crockery rattling in the back and Rick swearing as he struggled with a cranky gearbox and absence of power steering.

'So how come you were suddenly able to take time off?' she said, when they had settled into some sort of rhythm in the slow lane.

'I was getting to that,' Rick said grimly.

Cathy slumped in her seat. Just when she thought life was about to pick up again, it seemed this excursion together was a swansong to mark the end of their marriage.

'You're leaving me for Bekah Edwards.'

'What?' Rick swerved and nearly took them on to the hard shoulder. 'No, you dozy cow. I must be a hopeless bloody case as I still prefer you, so you're stuck with me.'

He reached out and squeezed her thigh briefly. 'Sometimes I think you'll never be satisfied until you've pushed everyone who loves you away. Cathy, you're not that little girl who got ignored when her baby brother came along. No one's going to lock you in your bedroom for hours at a time or run you cold baths any more. You're a grown woman with a family that loves you and it's about time you realised that and let us in.'

Don't let anyone get too close, that had been her safety mechanism. She dabbed ferociously at a tear that was threatening to spill over.

'I was afraid of what I might have inherited, that I might be capable of abusing the people closest to me, but I've ended up worse than them.'

Rick gave a dismissive snort. 'You'd have to go some to be worse than your parents.'

'I still made a fist of being a wife and mother, though. I don't know how you've all put up with me.'

'Stop beating yourself up! We're doing all right, aren't we? Look at Stevie, Miss Independence, making her way in the world and taking on all comers.'

'And May?'

He sighed. 'That's what we're about to find out. It's what Prince Bloody Charming's been doing that we've got to worry about. I never did like how he packaged May, selling her like some bloody object. And I bloody hated that song he put her up to singing.'

'We did all right out of it,' Cathy reminded him.

'Yeah, and that's another thing. We've got to stand on our own two feet and not before time. I've got no work, Cath. The job I had lined up has been put on indefinite hold because the client can't afford the upkeep on the place any longer, and everything else has dried up.'

'Rick? Have you—'

'Whatever you're going to suggest, Cathy, I've thought

of it. I've even tried pulling in a few favours to see if I can get some site work, but there's nothing doing. There's too many young blokes ahead of me.'

'But—'

'Sorry, love, you're going to have to be strong and we're going to have to pull together. Otherwise we're both going to be right up shit creek without a paddle.'

'Too late. I think we might be halfway there, Rick. The oil light's on. Doesn't that mean the engine's frying?'

Chapter Twenty-Five

The guests were crowding into Samphire, eager to sample the Regatta Platter and to enjoy the evening entertainment. From the numbers arriving it looked as if Matthew's chosen charity would receive a healthy donation from the event. Car doors slammed, and scraps of laughter and conversation floated on the breeze as they hurried towards the restaurant. May paused. The sunset, captured in the enormous glass windows as it blazed across the trembling waters of the creek, seemed particularly beautiful. A multitude of seabirds soared and twisted in the sky and her heart felt as if it was lifting with them. Or was that simply the effect of the man at her side, the warmth of his body close to hers and the familiar scent of him?

Bill stroked his fingers gently across her cheek and bent to brush his lips briefly to hers. 'You look so beautiful, I'm afraid to touch you,' he admitted, but came back for more nevertheless, before leading her into Samphire.

May smiled, relieved she'd got it right. Fond as she was getting of Little Spitmarsh, it wasn't exactly known for its exclusive dress shops, but at the same time she guessed that most of the guests at the restaurant would be more concerned about the food rather than what everyone else was wearing. She'd opted for a halter-necked jersey maxi dress from one of the chain stores, in a lovely turquoise blue which suited her skin tone and was subtly flattering. The secret support meant she didn't have to worry about a bra, and after giving the matter a great deal of thought she'd chosen a pair of cute but non-threatening silky knickers. Bill, she knew, would have fancied her even in a big ol' pair of cotton rich, high rise, full-on granny pants, but it was a good feeling, after trussing herself up to meet some of Aiden's expectations, to know that she would be acceptable just as she was.

'Who's a lucky boy?' she heard Matthew tell Bill in a low voice as he showed them to their table. Matthew himself was looking effortlessly sexy in a white tuxedo and scruffy Levi's, but Bill, beside him, made May feel she was the lucky one. She was a bit ashamed now when she thought about her initial reaction to him and how put off she'd been by the idea of sharing a small space with a big ginger builder. Now she thought how lovely the rich gold colouring looked against his dark navy jacket, though in truth he could shave his hair off and she wouldn't care. And when she felt the heat of his strong hand on the small of her back, gently guiding her through the throng of people, she felt safe, not trapped. As for the rest of him? If she thought too much about that she might not be able to eat her dinner, which would be a waste. Above all, though, Bill was a kind and caring man, and that, she thought, feeling her heart skip a beat as he looked at her, made a very pleasant change.

Before she could get too starry-eyed, waiters began to circulate with the Samphire Regatta Platter first course, an *amuse-bouche* of salmon and sour cream crostini. May let out a soft moan as it melted in her mouth, closing her eyes in rapture.

'I wish you wouldn't make that noise,' said Bill, laughing.

'Sorry,' she said, looking round worriedly, thinking that like Aiden, he was complaining about her embarrassing him.

He grinned and leaned closer, saying in a low voice, 'Not to put too fine a point on it, you moaning and groaning like that is playing havoc with my imagination, amongst other things. I have my breaking point, May, and picturing you in my bed, imagining making you cry out with pleasure is pushing me pretty close to it.'

'Don't hold back on my account,' she whispered back. 'We can go right now!' Then she thought of how cross Harry would be if they sneaked out of her husband's big fundraising event. 'Although – I vote you give Harry our excuses.'

Bill shook his head. 'We've got all night. And we've waited this long, so let's enjoy the evening.' Then he gave her a wicked grin. 'Just save some of that groaning for later.'

Bill stole a glance at May whilst she finished off the last crumbs of a miniature apple tarte Tatin with a small appreciative sigh. No airs and graces with May, he thought. What you saw was what you got; a sweet, funny, undemanding woman who made him feel good and whose company meant more to him with every minute they spent together.

It amused him now to think how wrong his first impressions were of her. Gold-digger? Not the May who enjoyed messing about in old boats and was happy to spend her summer in a small caravan. High-maintenance? Certainly not. There was none of that fussing around with her hair and nails or checking her make-up in the mirror every five minutes that bored him stiff with other women. And dishonest? He'd been wrong to doubt her when she'd insisted her ex was off the scene.

Looking at her across the table, he couldn't blame the guy for trying to hold on to her – already his life was brighter and happier because of her. His May, he knew deep down, was a one-man girl, who wouldn't be going home with him tonight unless she took her feelings seriously. But what about his feelings? He took a deep breath. No question about it. Their relationship might be at an early stage, but he'd fallen hard.

Flip, she'd turned his life upside down. He liked living alone, or thought he did, but now he felt lonely when May wasn't there. He considered himself an easy-going man, but now, he thought, scowling round the room, his hackles rose at the sight of more than one man eyeing May, wishing he could take her home. May herself seemed oblivious to the attention she was drawing in that jewel-blue dress in a flimsy fabric that clung to her breasts in stunning detail. Even Matthew, he thought crossly, hadn't been able to resist a second glance. And then she looked up under her dark lashes and given him a big wide smile that told him beyond doubt that he was the only man for her.

Reluctantly, he dragged his gaze from her and folded his arms as the lights dimmed to a single spot, signalling that the evening's entertainment was about to begin. Despite being impatient to go, Bill had to admit there was quite an atmosphere of anticipation building. Small white flames from the table candles added to the sense of theatricality, reflected in the floor to ceiling windows like snowflakes shimmering against the purple shadows of Campion's Creek. Chinking glasses were muted and the murmured conversations dropped to whispers as his old friend took the floor.

Matthew was a showman, he'd give him that, Bill thought, chuckling to himself. Commanding, confident in his impeccable white tux and jeans and utterly charming, as he regarded the assembled crowd with a lazily amused gaze until there was absolute silence in the room. 'And now, ladies and gentlemen ...'

Matthew's low, throaty voice even got May paying close

attention, Bill noticed, a tad put out, until she flashed another quick smile at him and reached out across the table to lace her fingers in his.

'Prepare to reset your minds before we meet tonight's special guest. Your mental image of the man you're about to hear may be of a fresh-faced kid in leather jeans taking the world by storm with the power of his voice that shocked and thrilled. He was the boy who became the accomplished front man holding stadium audiences across the US in the palm of his hands. The same man the music critics later said had sold his soul for commercial success and abandoned innovation. Or perhaps you'll only remember the headlines and the old, familiar story of addiction and decline. The rock star in his darkened room, creeping out once in a while to perform in little-known venues to an audience that had largely turned its back.'

He paused, letting his words take effect, and people watched him, their willing smiles turning to apprehension. 'Whatever impressions you have of this man, let me tell you now that the next forty minutes of your life will make you forget everything you ever knew about him. Ladies and gentlemen, for one night only, let me give you the one and only Thunder Harwich ...'

Bill nodded, admiring his mate for revving up his audience so effectively, but he only hoped he knew what he was doing or the evening was about to take a dramatic and mortifying nosedive. Matthew stepped back into the shadows and there was Thunder, sitting on a stool, his head bowed towards his ebony Gibson acoustic guitar. Scanning the room, Bill noticed the embarrassed faces; gazes dropped to the table, fingers tracing the bases of empty glasses. A collective holding of breath, as if everyone feared they were about to bear witness to a humiliating disaster.

And then just as the silence seemed to grow too hard to bear, Thunder started plucking out the sweet sad notes and everyone leaned forward in their seats. When he started to sing, he gave a wry smile as some of the audience recognised the lyrics of Nick Drake's 'Fruit Tree', the song about fame that some saw as a protracted suicide note in view of the writer's early death. In Thunder's hands it became both poignant and defiant, a declaration that the singer of this new interpretation was not going to lie down quietly.

By the time Thunder had gone through a repertoire of songs borrowed from artists from Neil Finn to Nick Cave, everyone in the room knew they were witnessing something extraordinary. Thunder's versions were stripped-back of any gimmickry; no showing off, nothing big or theatrical. They were personal, intimate songs about loss, delivered in a lived-in voice that resonated with a lifetime's worth of regrets.

'And here's one you haven't heard before,' he said, before breaking into a song that raised the hairs on the back of Bill's neck for its resonance with his own feelings.

'*Follow a star, starting again. When the voyage is over, will we still be friends? Say, we'll still be friends …*'

The chords died away and the applause was nearly loud enough to send waves surging across the creek. But if anyone in the room was surprised by what they were hearing, no one was more taken aback than Bill when Thunder paused in his set to explain what had changed his mind about hanging up his guitar for good.

'I met a girl, you see.' He smiled and people smiled with him, on his side. 'No change there, you might say. But this wasn't my girl, this was a singer-songwriter, a woman who'd had one hit and walked away from it all because she'd found fame such a demanding mistress. And whenever I heard her song played on the radio, I always thought it was a pity she'd lost heart in what she loved, that we weren't all hearing that voice any more. Now, it's different for me. I've been afraid to come back because everyone kept telling me what a talentless bastard I was, someone who'd lost it.'

A few people laughed, recognising themselves in his words. 'Yet, you folks have been kind enough tonight to give me a chance. To make me think I might not be a lost cause after all. And if you're wondering what happened to the girl who walked away from her success, she gave that song to me, so I'm really glad you like it because she's got far too much talent to let it go to waste. Even better, she's here in this room tonight and I'm hoping that together we can persuade her to face her fears and give the world a second chance to hear that sweet voice.'

Bill scanned the room wondering where the celebrity singer was, then he noticed Thunder was looking in their direction and seemed to be beckoning at May. Bill craned over his shoulder to see who was at the table behind them. Unless Carmen Moult, sitting there with an Amy Winehouse beehive, along with her husband Roy who had a very impressive quiff of his own, had a secret past life, this was beginning to feel very awkward. Poor old Thunder, he really needed to get his eyes tested.

Thunder was insistent. 'Come on up here, honey. Don't be shy now, you're among friends. Ladies and gentlemen, please give it up for Cherry!'

He really was losing the plot, Bill thought, shaking his head. Shame. And after his performance had been so well received too. He turned, smiling to May to see if she was shrugging off the unexpected attention with her usual good grace and humour … and froze. There was panic in her eyes and she seemed torn between folding herself into as small a space as possible and bolting for the door. He reached across to squeeze her fingers to show her everything was all right, and she let them rest there briefly, her eyes cast down to their hands clasped together. Then she looked up at him with an expression filled with regret.

'I'm so sorry,' she whispered, and let go.

People around them were smiling and putting their hands together in growing applause, then a delighted Matthew came bounding out of the shadows, lifting May out of her seat and wrapping his arm round her waist, and guided her towards Thunder.

Cherry? Comprehension hit him so suddenly, Bill felt as if he'd been punched in the stomach. Aware that a few curious faces and a couple of cameras were also turned on him, he forced himself to keep smiling until they'd lost interest. All the time his mind raced, rapidly readjusting to this new information.

Cherry: candyfloss pop princess. 'Chillin' in the Park': the feel-good summer anthem streaming all over the internet and pounding out of clubs, bars and wedding receptions everywhere. This was May who'd been sick over the side of a boat with him; the May who'd stoically kept steering through cold winds and churning seas which turned her face green. May, whose delicious curves took him all the way up to the edge of heaven. May was Cherry? Bill frowned as a picture started to form. In the small amount of television he ever managed to catch, even he hadn't missed clips of the girl in the music video. She was blonde then, and perfectly made up. A glamorous and remote singer in a white sheer dress with flowers in her hair. Then, as the images blurred into one, he wondered how on earth he hadn't known.

Careful to keep his expression neutral, he watched May, visibly trembling as she stood before everyone, and swallowed hard. Thunder played the intro to the song that all of them must have been able to sing in their sleep, except this version was a perky, quirky acoustic interpretation free from electronic wizardry. Shaken as he was, Bill still ached for her. In the growing tension, he willed her to overcome her nerves as Thunder repeated the same few bars, trying to encourage her to join in. Then, at last, hesitant and breathy as she started, May began to sing and Bill let go of the breath he'd been holding.

Even as he rooted for her, hoping that she would survive this very public and unexpected scrutiny, Bill could feel her slipping away from him. In three scant minutes, the May he was so fond of had blossomed into Cherry, a confident performer who beamed as she thanked the audience and then at Thunder, who mouthed a query at her. May nodded and together they began a heartbreaking version of Carole King's 'So Far Away' and when at last her eyes met his, Bill almost believed she was singing it for him.

As the last chords faded away, everyone got to their feet for a standing ovation, except Bill. This was Cherry's world now. If this was what she'd been missing and if it made her happy, he was happy for her. But in the noise and applause he slipped away unnoticed. He'd seen enough.

Chapter Twenty-Six

Early on Sunday morning, May concluded that at some point in the night, she *must* have fallen asleep because she wouldn't have pulled the knitted bedspread over her head otherwise. Not on such a sweltering night. Her subconscious mind, however, wasn't bothered about physical discomfort; it just wanted the emotional pain to stop.

She staggered over to open the caravan door and let in a welcome breath of air, then sat down to perch on the steps. Beyond the caravan everything was peaceful with no sign of the tumultuous events of the previous evening. The early morning sun was already strong on her bare feet and the tide was creeping up the banks chivvying pink-legged oystercatchers in their frantic search of the mudflats. May watched them with sympathy; there was every chance she was about to feel the force of events beyond her control too.

Last night's impromptu gig had been at first terrifying, then exhilarating as the mood of the audience changed. The point when they stopped holding back and embraced the music with her was always triumphant. It was a heady experience, even in a small venue, maybe more so when you were close enough to read the expressions on individual faces. She'd proved to herself she could stand up on stage without Aiden. But now she had to face the future without Bill. She rocked forward, overwhelmed with loss for a man, it seemed, she never really knew.

It was her own fault. She should have listened when he'd cautioned her against putting too much reliance on feelings that had boiled up in the intensity of a shared world at sea. Perhaps the only reason she'd come to think of him as someone she could lean on, a man who was strong and dependable, was because of her own frame of mind when she stepped aboard *Lucille* with him. Naturally, she'd had to rely on his great experience offshore because her limited sailing skills wouldn't have got them out the harbour. Yep, with hindsight it was easy to see why her body had put two and two together and concluded that the right answer was a very hot one on one.

But surely Bill knew her well enough to see how reluctant she'd been to join Thunder in the spotlight? When she'd looked back at him to see him smiling at her, she thought he was willing her on, sending her his support. So why had he walked out on her when she needed him most?

There were many reasons why she'd already decided, even before the text from Aiden that had destroyed the little self-confidence she had about her stage appearance just before the festival, that performing wasn't her first love. Touring exhausted her, especially the first one when the demands of travelling around the country on a tight budget meant nights sleeping in the van or the cheapest B&B, assuming they could find one that was open. Then there was the logistics of lugging equipment or worrying about someone else 'borrowing' it.

Aiden had pushed her hard, signing her up to anything and everything, trying to get a buzz going so that when the album was released there'd be a massive demand for it. Even when the single went stellar and 'Chillin' in the Park' made life on the road more comfortable, she'd never adjusted to the nocturnal hours or the feeling that she was living her life upside down.

What made it worthwhile was feeling the response to her songs. Seeing the audience lift their arms towards her as she stood on stage, hearing them applaud and call for more. Even 'Chillin'' for all its faults had made a lot of people happy. But not Bill, it seemed.

And that was another downside. Once her career took off, the men who tried to approach her after a gig increasingly saw the singer, not the woman. May felt as if they saw her as a potential conquest, someone to notch up on a bedpost, or, when she had the audacity to reject them, to criticise or poke holes in. And she already had Aiden to do that. When she tried to make friendly conversation – and there were many times on tour when she would have been glad of a friend – other men were simply too intimidated by her fame to engage.

Bill, she'd hoped, was strong and level-headed, sure enough of himself not to be bothered by all that – but he'd taken off at the first sign of her success. Maybe she should have told him about her alter ego sooner – but Bill's reaction was exactly the reason she'd been so hesitant. As much as she ached for him to hold her, as urgently as that demanding voice inside was prompting her to climb into the first taxi she could summon and get over to Bill's place and into his bed *now*, the fact remained that he'd turned his back on her.

And that was even before he'd known what a field day the press would make of her impromptu public appearance.

May started flicking through the websites on her phone. 'Cherry blossoms from pop star to sophisticated singer-songwriter in secret acoustic gig' beneath some grainy mobile footage of her and Thunder singing a duet. 'Cherry flaunts her curves in show-stopping dress' with a close up of her top-half. And, oh, Bill was going to love this one: 'Cherry and a male friend make quite a splash!' beneath a photo of his lips locked on hers as they embraced at the end of the regatta.

Even Thunder's ex-girlfriend had been quick to jump on the bandwagon, therefore providing the tabloid with a thin excuse to reproduce a photo of Paige in skimpy black knickers, pouting at the camera with her hands barely covering her breasts. 'Glamour model Paige Mosse, close friend of revived rocker Thunder Harwich, recalls seeing the happy couple on their luxury yacht in harbour only a couple of weeks ago. "They were low key about their affair," she told our reporter, "but anyone could see they only had eyes for each other."'

May blew out a deep breath and tapped out a text to Bill. He'd walked out on her, but she was going to be the bigger person and leave the door open – for a little while anyway. She didn't want Cecil thinking she'd forgotten him either. The final Parade of Sail as visiting yachts prepared to leave Watling's at the close of the regatta was taking place later that morning and she knew he'd be looking forward to seeing it. *Hope Cecil enjoys the show* she wrote to Bill. *Sorry I won't be there with you.*

In the creek a cormorant popped up struggling to swallow a gigantic mouthful. The feeding frenzy had begun – so who, thought May, switching off her phone, would be next to throw her to the piranhas?

As cheers sounded over at the yacht basin, May felt her throat tighten thinking about Bill, just a short walk away from her. All she wanted was to be wrapped in his arms, her cheek pressed against his chest, her senses revelling in all that was familiar and dear about him. If her feet would only follow her heart's instructions, she could have that now … but it wouldn't be what she needed. The Bill she thought she knew had been conjured up as a quick-fix solution, not as a man she could count on.

May got up and went inside the caravan. All of this was

make-believe too, a pretty little playhouse where grown-ups could go on a sentimental journey to a world that had never existed. As clever as the mix of retro and mod cons was, she was willing to bet that the attractions of caravan living began to pall after a week of rain or plummeting night-time temperatures. And as much as she would have liked to hang on to the rose-tinted glasses that had made it seem so charming and romantic, it looked as if it was time to get back to reality.

When she heard footsteps outside the caravan, May felt her heart leap with excitement. Bill! He'd got her text and had come to make up with her. It was difficult not to let her disappointment show when she skipped out to find Tyler, Harry's young assistant, approaching.

'Harry sent me down to see if you're okay,' he said apologetically.

'I've been better.' She tried to smile. 'But, hey, I'll survive.'

He gave her a quick, searching look. 'You were terrific last night. I didn't think your music was really my kind of thing, way too poppy for me, but I liked the stuff you did with Thunder. That "Follow a Star" song, was that really yours?'

When the voyage is over, will we still be friends? Say we'll still be friends.

She gave a short laugh. 'Yeah, that's the other side of me.'

He nodded, then hearing more noise from the boatyard, looked over his shoulder.

'Harry asked me to tell you that she'll catch up with you after the regatta, but she wanted you to know that the press are hanging around and making a bit of nuisance of themselves.'

May groaned. 'Oh, I'm sorry, I'll get packed up and get on my way.'

'No.' He gave her a quick reassuring grin. 'Harry's been throwing everyone off the scent telling them you were last seen heading off in a black Mercedes in the middle of the night. And you're safe here. Harry said to reassure you that the caravan's yours for as long as it suits you – if anyone's trying to find you, they'll have to get past us first.'

May didn't need to think about it. The more time she had to decide which way to jump next, the better. Even so, she was deeply touched by the kindness of people she barely knew. She swallowed hard, and Tyler touched her arm briefly.

'I told you, you were amongst friends here.'

Leaving her to it, he started to walk away then stopped and smacked his forehead.

'I nearly forgot, there's a couple just turned up in a beaten up old camper van claiming to be your parents. Looks as if some people will try any tactic to find you.'

Cathy and Rick, here? Had they seen the news already? Did they think the golden goose was about to lay more eggs? And then suddenly it didn't matter what motive had brought them there; they were her mum and dad and she wanted to see them.

The next day, May was still glad that her parents had given her a reason to linger in Little Spitmarsh. If she stayed put, there was always the possibility that Bill might show up at the boatyard and tell her he'd got it all wrong, an apology May was starting to realise she deserved just as much as the one she owed him. Despite her suspicions, her mum and dad had been completely oblivious to what the press was calling her 'secret gig' until they'd seen all the reporters. They'd seemed mildly surprised to learn that Aiden wasn't behind it, although their exchange of furtive glances seemed to suggest a mutual effort to back away from the subject of her career plans.

'This is what you want, is it?' Cathy asked doubtfully as they sat outside the caravan looking at the view. 'Won't you miss being in the spotlight?'

'I'm happier here, in the sunlight,' May replied. 'I want to be free.'

In a spirit of reconciliation, May guessed, Cathy had started insisting that losing the shop was a kind of release. Rick had taken a break too, so they could catch up on some of the travelling they'd always promised themselves. Little Spitmarsh was their first destination so they could see May before moving on.

As things stood, it was also likely to be their final destination for the time being. In a style typical of her parents, they'd hurtled off with very little in the shape of preparation and forethought, so the camper van had limped as far as the boatyard and then conked out. Harry had very gallantly agreed to let them use the facilities there until it was fixed. As a consequence, Rick, who'd been intrigued to find a slip of a girl, as he put it, in charge of the boatyard, now seemed to think she was a bit of an oracle. It amused May to see him meekly deferring to Harry's mechanical knowledge and consulting her about the best place to find spare parts for the VeeDub, especially when his ignorance of any other trade but roofing meant that nothing about their home ever worked for very long.

Cathy quickly got fed up of sitting around doing nothing. She wasn't really attuned to the beauty of nature. May suggested a stroll round Little Spitmarsh, which fell flat when they'd passed the upmarket tourist shops in the old town resurrecting all the angst about Soul Survivor. May's guilt and the voice inside that told her she could be doing more to relieve that situation was pushed to the back of her mind when they returned to Watling's only to bump into Cecil tugging a trolley full of provisions towards the pontoon.

'Cecil!' she greeted him, hoping to keep the conversation brief and breezy. 'How are you?'

'Better by the day,' he smiled, running an inquisitive eye over Cathy, who was in full rock chick mode in her skinny jeans and a pinstriped waistcoat over a white shirt.

'Hang on a minute,' said Cathy, bristling. 'You're not Cecil as in the skipper who was hoping to shed some inhibitions along with his business suit with my daughter, are you?'

'Erm,' said Cecil.

'No,' May said firmly. 'I'll tell you about it later, Mum.'

'I'm equipping *Lucille* for a serious sail while my nephew's not about to tell me what he thinks I can or can't do,' Cecil explained, nodding at the trolley. 'He's gone away for a couple of days on a job. Or so he says. I don't suppose you can shed any light on why he'd take off like that?'

'Perhaps something unexpected happened,' May suggested, blushing.

Cecil raised an eyebrow, but she headed him off before he answered his own question. 'Don't you think you should wait until he returns before you go sailing on your own?'

The raised eyebrow joined the other in a deep frown. 'Dear girl, I'm not an *invalid*,' he said, chewing the word around with considerable distaste. 'And I'm perfectly qualified to sail my own boat without my nephew's permission. All I require is someone to mind the shop for me while I'm away. The dear old soul who's been standing in for me's been called in to have her bunion removed at last. The pain's supposed to be dreadful afterwards, poor old stick, so she's going to be out of action for a good long while. That's the only thing stopping me.'

'I have a shop,' Cathy said beadily. 'I don't mind helping out while we're waiting for the car parts to turn up.'

May sighed. Now she'd be in Bill's even worse books. If there was such a thing. She introduced Cathy and Cecil. 'Yes, but you don't know anything about antiques, Mum. That's Cecil's trade.'

'Actually, I do,' said Cathy. 'I used to run a bric-a-brac stall on the market when your dad and I were first married, before we got Soul Survivor.'

'I don't think Cecil's stock could be described as bric-a-brac,' May said, hoping that was the end of the matter.

Cecil scratched his head. 'This *is* Little Spitmarsh, May, not South Kensington. There isn't actually much of a demand for Fabergé eggs and Ming vases. I'm sure your mother won't ruin me while I take the boat for a sail. Why don't you come to the shop, dear lady, so we can have a chat about it?'

'There,' said Cathy triumphantly.

'But Mum, you and Dad are only passing through,' May reminded her.

'Oh we're not in any hurry,' Cathy assured her, looking shifty. 'We haven't had a window of opportunity like this in years. Besides, you're here aren't you? And we want to see more of you.'

Cathy was so rarely demonstrative that the hug that followed was completely unexpected. Giving her mother's rather stiff frame a squeeze in return, May breathed in a nostalgic blend of white musk perfume laced with stale cigarettes.

'I'm packing them in,' said Cathy ruefully, seeing her face. 'I'm making a fresh start, May. I'm intent on turning over a lot of new leaves, beginning with tobacco.'

'Splendid,' said Cecil. 'I don't want you coughing over my valuable junk, I mean, antiques, now, do I?'

Before May could think of another reason to sabotage the arrangement, they were joined by Thunder, who had been to take another look round *Maid of Mersea*.

'I don't believe it,' Cathy murmured, going a bit pink. 'It's—'

'Maurice Cledwyn,' said Thunder, sticking out his hand. 'And this is my sister, Janice. I've come to show her round.'

'What did you think of the boat?' May asked politely.

Janice, who Marks and Spencer could snap up as a double for Twiggy if they needed an older model in a hurry, gave them a broad smile. 'She's a bit different to *Valhalla*, not quite what I was expecting!'

'Aw, she just needs some loving, like all of us,' Thunder said, affecting hurt.

'But what have we got here?' Janice said, stepping forwards to take a closer look at *Lucille*. 'Now this is *lovely*. Very pretty!'

Well, Cecil would be pleased with the compliment, thought May, casting a look at him to see how he was taking it. But Cecil seemed to have forgotten all about *Lucille* and was craftily eyeing Janice instead.

'Ding-dong!' he said, sounding very chipper.

Chapter Twenty-Seven

Bill could probably have driven back to Little Spitmarsh after surveying a fragile old wattle and daub building deep in the countryside, but it would have made a long day and there was no reason to hurry back. In just two days since May's unwelcome revelation, he'd had a bollocking from Matthew for walking out of his fundraising event, and one from Harry for walking out on May. Cecil was acting like a born again teenager. If he wasn't burning up to the speed limit round the country lanes in his Jaguar, he was surfing the internet ordering new gear and gizmos for *Lucille*. He'd also made it quite clear he didn't want anyone fussing around him. As for everyone's favourite pop star? Why would she want to hang around with a ginger builder when she, like Cecil, had rediscovered her mojo?

The house he'd surveyed stood on the outskirts of a picturesque market town where, on impulse, he booked himself in to the White Hart, another historic timber-framed building – arguably in better shape than the one he'd just left, depending on personal taste.

After a pint and a steak pie with chips in the restaurant, where he'd sat staring blankly at a large copper bed warmer on the wall, trying not to think about the space in his own bed, some of the emptiness inside had been filled. A quick tour of the town, noting that the prices in the antiques shops were far cheekier here than Cecil could have got away with, then a quiet read of a new political thriller he'd downloaded ought to ensure that he could drift untroubled to sleep.

Bill kicked his shoes off and stretched out on his lonely king-sized reproduction four-poster bed intending to catch the news headlines and inadvertently caught the end of some celebrity news round-up. Before he could press the controls to turn it off again, his hand was stayed by a horribly familiar song.

'Chillin' in the park
Just you and me
Having fun in the sun
You're the one for me
Inspiration
Jubilation
Don't leave me in isolation ...'

Sodding Cherry and 'Chillin' In the Park'. How May must have laughed to herself when he'd pushed his dad's guitar on her thinking he was giving her a hand with her career. And what had she made of his little lecture about self-belief? As for the woman whose body had been so hot and yielding under his hands, had that really been because of him or was that another role she'd been playing at too? *'Don't leave me in isolation, looks like love's our destination.'*

Repeat and fade to a happy end, he guessed, but not one that included him.

Whilst 'Chillin'' played in the background, reporters were pressing mics in the face of the couple who were on the red carpet for some music awards he'd never heard of. The tall, pink-haired female half of the couple was looking decidedly hacked off since everyone seemed to be more interested in the short dark-haired guy accompanying her, rather than her revealing pink lace frock.

'Tell us about the secret gig,' someone was yelling, 'Does this mean we're going to see more of your biggest star?'

Never mind the big star, thought Bill. He wouldn't mind seeing more of the lady in the lace dress. The short guy was obstructing what promised to be a great view, so it was even more disappointing when the cameras went in for a close up on the guy.

'Hey, what can I say?' he said, looking straight into the lens with a cocky grin.

Arrogant twat, thought Bill.

'It's very early days,' he drawled, baiting the reporters with a hint of knowledge withheld. 'As you know, Cherry's had a few issues recently …'

Cherry! Instantly, Bill sat up and turned up the volume.

The reporters pressed closer with a flurry of questions. The short guy raised a hand until there was silence again. He flashed a mocking smile before resuming his love affair with the lens.

'I've been keeping a close eye on her during her, er, her break to make sure she's been getting all the help she needs. I'm sure you can imagine what a difficult time it's been for everyone who cares about her, so it was a great relief to all of us that she coped so well with a carefully selected audience in an intimate setting. All I can really say is that the signs are looking good for her complete recovery.'

What a tosser! Bill resisted the urge to kick the telly. Implying she'd been in rehab. How was that supposed to help her career?

The cameras turned to the woman in the lace frock who, on closer inspection, wasn't half as attractive as Bill had first supposed, and nowhere near as lovely as May.

'Molly, you and Cherry are both signed to Pink Lix Records. The friendly rivalry between the pair of you is well known, but I'm sure you're delighted to hear your stablemate is on the mend. Is there any message you'd like to give her?'

'Yah,' the woman said in a cut-glass accent and with a smile that didn't reach her cold eyes. 'Take all the time you need to recover, babes.' She tossed back her pink hair. 'Don't rush back, will you?'

'Aiden? What about you?'

Aiden! That slippery, obnoxious, smarmy bastard was Aiden! Bill forced himself to stay calm before he burst a blood vessel. Besides, he wanted to hear what the man he'd come to detest had to say.

'Ah no, you don't catch me that way,' he chuckled into the camera. 'I don't need to use the media to send a message to Cherry, nor she me; we understand each other.'

After casting a last brooding smile into the camera, he turned his attention back to the woman he was, presumably, partnering. Instead of slapping his face, she meekly allowed him to grab her hand as they posed together in a blaze of flashing lights.

'That was Aiden Cavanagh, music mogul and founder of Pink Lix Records,' the newsreader said, back in the studio, 'talking about a possible comeback for Cherry.' The newsreader smiled at her male co-presenter. 'I wasn't sure Molly Gordon looked altogether pleased, did she? Still, there could be some exciting rivalry ahead if she and Cherry both have albums out at the same time.'

Bill turned off the TV and stared at the blank screen. So that was the man who exerted so much power over May. Why any woman in her right mind would fall for such an oleaginous little git, spouting utter bollocks – albeit in a very smooth accent – he failed to understand. Nor did he have to; the woman he thought he'd known didn't exist. So if Aiden was coming back for another bite of the Cherry that was fine by him.

*　*　*

Rick gave a strangled roar at the sight of Aiden flaunting his new squeeze on the telly, giving Cathy time to hit the button on the remote control before they added a wrecked TV to their debts. Especially one in such a posh room. With the camper van immobilised in the boatyard whilst they waited for the parts to turn up, Cathy quickly decided that the reality of life on the road was far less romantic than the idea of it. May had come up trumps and booked them in to Walton House, a stunning boutique hotel. Cathy did feel bad about May spending her money on them. Even though she seemed to be on very friendly terms with the owners, she suspected the 'mates rates' were still far more than she and Rick could afford.

Nevertheless, Cathy was enjoying herself again. After a successful introduction by Cecil to his shop, he'd been happy to leave her in charge whilst he made up for lost time pottering about in his boat. Antiques, she was surprised to find, with their individual stories and history, were inherently fascinating to her, unlike the wishy-washy new-age trinkets with their false promises that made her feel like a charlatan for selling them. There was far more meaning in the carefully wrought stitches of a simple sampler sewn by some long-dead hand than any of her crystals or temple bells.

'So have you told May to tell that little prick to get stuffed and forget about the shop?' Rick asked, buckling his jeans.

Cathy pulled a face in the dressing table mirror. Trust Rick to drop a clanger and disrupt her sense of contentment. 'With May being in the news I'm surprised he hasn't scurried up here by now demanding his pound of flesh. Although he appears to have his hands full with that Molly Gordon. She looks as if she'd give him a run for his money – especially once she sees May's face all over the press.'

'He might have to be a bit more careful with that one,' Rick growled, 'with daddy being an MP.'

Cathy squinted at the eyeliner on one lid, then started on the next. 'May's doing all right, isn't she?'

She leaned back, surveying her reflection and caught her husband's troubled gaze.

'I bloody well hope so,' Rick said, scowling.

Cathy pursed her lips together, struggling to control her emotions. She, of all people, should have seen Aiden's controlling behaviour for what it was: abuse that had stripped her daughter of her strength and confidence. Her neglect of her own child was shameful and still made her squirm when she looked into her heart, but maybe now she had the chance to put the past to rest.

Rick looked unhappy, but she hoped that picking up an unexpected job would help to take his mind off things. The scrappy little woman who ran Watling's was, as it turned out, married to a property developer who, on hearing that Rick was a roofer, had offered him a few days' work on an old chapel.

'May's not right, though, whatever you say,' Rick insisted. 'You only have to take a close look at her to see that something's eating away at her.'

Sometimes her husband was more perceptive than she gave him credit for, she admitted to herself. If it hadn't been for a rather interesting conversation she'd had with Cecil Blythe, she would have been more concerned, but now the future was looking rosier for all of them. Somehow the Starling family was going to emerge from this crisis stronger and closer than ever.

'Yeah, but it's not what you think,' she reassured him. 'It's nothing to do with Aiden Cavanagh, believe me.'

She turned round and got up to kiss her husband. 'I

promise you, May's going to be more than all right. Wait and see.'

Rick stiffened and held her away. 'Cath? What have you done now?'

'Me?' she complained. 'I haven't done anything. All I'm doing is minding a shop.'

The same evening, a couple of miles slightly further inland, Fiona felt it was well worth taking a small hit on the cost of accommodating May's parents since they were now in her debt. If May hadn't mentioned the sixteenth-century farmhouse her beau had just completed, she and Paul wouldn't be having this sneaky preview before it went on the market. Despite Thunder's generous offer for Walton House, there wouldn't be a lot of money to play with once they had paid off their debts, and now there was a baby to consider. Maybe they could come to a deal with the vendor which excluded the estate agents' fee? Fiona tried not to get too excited; it was important this was a joint decision.

They crossed the hallway into the first reception room where the evening sunlight slanting through the windows caught the expressions flickering across her husband's face.

'This is great, isn't it?' he said,

'It's lovely. And so beautifully restored,' she agreed. 'But can we afford it?' she asked, aware that there would be other pressures too when he went freelance.

'Let's see what the rest of it's like first.'

They reached the family bathroom and the house just kept getting better.

'I like that big bath,' said Paul, pulling her close. 'It's big enough for two … or even two and half.'

'Well if we do buy it we'd better make the most of it before we become three,' she smiled, feeling tears pricking her eyes because it felt so good to have her husband all to herself again.

Paul frowned. 'It's a great house, better than I dared hope we'd find, but are you sure you're ready to leave Walton House?'

'I'm more than ready,' she said firmly.

'It would mean we could stay close to Little Spitmarsh,' he said, clearly thinking aloud. 'Only this time, we'd have more time for each other, and the baby – and some money to play with too.'

Paul wrapped his arms around her and kissed her hair. 'There's just one more thing I haven't told you.'

Fiona felt herself tense. 'Oh Paul, haven't we both learned that keeping secrets doesn't work?'

'Hush,' he said, into her hair. 'This is one I've been saving. Call me selfish, but I've missed you. I was fed up with sharing you with other people, even before we got the chance to sell up, so I was determined to do something about it. I've been putting some money aside, which is why we've been particularly stretched lately.'

Another mystery solved.

'I wanted to surprise you – I've booked us a holiday, two weeks in the sun. Time to catch up before the move and before the baby comes ... What do you think?'

She pulled away and swallowed hard. To think, she had been guilty of fantasising about another man that time, when Aiden Cavanagh's seductive voice down a telephone line had suggested all kinds of adventures. And what a horrid little man he'd turned out to be. At least he seemed to have disappeared, leaving May in peace – something about Fiona's glimpse into their relationship had really bothered her. She'd been glad when May had confided she was moving on with the builder guy, so it was an awful pity to hear that their budding relationship had been crushed by the revelation of May's alter ego, Cherry, coming to light. But as Fiona reminded her, a truth that draws a tear is better than a lie that draws a smile. She nodded to herself; what May needed most was some time out in a place where she wouldn't be bothered. And if Aiden Cavanagh tried showing his face at Walton House again, he'd quickly find there were no vacancies.

'I think,' she said, lacing her arms around her husband's neck, 'that I'm a very lucky woman.'

Outside, they were about to close the door when Paul surprised her by scooping her up and carrying her over the threshold. 'We're in agreement then, Mrs Goodwin. You are a lucky woman and I'm a very happy man. Welcome to your new home.'

Chapter Twenty-Eight

As the green country lanes unravelled behind him, giving way to the subtle greys and golds of the coastal plain, Bill looked forward to getting home. A few days away, tacked on to the tail end of his site visit, should have recharged his batteries. But no matter how many stars the White Hart had been awarded or how highly commended the food, there was nothing like the thought of his own bed. A damn comfortable bed it was too; so perhaps he'd finally catch up with the sleep which was still eluding him. Some recreational activity before bedtime would probably help. Except the playmate he had in mind was May. The idea of anyone else taking her place only made him feel sad and weary, and how long had it been since the other half of his bed had been occupied anyway?

Instead he'd get in, open a beer and enjoy the peace unbroken by Cecil repeating the same old nautical stories. That one about crossing the Channel to see the eclipse in Cherbourg, for example, grew with the telling, he'd noticed. Even sharing the house with Cecil reminded him there were compromises to be made when anyone else was involved. So he was happy living alone with no one to moan at him about working erratic hours, trooping mud from construction sites across the floor or complaining about his snoring if he fell asleep on the sofa at the end of a long, hard day.

May wasn't afraid of getting her hands dirty and putting a bit of effort in. She'd pulled her own weight on the boat and hadn't expected him to do it all for her. And she hadn't complained about his snoring once. Although she could give nearly as good as she got in that department. He grinned to himself recalling the little puffing sounds that signalled when she was fast asleep. If only his temper hadn't got in the way of their night together, he might have had some fun teasing her about that.

Despite what people said about redheads, it took a lot for him to blow his fuse. Like discovering the woman he thought he knew so well didn't trust him enough to tell him the truth about herself. Even then he could partly understand why May had been so careful about guarding her privacy. It still hurt, though, to think that after everything they'd shared she could withhold something so important.

If he turned right at the next junction, he could detour to the boatyard to see if she was still about. But who would he find if he pointed the van in that direction, May or Cherry? He slowed down and weighed up the options. Home lay straight ahead, empty, silent and cheerless. Watling's to the right, with May, a smile in her honey-brown eyes, laughing perhaps, with Harry and Matthew, Georgia snuggled in her arms.

Bill was turning the wheel in the direction of the boatyard when his mobile rang. He pulled over to take the call.

'Harry? This is a pleasure. Is everything okay?' He braced himself and waited for Harry to tell him that May had packed up and gone. If only he hadn't been so pig-headed, he might have stopped her. He might, at least have salvaged friendship from the wreck of what they'd shared. How much harder would it be to apologise for his behaviour if she was halfway back to her old life? What if he never saw her face again, except as a remote figure on MTV?

'I'm sure there's nothing to worry about,' Harry said, sounding distinctly unsure. 'I wondered if your uncle had been in touch, that's all. He took his boat out yesterday morning without letting anyone here know where he was going or how long he'd be away. Do you want me to take the skiff out and have a quick look around?'

Bill went cold thinking of the warnings he'd been given by the hospital about the possible side effects of his uncle's operation. What if the stent graft had leaked, increasing the pressure on the aneurysm? Was Cecil out there now, alone, frightened and bleeding to death? Or unconscious and drifting helplessly out to sea?

'I'll be there in five minutes. I'm coming with you.'

He stopped the van in Watling's car park, his temples throbbing as if his head was being squeezed in a vice. Inland, the weather had been clammy and humid, but it wasn't much cooler on the coast. Black clouds hung stubbornly above steely grey choppy waters, resisting the efforts of a gusty wind to move them along. Whipping instead at the proud club burgees streaming from rigging shrouds, it threatened to shred them to tattered rags at any moment. Bill scanned the horizon, searching in vain for the needle of a mast piercing a pewter sky. When he opened the van door, the heavens opened as the tension which had been slowly mounting all day finally gave way. Hollows in the gravel surface formed instant pools, soaking the bottom of his jeans as he raced towards the pontoon where Harry was waiting. A cloud of white smoke rose from the stern of the skiff as she spotted him and started the outboard engine.

'Let me take over,' Bill roared above the noise.

'Barber or butcher?' Harry shouted back, nodding at his hair as she passed him a life jacket.

'Very funny.' He rubbed his shorn head with regret. It was obvious to him now that cutting off his hair because he suspected May didn't like the colour was a pretty futile gesture. One she'd never even know about, too. Then, a low grumble of thunder made them both look up.

'Harry, go in. I can do this by myself. Matthew won't be happy if you get struck by lightning.'

'For fuck's sake, Bill, I'm not some helpless little woman. The search will be easier with two pairs of eyes.'

'You have *never*,' Bill said emphatically, 'been "some helpless little woman". But you *are* a mum. What do you want me to tell Georgia when you're recovering in hospital if you get hit by three hundred thousand volts of electricity? Assuming you're still alive, that is.'

Harry gave him a scowl as black as the clouds above their heads. 'I won't *ever* forgive you for pulling that one,' she growled, clambering on to the pontoon.

'No, and Matthew wouldn't forgive me if I hadn't.'

The rain lashed against his face, half blinding him as he made sure Harry was safely back on the pontoon. And then he noticed she'd been joined by someone else in a yellow oilskin that was far too big for her.

'May,' he bellowed, 'what are you doing here? Go back to the caravan for crying out loud before you get drowned.'

'I'm coming with you,' she shouted above the noise of the engine. 'I want to help find Cecil and Harry's right, it'll be quicker with two of us. Please?'

'What good do you think you'd be? You're not playing *I'm a Celebrity … Get Me Out of Here* now. Cecil might be seriously injured.' And *he* would be seriously distracted. The last time he'd been distracted by May on a boat, he'd almost got himself killed by the boom.

'But I feel responsible for his disappearance. My mum's

been helping out at the antiques shop. He wouldn't have been able to go sailing if she hadn't been there to free him up.'

May's mother was in Little Spitmarsh? What was this, the Starling family outing? Bill shook his head. 'That won't work. It certainly wouldn't have stopped Cecil taking off in his boat if he was so minded. The trouble is he's become too confident too quickly. It's not your fault May so consider your conscience cleared and get back in the dry. I can handle this by myself.'

Before he could stop her, May scrambled in and squatted on the wooden seat opposite him. 'Swallow your pride, Bill,' she advised. 'You know what a good team we make on a boat. Stop wasting time and let's get going.'

Harry looked from one to the other then quickly untied the painter which was wrapped around a cleat and handed it to May.

'Good luck the pair of you. I hope he's all right.'

The labyrinthine nature of the creeks made it a tortuous search. As the navigable channels of one tributary after another grew thick with reeds and matted with marshland, Bill was increasingly aware of his uncle's fragility.

'We'll find him,' May smiled, peering at him under the curtain of rain dripping off her hood. 'He's probably tucked up somewhere safe, quite unaware he's raising concerns. I'm sure he didn't mean to worry any one.'

'That won't stop me giving him a piece of my mind when we find him.' Bill stretched his aching shoulders. 'How come you're still able to smile?'

'I was thinking about the regatta and how cross Cecil was not to win first place outright. He insisted afterwards we'd gone wrong in Peregrine Water, kept telling me that would have been the best place to take advantage of *Lucille*'s speed against *Rose of Grimsby*'s manoeuvrability.'

'No.' Bill shook his head. 'He's wrong about that. It was too tight an angle round Little Tern Island.'

'He reckoned if he had another chance he could outpace all the competitors ...' May paused and gave him an enquiring look.

Surely not? Had they missed the obvious? It was worth checking, but another rumble of thunder creeping closer reminded him he was putting May in danger every minute they stayed out there.

'We've come this far,' she urged, sensing his hesitation, 'what are you waiting for?'

The rain was lashing down as they turned into Peregrine Water. Lightning flashed, still some way off, but close enough to illuminate May's pale face beneath the yellow hood of the borrowed oilskin. It was time to get them to safety, he decided, when May gave a triumphant shout. There, riding out the storm, securely anchored in the shelter of Little Tern Island, was *Lucille*.

Bill felt inclined to thank the heavens even though they were pouring vast amounts of cold water all over them. Through the heavy drizzle, he could see the gold glow of the gimballed lights flickering from the cabin. It was a comforting sight on many levels, but his relief that the outward signs gave every indication that all was probably well on board fuelled his growing anger at his uncle's irresponsibility. May could have been electrocuted in the hunt for the selfish bugger, all for the sake of one quick radio call.

Slowing the engine so that they didn't create a huge bow wave which would rock Cecil's boat before he could rock it himself by giving his uncle a severe dressing down, he putt-putted closer. Abruptly, the torrential rain eased and as Bill's ears adjusted after the constant din he was stunned to hear music and laughter. He was even more surprised when he heard the sound of the doors that kept the cabin watertight sliding open, and suddenly there was Cecil, his head and shoulders popping up in the companionway. Another peal of laughter with a distinctly female ring followed, then he watched his uncle grapple with a bottle until there was a dull explosion and the soft plop of a champagne cork landing in the water.

Someone else squeezed up beside Cecil.

'Thunder's …' stuttered May, struggling to believe the evidence of her own eyes.

'It's all right, I think we're safe. The storm's passed now,' he assured her, boggling at the sight unfolding in front of him.

'No,' May whispered, 'I think it's only just beginning. That's Thunder's sister, Janice.'

'Jeez!' Bill muttered.

A shaft of evening sunshine had fought its way through the clouds after the rain and was lighting up Bill's brutal new haircut. If there was any heat left in it this late in the day, he'd have steam coming off his head soon, although judging from his expression he was already close to boiling point.

'Put your hood up and let's get out of here before they recognise us,' May urged him. And before Bill started wondering what might be going on over there. He had, May observed, a rather idealistic view of his uncle.

'I put your life in danger, just so Cecil could get laid!' He shook his head in disbelief.

Ah, too late.

'Slight exaggeration, Bill,' she observed. 'I'm alive and

kicking and as for Cecil? Well, I'm not brave enough to break up the party, are you? You don't know for sure what's going on over there, but it's not going to do any of us any good to go over and poke our noses in where we're not wanted,' she pointed out. Presumably though, Cecil hadn't sneaked off with Janice simply so she could trim his sails. 'Come on, let's go.'

To her relief, Bill obeyed and even kept the drum of engine noise down as they thudded back again in the direction of Watling's.

'Is nothing what it seems anymore?' he complained when they were back in the main channel. 'I don't know where I am with anyone. I mean, who's with me today; May or Cherry?'

'Oh, don't give me that!' she said, glaring at him in exasperation. 'There is no Cherry, she's just a fabrication. You know who I am, we've spent enough time together!'

'We've done that all right,' Bill agreed. 'Enough time for you to decide that I might have seen a little too much of you. Enough time to decide I was an embarrassing mistake. Enough time for you to decide you were better off with your influential, two-timing snake of a boyfriend.'

'Do you know, Bill,' she said, lifting her chin, 'that's one reason why I should be pleased you walked out on me. Because you always assume it's about money or influence with me! That's why my face didn't ring any bells with you when we first met, because you assumed I was some cheap little opportunist who was after your uncle's money! *Then* you decided I was making up to Thunder for his millions, and *finally* you accuse me of getting back with someone I never want to see again!'

The outboard coughed as it caught some seaweed, but May was still in full throttle.

'I was thrilled to bits,' she hissed, 'that you'd apparently been living under a rock for two years and had never even heard of Cherry. It gave me the chance to feel that we were just two ordinary people making a delivery trip, and I was grateful for a reprieve.'

'May,' Bill scoffed, 'we weren't exactly strangers by the time we reached Little Spitmarsh. Don't you think you could have trusted me with your secret by then?'

She rolled her eyes at him. 'You've seen how silly Matthew went when he spotted Thunder! Can you blame me for wanting to let sleeping dogs lie? Would you have treated me the same if you'd known? Most men don't. Either they can't see past the fantasy or they think I'm a gold mine.' She shot him an accusing glance. 'And besides, you let me take you at face value too. You were happy to let me go along with the illusion you were some sort of manual worker.'

'I *am* a manual worker!' Bill insisted. 'I just happen to own the company I work for and talk about what I do from time to time. You turned up your nose when you thought I was some labourer on a building site, though, didn't you?'

May felt a strong urge to smack his smug face. 'I wasn't turning my nose up at you, but because my dad's a roofer and it brought back memories of growing up in a house where nothing ever got done! We never knew what he was going to rip out next when he started a project, or more importantly, when it would ever get put back! He took the bathroom out during one set of my exams and I came home to find the loo was a bucket under the stairs until he worked out how to plumb in the new one.'

Bill had the grace to look at her a little more sympathetically, but now it was his turn to do some explaining.

'If anyone's been turning their nose up it's you!' she accused. 'You're the one who walked out on me, remember? Just when I was looking forward to us spending a romantic evening together! You might at least have stuck around long enough to tell me you'd gone off the idea.'

'I didn't think a fancy pop star would be interested in a ginger builder,' he said mulishly.

'Oh, so this is about your bruised ego, is it?' she cried, spreading her hands. 'I can't believe that the Bill I sailed with would have given up on me so easily. I was fond of that Bill, even when I thought he was a ginger builder.' She looked at his head reproachfully. 'Is that why you've practically shaved your hair off? Just when I was getting to like it?'

'You what?'

He watched her seriously, meeting her eyes with intent and she felt her breath go because he looked so sexy and she wanted him so much.

'Aw, Bill, for God's sake!' she murmured, standing up and moving closer. 'Just what do I have to do to prove it?'

As the ground tilted under her, May had just enough time to register that she had just done something very stupid before she tumbled over the side of the boat.

'What were you trying to do?' Bill was shouting as he hauled her back with some difficulty, not helped by the fact that her life jacket was now fully inflated. For a moment when she'd hit the water, she thought her chest had exploded, so it was quite a relief to find it was the life jacket and a comfort to know that the safety equipment worked and that their 'man overboard' drills had not been in vain.

'Did you think you'd round off your career by joining

the Twenty-Seven Club?' Bill was still roaring, 'along with Amy Winehouse, Jimi Hendrix, Richey Edwards and the rest? Just because it's the gold standard for a rock star's tragic death doesn't mean you have to join them!'

'Richey Edwards' body was never found,' croaked May. 'He might still be alive.'

'You better thank your lucky stars that you still are!' Bill bellowed. 'Although if the state of the tide had been different you might have been swept away instead of being stuck up to your knees in mud!'

'I've lost a shoe,' she noticed.

'Well, I'm not going in to find it and neither are you. Jeez, May, you're lucky that's all you lost.'

Bill was still muttering at her about how lucky she was not to have been drowned when they reached the landing pontoon at Watling's. May wished he'd stop going on, but she couldn't answer because of the lump in her throat. Her chattering teeth and the fact that she couldn't stop shivering were enough of a reminder of her rash behaviour without the additional humiliation of knowing that she'd spilled her feelings for him and not had a word of acknowledgement in reply.

Harry, who must have spotted them from the balcony of the converted boatshed where she and Matthew lived, was waiting for them. Her eyebrows steepled when she saw the state of May and she whistled softly under her breath.

'Cecil's fine,' Bill said, stony-faced as he handed Harry the skiff's painter. 'He's got some explaining to do when he comes home. And not just to me. But he's safe.'

Harry, hands on hips, looked from one to the other. 'I'm very glad to hear that, but what happened to you, May?'

May just shook her head. 'Nothing that a shower and a change of clothes won't sort out.'

That was it; she was done with Bill, boats and Little Spitmarsh. A dunk in cold water had certainly brought her to her senses. No more noodling around waiting for a ginger builder to notice her. Or waiting to discover what the real reason was behind her parents' innocent explanation of why they'd followed her; there was bound to be a sting in the tail somewhere.

The 'secret gig' had proved to her that she still didn't care for performing, but had also convinced her that her song-writing skills were still intact. Her next step, therefore, was to get dry, pack up and get back to doing what she did best. Only this time – once she had finally extricated herself from her current contract – without Aiden telling her what to do. May let out a deep breath and took a last long look at Bill as he climbed ashore. At least she'd have plenty of experience and material to draw from.

Chapter Twenty-Nine

Bill scowled at her and when she still didn't move, reached down and manhandled her from the boat. He probably had enough on his plate worrying about Cecil, May figured, when he still refused to speak.

'Come up to mine,' Harry said, glaring at Bill and stepping into the silence. 'You can have all the hot water you need there. And there's a spare bed. You'll be warmer there than the caravan.'

'Thanks, Harry,' said Bill, 'but given that she damn near drowned herself, I'm taking her back home with me where I can keep an eye on her.'

'At last,' said Harry with more than a hint of rebuke. 'I thought you were never going to get round to it. I was beginning to think you'd lost your mind as well as your hair.'

But May dug her heels in. 'Firstly, Bill, I'm quite capable of looking after myself, and secondly this isn't a romantic novel. It's not the old "bath and bed seduction scene back at your place" routine. I'm freezing cold, I've got seaweed in my hair and mud in all kinds of weird places, so if you think I'm getting in the van like this when everything I need is a short walk away, you've got to be kidding.'

'Run along then,' Bill said, shoving his hands in his pockets and walking away.

May watched him disappearing into the setting sun with a sinking heart, wondering if this was the last she would ever see of him, when he called back over his shoulder.

'Everything you need, eh? Good, enjoy it, will you? I'm going back to my comfortable warm home to run a long, deep, scented bath, tuck into a delicious hot meal and spread out in my big brass bed.'

'And when you get home,' May yelled, 'take a good long look at your lonely room, the single set of cutlery on the table and your big old empty bed and see how much you like it.'

That stopped him.

'And another thing,' she added, struggling against a lump in her throat. 'I've had exactly one important relationship in my life and it was pretty one-sided. A system of rewards and punishments for good and bad behaviour has nothing to do with love or trust, it's about manipulation and control. No one's going to treat me like a difficult child ever again.'

Bill turned, looking stricken. 'I'm not Aiden, and I'm not trying to belittle you in anyway. Jeez, May, I was scared I was about to lose you forever when you went over the side of the boat. I'm not angry with you – I'm angry with myself for not taking better care of you.'

'And were you angry with yourself when you found out about Cherry? Is that why you couldn't face me?'

Bill spread his hands. 'I'm not proud of myself for being jealous, but I was proud of you for standing up there when you were scared and so nervous. You performed like a true star. Whatever you decide to do next, wherever you go, I'll always be proud of you.'

'The only place I'm thinking of going right now,' May said, shivering, 'is home with you. But you'll have to ask nicely.'

'Please, May,' he said, drawing closer. He touched her face tenderly, 'come home with me, will you?'

'Hang on,' she said. 'Let me grab a change of clothes and I'll be right with you.'

'Halleluiah,' Harry muttered, unfolding her arms and turning towards home. 'About time too.'

A little later, May stood in the open French doors to Bill's garden, contented, warm and dry. The night was calm again with only the smell of rain on the grass and the glistening leaves of the honeysuckle against the glass to show for the afternoon's deluge. She lifted her head to the vast canopy of the East Anglian sky. As her eyes adjusted to the darkness, more stars emerged until a living cloth of glittering blue lurex floated and fluttered over her head. Trying to pick out the constellations, she found herself disoriented; the familiar landmarks had become unfamiliar. So many stars. Why hadn't she noticed them before? Had she been too busy or too blind?

When Bill came up behind her and put his arms around her, she leaned back against the broad expanse of his chest, luxuriating in his strength and the warmth of his body. She could smell soap and citrus and something that was uniquely Bill, familiar yet unfamiliar. The sea was barely a short walk away and they stood in silence listening to the waves drawing at the shingle shore. May could feel her own suspense echoed in that utter stillness before the release of water swooshing over stones.

'The sea will take all of this one day,' Bill murmured, his voice rumbling through his chest against her back.

'Hadn't you better take me to bed then,' she said, softly, 'before something else interrupts us?'

Bill's bedroom was lovely, tucked beneath the sloping roof with two Velux windows bringing them, it seemed, within touching distance of the starry sky. There was an oak floor, a white-painted tongue-and-groove ceiling ... and Bill's brass bed. Suddenly her confidence threatened to desert her. Then Bill folded his arms round her and held her close; constant, reassuring, filling her senses. Even the stars looked brighter.

'Is that a planet?' she asked as one in particular caught her eye.

'Where are you looking? Ah, I've got you. Now, see where the constellation Ursa Major, the Great Bear is, with the Plough in the middle. Okay? Now take the two pointer stars at the right – the end furthest away from the handle – and imagine a line going straight towards what you thought was a planet; that's the Pole Star, Polaris, and if you follow it, you'll always find true north. It's the star explorers use to find the way when there are no other land marks in sight.'

Like Bill, she realised, guiding her towards her destiny when she'd lost her way.

He turned her to face him and when she saw the desire in his darkened eyes, her breath caught in her throat. She couldn't believe that this lovely man, looking at her with such longing, would be anything less than patient with her. All the same, it was as well to warn him, she thought gloomily.

'It's probably a bit late to tell you this, but I hope I don't disappoint you,' she murmured apologetically. 'I haven't exactly had hordes of lovers.'

Aiden's demands had always made her aware of her lack of experience. To add to her growing misery, she was aware that she wasn't even wearing anything special. She hadn't been thinking straight when she'd thrown a few things in her bag at the caravan. Jeans and a T-shirt made a poor substitute for the blatantly sexy outfits and exotic lingerie Aiden preferred her to wear. Bill made a low noise of displeasure and shook his head as he reached out and gently cupped her face.

'What's that got to do with anything? My love, this isn't

about numbers; it's not about the past. This is you and me, here, now.'

He was so gentle and reassuring that May knew that it was going to be all right. Feeling better, she stepped back and started to remove her T-shirt. Emboldened by the heat that flared in his eyes, she moved slowly, lifting the thin material inch by inch before finally pulling it over her head and shaking out her hair. She heard Bill's breath catch and watched his eyes flood with desire as his gaze trailed across her naked breasts. He moved to touch her, but she admonished him softly, keeping him at a distance while she leisurely started to unbuckle her belt.

Teasing him with her body, slowly gyrating her hips in her silky briefs as she stepped out of her jeans, was, however, proving to be a tough call. The hot looks he was sending her made her hungry for his hands to follow where his eyes were roaming. She wanted to see and touch him in return because her imagination was running riot thinking about what he might do with that strong body of his, and she was burning up with the fire building inside her.

When she was almost at the point of being unable to contain her suspense, Bill, to her great relief, gave an impatient moan. His shirt was torn off in double quick time, rapidly followed by his jeans. Then it was May's turn to gasp. There was no doubt at all about how badly he wanted her. 'Blimey, Bill,' she giggled. 'Is that all for me?'

He threw back his head in a warm, sexy laugh. 'I'm all yours, May,' he said, pulling her towards his hot, hard body. 'Every bit of me.'

Much later, when they were both spent, she lay in his arms feeling blissful, letting the warmth enfold her body. Her eyelids fluttered and it was harder and harder to resist falling asleep.

'Goodnight, Bill,' she breathed, smiling as his lips brushed her forehead.

'Sleep tight, May,' he said softly, drawing the duvet over them.

'I love you, Bill.'

Instantly her eyelids flew open, but the room was in darkness. Where had that come from and had she really said it out loud?

'I love you, too, May,' Bill said, folding her into him.

Good, thought May, that was all right then, and let herself drift off secure in his arms.

The next morning, Bill was very loth to drop May back at Watling's, but his client was buying a second home in Little Spitmarsh and was only making a flying visit. Good thing it was only for a couple of hours, and he was looking forward to spending the rest of the weekend with May.

'Besides, I need to pack properly if I'm staying,' she said, kissing him goodbye. 'I'd like to wear something a bit more glamorous for you.'

Bill resisted the temptation to tell her she didn't need to wear anything at all to be glamorous, she looked amazing whatever she wore, but he was growing particularly fond of the May who came as nature intended.

He waved her goodbye and drove off to the Foo Fighters at full volume. Heck, he couldn't wait for this appointment to be over. He was like a teenager again, utterly lost, had been, in fact, way before the moment when May stood before him naked and trembling in the lamp lit room. With a backdrop of the night sky, a clear sapphire blue sprinkled with sparkling crystal, through the open roof lights beyond her and her hair falling in soft waves around her shoulders, she looked as if she had just wafted in from some fairy tale, except when he touched her she was warm, living and very real.

Thinking about it, he marvelled at quite how he'd managed to control himself, given how he'd been longing for her. He shook his head in wonderment, recalling a hot image of May rising and falling as she straddled him, her thighs clamped hard around his hips, her face ecstatic as he moved inside her. Then, as the tension rose, and her small moans built towards a crescendo, he'd flipped her over and plunged with her into the warm, velvety, explosive darkness, unknowing and uncaring of where to find new light, so long as she was there. Imagine where they could go next? Bill blew out a long breath. Imagining those kinds of thoughts while driving could get him into serious trouble. Besides, he didn't want to imagine, he wanted to know. And very shortly, he thought, grinning as he turned up the volume, he would begin to find out.

May smiled to herself as she turned away from the van. In a small way she was proud of herself for putting the past to rest. No more Cherry, just May – they'd got that one straightened out. And she'd satisfied a little of her curiosity too … and knew how good it felt to hear Bill say her name as he moved inside her, holding her in his dark gaze and driving her crazy. There was so much more she was yearning to discover. This was surely the start of a new voyage together, one with time and tide in their favour.

From her pocket, she heard her phone ring. Not Bill, missing her already, she grinned to herself looking at the name, but Fiona. Fiona who probably wanted to talk about the house she'd viewed the previous evening. Although it made her feel very guilty not to respond, May was so loved-up she knew her voice would give her away and for now she wanted to hug her newfound happiness to herself.

Even the elements seemed to have conferred their blessing on them. It was a beautiful morning after the previous day's storm, the sky a pellucid blue above sparkling water foaming with white peaks of still-turbulent waves. May slipped off her shoes to feel the cool shingle beneath her bare feet and ran her tongue across her salt-kissed lips. Being with Bill seemed to have sharpened her perceptions, waking her up after a long sleep and making her aware of so many sensual pleasures. But, goodness, she thought, overcome by a gigantic yawn, she was tired now. Definitely time, she smiled to herself, to get some rest so they could recommence their journey of exploration when Bill came to collect her later.

May trooped up the short flight of steps and was about to unlock the caravan door when she noticed it was ajar. Whatever could she have been thinking about – or not thinking about, since her mind was preoccupied by more pleasurable matters. At least she was fortunate to be in Little Spitmarsh. Anywhere else someone might have stripped the caravan of its contents. It wasn't that she was particularly worried about her own possessions, but it would be dreadful to imagine Harry's precious caravan vandalised, or how bad she would feel for Bill if anyone had made off with his father's guitar.

The only damage was to a driftwood heart which normally hung above the large window at the far end, and now lay in scattered pieces on the floor where it had dropped. If she was careful, she thought, gathering the bits together, she might even be able to mend it. She straightened up with relief. Then someone's hand closed over her mouth.

'Surprise!' Aiden whispered close to her ear. 'Pleased to see me?'

He pressed her hard against the thin wall, displacing a little model wooden sailing boat which fell to the floor from one of the shelves. Above the urgent drumming of her heartbeat, May tried to keep her breath steady. Perhaps he hadn't realised that with his hand still clamped across her mouth she could easily choke? She wondered about the possibility of shoving her free elbow into his rib and forcing him to let go, but that was a ridiculous thought, wasn't it? This was no random assailant, but a man she'd once thought she loved. Someone who had once looked after her.

'There,' he said, feeling her resistance give, 'that's better. Now we can catch up, at last.' He opened his fingers a fraction, then seemingly satisfied that she wasn't about to scream, took his hands away from her mouth.

'Couldn't you have phoned first, like anyone else?' she said, trying not to let him know how much he'd frightened her.

'Ah, don't tease me, May.' He sighed, clinging to her, the rise and fall of his chest against hers inescapable, his sandalwood aftershave making her head swim, driving out a lingering scent memory of Bill. Breathing heavily, he pressed his cheek against hers and ran his fingertips across her collarbone.

'You've been playing hard to get and not taking my calls. And you've been busy, so busy,' he crooned. 'The media's been buzzing with stories about you.'

Abruptly he pulled back, grabbed hold of her hand and forced her on to the bed. 'Come on. Come and tell me what you've been doing. Or who.'

May folded herself in the corner trying to protect herself

by squeezing in between the headboard on one side and the wall on the other. Unconcerned, Aiden bounced on the mattress beside her, stretching out and making himself comfortable. He looked up at her, his mouth curving into a smile. 'I warned you how unhappy I'd be if I found out you hadn't told me everything about your sailing trip, didn't I?'

'Aiden,' she said, determined not to let him push her around any longer. 'There's nothing to tell. And what I do is no longer any of your business. Now please go.'

'Have a think about that. See what you can remember.' He patted the space next to him. 'And while you do, lie down and have a look at this with me.'

May stayed put, but to her horror he pulled out his phone and flicked over to a porn site.

'Get out,' she ordered, trying to remain calm. 'Take your filth with you and get out now.'

Aiden raised his eyebrows. 'I can if you like, but then you won't get a sneaky preview before it gets posted on YouTube. I promise you, you'll want to see this.'

She wanted to tell him how disgusting he was, but the effort of trying to give the illusion of being calm was too much. She shivered, feeling the colour drain from her face and her hands grow cold as she prepared to face whatever was coming.

He sat up close beside her. 'Come on now, don't be shy. This is really hot stuff and I know you like a little fun.'

She waited, numb and sick for the torture to be over, so that he'd leave her alone.

'There now.' He smiled, running his hand down her thigh as he curled against her. 'So … who have we got here?'

May dragged her eyes to the screen to buy herself time. And then she saw what was playing out in front of her.

'Oh, look! A home movie,' he whispered close to her ear. 'A little reminder of happier times. Don't we make a lovely couple? And look at you? Oh, you're going to be very popular with all the boys when they see what you can do with those luscious—'

'Turn if off!' May demanded, lunging towards the phone.

'Oh, no you don't,' he sang, pulling her back down and grabbing hold of her hair. 'Come on now, May. Don't say it doesn't turn you on? I'm turned on – feel!'

She pushed him away and sank back, feeling the fight leave her body and the tears start to spill over. 'How could you? How could you film us making love? How could you abuse my trust like that?'

'It's not an abuse, it's a beautiful thing. A lasting souvenir of our love. So, we can either keep it to ourselves or share it with the world. It's entirely up to you, May.'

May watched her glimpse of happiness disappear, all her hopes shredded.

Then the door burst open and Cathy exploded in. 'Leave her alone, you nasty little shit!'

'Stay out of this, Mum,' May warned, afraid of the power Aiden now had over her.

'Why, look who it is,' he smirked. 'Why don't you come and join us? Let's see if your mum enjoys our film too. She's still got a great figure for an older woman.' He leaned back and considered the matter. 'Do you know I've never had a mother and daughter before? I think it's time I've found out what I've been missing.'

'You've got to be fucking joking!' Cathy hissed.

'I'm glad you think it's funny,' Aiden said with a warped smile. 'Did you tell May all about our little pact?'

'Oh don't try that,' May said. 'I already know you promised to give the shop back if I came running.'

'You didn't tell her?' Aiden chuckled. 'Ah well, guess I'll have to. How do you think I knew where to find you, May, when you set off on your little sailing adventure?'

May stared at her mother and grew cold. 'Mum?'

'You know how tedious your parents can be about money. Remember how they'd always be hanging round our flat looking for scraps? Of course you do! So how far do you think your mother would go to save her shop? Who do you think told me where you were – for a price?'

'Oh, Mum. Please say it's not true?'

'He's lying!' Cathy's face had gone white. She shook her head and opened her mouth, but the words took an agonisingly long time to come. 'It wasn't like that, May. I was thinking about your career. Aiden … he … told me you were in trouble and it would only get worse if you didn't face up to the situation.'

'You *sold* me to him?' May said, pushing past him and getting up.

'No, he tricked me,' Cathy insisted. 'He's taken the lot.'

'Ain't life a bitch?' Aiden said pleasantly. 'But just to show you there's no hard feelings, I'll think about letting you have it back, once May's safely tucked up at home with me. Shall we do that for your old mum, May? Are you going to make us all happy?'

May's eyes met Cathy's and she read the mourning for the loss of her business there, before it was masked. She found her rucksack and started packing.

'That's my girl,' Aiden said, stretching lazily. 'I like that you've put up a bit of fight, you were getting to be such a doormat. Let's go home and make some new films.'

'Don't do it, May. I don't give a stuff about the shop, it's not important,' Cathy said urgently, catching hold of her arm. 'I only want to do the right thing by you.'

May stopped what she was doing and stared at her mother. 'Yes? Well it'll be the first time ever.'

Cathy tried to hang on to her. 'Listen to me, May, I'm so, so sorry.'

May shook her off and Aiden jumped up. 'Come on, then,' he said, 'let's get out of here.'

Chapter Thirty

Bill, pulling into the boatyard, congratulated himself on his remarkable self-restraint. He couldn't wait to be with May again, to talk to her, to make love to her, to hold her close through the night. Heck, he just longed for them to have more time together. But, he'd forced himself to be patient and stopped off at Black Orchid on his way back from his appointment where he'd asked Frankie to make him up an enormous bouquet of cream roses and pale pink lisianthus. Frankie – who wanted to do something showy with birds of paradise and bamboo, had chided him gently for his lack of originality, but Bill insisted he was a traditional kind of guy.

He took one last look at the bouquet taking up most of the passenger seat and wondered whether to take it with him or leave it there as a surprise. The indecision was beginning to make him nervous – he hoped May liked flowers and didn't think it was some chauvinistic gesture to get her into bed. He shook his head. They had such a lot to find out about each other. If May was looking forward to them spending more time together as much as him, they were about to have a lot of fun.

Looking up, he froze at the scene unfolding in front of him. There was May hurrying along the towpath that led from George's caravan along Campion's Creek and round to the yacht basin. Her backpack was shoved over her shoulder and she must have been in a desperate hurry to get away from something because she was still wearing the same jeans and T-shirt he'd watched her take off for him only the night before. What the hell? Bill tensed seeing

Aiden Cavanagh following her, strolling along behind her as if he didn't have a care in the world.

May seemed to sense his gaze. She paused, lifting her pale face to him in mute appeal, and everything went into slow motion as the blood rushed to Bill's head. The man behind her smiled to himself when May stopped. He caught hold of her arm, roughly pulling at her to keep her walking, and grabbed the strap of her rucksack too, to drag May along with him, but by then Bill had leapt out the van and was running towards them.

'Stay out of this, Bill, please,' May pleaded as he ran towards her. 'So that no one gets hurt. You don't know what he can do.'

Cavanagh, still holding on to her, looked up with interest.

'Oh look, how sweet.' He smiled. 'Here's your sailing friend come to say goodbye to you. You'll pay later, my friend, for the liberties you've been taking with my girl, but as you can see we're busy right now. I saw your photo all over the paper – "Cherry's mystery man". The only mystery is what she saw in you. But there, we all like a bit of variety from time to time, don't we, May? He's a big ugly brute, though. Did you fancy a bit of rough?'

Anger ripped through him and Bill started towards the detestable little man taunting him.

'Don't, Bill,' May begged.

'No, don't, Bill,' Cavanagh mocked. 'Or May might be very sorry. Do you want to tell Billy Boy here about the little film we made together or shall I send him the link later? Or shall we all say goodbye to each other nicely and go our separate ways. What do you think, May?'

Bill watched in agony as May struggled with her emotions, helpless to ease her pain. And then she spoke.

'I think,' she began quietly, 'that you should leave now, Aiden. You're not going to hurt me ever again. I want you out of my life for good.'

'And if you know what's good for you, you'll think carefully about that,' he threatened, his face darkening. 'Don't forget that I know what's best for you.'

May shook her head and her voice grew in strength as she continued. 'No, you don't. I'm not an impressionable girl anymore. You can't turn on the charm and think you can make me feel special like you once did, because I've seen the ugliness within you. You used me. You made me believe that I had to please you because I was nothing without you. I thought I owed you, I thought you were acting in my interest, but gradually the small sacrifices I made for you became bigger.

'I thought you wouldn't let me go anywhere without telling you first because you *cared* about me. I thought you wouldn't let me go out alone because you couldn't bear to be parted from me. And on the rare occasions when I did manage to get out to see old friends, you convinced me that it was because you were worried about me when you'd turn up out the blue to check to see who I was with and if I was where I said I'd be.'

May's head drooped and Bill wanted to rush forwards and protect her, but wouldn't that make him as possessive and controlling as Aiden Cavanagh? The one person who knew what was best for her was May. All he could do was hold back and hope that she would keep finding the inner strength to fight her own battle.

She cleared her throat, and held her former tormentor in a steady gaze.

'Nothing you can do can hurt me now. I'm free of you. You have no hold on me. You can have your day in court and argue the toss about my contract if you like, but my own solicitor has advised me there's a sufficient case for me to counter-sue, so think about how much money you want to throw away. As for your sordid little film clip' — she shook her head sadly — 'if you decide to go ahead and desecrate an act of what I thought at the time was love and which clearly meant nothing to you, I won't hesitate to take out a cease and desist order against you.'

Bill's heart bled for her when he understood what she was saying and it took every fibre of his self-control not to step forward and punch the loathsome piece of shit's lights out. But May was standing her own ground, however sick she must have been feeling, and it was more important than ever for him to contain his raging emotions.

Cavanagh's lips curled into a smile. 'And by the time that happens it'll be far too late,' he drawled. 'I can spread the word to an awful lot of people and soon everyone will know what's really behind that sweet little girl-next-door façade of yours. Think of it as another helping hand with your career, May. Now that you're all washed up as a pop star, you could make it big as a porn star.'

'I don't think so,' said a steely voice from behind them.

Bill had been so busy worrying about May he hadn't noticed the slim dark-haired woman stealthily moving towards them.

'Mum, stay out of this.'

So this was May's mother? He struggled to see the resemblance between the brittle-looking woman in her rock chick black clothes and smoky eyes and May who always looked so gentle and approachable.

'You're not the only one with a camera,' May's mother sneered, holding up her phone. 'And I've just recorded your nasty little threats. You can have a day in court if that's what you really want. Only you'll be on trial for harassing my daughter, not just because of your despicable behaviour today but for every second you've bullied her and ordered her around over the last two years.'

'Fuck you!' Cavanagh spat, lunging at her. 'Give me that fucking phone!'

Before Bill could move, he'd grabbed the dark-haired woman's wrist and was twisting her arm up her back. She gasped in pain and the colour drained from her face.

'Leave my mum alone!' said May, jumping on his back. The older woman seized her opportunity to break free, but the phone slipped out of her grasp and clattered on to the wooden pontoon below them. There was nothing Bill could do to stop Cavanagh, who on seeing her trying to reach for the mobile, trod heavily on her outstretched fingers. At the same time, he jabbed an elbow in May's stomach, who, winded, fell back on the towpath.

'She's all yours, Billy Boy,' Cavanagh said calmly as Bill rushed towards her. He picked up the phone and juggled it in his hands. 'Though I'm not sure you'll want her when you see where she's been.' He hurled the phone into the yacht basin then smoothed his dark hair, adjusted his jacket and gave them a satisfied smile.

'Now go and fetch it,' said the dark-haired woman as she clambered to her knees, fell forwards and shoved him as hard as she could into the water.

May felt nothing as the police pushed him in the back of the car, even when Aiden searched for her and held her in his threatening stare. Where she had once looked to find love, all she saw now was how cold and soulless those dark eyes were. Whatever grip he'd once had on her was gone; he'd lost the power to hurt her ever again.

Of course, hearing him shrieking like an angry baby because he couldn't swim had stripped him of some of his authority. Since there really wasn't much of a chance of him drowning, May didn't feel too bad about leaving him to cool off. Bill had thrown him an emergency life belt and he was in easy reach of a pair of yachts and could have clung on to either of them. Harry, who'd been out with Georgia collecting parts for *Maid of Mersea*, had been furious to learn about the disturbance in her boatyard, and had wasted no time calling the police. When they fished him out, Aiden didn't look quite so dapper with his designer jacket all sodden and his pristine white shirt covered with oil from one of the boats. But none of that was important because May had discovered that the power to stand up to him lay entirely with her. She'd done it all by herself.

'I could murder him for what he's done to you,' Bill said, still visibly furious as the police car drove away.

'That won't be necessary and violence is never the answer.' She smiled, taking his hand. 'You've done more for me than you'll ever know, Bill. You've shown me that true love is unselfish. From the very beginning, when you put your life on hold to care for your uncle and gave him a reason to get well, I knew how generous and loving you were. And you had faith in me to help you deliver the boat, even though you knew nothing about me. Through you, I've found confidence and strength I didn't know I possessed.'

Looking up, she was touched to see tears in his eyes. He blinked them away rapidly and cleared his throat. 'You've kindly overlooked the fact I initially thought you might be after Cecil's money,' he said regretfully.

'And Thunder's, don't forget,' she added, seeing the old rocker wheeling towards them on an ancient pushbike.

'Bill,' he gasped. 'No offence, mate, but I'm going to have words with your uncle when he finally shows his face. Making off with my sister like that.'

A white Peugeot estate rolled into the yard and Fiona leapt out.

'You got my message, then,' she gasped to May.

'What?'

'When I saw who was in the police car just now, I assumed ... gosh, I'm relieved you're all right. I thought that man was going to make a nuisance of himself. He arrived at Walton House looking for a room and I told him we were full. He didn't like it at all.'

'Well, he's not going to be a nuisance to me ever again,' May said firmly.

A slamming of the car doors behind them and the appearance of Captain Flint wagging his tail and yapping excitedly told them that Matthew was also back and, to her surprise, he was accompanied by her dad, looking very proud of himself.

'That's nice, a welcoming committee,' he beamed. 'You must have known we've got something to celebrate. How do you fancy extending our stay here, Cathy? Matthew here thinks he can find some roofing work for me.'

Bill caught her eye and May nodded. 'I could do with a roofer,' he added.

'Excellent,' said Matthew. 'I knew you'd be pleased. Especially as I've found a tasty little project that'll be a quick money-spinner for us all.'

'If you regard all your clients as cash cows,' Fiona interjected, rolling her eyes, 'Paul and I might have to revise our offer on the farmhouse downwards.'

'Fiona, darling, I'm hurt that you could even think I meant you,' Matthew said, laying his hand on his heart.

'There'll be a bottle of champagne in the fridge when you move in to show there are no hard feelings.'

The flash of his dimple as he gave her a mischievous smile guaranteed instant forgiveness. No wonder Fiona went a bit pink and coy.

'So,' said Rick, looking at Cathy, 'what have you two been up to today? Anything exciting?'

May could see her mother take a deep breath and, letting go of Bill's hand, she crossed over to her, gave her a hug and kissed her. 'We've been catching up, haven't we, Mum? Having a bit of mother and daughter time.'

From the direction of the creek a yacht's hooter sounded and they all turned round to see *Lucille* slipping through the tidal gate.

'Right,' said Thunder, rubbing his hands. 'This better be good.'

Cecil, with the agility of man half his age, nipped ashore with the line while Janice did a very good job of neatly bringing *Lucille* alongside the pontoon.

'I say! Jolly good!' Cecil said, gazing at Janice with admiration. 'You are a woman of the most surprising talents.'

Then he spotted Cathy. 'Our plan worked, then?' he said, cocking his head at May and Bill and winking.

'What plan?' Bill and May said together.

'Cecil told me about how after he'd suddenly been taken ill, his nephew had gone in his place to fetch *Lucille*,' Cathy said, smiling. 'Afterwards, when Cecil was in hospital and it looked as if it might not be possible to carry out the operation because of his deteriorating health, Bill sat by his bed, encouraging him to get better by telling him about the boat, the trip and the wonderful girl he'd met, the one he couldn't live without.'

'Except you both seemed to be doing a jolly good job of doing exactly that,' Cecil bristled. 'Since it was the boat which brought the pair of you together, I thought if I disappeared in *Lucille*, you might be prompted into taking action. I hoped you might be concerned enough to come and look for me and, in doing so, realise what you meant to each other. But it seems you didn't even notice I was missing!'

Bill opened his mouth to speak, but May motioned at him to stop. Would Janice really want to hear that they'd unintentionally witnessed what looked like the prelude to a romantic evening? And looking at Thunder's face, it was probably better not to raise his suspicions about what she and Cecil might have been up to.

'Fortunately,' Cecil said, smiling. 'I took the precaution of asking this dear lady if she would like to join me for a trip aboard *Lucille*. And a very jolly time of it we had too.'

May thought fleetingly of what form of jolly time had been enjoyed aboard *Lucille*. Unfortunately, something similar must also have crossed Thunder's mind.

'I don't know about a jolly time,' he snarled. 'You'd better have a jolly good explanation about what you've been doing with my sister for the last two nights.'

'Nothing you need trouble yourself about,' Cecil said, haughtily. 'I would, however, like to make a small announcement and tell you all that this dear lady has done me the immense honour of agreeing to be my wife.'

Bill whistled softly. 'Fast worker. Congratulations to you both.'

'Some of us,' said Cecil, fixing him with a steely eye, 'know a good thing when we find it.'

Please don't, thought May, desperately hoping that Bill wouldn't be baited into an unwelcome declaration. It was too soon, too public, too scary to make that kind of commitment. Trying not to wince, she looked nervously up at him. He gave her a wry smile to show that he understood and wrapped her up in his strong embrace.

'And some of us,' he said, kissing her hair, 'just want to take our time appreciating the good thing we've found.'

Perfect, she thought, breathing him in. She was in the right place. Secure in Bill's love, free to be herself.

On a beautiful afternoon in mid September May waited impatiently in *Lucille's* cockpit for Bill to return with the last-minute supplies for their voyage. Work commitments had already meant they hadn't been able to get away quite as quickly as they'd hoped. Then they'd put off the trip for the chance of experiencing their first Little Spitmarsh Film Festival together. It was worth it, May sighed happily, to see Bill dressed up as the Sundance Kid for the final evening of the festivities, a favourite film character night at Samphire. He'd initially taken a little persuading, but was much more enthusiastic when she agreed to go as Ariel from the Little Mermaid.

Fiona and Paul, about to move into their new home, had come as Anthony and Cleopatra, although this Egyptian queen was sporting a little baby bump. Harry and Matthew were rocking Olivia Newton-John and John Travolta in 'Grease', and Thunder had made a few eyes water turning up as Tarzan.

May laughed to herself thinking about the interesting night she and Bill had when they'd got home. Now, while Cecil and Janice planned their future – although she and Bill noticed that the older couple seemed rather more keen on spending time together, now they had found each other, than running a B&B – they were free at last to take off for a week's idle sailing, taking advantage of the Indian summer to explore new shores. Together. She looked up as Bill came striding towards her, his lovely red hair glowing gold in the sunlight, and felt intense pleasure at the thought of spending some undiluted quality time with this wonderful man. She was all set to take the provisions from him when he jumped in beside her.

'Listen to this.' He grinned as he offered her his iPod, 'it's just become available so I've downloaded it.'

High tide and the summer rain
Hides your tears, conceals your pain
Cast off your past, learn to be free
Sail to your future, cast off with me
Follow a star, starting again
When the voyage is over, will we still be friends?
Say we'll still be friends

'I'm so proud of you,' Bill said, beaming and making May feel shy. If the spotlight had been entirely on her, she might have felt embarrassed, but Thunder had taken her lyrics and made the song all his own. His deep, careworn voice combined with all the mythology surrounding the redeemed rocker added a gravitas to her simple words which opened the song to all kinds of interpretations.

'He sings it so much better than I ever could,' she acknowledged.

'Not better, differently,' Bill reflected. 'I love your voice, and so do many other people. Are you quite sure you really want to give up on your singing career?'

'Look what happened last time I stood up in public and sang – you walked out on me.' She laughed and, seeing his stricken face, quickly put her arms round him. 'I'm much happier writing than performing. The last few minutes before I had to walk on stage to face an audience always tore me apart. I never overcame that fear even when they were people who'd paid to come and see me. Not even when I could hide behind a stage persona – especially one that never seemed to fit me.'

No, she thought fleetingly, she wouldn't miss Cherry, the sexy blonde alter ego Aiden had wanted her to be. In the end, after giving the matter very serious thought, May had decided not to take legal action against the man who had tried to control every aspect of her life. The threat of it had been sufficient for him to release her from her professional contract without a fuss and she had no taste for reliving every moment of the previous two years in court. Seeing him convicted wouldn't make her feel victorious. A few hours of community service probably wouldn't change his basic personality, she decided. What made her walk a little taller now was the knowledge that she'd found the strength and self-assurance within herself to break his hold on her. The decks were clear.

'And thanks to Thunder inviting me to write the material for his new album, I'll never have to worry about going back out on stage ever again.'

'I've been thinking about that. You'll probably want to be based in London, won't you?' Bill said, sounding as if he was trying to be brave.

'Why?' She shot him a look of disbelief. 'Why would I want to return to the south east when everything I need is here?'

Bill seemed to be too busy fiddling with his iPod to notice her meaningful look.

'Even Mum and Dad are selling up and moving here. I don't want to be too far from them now that Mum and I are getting on so well. Dad's got all that extra work, thanks to you, and Cecil's practically let Mum take the antique shop over permanently,' she added when he failed to respond.

'And we're following a star, starting again on our new voyage,' he said thoughtfully.

'When the voyage is over, will we still be friends?' she sang softly.

'Always.' He smiled and took a deep breath. 'I'll always be your friend, May,' he said, taking her hand, '*and* your lover for as long as you'll have me. Please understand that I never want to own you, May, or make you do anything you don't want to do, but I love you and I'm kind of hoping that one day, I could be more than just a friend or a lover to you. I'd like to be your husband and the father of your children. All you have to do when you're ready is say yes. Is that all right with you?'

May smiled up at him, happiness radiating through her. 'Yes,' she said, firmly.

About the Author

Winning a tin of chocolate in a national essay competition at primary school inspired Christine Stovell to become a writer! After graduating from the University of East Anglia, she took various jobs in the public sector writing research papers and policy notes by day and filling up her spare drawers with embryonic novels by night. Losing her dad to cancer made her realise that if she was ever going to get a novel published she had to put her writing first. Setting off, with her husband, from a sleepy seaside resort on the East Anglian coast in a vintage wooden boat to sail halfway round Britain provided the inspiration for *Follow a Star* and also her debut novel, *Turning the Tide*. Christine lives in Wales and has published numerous short stories and articles. *Follow a Star* is Christine's third novel with Choc Lit. Her others are *Turning the Tide* and *Move Over Darling*.

For more information on Christine visit:
www.twitter.com/chrisstovell
www.facebook.com/christinestovellauthor
www.homethoughtsweekly.blogspot.co.uk

More Choc Lit

From Christine Stovell

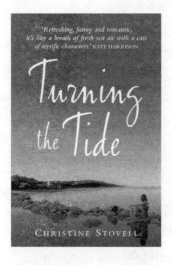

Turning the Tide

All's fair in love and war? Depends on who's making the rules.

Harry Watling has spent the past five years keeping her father's boat yard afloat, despite its dying clientele. Now all she wants to do is enjoy the peace and quiet of her sleepy backwater.

So when property developer Matthew Corrigan wants to turn the boat yard into an upmarket housing complex for his exotic new restaurant, it's like declaring war.

And the odds seem to be stacked in Matthew's favour. He's got the colourful locals on board, his hard-to-please girlfriend is warming to the idea and he has the means to force Harry's hand. Meanwhile, Harry has to fight not just his plans but also her feelings for the man himself.

Then a family secret from the past creates heartbreak for Harry, and neither of them is prepared for what happens next …

Visit www.choc-lit.com for more details including the first two chapters and reviews, or simply scan barcode using your mobile phone QR reader.

Move Over Darling

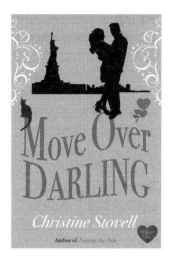

When is it time to stop running?

Coralie Casey is haunted by her past. Deciding it's time for a fresh start, she sets up 'Sweet Cleans', a range of natural beauty and cleaning products, and escapes to Penmorfa, a quiet coastal village in west Wales.

Gethin Lewis thinks he's about to put his home village Penmorfa behind him for good. Now an internationally-acclaimed artist living in New York, he just has to return one last time to wind up his father's estate.

But the village soon disrupts their carefully laid plans. As truths are uncovered which threaten to split the community apart, Gethin is forced to question his real reasons for abandoning Penmorfa, and Coralie is made to face the fact that some stains just won't go away.

Visit www.choc-lit.com for more details including the first two chapters and reviews, or simply scan barcode using your mobile phone QR reader.

More from Choc Lit

If you enjoyed Christine's story, you'll enjoy
the rest of our selection. Here's a sample:

Is this Love?
Sue Moorcroft

**How many ways can
one woman love?**

When Tamara Rix's sister
Lyddie is involved in a hit-
and-run accident that leaves
her in need of constant care,
Tamara resolves to remain
in the village she grew up in.
Tamara would do anything for
her sister, even sacrifice a long-
term relationship.

But when Lyddie's teenage sweetheart Jed Cassius returns
to Middledip, he brings news that shakes the Rix family to
their core. Jed's life is shrouded in mystery, particularly his
job, but despite his strange background, Tamara can't help
being intrigued by him.

Can Tamara find a balance between her love for Lyddie and
growing feelings for Jed, or will she discover that some kinds
of love just don't mix?

Visit www.choc-lit.com for more details
including the first two chapters and
reviews, or simply scan barcode using
your mobile phone QR reader.

Please don't stop the music

Jane Lovering

 Winner of the 2012 Best Romantic Comedy Novel of the Year

 Winner of the 2012 Romantic Novel of the Year

How much can you hide?

Jemima Hutton is determined to build a successful new life and keep her past a dark secret. Trouble is, her jewellery business looks set to fail – until enigmatic Ben Davies offers to stock her handmade belt buckles in his guitar shop and things start looking up, on all fronts.

But Ben has secrets too. When Jemima finds out he used to be the front man of hugely successful Indie rock band Willow Down, she wants to know more. Why did he desert the band on their US tour? Why is he now a semi-recluse?

And the curiosity is mutual – which means that her own secret is no longer safe ...

Visit www.choc-lit.com for more details including the first two chapters and reviews, or simply scan barcode using your mobile phone QR reader.

Sugar and Spice
Angela Britnell

The Way to a Hero's Heart …

Fiery, workaholic Lily Redman is sure of two things: that she knows good food and that she always gets what she wants. And what she wants more than anything is to make a success of her new American TV show, Celebrity Chef Swap – without the help of her cheating ex-fiancé and producer, Patrick O'Brien. So when she arrives in Cornwall, she's determined to do just that.

Kenan Rowse is definitely not looking for love. Back from a military stint in Afghanistan and recovering from a messy divorce and an even messier past, the last thing he needs is another complication. So when he lands a temporary job as Luscious Lily's driver, he's none too pleased to find that they can't keep their hands off each other!

But trudging around Cornish farms, knee deep in mud, and meetings with egotistical chefs was never going to be the perfect recipe for love – was it? And Lily could never fall for a man so disinterested in food – could she?

Visit www.choc-lit.com for more details including the first two chapters and reviews, or simply scan barcode using your mobile phone QR reader.

CLAIM YOUR FREE EBOOK

of

follow a Star

You may wish to have a choice of how you read *Follow a Star*. Perhaps you'd like a digital version for when you're out and about, so that you can read it on your ereader, iPad or even a Smartphone. For a limited period, we're including a **FREE** ebook version along with this paperback.

To claim, simply visit ebooks.choc-lit.com or scan the QR Code.

You'll need to enter the following code:

Q221404

Introducing Choc Lit

We're an independent publisher creating
a delicious selection of fiction.
Where heroes are like chocolate – irresistible!
Quality stories with a romance at the heart.

Choc Lit novels are selected by genuine readers like yourself.
We only publish stories our Choc Lit Tasting Panel want to
see in print. Our reviews and awards speak for themselves.

We'd love to hear how you enjoyed *Follow a Star*. Just visit
www.choc-lit.com and give your feedback.
Describe Bill in terms of chocolate
and you could win a Choc Lit novel in our
Flavour of the Month competition.

Available in paperback and as ebooks from most stores.

Visit: www.choc-lit.com for more details.

Keep in touch:
Sign up for our monthly newsletter Choc Lit Spread for
all the latest news and offers: www.spread.choc-lit.com.
Follow us on Twitter: @ChocLituk and Facebook: Choc Lit.

Or simply scan barcode using your mobile phone QR reader:

Choc Lit   *Twitter*   *Facebook*
Spread